Buckingham Palace Blues

Buckingham Palace Blues

An Inspector Carlyle Mystery

JAMES CRAIG

WITNESS
IMPULSE

An Imprint of HarperCollins Publishers

This book was previously published by Constable & Robinson in 2012.

EPub Edition NOVEMBER 2014 ISBN: 9780062365330

Print Edition ISBN: 9780062365347

10 9 8 7 6 5 4 3 2

Do not put your trust in princes, in mortal men, who cannot save. When their spirit departs, they return to the ground; on that very day their plans come to nothing.

Psalm 146. III–IV

Chapter One

'URGH.' JOE DALTON took a bite out of his fried-egg roll, chewed it a couple of times and spat it out of the window of the Austin FX4. Despite having eaten little for more than three days now, he could feel the bile rising instantly in his throat and knew that no food would stay down. Disgusted, he chucked the rest of the roll into the gutter and wiped his hands on his grubby Nickelback T-shirt. Gingerly taking the cardboard cup from the drinks-holder on the dashboard, he removed the lid and blew gently on his oily black coffee. He took a tiny sip and winced. *Horrible.*

Wearily he opened the cab door and climbed out. Pouring the steaming liquid down a drain leading into one of London's crumbling sewers, he then dropped the cardboard cup and its plastic lid into a nearby bin. Shivering in the cold, he went round to the back of the cab and opened the boot. Coiled on top of the spare wheel inside was the length of cord that he had been carrying around with him for weeks: three-strand 6mm white nylon – excellent shock-absorption properties, with a guaranteed break load of

750kg. With a sigh, he pulled it out, knowing that it was more than capable of doing the job required.

Sticking it under his arm, Dalton slammed the boot shut and walked towards the streetlight beside which he had parked the taxi. Looping one end of the rope around its metal pole, he tied it securely with a simple overhand knot. Stepping back to the cab, he tossed the rope through the driver's window, opened the door and got back in. After putting on his seat belt, he took a couple of deep breaths. Then he wound the free end of the rope round his neck three times, tying it off with the same kind of knot.

It was tight, but not too tight. The nylon cut into his neck, but he could still breathe. Gritting his teeth, he switched on the ignition and pushed the stick into first gear.

'Fuck it!'

Tears welling up in his eyes, he released the handbrake and stomped on the accelerator.

FERNANDO GARROS RETURNED his cup of tea to its saucer and idly watched the taxi driver getting in and out of his cab. He recognised the grinning face of Chad Kroeger on the guy's shirt and gave a small nod of approval. Nickelback were cool! Fernando had spent more than a day's wages to go and see them at Wembley the year before. The extra £20 for a T-shirt had been beyond him, but at least he had seen an awesome show. He hummed a few bars of 'Burn It to the Ground' before turning around, embarrassed, to check that no one had heard him. He needn't have worried; sitting by the window, he had Goodfellas café to himself. Apart from the cabbie, there had been no other customers through the door in the last hour. Xavi, the café's Spanish owner, had been fast asleep behind the counter for the last twenty minutes.

Yawning, Fernando checked his watch. It was almost 3.15 a.m. Closing his eyes, he folded his arms and stretched out his legs. He was in no rush. He had come off an eleven-hour shift as a hospital porter at St Thomas's and was enjoying his dinner (or was it his breakfast?) before he made the fifteen-minute walk back to the bedsit he had rented for the last eight years. Elephant and Castle wasn't the greatest neighbourhood to be wandering around in at night but, if he waited another half hour or so, he could be reasonably sure that all the gangbangers, nutters and general assholes who might otherwise try to impede his journey home would have gone to bed.

Xavi's snoring grew louder. Opening his eyes, Fernando finished the last of his tea and thought about helping himself to another cup. Deciding against it, he returned his gaze to the cabbie who had now returned to the relative warmth of his taxi. Fernando was amused by the way London cab drivers fussed over their taxis. He found it strange. True, the vehicles were expensive – £30,000 or more, he'd read somewhere – but even so, at the end of the day it was just another car.

'*Mierda!*'

Fernando almost fell off his chair as the cab suddenly shot backwards, jumped the pavement, knocked over a rubbish bin and crashed into the front window of a dry cleaner's.

Immediately, several alarms started ringing.

'What happened?' Xavi appeared at his shoulder, yawning, and went over to the door.

'Car accident.' Fernando then noticed the rope hanging from the lamp post, trailing along the pavement. He was fairly sure that hadn't been there before. Then he remembered the cabbie. It was hard to make out what was happening inside the vehicle, but it looked like the driver was slumped forward over the wheel. Maybe he'd suffered a heart attack. Meanwhile, something – a football? – had bounced into the road and come to a stop beside the upturned bin.

'Man,' Xavi scratched his head, 'you would have thought a taxi driver could drive better than that.' He stepped cautiously out of the door on to the pavement, and then into the empty road, heading towards the cab.

Feeling more than close enough to the action already, Fernando watched him cross the street towards the ball. Then, as an afterthought, he pulled out his mobile and dialled 999.

Chapter Two

It was a beautiful evening with the temperature in the low 60s, a bit chilly when the wind blew but as good as you were ever going to get in London on a Saturday evening in the middle of September. A darkening blue sky with only the occasional patch of cloud offered a sad reminder of the summer days past. Now was the steady, painful descent into autumn, and then winter beckoned.

Wiping his brow on his sleeve, Inspector John Carlyle took a swig of water from his plastic bottle as he jogged up The Mall, heading towards Buckingham Palace. Running was not really his preferred form of exercise, but it was cheaper than going to the gym. And just being outside helped clear his head.

He was glad to be out of the flat; his daughter and wife had been bickering all day, and he felt a sense of relief as he pounded the pavement. Alice was fast heading towards so-called 'tween-ager' status, twelve going on twenty-five, and several years of further conflict seemed inevitable. Carlyle felt bad that there wasn't more he could do to smooth things out between them, but he had learned a long time ago that there were severe limitations to what he could hope to achieve when it came to dealing with women, whatever their age and however well you thought you knew them.

Leaving the flat in Winter Garden House, he had taken an easy pace down Drury Lane, cutting through Covent Garden Piazza and Trafalgar Square, getting nicely into his stride as he dropped down from Carlton Gardens on to The Mall and made his way up towards Buckingham Palace. Carlyle was no royalist but he appreciated the grandeur of the surroundings. Having all this history on your doorstep was one of the perks of living in Central London. It gave you a sense of being at the centre of one of the great cities of the world. And, hand on heart, it *was* a great city. But, above all, it was *his* city. He had been born in London and, apart from a few unhappy but mercifully brief excursions into the provinces, he had lived and worked here his whole life. He was a London boy; it was the only place he had ever wanted to be.

Passing the statues of the Queen Mother and her husband King George VI, he veered on to the gravel cycle-path to avoid a couple of tourists taking photographs. As he did so, another couple stepped into his path and he was forced to do another little sideways dance, knocking him off his stride.

'*Tossers!*' he hissed under his breath, trying to get a bit of adrenaline going as he lengthened his stride. Looking up, he noticed that the Union Jack hanging from the flagpoles along either side of the road were interspersed with another flag that he didn't recognise, doubtless celebrating an official visit by some foreign head of state. Kicking on, Carlyle upped his pace as he approached the Palace itself. Nearing the junction with Marlborough Road, he checked the traffic-lights. They were on red, so he speeded up, not wanting to stop. But, as he did so, he saw the little green man that told pedestrians they could cross safely, disappear. Bollocks, he thought. But not wishing to lose his rhythm, he kept going.

Stepping off the pavement, his foot had barely touched the tarmac when a police motorcycle roared past, its lights flashing.

'Shit!' Carlyle quickly jumped back on to the pavement and started jogging on the spot, as if that had been the plan all along, ignoring the snickering of a couple of teenagers by his side. A few seconds later, there were some gasps from the gaggle of surrounding tourists, and cameras started whirring as a massive black Daimler slid past. All alone on the back seat, a little old lady in a pale yellow coat and matching hat sat staring into space. The limousine hardly slowed as it took a right and shot down The Mall towards the Palace, followed by another couple of police bikes.

Well, well, Carlyle thought, as he jogged across the now empty road. After more than forty years in London, I've finally seen the bloody Queen.

REACHING THE VICTORIA Memorial, he veered right. His plan was to complete two circuits of Green Park, and then head for home. It was already approaching 7.30 p.m. and the light was fading. The crowds were thinning and Carlyle could see only one other runner as he headed past Canada Gate and along Constitution Hill. To his right he heard a shout and turned his head to see a group of kids playing touch rugby. Their ball had landed a couple of yards in front of him. Picking it up, he passed it, quarterback-style, to the nearest kid, annoyed that his rhythm had been interrupted but happy for the pause. Taking a sip of water from his bottle, he looked around. Another kid, a girl, was sitting on a stone bench nearby while further on a man was walking his dog. Otherwise the place was fairly empty.

Another day in the city was slowly coming to a close.

His pace having slowed considerably, it was almost twenty-five minutes later when Carlyle passed the same spot for a second time. The man with the dog and the kids playing touch rugby had gone, but the girl was still sitting on the bench, staring into space. He eyed her as he approached – maybe nine or ten, short dark hair, a sleeveless flower-patterned dress and, he now realised, no shoes. She ignored him as he jogged past, the glazed expression on her face a study in inscrutability.

What's wrong with this picture?

It suddenly struck him that there was no one else within twenty yards of the girl.

No sign of any parents.

No playmates.

No one at all.

He jogged on another ten yards and came to a stop by a tree, letting his pulse subside while he drank the last of his water before tossing the bottle in a convenient bin.

Slowly he jogged back towards the girl, who still appeared lost in thought, and came to a stop a couple of yards in front of the bench.

'Excuse me?'

The child looked up at him but didn't say anything.

Carlyle stepped closer. Her eyes were like hard grey pebbles. 'Excuse me?' he said again. 'Are you okay?'

The girl lowered her gaze, but still she said nothing. As she folded her arms, Carlyle could see a series of black and blue marks just above each elbow. Some were faded; others looked fresh. Keeping a respectful distance, he knelt down in front of the child. 'I am John,' he said, a mixture of discomfort and anger rising inside him. 'What is your name?'

The child bit her lip and dropped her chin close to her chest, shaking her head.

'I am a policeman.' He was conscious of having no ID on him, but that couldn't be helped. 'Are you lost? Do you need any help?'

The girl's eyes welled up and a single tear ran down her left cheek. Carlyle's heart sank. He stepped back and looked around. It was getting properly dark now. The cars speeding by had their headlights on and the Palace behind him was bathed in floodlight. Doing a slow pirouette, he scanned though 360 degrees. Still there was no one else in sight who looked like they might belong to this kid. Fuck, he thought, what a pain in the arse. With a heavy sigh, he pulled his mobile from the back pocket of his shorts and called the station.

George Patrick, the fairly new desk sergeant at Charing Cross police station, answered on the first ring. 'Desk!'

George was probably older than Carlyle, but he was enthusiasm personified compared to his predecessor, Dave Prentice. Earlier in the year, Prentice had finally realised his lifelong ambition by retiring to the eastern suburb of Theydon Bois. Not a minute too soon, thought Carlyle. The inspector had not missed the moaning old sod once since he had left.

'George,' he said, 'it's John Carlyle. I'm in Green Park, just past the Canada Gates on Constitution Hill. There's a young child here who appears to be lost.' He lowered his voice a notch. 'She looks a bit . . . zonked out, so there may be more to it than that. Can you send a car?'

'Let's see . . .' There was the rustling of papers in the background. 'I'm not sure we've got anyone spare at the moment, but I'll find you something.'

'Thanks. Who's on duty at the moment?'

More rustling. Then Patrick read out a list of names.

Carlyle thought about it for just a second before making a decision. 'Send Nicole Sawyer.' Sawyer was an extremely pleasant, extremely overweight Afro-Caribbean WPC. At twenty-nine, her social skills were far better than Carlyle's and better than those of just about anyone else he had ever worked with. She might not be able to catch any criminals running down the street, but she certainly had the knack of simply talking them into giving themselves up. If anyone could be considered the acceptable face of the Metropolitan Police Force, it was Nicole. 'See if you can get her down here as well.'

'Okay.'

'Call me on my mobile when they're on their way. And check if there have been any reports today of a missing girl. She's aged about eight or nine, I'd reckon. Grey eyes and short dark hair. Wearing a flowery dress.'

'I'll check.'

'Thanks. See you later.' Carlyle ended the call and dropped the phone back in his pocket. As he did so, he became aware of someone hovering just behind him.

'Alzbetha!' cried a very pukka English voice that contained more than a hint of irritation. 'Come here! What have I told you about talking to strangers?'

Carlyle turned round to face a handsome man in his late twenties or early thirties. He had light, sandy hair receding at the temples, with sharp blue eyes and slim build. Carlyle put him at around five foot ten. His black suit looked expensive – Armani, maybe – as did his azure-blue shirt, which was open at the neck, and his black penny loafers.

'Who are you?' the young man asked, not trying to hide his annoyance now.

Carlyle stepped protectively in front of the girl. 'Who are *you*?'

The man looked flummoxed for a second. 'I am the girl's . . . uncle.'

That's a lie straight off the bat, thought Carlyle, whose dislike of this posh-sounding gent in front of him was already fully formed. 'Is that right?'

'Yes, it is.' The man nodded theatrically. He held out a hand towards the girl. 'Come.'

Alzbetha slipped off the bench but did not make any move towards her 'uncle'. Carlyle put a hand on her shoulder and felt the girl flinch. He thought of his own daughter – who was not much older than this kid – and a sense of rage rose within him. He kept his hand on her shoulder and tightened his grip. You are going nowhere, he thought, not with that tosspot.

He plastered a smile on his face that was more like a grimace and looked the man directly in the eye. 'I'm afraid you'll have to wait for a moment.'

'Is that right?' the man now yelled. 'And what business is it of yours?' He took half a step forward, as if contemplating a quick right hook to Carlyle's jaw.

'I am a police officer,' Carlyle said quietly, ignoring the phone which had started vibrating in his pocket. In the distance, he could hear a siren approaching quickly up The Mall. He gave silent thanks to George Patrick and stood his ground, still keeping a firm grip on the girl's shoulder.

'This is ridiculous!' But the man had heard the siren too, and Carlyle could see that he was unsure now about what to do.

'I think we need to discuss this down at the police station.' This time, Carlyle's smile was more genuine. The siren was getting ever louder. The car would be here in a matter of seconds. He took his hand from the girl's shoulder and stepped towards the other man. Immediately, she shot off, heading deeper into the park, in the direction of Piccadilly. Both men eyed each other, wondering who would be the first to give chase. When it was clear that his adversary was not going to move, Carlyle turned and headed after her.

The girl had a sharp turn of speed. By the time Carlyle got going, she had a start of maybe twenty metres. After tripping over a drain-cover, it took him the best part of a minute to catch up with her. Once he did, however, she stopped in her tracks, with a resigned look on her face, and let him lead her back to the now waiting police car.

Nicole Sawyer gave them a friendly greeting and ushered the girl carefully into the back of the car.

'Where's the bloke?' Carlyle asked, looking around for the young man in the expensive suit.

Sawyer eyed him quizzically. 'What bloke?'

DECLINING THE OFFER of a lift back to the station, Carlyle took a direct route home to Winter Garden House, running the whole way in a little over ten minutes. After a quick shower, he threw on some fresh clothes before grabbing a banana and a couple of Jaffa Cakes. As he headed back out the door, he stopped to give his wife the briefest of explanations about what had happened in the park.

'Poor girl.' Helen grimaced, glancing up from the television. 'God knows what they've done to her.'

Not interested in stopping to discuss who 'they' might be, Carlyle just shrugged and gave her a quick kiss on the forehead. 'I'll be back as soon as possible,' he promised limply.

'Sure.' From years of experience, she knew that 'as soon as possible' could mean anything between half an hour and three or four days. Blowing him a half-hearted kiss in return, she returned her attention to the television.

FIFTEEN MINUTES LATER, he was standing in one of the 'friendly' interview rooms located on the third floor of Charing Cross police station, which looked out over Agar Street. The girl was now sitting at a table, happily munching a bag of cheese and onion crisps and doodling in a colouring book that Nicole Sawyer – God bless her – had rustled up from somewhere. Also on the table were the remains of a chocolate bar and an empty Coke can. If Alice gobbled that lot, Helen would have a fit, Carlyle thought. This, however, wasn't the time or the place to be too choosy about the child's diet.

Standing by the window, Sawyer had her back to him. She was talking on the phone and he could tell by her hushed tone that it wasn't about work. Catching his reflection in the window, Sawyer quickly ended the call and turned around, signalling that they should step into the corridor. Finally acknowledging his presence, the girl looked up, gave Carlyle a wary stare and went back to her drawing.

Outside, Carlyle waited for Sawyer to close the door behind her. 'Has she said anything yet?'

Sawyer shook her head. 'Nothing I could understand. She did say something, but it wasn't English.'

'So she's foreign?' Carlyle asked in surprise, thinking about her very English 'uncle'.

'I suppose so,' Sawyer shrugged.

'Have we got a translator?'

'Nothing doing till tomorrow morning,' Sawyer said. 'Do you have any idea where she's from?'

'Not a clue.' Carlyle said. 'What about a doctor?'

'On the way . . . apparently.'

'Social Services?'

Sawyer rolled her eyes to the ceiling. 'We've left a message. No one's picking up, as usual.'

'Christ!' Carlyle hated dealing with Social Services. Almost without exception, the social workers he came across were unmotivated and uninspiring, he thought, always looking to do the bare minimum while hiding behind the rule book, their union agreements and political correctness. As far as he could see, it was a profession where everyone hated their job and couldn't wait to retire on some grossly inflated public sector pension. Looking forward to his own pension, Carlyle was fairly ambivalent about that ambition. What he couldn't abide was the general reluctance to earn their corn while they were still working.

Sawyer looked at her watch theatrically. 'Sorry, Inspector,' she said, 'but my shift ended half an hour ago. I need to get home.'

'No problem,' Carlyle replied, through clenched teeth. Now *he* was left holding the baby. Literally. He resisted the temptation to point out that he himself wasn't supposed to be working at all today. 'See you tomorrow.'

'Yes. Thanks.' Sawyer turned and propelled her fat arse along the corridor as fast as possible, before Carlyle changed his mind and condemned her to some more involuntary overtime.

Stepping back into the room, Carlyle took a seat opposite the girl. She stared at him for a moment, then glanced at the door, as if she was weighing up whether she could try and make another break for freedom.

Carlyle leaned back in his chair. What the fuck do I do now? he wondered.

The girl picked up a red crayon and began smearing it across the paper.

With some effort, he tried to assume what he hoped was his friendliest demeanour. 'Hello, again,' he said gently. 'Remember me? I'm the man from the park.' He pulled out his warrant card and slid it across the table. 'I'm a policeman. My name is John.'

The girl looked at the ID but did not touch it.

'What's your name?' What had the guy called her back at the park? Alzbetha? 'Elizabeth?'

The girl looked at the crayon, squeezing it so tightly between her fingers that it snapped in two.

'Is that your name?'

Carlyle watched her eyes welling up. Her bottom lip trembled. He leaned forward, waiting for the words to spill out.

Suddenly, she wiped her nose and looked at him defiantly. 'We fuck now?' There was no hesitation in her tone. It was almost a challenge.

'What?' Carlyle pushed himself away from the table, wanting to pretend that he hadn't heard what he had just heard.

The girl stood up. 'You want?' she asked, trying to put on an approximation of the same cut-glass accent spoken by the man in the park. 'We fuck?'

WITHOUT ANOTHER WORD, Carlyle left the room. Closing the door behind him, he headed a couple of yards down the corridor. Standing in front of a road safety poster, he headbutted it twice.

Ow!

The pain felt good. After it had subsided, he pulled out his mobile phone and called the desk downstairs. 'Is the doctor here yet?' he asked, feeling more than a little desperate.

'Two minutes,' Patrick replied.

'Who is it?'

'Weber.'

Carlyle knew Thomas Weber. He was a very nice guy. German. Very thorough. Very professional. Not the man for this job, though. 'Get me a woman,' he said.

'What?'

'Trust me,' Carlyle hissed, fighting to keep his tone even. 'It should be a woman.'

'But Weber is on call . . .'

'I don't care if the King of fucking Siam is on call,' he ranted. 'Get – me – a – woman doctor. *Please*.'

'Inspector . . .'

Calm down, Carlyle told himself. Just calm down. Shouting won't get you what you want. He took a deep breath. 'Look, George, I'm sorry but this could be nasty. Really nasty. Not the usual day-to-day bullshit that we have to put up with. It's important and it's urgent. I'll stay with the kid till we get it sorted. See what you can do.'

'Okay.' Patrick slammed the phone down in a *fuck you too* kind of a way.

Carlyle stood in the corridor, feeling dizzy. For want of anything better to do, he went back into the interview room. The girl had abandoned her colouring book and was now crayoning on the table. This time, she didn't even acknowledge his presence. Leaning against the wall, he watched her destroy one crayon after another until there was nothing left but a pile of stubs. When there were none left, she sat back in her chair, folded her arms and admired her handiwork. It looked pretty good to Carlyle. Maybe they should take the table over Waterloo Bridge to Tate Modern.

'Elizabeth,' he said, more to himself than to the girl, 'where the hell are you from?'

She rolled one half of the broken red crayon across the table, muttering something under her breath that he didn't catch. She sounded Eastern European. Russian maybe? Polish? He didn't know. The kid looked European, but she wasn't speaking French, Italian, German or Spanish. Presumably she wasn't from Scandinavia. He had never heard of children – or anyone else for that matter – being trafficked from there.

He was still mulling it over a few minutes later, when Thomas Weber arrived. The doctor was accompanied by a small, mousy-looking WPC Carlyle didn't recognise. She smiled wanly but said nothing. Seeing the annoyance on the inspector's face, Weber held up a hand before Carlyle could say anything. 'I know what you asked for,' he said firmly, 'but I'm all you've got.'

Carlyle studied the tired-looking man in front of him and nodded sheepishly. Now was not the time for any more shouting.

'Okay.' Weber looked at the little girl and smiled. 'Let's go downstairs.'

The WPC took the girl by the hand and led her out of the room. Carlyle let Weber go next and brought up the rear.

On the first floor was the station's 'medical suite': a couple of rooms that had been kitted out in a fair imitation of a GP's surgery. Once they got there, Weber turned to Carlyle. 'It's probably better if you let us handle this from here. Why don't you go and get a cup of coffee and come back in half an hour?'

'Will do,' Carlyle agreed, secretly quite relieved.

WHILE THE CHILD was being examined, he nipped out of the station and headed for a nearby bookstore on New Row that he knew would still be open. The children's department was in the basement. With help from a friendly assistant, he found a copy of *My First Atlas* and a couple more colouring books – one with pictures of ballerinas, the other of princesses. The books made him smile; they were the kind of thing he would have bought for Alice only a couple of years ago. Then he remembered the girl back in the station, and the smile died on his face.

'Is there anything wrong?' The assistant seemed genuinely concerned by the thunderous look on Carlyle's face.

'No, no,' replied Carlyle almost absentmindedly. 'Thanks for your help. That's just what I was looking for.'

Back at the station, the doctor was already waiting for him outside the medical suite. As he approached along the corridor, Carlyle could see from the look on Weber's face that things were at least as bad as he had feared. Squeamish at the best of times, the last thing Carlyle wanted was a discussion of the ugly details.

'One for Social Services?' he asked quickly, before Weber could say a word.

Weber nodded solemnly. 'I'll give them a call straight away.'

'Good luck with that,' Carlyle growled. 'What am I supposed to do in the meantime?' It was a stupid question, the result of tiredness and frustration.

'I'll be as quick as I can,' Weber said evenly, picking up the briefcase at his feet and heading for the stairs.

Gritting his teeth, Carlyle watched him go. Not for the first time, he cursed himself for getting into this type of situation. His stomach rumbled and he realised that he was starving. The station canteen would be shut by now and he would need to go out again if he wanted to get something to eat. He thought it through. If he took the girl with him, it would be a breach of protocol. On the other hand, maybe it would help her open up a bit. Carlyle doubted, however, that her English extended much beyond the terrifying handful of words she had already come out with. But maybe, just maybe, he could start to build up some trust with her over a burger and some chips.

Bracing himself, he stepped into the medical suite. The WPC jumped up from her seat, nodded in his general direction and quickly left the room. In the corner, he could see the girl asleep on the examination table. She lay with her back to him and was wearing a paper gown. In the silence of the room, he could hear her snoring quietly. Carefully placing the books on an empty desk on the other side of the room, he found a blanket in a cupboard and gently placed it over her. For a while he stood there, watching the slight rise and fall of her chest. A pretty girl, though. Almost all kids are pretty at that age, he mused. Eyes closed, and without the frown, she looked at peace for the first time since he'd met her.

Switching the light off, he sat down on the chair vacated by the WPC. His stomach rumbled again. He told it to shut up. It didn't matter how hungry he was; all that he could do now was wait.

WAKING WITH A start, Carlyle slowly came to terms with the darkness. After a while he could vaguely make out the time, by the clock on the wall. He groaned when he saw that it was 2.15 a.m. Rubbing the back of his neck, he got reluctantly to his feet and ran through a mental checklist of all the places where his body ached. It was a long one. The girl was still fast asleep, curled up in the foetal position, her breathing steady.

Stepping quietly out of the room, Carlyle checked his phone. To his dismay, he had four missed calls and a text message from his wife – *Where are you?* – timed at just after 11 p.m. Carlyle yawned. How had he slept through all that? Par for the course. He had a very mixed record with mobile phones. Sometimes he could go for days without managing to pick up any of his calls. It drove him – and everyone else – mad.

Now was not the time to call Helen back. He felt an ache in his bladder and realised he needed to piss. After a trip to the gents, he headed downstairs to the front desk. By now, George Patrick had gone off shift. He had been replaced by Gerry Armstrong, an Irishman Carlyle knew reasonably well. Beyond the security doors, the reception area was relatively empty for Saturday night–Sunday morning. There were a couple of drunks and one guy with blood oozing from a cut above his eyebrow, but it seemed that tonight the loser count was relatively low.

'Gerry,' he nodded in greeting. 'Quiet tonight.'

The desk sergeant looked up from an early edition of the *Sunday Mirror*. 'John,' he replied, sounding far too cheery for this time of night. 'What are you doing here?'

Carlyle explained the situation.

'Christ!' Armstrong exclaimed. 'No one told me. Mind you, I was a bit late in getting in tonight.'

Maybe you should read the duty log then, Carlyle thought. But he let it slide. It was too late and he was too tired to allow himself to get annoyed again. 'That's okay. But I need you to get one of the PCSOs – a woman – to sit with the kid for an hour or so. She's asleep now, but just in case she wakes up. I'm going home to get a bite to eat and pick up some stuff. Then I'll be right back.'

Police Community Support Officers, known as 'plastic policemen', were staff hired to help with the grunt work. Regular officers, like Carlyle, generally had a very low opinion of the plastics. Bored, with no power to arrest suspected criminals, they were responsible for most cases of gross misconduct among Metropolitan Police staff. Carlyle avoided them wherever possible. For now, however, they would have to do. Surely even a PCSO was capable of looking after a sleeping kid for an hour.

'No problem,' Armstrong said. 'They're all in the smoking room, watching videos, anyway.'

Safer than having them on the streets, Carlyle thought. 'Thanks. And could you call Thomas Weber for me? See if he's made any progress with Social Services.'

'Will do.' But Armstrong had already returned his attention to his newspaper – a story about some bisexual, drug-dealing minor member of the royal family – and Carlyle realised that he had been gently dismissed. Zipping up his jacket, he headed off into the night.

THE GIRL FINALLY awoke just after seven in the morning. If not exactly happy to see Carlyle, she didn't immediately try to make a dash for the door. Taking the clothes he had brought for her – some of Alice's cast-offs that Helen hadn't found a home for – she dressed quickly. When she was finished, he looked her up and down, feeling a small stab of satisfaction at a job well done. Even in the middle of the night, he had managed to come up with a reasonable ensemble – jeans, sweatshirt, trainers – without waking up either wife or daughter, which was a major result.

He opened his mouth and pointed a finger at his tongue. 'Food?'

The girl nodded.

'Good.' Carlyle smiled, happy to be making at least a little progress. He held out a hand, but the girl refused to take it. Ignoring the snub, he stepped over to the door. 'Come on, let's go and get some breakfast.'

Official police protocol or not, they had to eat. Carlyle knew that the only place open at this time of a Sunday morning would be the Box café on Henrietta Street, a minute from the station, just down from the piazza. As they arrived, the owner was just opening up. He nodded his welcome as they slipped inside and took a table by the window. The girl immediately grabbed the outsized laminated menu and scrutinised the pictures, before pointing to the Full English Breakfast. 'Two English, please,' Carlyle called over to the owner. 'I'll have a coffee and she'll have orange juice.'

While they waited for their food to arrive, Carlyle showed the girl the books that he had bought for her the night before. Looking through the colouring books, the girl muttered unhappily under her breath and Carlyle realised that he hadn't brought along any pens.

'Sorry,' he shrugged.

Seeming to ignore him, the girl carefully put the books to one side.

'Here.' Carlyle picked up the atlas and offered it to her. When she didn't take it, he opened it, found the pages covering Eastern Europe and laid it down in front of her. 'Is this where you are from?'

The girl scanned the countries without showing any sign of recognition. Carlyle tapped Russia on the page and pointed at the girl. 'Russia,' he said clearly. 'Are you from there?'

She shook her head and turned to the next page. They were interrupted just then by the arrival of two large plates of food and both spent the next five minutes eating in hungry silence. Carlyle ate quickly and methodically, swallowing his last piece of toast and washing it down with coffee while the girl was still munching on her second sausage.

In the end, she was not able to eat all of her breakfast. Never one to let food go to waste, Carlyle quickly swapped plates. Eyes down, he began gobbling up the girl's leftovers. As he finished off the last mouthful of beans, he looked up. The girl gave him a dirty look.

'Sorry,' Carlyle grinned, 'but I was still hungry.' To his left, he noticed that the owner was placing a tray of Danish pastries on the counter. They looked good. Carlyle gestured at the tray. 'I'll have one of those and another coffee. Thanks.' He turned back to the girl. 'Would you like anything else?'

She showed him another picture on the menu. 'Ice cream.'

What an interesting English vocabulary you have, Carlyle thought. He turned to the owner: 'Ice cream for breakfast it is.'

The owner nodded. 'We have vanilla, strawberry, pistachio, chocolate . . .'

'шоколад!'

'шоколад? Chocolate?' The man smiled. 'Okay . . . chocolate.'

The girl slid out of her chair and the pair of them disappeared behind the counter. Carlyle heard boxes being shifted around and some giggling, before the girl returned triumphantly with three massive scoops of chocolate ice cream.

He watched her demolish the first scoop before standing up and stepping over to the counter, where the owner was lifting his pastry from the tray.

'What language was that you were speaking?' Carlyle asked quietly.

The man looked at him in surprise.

Carlyle pulled his ID from his pocket but didn't open it. 'You know that I am police?'

The man placed Carlyle's Danish on the counter. 'Yes.'

'So where are you from?'

The man turned to the Gaggia coffee-machine. 'I am from the Ukraine. More than twenty years now. And so is the girl.' He gave the policeman a stern look. 'You should know that.'

I do now, Carlyle thought. Thank you.

By the time Carlyle returned to the table, the girl had finished her ice cream. He handed her a napkin and gestured for her to wipe her mouth. As she did so, his phone started vibrating. There was no number ID, but he picked it up anyway. 'Hello?'

'Inspector Carlyle?'

'Yes.'

'This is Hilary Green of Westminster Social Services. What are you doing?' The woman sounded as annoyed as he himself felt.

Waiting for you, love, Carlyle thought, as I have been for the last twelve bloody hours.

'Where are you?'

He bit his lip and took a deep breath simultaneously. Then he told Ms Green that they would be back at the station in two minutes.

While he paid the bill, the girl re-opened the atlas and started flicking through the pages. She stopped at a map of the United Kingdom, surrounded by little drawings of famous landmarks. Holding up the book, she pointed to Buckingham Palace: 'мій будинок.'

'What?' Carlyle looked at the café-owner for help.

'Ось де я живу!' the girl yelled.

'She's a little princess,' the café-owner laughed. 'She says that she lives in Buckingham Palace!'

Chapter Three

STANDING ON THE steps of Charing Cross police station, Hilary Green's eyes narrowed as she watched them come round the corner of Agar Street. The social worker tossed her cigarette on to the pavement and stubbed it out with the toe of her shoe before kicking it into the gutter. Glancing at her watch, she cursed the pair of them for destroying her Sunday.

Carlyle watched her exhale the smoke she had been holding in her lungs and start coughing. Hilary Green looked to be in her mid-thirties, a fake blonde wearing too much make-up, with a face that would curdle milk. She was wrapped in an oversized winter coat and shivered noticeably as they came closer, even though it was barely autumn proper and the weather was still mild.

Green observed them approach with an air of weary suspicion. The child had the kind of vacant, expressionless face that she had seen a million times before, and the policeman was just another copper who would be all too happy to dump this additional pile of shit in her lap.

'Carlyle?' she asked, as they reached the foot of the steps.

The policeman nodded.

Green looked the girl up and down. 'Is this her?'

No, Carlyle thought, I've got another one under my desk. 'Yes.' He gave the girl a gentle pat on the head and was gratified when she didn't flinch. 'Her name is Alzbetha or Elizabeth . . . I think. Something like that. She hasn't said much.'

'Hello, Elizabeth.' Green greeted the child with no obvious enthusiasm.

'She doesn't have much English.'

Green eyed him carefully. 'But she has some?'

'Not really,' Carlyle said. 'I'll put it in my report.' He felt the girl step closer to him and reach for his hand. There was a look of boundless resignation in her grey eyes and his heart sank. He turned to the social worker. 'Have you spoken to Dr Weber yet?'

'Not yet,' the woman said defensively.

'You should.' He gestured towards the girl. 'She's been badly abused.'

Green nodded, like that was fairly normal in her line of work. It probably was.

INSIDE, CARLYLE SAT at his desk watching Green laboriously fill in a series of forms.

Finally, with the tiniest of flourishes, she finished the last sheet of paper. 'Right, you just need to sign here . . .'

Carlyle looked at the girl – playing intently on a nearby computer – and then he looked at Green. Did he really want Social Services to walk off with the kid? Green sensed his hesitancy and looked at him, her expression defiant. They both knew that he had no choice. Carlyle took her pen and limply scribbled the remotest approximation of his signature he could manage on the line next to where the social worker had made a little cross.

'Thank you,' Green said, scooping up the pile of papers and dropping them into her bag. She stood up and turned to the girl. 'Elizabeth, we need to go now.'

You don't even know for sure that's her name, Carlyle thought. He felt sick. 'Where are you taking her?' he asked quietly.

Green looked vaguely annoyed at the question. 'I need to go back to my office, and then we can see if we can allocate her a place in an interim facility.'

Interim facility? How cosy.

'It depends where we've got some space,' Green continued.

'Let me know.'

Green zipped up her bag. 'Of course.'

Carlyle ticked off the To Do list in his head. 'I need to file my report, look at the findings of Dr Weber and also locate an interpreter.' He wondered about going back to the guy at the Box café, but that would fall foul of Social Service protocol. 'I assume that the council has Ukrainian speakers on its books?'

Green shrugged.

'The Met,' Carlyle said, gesturing at his computer, 'has two. One has been off sick for three months. The other is away on holiday. Maybe you could help us out on that score?'

'Inspector,' she said sharply, her mouth curling up at the edges, 'I have to look after almost a hundred kids at any one time. I reckon that an average group of children speaks something like twenty different languages.'

'Wow!' Carlyle made a belated and insincere stab at empathy.

'With Ukrainian, make that twenty-one,' Green went on. 'Working on the basis of limited communication is normal. I will do my best.'

'Thank you.'

'What we really need to do is find someone in the girl's family.'

'Of course.' Yawning, he opened a drawer in his desk and pulled out a small box of business cards. Removing a couple, he stood up and handed one to Green. 'Call me when you know where she is going to stay. I will come and visit her this afternoon.'

The woman dropped the card in a pocket, saying nothing.

Carlyle went over to the girl and crouched beside her. When she kept her eyes firmly on the computer screen, he touched her shoulder. 'This lady,' he said softly, when he had her attention, 'is going to find you somewhere to stay.' He tried to smile. 'Somewhere nicer than this.'

The girl's eyes began to well up, and Carlyle had to grit his teeth to stop from doing the same. It was one of those relatively rare moments during his professional life when he felt totally inadequate as opposed to just inadequate. He had found her and now he was abandoning her. She had become his responsibility, and here he was passing the buck.

'Here . . .' his hand trembled slightly as he handed over his card. 'This is me.'

She held the card between her thumb and forefinger, without looking at it. He gently took it back from her and put it carefully in the pocket of her jeans. Sensing Green hovering impatiently behind him, he gave the girl a pat on the arm. 'Don't forget your books. I will come and see you this afternoon and bring you some pens, I promise.'

Slowly the girl slid off her chair and followed the social worker to the stairs.

With a mighty sigh, he watched them go.

WHEN HE GOT home, there was a note from Helen saying that she had gone out with Alice to meet some friends at Coram's Fields, a playground for children up towards King's Cross. He thought about heading up there to meet them but now exhaustion got the better of him. Taking off his shoes, he collapsed on to the bed, still fully clothed. Keeping his eyes tightly shut, he tried to clear his mind and get some rest. Sleep, however, would not come. After about twenty minutes, he bowed to the inevitable and got up again. Following a shave and a change of shirt, he made himself a couple of slices of toast with marmalade. Washing them down with a cup of coffee, he planned out the remainder of his day.

Returning to the station, he typed up his report. It didn't take long – there really wasn't much to say. He had just printed out a hard copy when an email from Thomas Weber pinged into his inbox. With some trepidation, Carlyle opened the attachment and read the doctor's own report following his session with the girl the night before. Weber had been far more detailed than Carlyle; indeed, Weber was far too detailed for Carlyle, whose squeamish-ness had, if anything, become worse over the years. A quick scan showed that all of his worst fears had been realised. The girl had been physically and sexually abused, probably over a period of several months. Her right forearm had been broken too, an injury that had only recently healed. He felt a surge of adrenaline and hatred for the people who had done this. Someone has to pay, he thought. This is not something that you can just let slide.

After correcting a few typos in his own report, he attached both documents to an email and sent it to his boss, Commander Carole Simpson, along with a covering note that said he would give her a call to discuss things later in the day. Next, he called Hilary Green; her voicemail kicked in immediately and he asked her to call him with the address where the girl was staying. Finally, he Googled various translation services looking for someone who could speak Ukrainian. He tried a couple of numbers, but no one was picking up on a Sunday.

Putting down the phone, he sat back in his chair and closed his eyes. Where do you go from here? he wondered. He laid out the events of the last eighteen hours in sequence: the girl, the posh bloke, the evident abuse – no Missing Person report.

Mm.

No immediate lines of enquiry popped into his head. This type of thing really wasn't his area of expertise. He would need some help – but who could he reach out to? For want of anything better to do, he picked up the phone and called his sergeant, Joe Szyszkowski.

Joe was, as far as Carlyle knew, the only Polish sergeant working in the Metropolitan Police. At least, Joseph Leon Gorka Szyszkowski was second-generation Polish, having been born in the UK. Brought up in Portsmouth, he came to London to study geophysics at Imperial College. For reasons Carlyle didn't understand, he decided to join the Met after graduating with a good 2:1 degree. More British than Carlyle was (or, at least, felt), Joe had an Indian wife, Anita, and a couple of quintessentially English kids, William and Sarah. However, despite all of this, there was still a strand of the sergeant's DNA that was deeply, irredeemably Polish i.e. dark, pessimistic and Catholic. This contributed to a sense of detachment, irony and, perhaps just as important, fatalism, which for Carlyle made Joe a perfect colleague.

Joe picked up after four or five rings. 'Boss . . .' he began warily.

'Joe,' Carlyle replied, 'sorry to disturb you on a Sunday.'

'No worries.' Joe lowered his voice. 'We've got the in-laws round, so disturb away.'

'Do you know anyone working in Vice at the moment?'

There was a dramatic pause. 'You haven't been caught with your pants down, have you?'

'Seriously . . .'

'One or two,' Joe laughed. 'Why?'

Carlyle outlined the situation. There was another pause.

Like Carlyle, Joe was a family man. He knew how seriously his boss would take this case. 'Let me make a few calls.'

'Thanks, Joe. I appreciate it.'

'Do you want me to come in?'

'Maybe later. At the moment, I'm just trying to work out a plan of action.'

'Sounds like it will end up on Vice's desk, anyway,' Joe mused.

'I don't care whose fucking desk it ends up on,' Carlyle said firmly. 'I will see this one through to the bitter end.'

A COUPLE OF minutes later, Carlyle's mobile started vibrating in his hand. 'That was quick!' he said.

'Eh?' It was Helen.

'Sorry,' Carlyle said quickly. 'I thought you were Joe.'

'Sorry to disappoint.' Her voice was tart.

'N-no, it's not like that,' he stammered, trying to keep the irritation from his voice. 'It's just that it was a difficult night.'

'That's okay,' she said, adopting a more conciliatory tone. 'You can tell me about it tonight. I'll make us a family dinner once we get home. Alice fancies pancakes.'

'Nice!' Carlyle smiled. He always fancied pancakes.

'I just wanted to tell you that we are going to stay out for a while longer,' Helen continued, 'seeing as it's such a nice afternoon.'

'It is?' All Carlyle could see out through his window was a sooty brick wall.

'Yes, it is,' she laughed. 'You should get out more.'

'Yes,' he agreed. 'I should.'

His wife sighed. 'Whatever you're up to, don't overdo it, John.'

'Me? Never.'

'You know what I mean.'

'Yes, yes. Don't worry. I'm fine.'

'Good. We'll see you later.'

Chapter Four

CAROLE SIMPSON WALKED out through the gates of Opel Open Prison and gazed in the general direction of the sea, breathing in deeply. The sea air outside the prison fence was just the same as that on the inside, but somehow it felt better . . . much better. Another visit over, she could get back to the 'normal' part of her life. The routine of visiting her husband was now well ingrained but it still made her feel uncomfortable. Every second Sunday, she would make the trek down from London to the South Downs to spend a couple of hours walking around the prison grounds with Joshua, talking about their respective jobs – hers running a pool of seventy detectives for the Metropolitan Police, his teaching fellow inmates mathematics – and their plans for rebuilding their life together once he got out.

Release for Joshua Hunt – aka Mr Carole Simpson – was still quite a way off. He was almost eighteen months into a seven-year stretch for fraud, conspiracy to defraud and embezzlement. Even with time off for good behaviour, it would be at least another year, more likely two, before he could begin to think about parole.

However long it was, she could wait. Alone in the outside world, Simpson was surviving perfectly well – far better than she might have imagined back when Joshua's investment firm had collapsed and he was arrested.

When they'd seized his assets and hit him with a £15 million fine, she had been forced to radically downsize, moving from an elegant house in Highgate to a modest two-bedroom flat in Hammersmith. The fancy restaurants, the charity dinners and the celebrity 'friends' were a thing of the past as well, along with the expensive holidays in the Caribbean, Italy and South Africa. But the new reduced lifestyle didn't bother her in the least. The most important thing was that she was still working; she had kept her rank and most of her responsibilities. As a commander, she was still one of the thirty or so most senior women on the Force. There would be no more promotions – the dream of making deputy commissioner was over – but she hadn't been kicked out.

That had been a major surprise. On the one hand, she had not been involved in any of her husband's financial misdeeds. On the other hand, she had become a major embarrassment to the Met. As such, she had been expecting the boot. But they had bottled it, and Simpson had gruffly declined to fall on her sword.

Walking away with her tail between her legs would have been seen as an admission of guilt. More importantly, it would have left her with nothing to do. Simpson knew that retirement would have bored her out of her skull. Barely into her fifties, she had a good decade of productive working life left in the tank. By standing her ground, she would at least be allowed to retire at a time of her own choosing, which would be as late as possible.

Even the annoyance of being dubbed 'the clueless copper wife of Britain's biggest conman', as one tabloid newspaper so elegantly put it, had dissipated over time. The world still kept turning. The thing was, Simpson realised, that she still didn't really know if Joshua was a fraudster or not. As far as she could make out, he had been doing the same things all through the good years, when he was hailed as a hero and a genius, as he had when things went south. It was just that the market had gone bad. No one had cared what he had been up to when he was making them money.

When the market crashed, however, the hunt was on for someone to blame. What was the saying? *When the tide goes out, you see who's been swimming naked.* Well, Joshua, it seemed, was wearing not a stitch. But then neither were plenty of other people. Now the whole world had seen his hairy arse. Well, so be it. He was her husband. She was sticking with him the same way she was sticking with the job; she had too much of her life invested in their marriage – almost twenty-five years – to cut and run now.

Reaching the car park, Simpson pulled out her keys and watched the other prison WAGs as they headed for their cars. She hadn't spoken to a single one of them in all the time she had been coming here. Most of the other wives and girlfriends were much younger than her. They looked harder, but at the same time seemed relaxed about their fate.

A couple of them – all blonde hair, high heels and short skirts – were laughing and joking as they headed for their cars, casually going about their business here as if they were simply visiting the supermarket or the hairdresser's. What were their husbands in for? Nothing too terrible, Simpson supposed, if they were in an open prison. *Nothing too terrible?* She laughed at herself: what a thing for a copper to think!

She reached her car and opened the driver's door. On the seat lay her mobile phone. It must have fallen out of her pocket when she was getting out. Cursing her absentmindedness, she picked it up. Immediately, the phone started vibrating in her hand.

'Hello?'

'Carole? It's John Carlyle.'

'John,' she said warmly. 'How are you?'

'Fine,' Carlyle replied. 'And you?'

'I'm good,' Simpson said evenly.

A seagull started yapping overhead. 'Are you at the seaside?' Carlyle asked.

'Yes, I've just come out from visiting . . .' She stopped short. Their relationship had warmed considerably since Carlyle had been one of the few, one of the very few people on the Force to offer her any sympathy and support after Joshua was nicked, but the relationship was still a formal one. Professional. There was a better understanding between the two of them, but they still weren't close.

'How is Joshua?' Carlyle asked, not picking up on her sense of discomfort as it came down the line.

'He's fine.' Simpson sighed. 'Sometimes I think he quite likes it in there, with all his books and his small group of students to teach, and no distractions from the outside world.'

When you put it like that, Carlyle thought, it sounds quite good. Like a little holiday. 'He'll be out in no time.'

Yes, he will, Simpson thought, not altogether happily. 'What can I do for you, John?'

'Well . . .' Carlyle quickly outlined what was contained in his report.

Jamming the phone between her shoulder and her ear, Simpson rummaged in her bag until she found her BlackBerry Curve 8900. Scrolling down through her emails, she opened the latest one from Carlyle. 'I've got it here. Let me read it tonight and we can discuss it tomorrow.'

'All right,' said Carlyle, trying to ignore the stab of impatience that he felt.

'But,' Simpson continued, tossing the machine onto the passenger seat, 'it sounds from what you've said as if we should hand this one over.'

No bloody way, Carlyle thought. Not a fucking chance. 'Maybe,' he said.

'The girl is now in care,' Simpson said. 'You don't think it's a domestic, so you should speak to Vice.'

'Joe is doing that right now,' Carlyle said, wondering now if that was such a good idea.

'Good.' Simpson eased herself into her seat. 'Let me know how that goes. It's best that the right people handle it.'

Meaning: *it sounds nasty, it looks like a dead end, the kid'll probably get sent back home, so let's make sure we can pass the buck.*

'Sure,' he said, as casually as he could manage. 'In the meantime, I thought that I would check in with some of my old friends in SO14.'

There was a pause on the line. He heard some muffled noises in the background as she closed the car door, smiling as he imagined his boss banging her head on the steering wheel. 'John,' she said finally, 'you don't *have* any friends in SO14 – old or otherwise.'

'Yes, but—'

'Anyway, why would you want to talk to the Royal Protection Unit about this?'

'Because that's where I found the girl.'

'You found the girl in Green Park,' Simpson corrected him. 'Thousands of people use Green Park every day. The Queen, as far as I know, is not one of them.'

'The girl said she lived there,' he persisted. 'At Buckingham Palace.'

'That's what you *think* she said,' Simpson snapped, tired of holding this conversation on what had been a stressful day to start with. 'Even if that's what she did say, so what? She's a little girl. All little girls want to be a princess and live in a castle.'

'I know—'

'Look, John,' she sighed. 'I—'

'I know,' he repeated hastily. 'I know.'

Simpson looked out at the grey horizon. 'You say that you do, but then you act like you don't.' She felt herself slipping into schoolteacher mode, but kept going anyway. 'It's like my dad used to say: you should ignore everything that a boy *says*, and pay very close attention to everything that a boy *does*. Best advice I ever had. And it applies just as well to my professional life as it ever did to dating boyfriends. I remind myself of it every day.'

I must remember to tell Alice that one, Carlyle thought.

'Leaving aside the fact that, based on what you've told me, you have absolutely no grounds for snooping around Buckingham Palace,' Simpson continued, on a roll now, 'your history with SO14 is such that I can't honestly believe that there is anyone there who would even give you the time of day.'

'Are you telling me to abandon this child?' Carlyle asked.

'No one is abandoning anything,' Simpson said, aggrieved. 'From what you have told me, she is not your responsibility any longer.'

'I found her.'

'John . . .'

He kept pushing. 'Nine years old.'

'Don't come all Mother bloody Teresa with me, Inspector Carlyle.' Despite herself, Simpson laughed audibly, allowing them both to step back from the row that was brewing.

Interesting, Carlyle thought. Having a husband in prison has helped her develop something approaching a sense of humour. 'Look, all I'm saying is—'

'Don't push me, John. Let me read the report tonight, and we'll discuss it tomorrow.'

'Okay.' He knew that was as much as he could hope to get right now. 'Have a safe journey back to London.'

'Thank you.'

Ending the call, he dropped the phone back in his pocket. 'Score draw, mate,' he said to himself. Maybe he had expected too much from the 'new', humbled Commander Simpson. At least, however, he could say that he had kept her in the loop. He could argue his case again tomorrow. And, in the meantime, he could continue with his enquiries.

HE PICKED UP a message from Green confirming that the girl had been taken to a small 'interim holding facility' i.e. hostel on Bolsover Street, just south of Regents Park. Carver House was a four-storey Georgian building containing six bedrooms and thirteen beds. It was used as emergency accommodation for children between eight and twelve while Social Services sorted something more permanent for them, whether a foster home, a 'special school' or maybe deportation.

Before heading up there, Carlyle made another trip home – Helen and Alice were still out – and 'borrowed' some colouring pens and a small cuddly rabbit that he was fairly sure his daughter hadn't looked at for at least five years.

The walk up to Bolsover Street took him about twenty minutes, ideas bouncing around his head in a random, desperate fashion. He might not be able to solve this case but he was clear that he still had to help the girl. If he couldn't do that, he was lost. He was a copper with the full weight of one of the world's biggest and well-resourced police forces behind him. If, despite all that, he still couldn't protect a little girl, what was the fucking point?

Standing on the doorstep of Carver House, he felt tired and anxious. He rang the buzzer and waited. No one came. He rang it a second time, and then a third. In the end, he just kept his thumb pressed down and let it ring incessantly.

'Okay! Okay!' Finally the door clicked open. A gaunt, middle-aged woman wearing a dark pink tracksuit and green trainers peered out at him. 'Yes?'

Carlyle retreated down a step, flashing her his badge. 'I'm Inspector Carlyle of the Metropolitan Police. I'm here to see Hilary Green from Social Services.'

'It's like Piccadilly Circus here today,' the woman grumbled.

'Hilary Green,' repeated Carlyle impatiently.

'She's not here,' the woman replied. 'Her shift finished hours ago.' She tut-tutted. 'Poor woman, do you know how much over-time she has to do each and every week?'

Biting his tongue, Carlyle made a face that might have been a grimace, might have been a scowl. 'Is the girl here?'

Leaning against the doorframe, the woman folded her arms. 'Which one d'ya mean? I've got five of them here at the moment.'

'The one that Hilary brought here earlier. The Ukrainian girl.'

'Ukrainian, is she?' The woman sniffed. 'Why am I not surprised? We get all sorts here.'

'Look,' Carlyle snapped, 'I don't need the social commentary. I just want to see the girl.'

Shocked, the woman took a step backwards, as if getting ready to slam the door in his face. He quickly jumped up a couple of steps and put his foot in the door.

The woman eyed the rabbit in Carlyle's hand then stared at him suspiciously. 'Who did you say you were again?'

With a sigh, Carlyle took out his warrant card a second time and thrust it in her face. 'Carlyle,' he said slowly. 'I work out of the Charing Cross police station. Maybe I should ask you for *your* ID.'

'Okay, okay.' The woman moved back out of the way. 'Keep yer hair on.'

'Now,' Carlyle hissed through gritted teeth, 'can I see the girl?'

The woman edged back further. 'She's not here either.'

'*What?*'

'Your colleague took her about an hour ago. Not long after Ms Green left.'

Carlyle frowned. 'What colleague?'

'The other policeman.' The woman still gripped the handle of the door tightly. 'He was far more polite than you.' She looked Carlyle up and down. 'Far better dressed too. Much more of a gentleman.'

'For fuck's sake!'

'He didn't swear either.'

'Fuck!' Carlyle hurled the rabbit at the woman, who ducked out of the way.

'Hey!' she cried. 'I'll report you for that. Wait 'til I tell Ms Green what you did.'

Carlyle stepped inside, slamming the door against the wall. Ignoring some whispering at the top of the stairs, he demanded of the cowering woman: 'This "colleague" – what did he say his name was?'

She made a hissing noise, but said nothing.

Carlyle had to resist the almost overwhelming temptation to give her a kick. 'Did he show you a badge?'

Arms wrapped around herself, the woman nodded.

'What did it say?'

'I don't know,' she whimpered. 'It was like yours.'

'What did he look like?'

'I dunno.' The woman gingerly lifted a hand to her face and wiped a tear from the corner of her eye. 'Like I said, he was smarter dressed than you.' She began edging away from Carlyle. 'Taller. Blond hair. Younger.'

'English?'

'What?'

'Was he English or was he a foreigner?'

'Oh, he was English. He had a very polite accent.'

'Posh?'

The woman nodded. 'Very posh.'

'Where did he say he was going?'

The woman thought about it. 'He said he had to take the girl back to the police station for some more questions.'

'Which station?'

'He didn't say.'

'And you just let him go?'

'He was a policeman,' the woman whined.

'How many posh policemen do you know?' Carlyle snarled. 'And what about the girl?' he asked. 'How did she react? Was she happy to see him? Did she go willingly?'

The woman said shamefacedly, 'I didn't see her. I was in the back making a cup of tea. They'd gone before I returned.'

'Jesus *fucking* Christ!' Carlyle sat himself down on the bottom stair with a thud and the woman scuttled into the rear of the house. If she's going to try and raise someone from Social Services, good luck to her, he thought. Breathing deeply, he waited for the anger inside him to subside so that he could start to think.

'Mister?'

Carlyle looked round to see a girl, maybe the same age as Alzbetha, standing at the top of the stairs. 'Hello,' he said. 'What's your name?'

'Sally.'

'Nice to meet you, Sally,' he said, giving her a limp wave. 'I'm John. I'm a policeman.'

'I know. I heard you tell that woman.' Cautiously, she came down towards him. 'Can I have those pens?'

Carlyle looked at the packet in his hand and passed it over. Picking up the rabbit from the hall floor, he tossed her that as well.

'Thanks.' The girl held her new presents tightly to her chest and retreated slowly up to the top of the stairs. 'I saw the man take that girl.'

'Oh, yes?'

'She didn't want to go. She tried to hit him, but he stuck her under his arm and carried her down.'

'This man,' Carlyle said gently, 'what did he look like?'

The girl looked him straight in the eye. 'He looked like a prince.'

'I see.'

'Yes.' Sally turned and disappeared. Moments later, she came back with a colouring book. Carlyle recognised it as one of the books he had bought for Alzbetha the night before. She pointed to the cover, where a prince and a princess were dancing in front of a castle. 'He looked like him.'

Chapter Five

'INTERVALS' IN THE Queen's official programme allowed opportunities for the State Rooms of the Palace to be opened up to the public. With more than four million people taking the tour, it was a nice little earner for one of the richest families in the world. Helen had taken Alice there the year before and had come back moaning about the cost and the petty officiousness that had seen the child's bottled water taken away from her on 'security grounds'.

Today there was still more than an hour to go before opening time, and the queue of tourists patiently waiting outside Buckingham Palace Mews numbered only a dozen or so. Walking quickly past them, Carlyle headed for a small side entrance twenty yards further along Buckingham Gate. As he approached, the door opened and a small man in a green cap and uniform ushered him inside. Nodding to him, Carlyle carried on down a passageway and round a corner. Five yards further on, he showed his ID to another guard sitting in a small Perspex booth. Next to the booth stood a metal detector. Behind that was a floor-to-ceiling turnstile, of the kind you usually saw at football grounds.

'Who are you here to see?' The man in the booth said it into a small microphone, his voice tinny and distorted by feedback.

'Charlie Adam.' Carlyle glanced at the CCTV camera above his head and waited as the guard consulted a list of names printed on a sheet of paper. 'He's expecting me.'

After some searching and a bit of head-scratching, the man finally located the right name. 'Carlyle, yes.' He picked up a phone.

'Don't worry,' Carlyle smiled. 'I know where I'm going.'

The man shrugged. 'Protocol.'

'Fair enough.' Be cool, Carlyle told himself. You don't want to get thrown out of here again.

Someone answered at the other end of the line. 'I've got Mr Carlyle here,' the guard announced. 'Yes, *Inspector* Carlyle. Okay, I will.' He put the phone down carefully, as if he was scared that it might break, and nodded to Carlyle. 'You can go in.'

'Thanks.'

After emptying his pockets, Carlyle stepped through the metal detector which, happily, did not go off. After first recovering his keys and his change, he was clicked through the turnstile by the guard. On the other side, the passageway continued for a few yards before he proceeded through another door, emerging into a cobbled courtyard about half the size of a football pitch. The smell of fresh horse manure told him that the stables were still where he remembered them. Glancing to his left, he could see a couple of horses happily munching on some hay. To his right was the Royal Mews, and on the far side of the courtyard was a collection of offices used by members of the Royal Household and other Palace workers. Dodging several large piles of horse shit, he set off across the courtyard, heading for a flight of stairs in the far left corner.

JUST AFTER THE turn of the millennium, Carlyle had been assigned to Royal Protection Duties. What was supposed to be a three-year posting ended after less than two. It had been, by some considerable margin, the worst time of his professional life.

SO14 was arguably the most boring posting in the Met. The job consisted solely of babysitting some of the most over-privileged, least self-aware people you could imagine, from a threat that largely consisted of over-zealous grannies and the odd harmless nutter. No one had been interested in blowing up royalty since he was a boy; and now even the most senior royals were just an extension of the ubiquitous celebrity culture that seemed to hold the whole country in its thrall. There were so many of them, too: not just the Queen and her immediate family, but dozens of hangers-on, known as 'collaterals', who the average man and woman in the street had never heard of. Together, they helped drive the annual cost of SO14 up to an estimated £50 million; *estimated* because the actual number remained a State secret that even the Freedom of Information Act could not access.

Carlyle had never given any of this a moment's thought before he joined SO14. After almost twenty years on the Force, he had become used to being shunted around from place to place. Once he arrived among the horse shit and the tourists, however, it was a different story. Working in SO14 was not policework as Carlyle understood it. Basically he was there to be used as a gofer, a servant and a general dogsbody. The amount of actual policework involved was approximately nil. What there was, however, was the opportunity to make a bit of cash on the side. Sidelines included flogging the odd royal trinket on the internet and hosting informal tours of the Palace when the owners were away. During Carlyle's time there, one PC had even charged a mate £200 so he could shag a girl on the back lawn. Urban legend had it that one of the Queen's corgis had almost choked on the discarded condom.

From the off, Carlyle had been bored silly. So he made a concerted effort to get transferred out of the unit as quickly as possible. However, his lack of connections and good will meant that the harder he tried to get out, the more he was reminded that he would have to complete his full term. Carlyle being Carlyle, however, he would not take 'no' for an answer. In the end, he managed to secure an early release. But only by nearly ending his career in the Police Force full-stop.

Having to chaperone the younger royals when they went out on the lash was the worst part of the job. Watching them drop the equivalent of more than a month's salary in some Chelsea nightclub, and then stagger out much the worse for wear, to provide fodder for the paparazzi, was simply soul-destroying. One night, Carlyle's charge, a wretched collateral who was something like twelfth or thirteenth in line to the throne, stumbled blind drunk out of Pomegranate, a fashionable watering-hole – like a school disco but with silly prices – and started rowing violently with his girlfriend. The woman herself, a nice but dim deb from the Home Counties, burst into tears and fled into the night. While Carlyle's partner chased after her, Carlyle stayed with the boy. Five or six snappers immediately surrounded the young man, like hyenas round a wounded zebra, flash guns illuminating the darkened street. Before he could intervene, Carlyle watched with a mixture of horror and amusement as the young royal stepped forward and took a swing at one of the photographers. Unfortunately for him, the photographer in question was Alex Hutton, a South African soldier who had spent a couple of years in the French Foreign Legion before accepting the much tougher assignment of working for a British tabloid. Just for a moment, Hutton completely forgot where he was. As his training kicked in, he stepped outside the intended punch and downed his assailant with a swift right to the stomach, following by a crunching left to the nose.

'Ouch!' Carlyle grinned. He was enjoying himself for the first time that day. 'That has got to be a major breach of royal etiquette.'

The young royal collapsed on the tarmac in a bloody heap and began vomiting. While Hutton and the other photographers moved in for their close-ups, Carlyle slowly counted to thirty, before stepping in among them and leading the groaning youth to a nearby car.

On the drive back to the Palace, Carlyle's passenger slowly recovered his breath in the back seat. 'Where the hell were you?' the boy hissed, still holding his nose. 'I've lost a fucking tooth . . . and I think that bastard has broken my nose!'

Carlyle glanced in the rear-view mirror at the puffy-faced hooligan, and smiled to himself.

'Fucking useless plod! You people are all the same . . . I'll have your bloody goolies for this!'

Carlyle said nothing.

Once he got back to the Palace, he handed the boy over to the servants and headed to the SO14 office to write his report. This would be all over the papers in a couple of hours and Carlyle knew that he had to get his explanation in first. In considerable detail, he described how the snapper had acted solely in self-defence, and stressed that the young royal had been 'instantly' rescued from the consequences of his folly.

The next day, Hutton was arrested, charged with grievous bodily harm and threatened with deportation.

Two days later, Carlyle himself was suspended.

With half a dozen witnesses, and dozens if not hundreds of photographic images to support the snapper's defence, the Crown Prosecution Service quickly realised that this was one case they did not want to bring to court. Knowing the score, the snapper's lawyer politely but firmly refused to settle, and waited for the CPS to fold. In the end, it took more than three months for the charges against Hutton to be dropped. Shortly afterwards, Carlyle received a letter from the Police Federation saying that he would be returning to duty the following week. That was the good news. The even better news was that he would be going back to Charing Cross. His unhappy stint at Buckingham Palace was over.

Unable to believe his luck, Carlyle had to restrain his glee when the union representative gave him a call to tell him that he had been very lucky: he had kept his job and his pension was secure – but he had *used up all his last chances*, whatever that meant. Being an inspector at Charing Cross would be the end of the line. That's fine by me, Carlyle thought, just as long as I don't have to deal with these idiots any more.

AT THE TOP of the stairs, Carlyle turned right and headed for the door furthest along. Taking a deep breath, he knocked.

'Come!'

He stepped inside and smiled at the chief superintendent sitting primly behind the desk in his small, cluttered office which enjoyed a fine view over the carefully manicured lawns on the west side of the Palace. Normally used for landing the royal helicopter, the lawns also provided the setting for the Queen's annual garden parties, and were large enough to take 8,000 people at a time for tea and cucumber sandwiches.

'John Carlyle,' he announced.

'Charlie Adam.' Standing up, the man leaned over the desk to offer his hand.

The senior SO14 officer on site, Adam was not much more than five foot six, round and totally bald. The lack of hair made him hard to age, but Carlyle reckoned him to be in his late fifties. 'Thank you for seeing me.'

'My pleasure.' Adam smiled. They shook hands. 'Take a seat,' he said, sitting down himself. 'Cup of tea?'

'No, thank you.'

'Are you sure?' Adam pulled a 'Coat of Arms' tea caddy from a drawer and waved it at Carlyle. 'These are HRH Originals. Top-notch organic stuff.' Opening the lid, he pulled out a bag and held it in front of his nose. 'The leaves are rolled on the thighs of West Country virgins, or something.'

'I didn't know there were any virgins in the West Country,' Carlyle leered.

'Probably not,' Adam grinned, 'not after about the age of ten, anyway. Still, it's good stuff. A tin like this sells for seven quid in the tourist shop.'

Carlyle held up a hand. 'I'm fine.'

Adam placed the caddy on his desk, adjusted his tie and sat up straight. 'So, you are the infamous John Carlyle.'

Carlyle grimaced. 'Hardly infamous.'

'Don't be so modest,' the chief superintendent smiled slyly. 'They still talk about you round here.' He mentioned a few names from the past. 'I'm guessing that you're not looking at coming back.'

Carlyle winced. 'No.'

'Just as well,' Adam conceded. 'So, what is it that I can do for you?'

For what seemed like the hundredth time, Carlyle explained the story of the young foreign girl he had found just beyond the gardens outside.

Adam listened intently, fingers pressed together as if in prayer. 'That's very interesting, Inspector,' he said, once Carlyle had finished, 'but what has it got to do with us?'

Good bloody question, Carlyle thought. 'There are two things . . .'

'Yes, yes.' Eyes shining, Adam sat up further in his chair.

He should get a cushion to sit on, Carlyle thought.

'First, the girl said she lived here.'

'Hah!'

'Yes.' Carlyle gave a small nod. 'Then there's the guy who claimed he was her uncle.'

Adam smiled benignly. 'Did you actually see him exit or enter the Palace?'

'No.'

'There are more than five hundred people working in here at any given time . . .'

'I know that.'

'At the weekend, there was a State Banquet for the Sultan of Brunei, so you can double that figure – even triple it.' Adam laid his palms on the table. 'Then there are the tourists . . . and that's just inside.' He let out a long breath. 'Outside, goodness knows how many people are milling about at any given time. You, my friend, really are looking for the needle in the haystack.'

'Fore!'

The sound of breaking glass was followed by the angry whinny of a horse.

Carlyle rose halfway out of his chair and peered through the window. In front of the shrubbery, three men stood holding plastic buckets in which they were collecting the golf balls being pinged across the lawn by a gent in a tweed cap, standing two hundred or so yards away. 'I see the Duke still likes to practise his game in the back garden.' He smirked.

Adam groaned. 'His youngest son has just taken up the game, too. If anything, he's even worse than his father.'

'Are those your guys on ball collection duty?' Carlyle asked, sitting back down.

Adam coloured slightly, but did not respond.

'A great use of public money, I reckon.'

'Ours not to reason why, Inspector,' Adam bridled. 'Is there anything else I can help you with?'

'I was wondering,' Carlyle said, 'if I could have a list of all staff currently working at the Palace – including the SO14 roster, of course.'

'Why?'

'I would like to speak to everyone who was on duty on Saturday night.'

Adam frowned. 'Is that really necessary?'

Carlyle shrugged. 'I have to start somewhere.'

'Inspector,' Adam let out an exasperated snort, 'I have just explained how many people we have here, as if you didn't already know that. It would take forever to interview them all. And because of what? A hunch?'

Carlyle said nothing.

Adam raised an eyebrow. 'How much manpower would such an investigation require? How much time?'

Carlyle smiled weakly but said nothing. After almost thirty years in the Metropolitan Police, he knew that efficiency and value for money were alien concepts to the Force. The only time anyone ever raised cost as an issue was when they wanted an excuse to stop you from doing something.

'I have to say,' Adam continued, 'that it sounds like a complete waste of time to me. And there was me thinking that you seemed so keen on seeing the efficient use of public funds.'

'It's *my* investigation,' Carlyle replied evenly. 'I would also like to see the CCTV images taken from the Constitution Hill side of the property around the time I found the girl on Saturday night.'

Adam eyed him carefully. 'Does Carole Simpson know about this?'

'Yes.' Carlyle nodded. It was, he decided, kind of true.

Adam sat back in his chair and stared at his precious tea caddy. 'Well,' he said mechanically, 'if the commander sends me a formal request, in line with the established and agreed protocols, I will see what I can do.'

Carlyle realised that this was the best he was going to get. 'That is very kind.' He smiled as he stood up. 'Thank you very much for your help, sir.'

'My pleasure,' Adam said, reaching across the table and offering him another limp handshake. 'It's good to meet you at last. I must say, I'm glad you weren't here on my watch. We run a tight ship here now.'

'I'm sure you do,' Carlyle said politely. 'I'm sure you do.'

HE GOT BACK to the office to find a stack of documents sitting on his desk. On top of it was a large yellow Post-it note. Carlyle read the scribble – *Don't ask where these came from and burn after reading, Joe* – and laughed. Sitting back in his chair, he put his feet up on the desk and flipped through the papers. They contained summary details of everyone currently working in Royal

Protection. It wasn't as much information as Charlie Adam could have provided, but it was a start.

In all, SO14 had more than 400 officers, including 256 on active duty: of these, 152 currently worked primarily in London, 60 worked at Buckingham Palace itself and 14 had been on shift the previous Saturday evening. For each officer, he now had a name, rank, summary career details and a passport-style photo. He looked through the 14, then the 60, then the 152, but none of them was the posh man from the park. Relief mixed with frustration; the idea of a police colleague being involved in something like this would have been simply too dispiriting – even for a hardened cynic like Carlyle.

After a couple of hours of careful sifting, he was left with three sorted piles. By his left hand was one for the 126 officers he didn't know, plus another for the 25 he did. The former had no obvious reason to help him with his enquiries; the latter, he was fairly sure, wouldn't even piss on him if he was on fire. The third selection to his right was very much smaller. It consisted of just one person; the only person he knew who might, perhaps, be willing to give him some help.

THE NUMBER RANG for what seemed like an eternity before the voicemail kicked in: *This is Alexa Matthews. Leave a message and I might get back to you in due course.*

Friendly as ever, he thought. 'Alexa, this is John Carlyle. Long time no speak. Give me a call – I'm still at Charing Cross. I wondered if I could ask you about something. Thanks.'

Two minutes later, his phone rang.

'Hello?'

'John,' Carole Simpson said shrilly, 'what the hell are you doing?'

'Er . . .' Carlyle shifted uneasily in his seat. 'What do you mean?'

'You know exactly what I bloody mean,' she snapped. 'I've just got off the phone to Charlie Adam.'

'Did he try and sell you some organic tea?'

'What?'

'Nothing.'

'I'll tell you what he did do,' Simpson said crossly. 'He told me, very politely but very firmly, to keep you under control.'

'I'm always under control,' Carlyle joked.

'John, please, try and *listen* for once. Adam asked me why you thought you could just bowl up to SO14 and basically look to put the whole bloody lot of them under investigation when you've got absolutely no reason to do so. When it's not even your case.'

'What did you say to him?'

'What *could* I say?'

There was a pause.

'Have you read my report?' he asked finally.

'Adam made it very clear that you are not welcome over there. He doesn't want you wasting any more of his time.'

'Have – you – read – the report?'

'Er . . .'

At least she can't bring herself to lie, Carlyle thought, which puts Simpson a cut above a lot of people I know. 'A child has been physically and sexually assaulted,' he said grimly. 'And now she has been kidnapped. This is a very serious investigation. A young child suffering horrible and despicable abuse – and yet no one seems interested. No one seems to give a flying fuck.'

There was another longer pause while Simpson thought of something to say. Finally she asked: 'What about Social Services? What about the social worker?'

'She knows nothing,' Carlyle snorted. 'She wasn't there when the kid was snatched. Still, it hasn't stopped her taking stress-related sick leave. She'll probably be off for months.'

'Have you heard anything from Vice?'

'Not a dickie-bird.'

'Okay.' Simpson let out a deep sigh. 'I'll read the report right now. Come up to Paddington in an hour.'

THE TWO MEN stood in the doorway and looked at the sullen girl sitting on the bed in front of them. A single low-energy bulb hanging from the ceiling above her head bathed the room in a grubby light that hid the dirt and the flaking paint on the walls, but only added to the sense of gloom. Outside, from the suburban North London street, came the constant hum of traffic. Inside, there was nothing in the room apart from the girl and the bed. It looked like a prison cell. It *was* a prison cell.

'So . . . what shall we do with her?'

The older man looked surprised at the question. 'It's business as usual. We have bills to pay.'

'Isn't that a bit risky?'

'What do you want to do? Shut the whole thing down?'

The younger man looked at the business card in his hand. 'No, but—'

'You worry too much. The police will lose interest very quickly. They had already handed the kid over to Social Services before you got her back.'

'That's *how* I got her back.'

'So everything now is sorted.'

'It's just so damned annoying to have this type of problem.'

'It's nothing. Think about it from their point of view. They have lost the girl, and they have no leads. The last thing they want is anyone asking questions about how they managed to lose a nine-year-old girl who was supposedly in their care. Within a week they will have forgotten that she even existed.'

The girl was quiet, resigned now. It was almost as if she was in a trance. The older man marched over to the bed and pulled her upright by the hair. 'No more running away,' he hissed.

The girl started screaming.

'Calm down!' The younger man gently freed her and she slumped back on to the bed. 'She can't understand you anyway.'

The older man made a fist. 'Oh, yes, she can, the little bitch! It's time that she earned us some money.'

The younger man stepped back out of the room. 'She will. In the meantime, if it's bothering you that much, see what you can find out about the policeman who found her. If it comes to it, we can have him dealt with.'

Alzbetha rubbed her tingling head as she watched the two men leave the room. The door clicked shut behind them and she heard the key turn in the lock. Pulling her knees up to her chest, she began slowly rocking backwards and forwards on the bed. Looking round the bare cell, she wished that they had at least let her bring her colouring book. She hoped that the nice man who had bought it for her would come and get her, but she knew that he wouldn't.

SITTING IN SIMPSON's office in Paddington Green police station, Carlyle noticed that she had removed the picture of her husband from her desk. As far as he could tell, the photo had been the only personal touch she had ever allowed herself in all the years spent in this cramped, over-heated office. Now it was gone, presumably never to return. Wondering why she hadn't filed for divorce, he quickly concluded that it was none of his business. He wasn't really that interested anyway.

Simpson sneezed, bringing him back to the present.

'Bless you.'

'Thank you.' She looked up, as if awaiting some barbed comment.

Carlyle said nothing. Returning her gaze to the desk, she made a scribble on a memo. Arms folded, he waited for her to read the various reports and tried not to look bored.

After a couple more minutes, she pulled a file from the bottom of the heap and flipped it open. Quickly, she scanned the text in the hope that it had somehow changed since she had read it last. It hadn't. With a sigh, she closed the file and pushed it across the desk towards Carlyle. 'We don't have a lot, do we?'

'No.'

'What other work have you got on at the moment?' It was an admission of defeat.

Trying not to smile, Carlyle ran through a dispiriting list of misdemeanours and anti-social behaviour that he was supposed to be sorting out.

'Fine,' Simpson said. 'Go and talk to Superintendent Warren Shen in Vice. I've sent him a copy of your report. He'll decide if there's anything they can do. In the meantime, feel free to shake things up a bit. See what you can find.'

'Okay.' Carlyle grinned.

'You are right,' Simpson sniffed, 'this *is* horrible. We should give it some of our time.'

'Thank you.'

'But if you find you're not getting anywhere,' Simpson said flatly, 'don't drag it out.'

Chapter Six

CARLYLE WALKED OUT of the train station, heading in the direction of Windsor Castle. According to a tourist brochure he had read on the train, Windsor Castle was the Official Residence of Her Majesty the Queen and the oldest and largest still-occupied castle in the world. At the moment, however, the old girl wasn't at home. Rather, she was on a state visit to Costa Rica, doing whatever it was that you did on state visits. During his time in Royal Protection, Carlyle had never travelled anywhere more exotic than Cardiff. That was more than far enough away from home, where he was concerned. Anyway, wasn't Wales considered a kind of foreign country these days?

It had turned cold. When the wind blew, Carlyle realised it was time to be breaking out his winter wardrobe. Walking through the town centre, he buttoned up his raincoat and lengthened his stride. After five minutes, he turned down Peascod Street and headed for the Royal Joker public house.

The Royal Joker occupied the ground and lower-ground floors of a nondescript 1970s office block. Given that it was barely eleven o'clock in the morning, Carlyle was not surprised to find the place completely empty when he stepped inside the pub. On the wall at the back was a sign pointing to a games room and the beer garden. Nodding at the girl cleaning the tables, Carlyle went through the main bar and down some stairs into a large room that, if anything, seemed even colder than the street outside. At the far end, a pair of French windows led out on to a patio on which stood a few forlorn plastic tables. Inside, a couple of tatty leather sofas sat next to a wall. Above one was a large poster of Mount Iron in Wanaka, advertising holidays in New Zealand. In the middle of the room was a coin-operated, red-topped pool table. A handwritten sign on the side said £2 a game. Two half-empty pints of lager stood on the rim of the table, next to a small cube of blue chalk.

Ignoring his arrival, two women were engrossed in a game that had clearly just started. The one leaning over the table was bulky, with a low centre of gravity. Her short dark curly hair and pained expression gave her more than a passing resemblance to Diego Maradona in his post-playing days. One foot off the ground, she bent forward, searching for the right angle for her next shot. Watching her intently was her companion, a tall, thin woman in black jeans and a black T-shirt. With too much make-up and violently black hair, she looked to Carlyle like a Goth pensioner. He was pretty sure she was the girlfriend. He remembered meeting her once or twice during his time in Royal Protection but couldn't remember her name. Studiously ignoring him, she picked up her pint and took a dainty sip.

With a grunt, the woman at the table over-hit her shot and watched the cue ball slam into the middle pocket and disappear. 'Shit!'

'Unlucky,' Carlyle said, stepping towards the table.

Alexa Matthews slid away from the table and turned to face him. 'Fuck off.'

Making an effort to almost smile, he looked her up and down. They were about the same height, but she was twice his width. Wearing a pair of biker boots, torn jeans and an Iron Maiden T-shirt, she looked every inch the off-duty copper that she was. Matthews had been dressing the same way for at least twenty years. In his opinion, the nose ring and the three piercings in each eyebrow didn't really suit a woman in her late forties. Presumably she took them out when she went on duty.

'What are you doing here?' she scowled, grasping her pool cue tightly.

'I wanted a word,' Carlyle said evenly, glancing cautiously at the cue. 'I left you a message.'

'And I didn't reply,' Matthews said. 'Didn't that tell you something?'

The other woman had retrieved the cue ball and proceeded to pot a couple of colours in quick succession.

Matthews glanced at the table and grimaced. Turning back to Carlyle, her eyes narrowed. 'And now you've put me off my game,' she said, without even the hint of a smile.

The other woman moved round the table for her next shot, gently shooing Matthews out of the way, forcing her to step closer to Carlyle.

'Now that I'm here . . .' he started.

'You shouldn't have come,' Matthews hissed.

'Now that I am here,' he repeated, 'I wanted to ask you about something important.'

Matthews tossed her cue on to a nearby sofa and picked up her pint. 'I don't want to talk to you.'

'It's important,' he repeated, not wanting to plunge into the details.

'Maybe to you.'

'Seriously.'

'It was always important with you, Carlyle,' Matthews sneered. 'Wasn't it?'

Carlyle ignored the barb. 'I just need some up-to-date information on SO14.'

'What?' Matthews snorted. 'You still trying to fuck the unit up? I thought you'd given up on that one a long time ago.' She grinned at her companion. 'Around about the time you got your fucking head kicked in.'

The other woman looked up from the table and laughed, before quickly potting a green.

Carlyle gazed at his shoes in an attempt to hide a rueful grin. His mind went back to the night when a couple of his SO14 colleagues, incensed by his lack of 'team spirit', had dragged him out into the Palace stables for a good beating. They had just been working up a head of steam when Matthews had appeared with a couple of royal footmen, and hauled them off. Carlyle had been left with just a few cuts and bruises, and a medium-sized dent to his pride.

The next day, he had gone to thank her, but she had waved him away. 'I did it for them,' she had said, 'not for you. You're not worth anyone risking their career for.'

Matthews drained the last of her pint. 'Just because I saved your arse that time doesn't mean I'm your friend.'

Carlyle held up a hand in supplication. 'I know.' He watched the other woman sink the last ball and drop her cue on the table.

Matthews held out her empty glass and nodded towards the bar. 'Why don't you get me another one, Heather? I'll be out in a minute.'

Heather? That was it: Heather Ramen. Or Raven? Or Ramsden? Something like that. A 'performance artist' back in the day. Carlyle wondered if she still 'performed'.

Heather grunted as she took her pint pot and wandered off.

Matthews waited until she had left the room before turning to Carlyle. 'You always were a right cunt, causing trouble, winding everyone up.'

'Maybe.' Carlyle shrugged. 'But things are getting worse in SO14, aren't they?'

Matthews picked up the cue ball and weighed it in her hand like she wanted to smash his skull with it. 'What would you know about it?'

'It's come up during an investigation.'

'Bollocks. You're just shit-stirring.' Matthews reluctantly tossed the ball back on the table. 'You should leave SO14 alone. It's not your problem any more. And it's not mine either. I'm leaving. Transfer out next month.' She pointed a stubby index finger at him. 'So I don't want any aggro.'

Carlyle stood his ground. 'This is a formal investigation, Alexa. I'm well within my rights to come and see you at work. Or at home.'

She studied him doubtfully.

'If I wanted to cause you and your girlfriend any aggro,' Carlyle continued, 'I wouldn't have trundled all the way out here to make a discreet social call at eleven o'clock in the morning.'

Matthews bristled. 'Leave Heather out of this, you tosser. I've been out for a long time. Everyone knows I'm a dyke. So what?'

'It wasn't a threat,' Carlyle said mildly.

'Yeah, yeah.' Matthews glanced in the direction of the bar. For a moment, she clearly turned something over in her mind.

Carlyle waited.

Heather had decided to take her time. Matthews cursed under her breath.

Carlyle looked at his shoes.

'Joe Dalton,' she said finally.

'Joe Dalton?' Carlyle made a face. 'Who's Joe Dalton?'

Matthews pawed at a stain on the carpet with her boot. 'Joe was in SO14. Did a bit of moonlighting in his brother's taxi. Topped himself a couple of months ago.' She rubbed her eyes. 'Decapitated himself in his cab.'

Carlyle thought about it for a moment. 'How did he manage that?'

'It was in the papers. You might have read about it.'

Carlyle shook his head. 'No, I don't think so. What's Dalton got to do with all the shenanigans going on at SO14?'

She shot him a look. 'That's for you to work out. You're the bloody detective. Jesus!'

'Okay.' Carlyle sighed. 'If I'm the bloody detective, where should I start bloody looking?'

Despite herself, Matthews grinned. 'Go and talk to his girl-friend. A woman called Fiona Allcock.' The grin stretched into a leer. 'As in all-cock.'

'Where do I find her?'

'It shouldn't be difficult to track her down. She's famous.'

'Famous?'

'Just Google her.'

Fucking Google. Suddenly it was the world's number-one police tool. How did any criminals ever get caught before it existed? Carlyle thought about it. 'It's a fairly common name. How will I know if I've got the right Allcock?'

'Jesus!' Matthews groaned. 'You're still as annoying as ever.' Then her grin reappeared, this time wider than before. 'Try Googling "Allcock" and "animals". See what you get. Just don't let the wife catch you doing it.'

Carlyle raised an eyebrow.

'Off you go.' Matthews laughed, sticking a couple of coins in a slot in the table and releasing the balls for another game. 'That's your lot. And don't come back here again. Next time I *will* brain you. And that's a promise.'

SUPERINTENDENT WARREN SHEN was standing in the storeroom on the first floor, above the Vintage Magazine Shop in the heart of Soho. Yawning, he flicked the fringe of his shoulder-length blond hair out of his eyes. Six foot one inch tall, rake thin, dressed in jeans and a Bruce Lee *Fists of Fury* T-shirt, he looked like he was barely into his twenties when, in fact, he would reach forty in little more than six months' time. A seventeen-year police career, the last six of them in Vice, had not yet eaten away at his boyish good looks. What it had done to him on the inside was, however, another matter entirely.

Out of the window, Shen eyed the entrance to the Soho Parish Church of England primary school, on the other side of Great Windmill Street. It was coming up to leaving time and a small group of mothers, a couple of them minding younger children in pushchairs, were standing by the gate to collect their kids. Every couple of minutes, one of the girls from the Fun Palace strip club next door would venture out into the street and remonstrate with the waiting mothers, inviting them to fuck off lest they put off potential punters wandering up the street.

This was a scene that Shen had witnessed many times before. The strip clubs, sex shops and hostess bars on Great Windmill Street regularly complained about the potential for the school run to interfere with their passing trade. With no obvious sense of irony, one of the shop-owners – Soho's self-proclaimed number one dildo merchant – had complained to the local paper that the school 'lowered the tone of the neighbourhood'. On the one hand, it was quite funny. On the other it made Shen pine for the good old days (approximately twenty or so years before he started on the Force) when you could simply round up the filth-peddlers and the perverts and haul them back to the cells for a good kicking.

In the face of this onslaught, one of the mothers – an evangelical Christian called Mary Mack – once had the temerity to fight back. Mack organised a petition and launched a campaign for a fifty-yard 'smut-free zone' around the school. It was a good idea but, given the economic realities of the neighbourhood, one that never had the remotest chance of being realised. Instead, the poor misguided woman had found herself singled out for particular abuse.

Only a week earlier, Mrs Mack had been sexually assaulted and pelted with dogshit by a group of disgruntled sex-industry workers. When the *Evening Standard* had put the story on its front page, it had caught the attention of someone sufficiently senior at New Scotland Yard for action to be demanded. Shen had been tasked with arresting the culprits and sending a clear signal to the good citizens of Soho that there were limits of indecent behaviour beyond which even they could not go without the risk of official sanction.

Needing to catch the perpetrators in the act, Shen had been surprised and delighted when Mrs Mack agreed to come back for more punishment. Before she could change her mind, he had put in place a highly sophisticated sting operation that basically involved her lingering outside the school gate, waiting to be abused again.

Shen brought the Motorola radio to his mouth as he watched a fat peroxide blonde come out of the Fun Palace and on to the pavement. She was followed by one of the strip club's bouncers, a skinny, shaven-headed bloke in a Britney Spears T-shirt.

'Here we go . . .'

As the duo headed towards their target, the other mothers moved quickly away. Shen watched the by now familiar angry exchange that followed. Waiting until the bouncer put his hand on Mack's shoulder, he spoke into the radio: 'Okay. Move in. Arrest them both. Make sure we try and keep them in custody longer this time.'

As the two miscreants were bundled into a police van, the kids began heading out through the school gates. Shen thought of his own kids safely ensconced in the South London suburbs, and gave a silent prayer of thanks. By all accounts, Soho Parish was a very good school. But you had to be a certain sort of parent to send your kid there and have to put up with all the neighbouring shit, both metaphorical and physical.

Shen turned to Carlyle who was sitting on a sofa, reading the evening freesheet and worrying about Fulham's chances of avoiding relegation this season. 'You live round here, don't you?'

Carlyle nodded, but didn't look up from the paper. 'Yeah. About five minutes down the road. The other side of Cambridge Circus.'

'Kids?'

'One. A girl.'

Shen gestured in the direction of Soho Parish. 'She didn't go there, did she?'

'No. The wife looked at it though.'

'I wonder what all the kids make of it.'

Carlyle finally closed his paper, folded it up and stuck it in his jacket pocket. 'What? All the sex shops and stuff?'

'Yeah.'

'I suppose what you know is what you know,' Carlyle said. 'If you make this neighbourhood boring and mundane, then it loses any glamour and attraction.'

'It's a theory, I suppose.' Shen stepped away from the window and moved into the centre of the room. 'Anyway, I read that report Simpson sent me. Interesting . . . Do you really think the girl you found had been inside Buckingham Palace?'

Carlyle shrugged. 'It's a possibility.'

'A rather far-fetched one.'

'Maybe. I dunno.' Carlyle stiffly pushed himself up out of the sofa and on to his feet. 'The more I think about it, the more I think, Why not? Given all the other shit that people do there, it would make a perfect location for some evil bastard to get up to something like that.'

'It would be a new one on me,' Shen said. 'But we'll make some enquiries. Any leads on the girl?'

Carlyle shook his head. 'Not yet.'

Both men knew it was a minor miracle that she had been found once. There was next to no chance now that she would ever be seen again.

'What about the Ukrainian angle?' Carlyle asked.

'Obviously,' Shen said, in the kind of flat tone you adopted when giving a speech to the local Residents Association, 'we get a lot of Eastern Europeans – people-trafficking and prostitution. They come from all over, including the Ukraine. Kids are less common, but not unheard of.' He coughed. 'There is one guy we'll go and talk to, name of Ihor Chepoyak.'

'Who he?' Carlyle asked.

'A bad guy straight out of Central Casting. He is reputed, among other things, to have decapitated two of his girls with a blowtorch.'

'Nice.'

'Never been able to lay a finger on him,' Shen said wistfully. 'So far, at least.'

'Do you think you'll get anything out of him?'

'No idea,' Shen said, 'but he's just about the only Ukrainian I know.'

Carlyle gave Shen a quizzical look.

'You've got to start somewhere.' Shen grinned. 'Anyway, how many Ukrainians do you know yourself?'

Fair point, Carlyle thought. 'Can I tag along,' he asked, 'when you go and see him?'

'Why not. I'll let you know when I get an appointment.'

An appointment? Carlyle wondered.

'Thanks.'

'No problem.' Shen patted the inspector on the shoulder and headed for the door. 'Meantime, I need to go and sort out these shitheads we've just nicked.'

Chapter Seven

SITTING AT HIS desk on the third floor of Charing Cross police station, Carlyle flicked through the autopsy report on Joe Dalton, the decapitated part-time cabbie. It was clear that the case had been written off as a straightforward suicide, so the investigation had been perfunctory in the extreme. Both cocaine and ecstasy had been found in Dalton's system, but this had attracted no comment whatsoever, either from the pathologist or from the officer investigating the case. For his part, the inspector could let that slide. Getting coked up before you topped yourself seemed quite reasonable. The thing that *really* surprised Carlyle was that this case had been closed as a result of the intervention of SO14. Chief Superintendent Charlie Adam himself had signed off the final report, whereupon it had been completed and sent off to the central archive within less than a week.

Joe Szyszkowski ambled up to the desk, grazing on a chocolate doughnut. 'I checked the newspapers,' he explained, once the last of the sugary snack had been polished off and he'd licked his fingers clean in a frankly disagreeable manner. 'There were a couple of mentions of the . . .' he paused, grasping for the right word '. . . accident at the time when it happened. But no follow-up. And, bizarrely, no one mentioned that Dalton was a copper.'

'It seems unusual that SO14 got involved in the investigation,' Carlyle mused.

'Very,' Joe agreed.

'Why not just leave it to the locals?'

'Maybe they just wanted to sit on the drugs thing. That could have come back on them. I'm sure a spate of "random" drugs tests over at the Palace wouldn't have gone down too well.'

'Maybe not.'

Joe scratched his ever-expanding belly. 'I spoke to the original investigating officer, down at Elephant and Castle. He arrived on the scene about twenty minutes after it was called in. Also spoke to the guy who saw it happen. Even though there was no suicide note, it sounds like that is definitely what it was.'

'Yes,' Carlyle said. 'The question is, why did Dalton feel the need to top himself? He had no problems that anyone seemed to know about – no money worries, no history of mental illness. Okay, so he did some drugs, but plenty of coppers do. In Dalton's case, it seems to have been purely recreational, and kept well under control. He turned up for work when he was supposed to and always put in a regular shift.'

'Hadn't taken a single sickie this year, apparently,' Joe put in.

Carlyle raised his eyebrows. They both knew that a copper who didn't take regular sick leave was a rare creature indeed. Slack rules and a 'sick-note culture' meant that the average British policeman took as much as an extra three weeks a year off for supposed illness. And then, at the end of it all, around a third of *all* police retired early due to 'ill-health'. The scam was so institutionalised that it was widely considered a legitimate part of the job. Carlyle hated the lazy, skiving mentality behind the numbers, but even he knew better than to open his mouth and express an opinion on it. If Dalton was one of the few coppers not on the skive, that suggested he liked his job and took it seriously. 'So, there was nothing to suggest a problem with the execution of his duties?'

'Apart from the fact that he was moonlighting and doing X,' Joe pointed out helpfully.

'At least he didn't pass out in front of Her Majesty,' Carlyle grinned.

Joe laughed out loud. 'Or try and mount the Duke of Edinburgh, while under the misapprehension that the old bugger was Charlize Theron.'

'Urgh!' Carlyle made a face. 'Enough already! It would take more than ecstasy to mistake Big Phil for Charlize Theron. Seriously though, it must have something to do with the missing girl.'

'Could be.' But Joe was clearly not convinced.

'That's the direct implication of the steer which Alexa Matthews gave me.'

'Why don't we just press her for more information?'

'I got as much out of her as I could,' Carlyle said tartly.

'Want me to have a word with her?' Joe asked.

Carlyle shook his head. 'No . . . maybe – well, not yet. We've still got plenty of other leads to follow up.' His train of thought was interrupted by the phone on his desk starting to ring. He leaned over and picked it up. 'Hello?'

'John? It's Warren Shen.'

Carlyle jumped to his feet. 'Are we on?'

'Yes, we are. Can you meet me at Chalk Farm tube station in half an hour?'

'Yes. See you there.' Grabbing his coat, Carlyle turned to Joe. 'That was Shen.'

Joe looked at him blankly.

'The guy from Vice.'

'Okay.'

'I'm off to see this Ukrainian mobster that he knows. Let's have another chat when I get back.'

'Right.'

'In the meantime, see if you can find out anything about a woman called Fiona Allcock. She was Dalton's girlfriend. She's into animals, apparently.'

Joe raised an eyebrow.

'I know, I know.' Carlyle chuckled. 'I thought you'd like that. But try to avoid getting your computer closed down by IT. It'll take you weeks to get your access restored.'

'Good point.'

'Just see what there is. We'll talk when I get back.'

IN THE EVENT, Carlyle – more than ten minutes late himself – had to wait almost twenty minutes outside Chalk Farm tube station before Shen pulled up behind the wheel of an aged white BMW. Carlyle jumped into the passenger seat, and nodded to the two very large blokes squeezed into the rear.

'Constable Hamilton and Sergeant Frost,' Shen told him, glancing at the rear-view mirror.

'John Carlyle.'

The two men grunted acknowledgement.

'I've explained to them who you are – and why you're here,' Shen added.

Carlyle fastened his seat belt. 'So we're going in mob-handed?'

Shen pulled away from the kerb into some late-afternoon traffic. 'When it comes to Ihor, this is not mob-handed,' he said, casually cutting in front of a number 168 bus and heading north up Haverstock Hill.

Taking a right turn past the Royal Free Hospital, they turned east, heading away from the bourgeois splendour of Hampstead towards the somewhat grittier delights of Kentish Town. After about five minutes, Shen turned the car into Arkan Street, a mix of blocks of council flats, offices and light industrial units. After slowly making his way almost the full length of the pothole-ridden road, he brought the car to a halt, parking it in a motorcycle bay outside a decrepit-looking café called Janik's.

Inside, the place was empty. Hamilton and Frost took a table near the door, nodding eagerly when the woman behind the counter offered them coffee and a selection of *babka* cakes. Tempted by the cakes, Carlyle reluctantly followed Shen into a small room at the back. There, sitting at a round table, casually smoking a Marlboro was a huge, shaven-headed man dressed in a black leather jacket and a grey shirt which was open at the neck. Apart from the table and a couple more chairs, the room was bare. Behind the giant was another door. It was open a couple of inches, and Carlyle noticed some movement behind it. He glanced at Warren Shen but his colleague seemed relaxed enough. It looked like the superintendent had been here many times before.

The man nodded towards the two spare chairs and waited for the policemen to sit. Just then, the woman brought in a tray carrying three double espressos and three plates of *babka*, covered in melted chocolate. Placing the tray on the table, she quickly and silently retreated into the main café, closing the door behind her.

'Gentlemen.' Ihor Chepoyak gestured at the table. His accent was more North London than it was Kiev. 'Please.'

'Thank you.' Shen picked up a demitasse and took a sip of coffee.

Carlyle pounced instantly on one of the cakes and took a deep bite. He took care to chew it several times, savouring the taste before swallowing. 'Delicious!'

Chepoyak nodded happily.

Quickly finishing the *babka*, Carlyle resisted the temptation to ask Shen if he would be eating his. Indeed, he could have easily eaten all three. Instead, he settled for draining his espresso and sat back, ready to watch the show.

Chepoyak stubbed out his cigarette in an ashtray advertising Khortytsa Vodka and drank the rest of his coffee. 'So, Superintendent,' he asked, 'to what do I owe this pleasure?'

'Well . . .' Shen cleared his throat. 'This is my colleague, John Carlyle.'

Chepoyak ran a meaty hand backwards and forwards across the top of his head. As he did so, his eyes narrowed until they were almost slits. 'So we have a new face in Vice?'

'No, no.' Carlyle shook his head. 'I work out of Charing Cross. Superintendent Shen and I simply have a common interest in a particular case.'

Chepoyak folded his arms and leaned back in his chair. 'Which is what?'

'We are looking for a Ukrainian girl,' Shen said evenly.

Chepoyak leaned even further back in his chair. 'There are lots of girls,' he smiled.

'This one is very young,' Carlyle explained. 'Just eight or nine years old.'

Chepoyak made a face that said, *Ah, well, it takes all sorts* . . .

'She was trafficked,' Carlyle said quickly. 'She was abused.'

'I know, Ihor,' Shen said diplomatically, 'that you would not have anything to do with such business.'

Chepoyak leaned forward in his chair and dropped his forearms on the table. 'That's good to hear, Superintendent. I wouldn't want you thinking you could come here to ask for my help and also insult me at the same time.'

'Of course not.' Shen's smile was brittle yet sincere. 'We would never do that.'

'You might not like me,' Ihor said with a shrug, 'but I do good work back home. I build nurseries, I fund orphanages.' He stuck a hand inside his jacket. Carlyle tensed slightly, but all that came out was an A5-sized piece of paper which had been folded in half. He unfolded the photograph and tossed it across the table; it landed on Carlyle's empty plate. It showed two rows of children, maybe forty in total, with a couple of teachers in their midst. They stood under a large tree, in front of a long, low hut that could have been a classroom. 'My kids.'

Carlyle scanned the faces, trying to see if he could find Alzbetha among them, but the image wasn't clear enough, and there wasn't enough time. Chepoyak let the two policemen peer at the picture for only a few seconds before scooping it back up and returning it to his inside pocket. 'That is the Hnizdechko Orphanage Number 3, in the city of Pryluky. Do you know what Hnizdechko means?'

Carlyle looked at Shen, who made a face and shrugged. 'No,' he said quietly. 'What does it mean?'

'It is translated as "Little Nest".' Chepoyak snorted. 'Little fucking nest – hah! It is a total shit-hole. Without me, they have nothing. The situation is terrible. Truly terrible.'

'Which is why you come over here,' Shen prompted.

'Yes. From here, I can make money. I can make a difference. There are a quarter of a million children in orphanages in the Ukraine. Some have lost their parents. Others have just been abandoned. Alcoholism, drug abuse, prostitution – we have it all.'

Maybe that's why you're so good at what you do, Carlyle thought.

Chepoyak looked at the two policemen. 'Like you two give a fuck about who I am and where I'm from,' he continued in a grim voice. 'It is a scandal what happens to those children – a disgrace. The only time you hear about all this shit over here is when some pop star or actress goes to my country and tries to adopt one of them.'

'So you do a lot of charity work?' Carlyle asked, wondering how to get the conversation back on track.

'I do what I can.' Chepoyak shrugged. 'The government, of course, does nothing. There is never enough food, never enough clothes, never enough shoes. The children suffer from poor nutrition; they get ill but they don't have medicine when they are sick. All the orphanages depend on charity for survival. It is a living hell.'

'This girl could have come from an orphanage,' Carlyle mused.

'It's possible. I wouldn't know about it, but I can ask around.'

'If you hear anything . . .' Shen interjected lamely.

'Yes, yes, of course.' Chepoyak waved a hand dismissively.

What exactly was the point of this meeting with Ukraine's answer to Robin Hood? Carlyle was wondering where his investigation could go from here when there was a sudden kerfuffle outside, and two women burst in. They were followed by a man who looked like a much smaller version of Ihor.

Carlyle glanced back out into the main café. Hamilton and Frost were both happily shooting the breeze, apparently oblivious to the new arrivals. *Just as well it's nothing serious then, boys,* he thought sourly.

Chepoyak said something to the mini-him, and the other man disappeared somewhere into the back. The women then took a seat at the table on either side of the boss. Both were bottle-blondes; one with a page-boy cut, the other with her hair longer and tied up in a ponytail. Each wore plenty of make-up and each had a smouldering cigarette dangling from her lower lip. The pair of them wore warm-looking winter overcoats, buttoned up to the neck. Without being able to see what was concealed under-neath, Carlyle marked them down as a pair of Eastern European hard bodies, the kind of girls that had swamped the prostitution market in London over the last decade or so.

The only real difference between the two of them was in the eyes. Whereas the ponytail had dark, dead eyes, black as coals; page-boy's blue irises sparkled with curiosity and mischief.

Throwing an arm round each of his girls, Chepoyak smirked at the policemen and raised his eyebrows suggestively.

Shen glanced quickly at Carlyle and held up a hand. 'Thor, you know we don't take freebies.'

The one with the dead eyes glared at Shen. Her companion kept her amused gaze fixed on Carlyle.

'We are looking for a girl,' Carlyle repeated for the benefit of the women, 'maybe as young as eight or nine. A Ukrainian girl brought to London and pimped out to rich men.'

'I told you,' Chepoyak said, pushing back his chair and getting slowly to his feet, 'I don't know anything about it. But I will . . . how do you like to say it,' he grinned, 'make some investigations.'

Shen stood up. Carlyle followed suit.

'That is much appreciated,' Shen said, extending a hand. 'Thank you for your time.'

Chepoyak shook his hand vigorously. 'No problem,' he said. 'Any time.'

Chepoyak and the women followed the two policemen out into the café. At the counter, Carlyle looked longingly at the remaining cakes sitting on a plate behind the glass. Digging into his trouser pocket, he found a handful of change. Smiling at the silent woman behind the counter, he pointed at the *babka*. 'Could I take two of those?'

The woman nodded. Picking up a paper bag from the shelf behind her, she carefully picked out a couple of cakes from the plate.

Not sure about the price, Carlyle placed four pound coins on the top of the counter.

'Please!' Chepoyak stayed his arm. 'There is no charge.' He said something to the woman that Carlyle didn't understand. He held out a hand again. 'Until the next time, Inspector . . .'

'John Carlyle.' Carlyle shook his hand.

'Ah, yes.' Chepoyak had already turned away and was heading towards the back room. 'Inspector John Carlyle, I will see you next time.'

Carlyle watched him disappear and accepted the bag of cakes from the woman, leaving the small pile of coins on the counter as a tip. Shen and the others had already gone outside and he heard the BMW's engine start up.

'You have a sweet tooth, Inspector?' The girl with the sparkling eyes had appeared at his shoulder.

'I'm afraid I do,' Carlyle admitted.

The girl nodded sympathetically. 'I also love a nice pastry. Perfect with a coffee.'

'Yes.' Carlyle couldn't agree more.

'In fact,' she sighed, 'I could do with an espresso right now.' Turning to the woman behind the counter, she pointed at the ancient-looking Gaggia by the wall. 'Anichka, could you get me one, please? A double.'

The woman grumbled under her breath before turning away from the pair of them to work the battered machine. As it rumbled noisily into action, Carlyle flinched slightly as he felt a hand on his backside. Holding his breath, he let the girl slip something into the back pocket of his jeans.

She studiously ignored his quizzical look, instead peering over the counter in anticipation of the arrival of her coffee. 'Maybe just a little hot milk, too, if that's possible . . .'

Remembering to exhale, Carlyle turned on his heel and left.

Chapter Eight

HELEN GAZED OUT of the window, looking south across the river, towards the London Eye. She watched Carlyle enter the tiny kitchen and grab a couple of Jaffa Cakes from a box sitting on top of the microwave. Waiting until he had stuffed the first one in his mouth, she waved the business card in her hand. 'What is this?'

Carlyle swallowed. He felt the chocolate from the second Jaffa Cake melting on to his fingers. 'It's a girl's phone number,' he replied as casually as he could manage, resisting the urge to make a grab for the card itself. He knew that his only way out of this situation was a careful blend of insouciance and full disclosure. 'She's a Ukrainian prostitute. I met her yesterday.' He took a nibble from Jaffa Cake number two. 'On business.'

'Yours? Or hers?'

'Mine, obviously.'

Somewhat reluctantly, she handed him back the card and he slipped it into the pocket of his jeans. He waited patiently as Helen sipped her green tea and made a show of looking her husband up and down. She had never tried to set any rules when it came to his job, but she had always been secretly relieved that he had managed to steer clear of working in Vice. There were plenty of other things he could do on the Force where there was much less in the way of temptation. This latest case was making her uneasy, but she knew that she had to try to keep things light. He was a policeman, after all. He had always been a policeman, even before they had met. There were limits to how far she could circumscribe his career. 'Do many working girls give you their phone number, Inspector?'

'Only when they're on the game,' he deadpanned, confident – well, *reasonably* confident – that she was taking things in the right spirit.

Helen looked at the card again. 'Why did *Olga* hand it over to you?'

'I dunno,' Carlyle shrugged, careful not to mention precisely *how* it had been handed over. 'Maybe she can tell us something about the missing kid. God knows, we need a break.'

'There's something else.' Helen abruptly changed the subject.

'Oh?' Carlyle's heart sank. He didn't need 'something else' at the moment.

'Yes,' she said, cradling her mug of green tea while gazing out the window. 'They've had more problems at Alice's school.'

'That's not really a surprise.'

All schools had their dramas, but Carlyle had to admit that his daughter's school – City School for Girls in the Barbican – really did seem to push the boat out in that respect. He thought back to the time when the police had been phoned after two of the pupils had called in a bomb warning. Happily there was no actual bomb, but a subsequent police sweep of the classrooms had turned up no less than eight bags containing dope of one sort or another. The headmaster had implemented a very public crackdown. More than a dozen girls had been expelled, and all the parents had received a letter informing them that anyone found in possession of cannabis or any other drugs would face a similar fate. With cannabis being reclassified from a Class C to Class B drug, the headmaster added that 'any student found to be in possession of cannabis will be arrested and taken to a police station where they can receive a reprimand, final warning, or charge depending on the seriousness of the offence'.

Helen had forbidden Carlyle from writing back and pointing out to the headmaster that no police station in the city would welcome the receipt of his errant charges, and that he should maybe look to try and put his own house in order by himself. On reflection, he realised that Helen was right: this was not the kind of issue to pick a fight over. Anyway, if Alice ever got involved in drugs while at school, the headmaster would be the least of her worries.

'What's happened now?' he asked wearily.

'Another two girls have been expelled.'

Carlyle shrugged. That was hardly hold-the-front-page news.

'One of them,' Helen continued, 'was in Alice's class.'

'Shit.' Carlyle frowned. 'She's what – not even a teenager.'

'I know.' Helen stepped away from the window and stood beside him, resting against the workbench. 'I spoke to one of the other mothers today, and she says that they think that girls as young as eight could be involved.'

'Bollocks.'

'I don't know, John.'

Carlyle stuck an arm round his wife's shoulder. 'Come on . . .'

'I know, it seems ridiculous. But everyone's getting a bit paranoid about it.'

Carlyle grinned. 'Maybe some of the parents have been smoking too much skunk themselves.'

She gave him a gentle punch in the ribs. 'That's not funny.'

'Sorry.' He stood up straight and folded his arms, as if to show that he was taking it seriously. 'Have you spoken to Alice about it?'

'We had a chat.' Helen reached over and placed her mug in the sink. 'She didn't tell me much, but at least we had a bit of a conversation. She didn't storm off in a huff – which makes a change these days.'

'So what did she say?'

'According to Alice, everyone in the class knows about it. The girl who's been expelled isn't one of her friends, and had been hanging out with some older kids. She says no one else in her class has tried anything.'

'So far.'

'Anyway, Alice says she's really not that interested.'

'I can easily believe that.' Carlyle leaned over and kissed the top of his wife's head. 'She's basically a sensible kid – gets it from her dad.'

Helen didn't smile. 'I know, but . . .'

'Shall I talk to her?'

She gave his arm a grateful squeeze. 'When it comes up, and only when she's happy to have the conversation. Don't just jump in there and force her to clam up.'

Me? Carlyle thought. When did *you* become the expert in communicating with our little tweenager? He felt a familiar bubble of frustration in his stomach, and waited for it to pass. 'Okay.'

She was obviously alert to the dark look clouding his face. 'Promise?'

'I promise.'

HALFWAY DOWN WILFRED Street, a two-minute walk from Buckingham Palace, Alexa Matthews propped herself up against the wall in the alley next to the Drunken Friar and lit the last cigarette from the packet of twenty Lambert & Butler Silver that she'd bought from the machine inside the pub barely three hours earlier. Inside, she could hear the bell being rung for last orders. Alexa groaned and took a greedy suck on her ciggie. A 'quick drink' after work with a few colleagues coming off shift had turned into a proper session. After five or six pints of Stella, and a couple of vodka chasers, Alexa had to admit that she was well and truly bladdered. The two pork pies she had scoffed half an hour earlier hadn't been such a good idea, either.

In her jacket pocket, she could feel her mobile buzzing. Alexa didn't have to look at it to know who it was. Heather, her girlfriend – who had been expecting her home four hours earlier – was well pissed off. Reaching into her pocket, Alexa read the latest abusive text.

Where are u u stupid cow?

'Fuck off!' Alexa slurred to herself. Given the turn of events, she wondered if it would be worth going home at all. Would it be better to grovel tonight? Or in the morning? If needs be, she could kip in one of the empty stables back at the Palace – it wouldn't be the first time. Taking a long drag on her fag, she tried to think herself sober.

'Hey, Alexa!'

'Shit!' Cursing under her breath, Matthews looked up to see three men, all wearing jeans and bomber jackets, coming out of the side door of the pub and walking towards her. The group was led by the avuncular figure of Tommy Dolan, a sergeant in SO14. Dolan had been drinking with them for an hour or so. The other two she didn't recognise. She didn't even remember them being in the pub earlier in the evening.

'Not going to puke, are you?' Dolan stopped five feet short of Matthews, ready to dodge any flying vomit.

'What do you want, Dolan?' Matthews slipped her phone into a pocket and eyed the sergeant carefully.

'Just checking you were okay.'

'Yeah, right.' Matthews took a deep breath and tried to fight off the nausea. Like everyone else in SO14, she knew that Dolan was trouble. The best way to deal with him was simply to keep out of his way. When he had appeared at the bar, she had vowed to make a sharp exit. Then someone had bought another round and she had stayed. Now that wasn't looking like such a clever decision. Instinctively, she looked over her shoulder. Behind a pile of rubbish was a brick wall, at least twenty feet high. The only way out was to head back the way she had come.

She took a final drag on her cigarette and tossed it in the direction of Dolan's trainers. Out of uniform, he looked nothing much: a squat bloke, five foot ten, in reasonable shape given that he was already well past fifty, with a number-one cut that made his silver hair shine under the orange glare of the streetlight at the open end of the alley. Dolan, thirty-year veteran of serving Her Majesty and her dysfunctional family, was the man who actually ran things on the other side of Buckingham Gate. The Charlie Adamses of this world might come and go, but Dolan was omnipresent. While Adam might be nominally running the show, it was Dolan who was in charge of all the money-making scams that had been carefully built up over the years, like the private tours, illicit parties and souvenir sales.

On the nights when he would sit out on the back lawn and get pissed on Pol Roger Cuvée Winston Churchill, the sergeant liked to joke that he was 'the most important person in the whole bloody Palace'. The really funny thing was that this was probably true. Dolan was very protective of his mini-empire. He didn't like anyone who didn't share his view of SO14 as a nice little earner, wouldn't put up with anyone who rocked the boat. And he was deeply suspicious of anyone who ever asked for a transfer.

'Where's your girlfriend?' Dolan sneered.

Matthews ignored this, replying instead, 'What can I do for you, Tommy?'

Without saying a word, Dolan moved to his right, allowing one of the men behind him to step forward and slam a fist into Matthews's stomach. Sinking to her knees, gasping for air, she felt the pool of lager rebelling in her stomach. A second later, she was retching violently, sending a stream of vomit bouncing off the sticky tarmac.

'Fuck!' Dolan laughed, dancing away from the oncoming mess.

Her attacker then dodged to the side and gave her a firm kick in the ribs.

Happy to stay in the background, the third man laughed too.

Leaning as far forward as he dared, Dolan hissed, 'You always were a skanky bitch, but why did you go and talk to that fucking wanker John Carlyle? That was really stupid.'

Matthews tasted the puke in her mouth and gagged again. Trying to push herself up, she vomited for a second time. One of her ribs felt like it might be broken. Through the haze of pain she cursed Carlyle. You've dropped me in it again, she thought, you stupid, fucking twat. Looking up at Dolan, she groaned, 'I dunno what you're talking about.'

Dolan reached down and grabbed her by the hair. 'You're a lying fucking slag.'

'Fuck! Tommy, for fuck's sake!'

Dragging her through the mess, he pushed her face down until she was prostrate on the stinking ground. 'What did you tell him?'

Feeling the world spinning around her, Matthews tried to close her eyes. If she could ignore her tormentors . . . if she could go to sleep, maybe all this would stop.

Dolan gave her another hard kick. 'What did you tell him?'

'Nothing,' she mumbled. 'I told him nothing.'

'Do you want us to go round your house and have a word with your missus?'

'Leave Heather out of this . . .'

A boot glanced off the side of her head and, finally, she felt the world slipping away. As they set about her in earnest, she began dreaming of the stars.

Chapter Nine

SITTING ON THE kitchen floor, Carlyle dialled the number on Olga's card and listened to the call girl's mobile ring for what seemed like an eternity. It was 10 a.m. and he wondered if she might still be in bed. Waiting for the voicemail to kick in, he was surprised when someone finally picked up.

'Da?'

'Olga?'

'Yes, darling,' her voice purred down the line, 'this is Olga. What can Olga do for you?'

Carlyle could hear voices in the background; maybe she could talk freely, maybe she couldn't. It dawned on him that he couldn't even be sure that he was talking to the right woman. Still, he ploughed on: 'You gave me your card the other day . . .'

'I give my card to a lot of people,' she laughed. 'You want business?'

Someone chortled in the background.

Was this a game? 'Er . . . yes.'

'Good,' she said seductively. 'What would you like?'

If his wife could hear him now . . . Carlyle felt himself blush ever so slightly. Thank God Helen was at work. 'Er, what do you suggest?'

'I don't do anal,' she said quickly.

More laughter.

Carlyle felt himself getting flustered. 'But I didn't—'

'And, always, we use a condom.'

'Okay.'

'Don't worry, darling, I will show you a good time. You must be horny, for wanting it at this time in the morning.' The laughter grew louder. 'Where are you?'

'Covent Garden.'

'Which hotel?'

'Er . . .'

'Ah. Good.'

'Huh?'

'I know it well,' she told him. 'I meet you in the lobby of the Garden Hotel in forty-five minutes. Is £175 for an hour, plus my taxis, plus my tip.'

'Tip?' Carlyle asked, belatedly getting into the spirit of the conversation.

'*Da*,' she giggled. 'My tip for making you . . . *explode*!' The laughter reached a crescendo. Olga waited until the hubbub had subsided. 'Consider it a performance-related bonus.'

'What if I don't explode?' Carlyle joked. 'Do I get a discount?'

'Don't be cheeky. I see you soon.' The phone clicked and she was gone.

Carlyle sat there for a moment, wondering what to wear.

PUTTING ON HIS best suit, a navy Paul Smith number that he'd snapped up for eighty quid several years earlier from the Oxfam shop on Drury Lane, he headed out of the flat. Ten minutes later, he was walking through the revolving doors of the Garden Hotel.

The Garden was situated on St Martin's Lane, just up from Trafalgar Square and round the corner from Charing Cross police station. A boutique hotel fashioned out of a 1960s office block, it was, according to its brochure, *a manifestation of the emotional zeitgeist of the city.* That automatically made it the kind of place that Carlyle himself could never afford to stay in. At the same time, he had spent quite a bit of time pacing the lobby over the years, for one reason or another, so he knew many of the staff by sight if not by name. Giving the doorman a swift nod, he scanned the lobby itself and the Light Bar beyond, in case Olga had arrived early. When it was clear that she wasn't there, he headed towards the foppish-looking gent who was sitting at a tiny desk behind one of the lobby's pillars, with a look on his face that suggested he was half reading the copy of *Country Life* propped up in front of him and half-staring into space.

Over the top of his magazine, Alex Miles watched Carlyle approaching. As chief concierge at the Garden, Miles had acted as the hotel's senior fixer for their more important and demanding guests for over a decade. When it came to doing his job, policemen were a minor irritant. They had to be managed carefully.

Miles gave up on the article he'd been half-reading about the history of highwaymen and replaced the magazine on the desk. Almost managing to keep the look of disappointment off his face, he forced himself to his feet as Carlyle reached the desk. Straightening up the jacket of his grey pinstripe suit, he extended a hand. 'Inspector . . .'

'Mr Miles,' Carlyle replied cheerily. 'And how are you today?'

Miles eyed him warily. 'I'm fine. What can I do for you?'

Happy to dispense with any further pleasantries, Carlyle got straight to the point. 'I need to borrow a room for a couple of hours. A nice one.'

Miles raised an eyebrow but didn't smile. 'Why?'

'I'm meeting a prostitute,' Carlyle said casually.

Miles raised both eyebrows.

Carlyle smiled faintly. 'It's a professional meeting.'

'Of course,' Miles said smoothly. 'Can I get you a packet of condoms as well?'

'That won't be necessary,' Carlyle told him. 'But our meeting needs to look kosher. She'll be here in ten minutes.'

The concierge stared at him blankly.

'Consider it a deposit at the favours bank,' Carlyle murmured. 'A small deposit that represents a tiny nibble at your massive overdraft there.' A few years earlier, Carlyle had overlooked an unfortunate indiscretion occurring in one of the rooms upstairs involving the concierge himself, two transvestite hookers and a large quantity of unusually pure cocaine. The evidence was still safely locked away at the station, and could be brought out at any time. It was preferable, however, to leave it there and be able to call on Miles's services now and again.

'But—'

Carlyle gave him a sharp look. 'Do we need to examine the ledger?'

Miles looked at his shoes. 'No.'

'Good.'

'Okay.' Miles sighed, before heading off across the lobby. 'Let's see what we've got.'

Following at a discreet distance, Carlyle watched Alex Miles step behind the reception desk. After a brief conversation with the extremely pretty black girl on duty, he pulled a key card out of a drawer and activated it.

While Miles tapped away at a computer, the girl gave Carlyle a suspicious look. Pretending not to notice, he waited for Miles to beckon him over.

Miles nodded at the card. 'There you go. That'll get you into the penthouse suite. Top floor.' He cleared his throat. 'For people with money, it normally costs two grand a night.'

Fuck me, Carlyle thought. Two grand for a night in a hotel? 'I won't be there for a whole night,' he said, somewhat wistfully.

'Don't make a mess on the sheets,' was Miles's only response.

Carlyle popped the card into the breast-pocket of his jacket. 'I'll meet her in the lobby. When the lady comes in, give her a discreet once-over. We'll have a little chat when I'm done upstairs. I'd be interested to learn if you already know her. If not, maybe you can find out something about her.'

'Don't want much, do you? What's her name?'

'Olga.'

'Yeah, right. What's her *real* name?'

'Dunno,' said Carlyle, flopping down on a sofa. 'But I'm sure that I can find out.'

'The world's greatest policeman,' Miles grumbled, slouching off towards his desk.

'I know,' Carlyle smiled, closing his eyes and letting his mind wander, listening to the expensive tap-tap-tap of Miles's leather shoes on the limestone floor as he walked away.

'Hey! Wake up!'

Carlyle felt a sharp pain in his shin and sat up quickly. He rubbed his eyes and saw Olga standing over him, a cheeky grin on her face.

She looked around, making sure no one was in earshot. 'You're supposed to fall asleep after our business, not before.'

'Did you just kick me?' After rubbing his leg, Carlyle struggled to his feet, catching a glimpse of Miles sniggering from behind his desk.

'Come on,' Olga said, taking him by the arm and marching him to the lifts. 'I assume you've got a room.'

'Of course.'

'Perfect.' She stood on tip toe and kissed him full on the lips, before pressing the call button.

Blushing violently, Carlyle took a step backwards. 'What did you do that for?'

'We have to look the part,' Olga giggled. She arched an eyebrow back in the direction of Alex Miles. 'Hotel security is checking out more than just my arse.'

'Mmm . . .'

'Did I tell you that kissing costs extra?' she said brightly.

'Extra?'

'Yes. Another two hundred pounds. And no tongues.'

'Christ!' Carlyle wished the lift would hurry the fuck up. Not daring to make eye-contact with the concierge, Carlyle kept his gaze firmly on his companion. She was wearing jeans and black cowboy boots, with a grey silk blouse and a tailored navy jacket. There was an expensive-looking watch on her wrist and a thin gold chain around her neck. Discreetly, he sniffed her perfume. He had no idea what it was, but it was nice and doubtless costly. All in all, she fitted in with her surroundings perfectly.

They rode in silence to the top floor. Exiting the lift, Carlyle stepped across the lush carpet and inserted the key card into the door. To his relief, there was a click and he was able to push it open. Stepping inside the suite, he switched on the lights and glanced around. Decked out in the same minimalist style as the rest of the hotel, the room seemed bigger than his entire flat.

Coming in behind him, Olga let out a small shriek of delight. Dropping her bag on the bed, she trotted off to inspect one of the side rooms.

Perching on the end of the bed, Carlyle waited patiently while she completed her tour.

Five minutes later, she returned carrying a handful of toiletries and a selection of spirits from the mini-bar. Dropping them into her bag, she flopped down beside him.

'Like it?' he asked.

'It's really cool!' she laughed, angling a toe of one boot in his general direction.

'You can have it for the afternoon. They won't kick us out for a while.'

She propped herself up on one arm. 'Why? You wanna fuck?'

Again he felt himself blush. 'No, no. I was just saying.'

'Whatever.' She glanced at her watch. 'We've got about forty minutes. If I stay longer, Ihor will wonder what is going on. He will want to see more cash.' She traced a line on the back of his jacket with her finger. 'So I can't stay for longer than the hour – unless you decide to pay me more.'

'So . . . how do you know Ihor?'

She smiled. 'I met him in church.'

'Church?'

'Yes, the Ukrainian Catholic Cathedral in Mayfair. I was at the christening of the daughter of a mutual friend. Ihor was there with his family. He is a big family man. For him, it is everything.'

Carlyle thought about that for a moment. 'And you joined the family?' he asked, prepared to go along with this lie.

'In a manner of speaking,' she pouted. 'It's quite an extended family, but it works well for me.'

'Fair enough.' Carlyle shifted uncomfortably on the bed. 'I'm not making any judgements.'

'I don't care one way or the other about what you think. It is *my* relationship.'

'A working relationship?'

'A *professional* relationship.'

'And he takes what? Half of your income?'

'That's one way of looking at it.'

'What's the other?'

'Haven't you heard of *SuperFreakonomics*?'

Carlyle frowned. 'Super what?'

'*Super-Freak-onomics*.' She bounced on the bed like an excited child being given a chance to show just how clever she was. 'It's a book by an American professor. You should read it.'

'Mm. I'll add it to the list.'

'What list?'

'The list of books I *should* read.'

'It's good. A client gave me a copy.'

A book? What kind of punter gives a working girl a book? And what kind of girl reads it? He felt he was being given some kind of red flag, but wasn't sure what it signified.

'One of the chapters is about how prostitutes do better with pimps.'

Just what I need, Carlyle thought, a pseudo-intellectual hooker dosed up on American pop sociology. 'Uhuh . . .'

Olga closed her eyes, as she dug the key points out of her memory. 'This guy says that a pimp is just like an estate agent.'

On the other hand, maybe the guy did have a point. 'Now that you mention it,' Carlyle grinned.

Ignoring him, she ploughed on, 'Because they both market your product to potential customers.'

'Why don't you use the internet like everyone else?'

'I'm an old-fashioned girl,' she said primly. 'I won't be doing this forever and I don't want to leave an electronic trail. I work strictly by referral. Strictly cash. When I'm gone, I'm gone. No one will be able to find me.'

Good luck, love, Carlyle thought.

'Strictly cash,' she repeated, holding out her hand.

'Ah, yes. The money.' He reached into his trouser pocket and pulled out a slender wad of twenty-pound notes.

Reaching over, she took the money and counted it carefully before zipping it into a side-pocket of her bag. 'No tip?'

'I'm not going to explode.' Carlyle sniffed.

'You don't know that yet.' She slid off the bed and stepped in front of him, holding out her hand. 'Give me another fifty.'

'Come on,' Carlyle groaned.

Olga stood her ground. 'Come on? *You* come on! This is my time we're talking about.'

'Okay, okay.' Carlyle sighed wearily and stuck his hand back in his pocket. 'I suppose a receipt is out of the question?' he asked, handing over his remaining money.

'You suppose right,' Olga smiled. 'Thank you.' Sticking the money in her pocket, she sat down next to him on the bed. 'Okay. Now we've got that out of the way, what do you want to know?'

'What can you tell me about the girl?'

She edged along the bed slightly and turned to look at him. Her eyes seemed to have lost their sparkle, the smile on her face now looking forced and tired. 'There are many girls. I am one myself. Sometimes it's not nice, but it's better than the alternative . . .'

'Yes,' he nodded, hoping that she would hurry up and get to the point.

'But the children, this is something else.'

'Is Ihor responsible for bringing them over?'

'Sometimes.'

'So all that stuff about helping kids in orphanages is fake?' Carlyle asked. 'Is it just a front for people-trafficking?'

'No – he does pay for things. But there is also business to be done.' She made a face, like it was obvious and logical. 'He sees the two things as separate.'

'Who does he work with?'

She thought about it for a moment, and Carlyle wondered if she was trying to remember a script. It crossed his mind that this could all be a set-up. Maybe she was actually lying to him, but he would have to run that risk. It wasn't like he had a lot of other leads to follow.

'Ihor has business associates here in England,' she said finally.

'And who are they?'

'I don't know.'

Carlyle wondered about the posh man he saw in Green Park. 'English?'

'I guess so. Ihor knows lots of people. All different kinds. He likes to talk about how he doesn't just mix with scumbags and losers. He knows nice people, too. Some of them might be English.'

'What about the not so nice people? What about the people who go after children?'

She made a face. 'The young ones are only for very special clients. Very important men, Ihor says. That's the thing for these guys. It's not just about the sex. They can fuck any woman they want, so it has to be more edgy. They want under-age, they want exotic locations . . . whatever can give them a bigger, better buzz.' She held his gaze for one, two seconds. 'That's what it's about – the buzz.'

Carlyle thought about that for a moment. 'Which "exotic" locations?'

She shrugged. 'I don't know.'

'Give me some examples.'

She threw her hands in the air. 'The London Eye is quite popular. They book a whole pod and have a bit of a party.'

'Where else?'

'I heard Ihor boasting one time that a guy had paid ten thousand pounds to do it in the House of Commons. He even brought his own rent boy!'

'Sounds like your average MP,' Carlyle murmured. 'What about Buckingham Palace? Did anyone ever do it there?'

Olga thought about it for a moment. 'Maybe. Why not?'

'But have you heard of it?'

'No, but it's a good idea.' She patted him on the shoulder. 'Maybe I will suggest it to Ihor.'

Carlyle wondered what he was actually getting for his money here. 'Okay, what about my girl?'

She looked at him blankly.

'The girl I found in the park – Elizabeth, or Alzbetha or something.'

'There were a couple of young girls recently. I saw them at a house of Ihor's, near the café.' She reached into her bag and pulled out a scrap of paper, handing it to him. 'That's the address.'

'Are they there now?'

She shook her head. 'I wouldn't have thought so. It was several weeks ago.'

Before the Green Park incident, Carlyle thought. 'After I found Alzbetha, someone went to the care home she was in and kidnapped her.'

Again, Olga shook her head. 'I don't know anything about that.' She glanced at her watch. 'I have to go now.'

'That was a very quick forty minutes.'

'Darling,' Olga pointed out, 'usually when I go to work, it is five minutes total maximum.' Her grin grew bigger than her face. 'The clients! They simply cannot control themselves!'

Feeling not very much in control himself, Carlyle looked at the scrap of crumpled paper in his hand. 'That's not much for my money.'

'That is easy for you to say.' Her eyes narrowed. 'For me it is a lot. I take a big risk talking to you.' Standing up, she grabbed the bag and slung it over her shoulder.

'Fair point.' Carlyle got to his feet. 'Don't worry, no one else will know about this conversation. We'll check out this address. But see what else you can find out in the meantime.'

'Sure.' Olga turned to him as she reached the door. 'I will do what I can.'

As the door closed behind her, Carlyle flopped back on the bed, wondering what else he could do in his expensive hotel room.

THE PHONE WAS ringing.

The phone . . .

. . . was ringing.

Slowly, Carlyle came to his senses.

Sitting up on the bed, it took him a moment to realise where he was. He yawned. Then he noticed the time on the clock: 4.23.

A.m. or p.m.?

'Fuck!' He scrambled across the extra-king-size duvet and grabbed the handset. 'Hello?'

Alex Miles sounded more than a little peeved. 'What the hell are you still doing up there? Your girl left hours ago.'

'I . . .' Carlyle let out another yawn. 'I must have dozed off.'

'I told you not to mess up the sheets,' Miles grumbled.

'Don't worry,' Carlyle snapped back. 'I fell asleep on top of the bed. What time is it?'

'It's past four in the afternoon. Time for you to check out.'

'Okay, okay. Thanks for the alarm call. I'll be down in a minute.'

After washing his face and helping himself to a Toblerone from the mini-bar, Carlyle sheepishly made his way down to the lobby. Alex Miles was still behind his desk, his *Country Life* having been replaced by a copy of the evening paper. This time he didn't get to his feet. 'Well, well,' he said, looking over the top of it. 'Good afternoon, Sleeping Beauty.'

Carlyle placed the key card on the desk. 'Thanks for that.'

'If you've been using the porno channels,' Miles smirked, 'I'm gonna have to bill you.'

'Genuinely, I fell asleep. What did you think of the girl?'

'Nice.' The grin on Miles's face crumpled into a leer. 'Can you let me have her number?'

'Seen her before?'

Miles carefully folded the newspaper and dropped it onto the floor beside his chair. 'I don't think so. What's the story?'

Carlyle thrust his hands into his pockets. 'There isn't one yet. Have you got her on CCTV?'

'Of course.' Miles pulled open a drawer and took out a couple of sharp A5 images that had been run off on a computer printer. He handed one to Carlyle and kept the other for himself. Carlyle recognised the back of his own head. The shot had been taken while they were waiting for the lift to take them up to the penthouse. The image didn't do Olga full justice but it was a fair likeness.

'One for you,' Miles said, 'and one for me. I will ask around.'

Carlyle folded the sheet of paper and placed it in his pocket. 'Thank you.'

'And now, I'll go and check the CCTV up in the penthouse suite.'

'What?' Despite his complete and utter innocence, Carlyle felt himself blush.

'Don't worry,' Miles laughed, 'only joking. People don't pay two grand so we can spy on them – more's the pity.'

'Ha, ha,' Carlyle said stiffly. 'Thanks again for your help with this. Let me know if you hear anything.' Without waiting for Alex Miles to embarrass him any further, he then turned and headed for the street.

Chapter Ten

'AND WE WOULD like to thank our British guests who are here today, from the Anglo-Ukrainian Friendship Society delegation in London . . .'

Shivering inside his black cashmere Ede & Ravenscroft overcoat, Gordon Elstree-Ullick stifled a yawn and tried to tune out the heavily accented drone of the Director of the Sandokan International Children's Camp. Sitting on a low podium at the front of the assembly room, he watched a grey cloud drift across the dirty sky outside the windows. Feeling his eyelids dropping, he dug a fingernail into the loose flesh by the thumb of his left hand in order to stay awake. His mind began to wander . . . somewhere out there, not all that far from where they were sitting, the Light Brigade charged into the pages of history during the Crimean War. Elstree-Ullick smiled to himself at the thought. According to family lore, his great-great-great-grandfather had his left bollock shot off during the Battle of Balaclava.

Balaclava had been a typical British cock-up: the cavalry charging up a valley strongly held on three sides by Russians with heavy guns. End result: 250 men dead (not to mention 400-plus horses) lost for no gain whatsoever. By comparison, Great-greatgreat-grandpa had got off lightly. Elstree-Ullick shuddered at the thought of what might have happened if the old bugger had lost both his balls. Balaclava – that was what? About 150 years or so ago. Did we win? He had no bloody idea.

'. . . our bonds of friendship shall never be cut asunder . . .'

Cut asunder? What was the old fool talking about now? The combination of last night's vodka and the strain of keeping a constant smile on his face threatened to overwhelm him. The director's farewell speech had already been going on for more than twenty minutes and, if past experience was anything to go by, it would drone on a while longer yet.

Elstree-Ullick had heard it all so many times before. This latest trip had lasted three days; in that time he must have listened to almost a dozen speeches from camp workers and local dignitaries. All of them followed the same pattern: they would bemoan, at length, the fate of their country, quickly thank the Brits for the aid that they'd brought from London, and then launch into an impassioned plea for yet more of the same.

'The need now is greater than ever . . .'

Why didn't any of these bastards get off their backsides and do something for themselves? All they seemed capable of was sitting around waiting for handouts.

Finally, there came a smattering of applause. Elstree-Ullick nodded politely as he scanned the young audience. Sandokan was not international. And it was not a camp. All the kids came from inside a 100-mile radius. Their parents were dead, or they had abandoned their offspring. It was an orphanage straight out of a Dickens novel, housing almost four hundred children between the ages of six months and eighteen years. More than a hundred of the older ones were gathered here today. Scrubbed and dutifully silent, they were being closely watched by staff who were more like security guards than teachers.

Elstree-Ullick knew well enough that the children were given no education or training for the outside world. And what an outside world! Ukraine was your standard post-Soviet nightmare, with no jobs and no hope. Things would never change here, except to get worse – which was why he kept coming back.

Scanning the room, he looked at the blank faces waiting to be told when to start clapping again. He watched a boy on the front row stubbornly pick his nose with his index finger. On this trip, the children seemed even more introspective and sullen than usual, which was saying something. Finding a couple of 'special cases' to take back with them had been harder than ever. Nor was it clear that he would find a buyer back in London. Elstree-Ullick was only too well aware that he was on the cusp of falling out of step with the zeitgeist. The 'Eastern European' was no longer a badge of quality. The Ukrainian market was moving out of fashion. He could easily end up losing money on this trip. It was time to move on.

Market forces were not the only consideration. The fact that a dossier concerning alleged child sex abuse at Sandokan had recently been transferred to the Ukrainian Prosecutor General's Office was another compelling reason to seek pastures new. The very night that Elstree-Ullick had arrived in the country, a Regions Party MP called Roman Popov had claimed on national television that children as young as six had been raped at this centre. Rumours were already circulating about children being sold as sex slaves to Western countries. Elstree-Ullick was pretty sure that the Deputy Prosecutor,

General Dmytro Gazizulin, a local Robocop determined to make a name for himself, would quickly and painfully get to the truth. A Presidential election was looming, and this investigation supplied local politicians with quantities of mud to throw at each other. If the truth – or anything approximating it – came out, the best that his friend the Director here could hope for would be a long and brutal prison sentence. Elstree-Ullick had no intention of joining him in a Ukrainian cell. He did not want to be within a thousand miles of Kiev when General Gazizulin came calling. It was only due to the fact that the State Security Service was so totally corrupt, that they were not all in jail already, himself included.

'God bless you all! . . .'

The sudden applause woke him from his reverie. Groggily, he got to his feet and stepped across the podium to shake the Director by the hand. A bell sounded and the children quickly filed out through the exits. Within a minute, the room was cleared apart from four girls sitting silently in the back row, gazing into space. The Director eyed the girls thoughtfully for a moment before turning to face Elstree-Ullick. Without saying anything, the Englishman pulled a small white envelope from his jacket pocket and handed it over. Grasping the envelope tightly, the Director bowed his head and disappeared through a back door.

'I really need a stiff drink,' Elstree-Ullick muttered to himself. Stepping down from the podium, he walked slowly towards the rear of the hall under the suspicious gaze of his four new employees.

ALEXA MATTHEWS STOOD in front of the chief super's desk, waiting for the smug little bastard to invite her to sit down. Outside, she could see a couple of gardeners trimming the lowest branches of an oak tree. She idly wondered what it would be like to wield one of their chainsaws on Tommy Dolan and his chums.

After a few more seconds scribbling notes on a pad for effect, Charlie Adam looked up at her with his solemn face on. 'Well?'

Well, what? she thought angrily, concentrating hard as she tried to stop herself swaying in time to the throbbing in her head. Her whole body ached and she was acutely aware that, even in uniform, she looked a complete mess, with a bust lip and a peach of a shiner around her left eye. Even before you considered the bruises all over her body, the bruised ribs and the broken hand, Alexa looked like she'd been on the wrong end of a beating. Which, of course, she had.

'I've read Dolan's report,' Adam continued. 'What do you have to say for yourself?'

Matthews focused her gaze on a spot on the wall a foot above Adam's head. 'I was going about my lawful business when I was assaulted, sir,' she replied in a matter-of-fact manner.

Adam tapped a sheet of paper lying on the desk with his index finger. 'That's not what it says here.'

Big fucking surprise, Matthews thought. She hadn't read Dolan's work of fiction but she could guess well enough what it said. She took a deep breath. 'No, sir.'

'It claims here,' Adam said, the annoyance in his voice clear, 'that you got blind drunk and attacked a couple of your colleagues.'

Which would be why I am the one who is black and blue, Matthews thought grimly, and none of them have so much as a scratch. 'What about the CCTV, sir?' she asked quietly.

'What?' Adam looked bemused by the question.

'The pub has CCTV that covers the full length of that alley,' Matthews explained. 'The footage will confirm my version of events.'

Adam glanced again at the papers on his desk. He ran a finger down the top sheet until he found what he needed. 'The CCTV camera wasn't working.'

How convenient.

'Apparently it's been defective for months, if not years,' Adam said coolly. 'Which you would doubtless know, given that, by all accounts, you go drinking in the Drunken Friar most nights of the week.'

What I know, Matthews thought, is that I've been done up good and proper. She tried to calm herself down. You're almost out of here, she told herself, so don't make a fuss.

Adam flopped backwards in his chair, sighing loudly. 'This is simply not good enough. Do you have anything else to say for yourself?'

'No, sir.'

'This is a disciplinary offence.'

'Yes, sir.'

'The investigation process will take time.'

'Yes?' Matthews wondered where this was going.

Adam dropped his gaze to the desk. 'In the meantime, you will be staying in SO14. I have decided to pull your transfer.'

'But—' Matthews began to protest.

Adam held up a hand to silence her. 'Take it up with your union rep if you wish. I am not going to risk letting our dirty laundry be aired outside the unit. This matter will have to get sorted out fully before you leave.' He looked her in the eye. 'Indeed, as I am sure you are aware, the investigation into this violent outburst may result in you leaving the Force altogether.' He folded his arms in the manner of a headmaster dismissing a troublesome pupil.

Fighting back her tears, Alexa Matthews got to her feet and stumbled towards the door.

Chapter Eleven

IN NO WAY did number 75 Thane Villas look like a desirable residence. It stood on a terraced street located between Seven Sisters Road – the rat-run less commonly known as the A503 – and the main railway line into the centre of the city. It was a four-storey bay-fronted terrace house set six feet back from the street behind a small patio area and a massively overgrown hedge. On the pavement, an overflowing rubbish bin stood sentry by the gate, next to an ancient, rusting Vespa scooter with two flat tyres which was propped up against a low wall. The windows of the house were caked with grime, and a pile of discarded junk mail sat outside the front door, which itself was crying out for a new coat of paint.

The whole property clearly needed some serious attention, but it was unlikely ever to get it. Even before the property slump, this part of North London was a long way off becoming gentrified. This was a low-income neighbourhood. Number 75 was the only property in the street that had not been chopped up into tiny flats to accommodate a transient population of students, immigrants, minimum-wage foot soldiers and benefits scroungers.

The neighbourhood also enjoyed one of the highest crime-rates in the city. Yellow police signs asking for witnesses to the latest assault, or worse, were commonplace. One Saturday night, a council survey had recorded an incident of 'anti-social behaviour' – anything from pissing in the street to attempted murder – every forty-three seconds. It was the kind of place which, if you could afford to, you quickly moved out of.

Carlyle stood in the gloom of a downstairs bedroom, listening to Warren Shen's men bounce up the stairs. Doors were banged open and he could hear the sound of their boots thumping across the bare floors of the rooms above. Flexing the toes in his aching right foot, he wondered if he should have been quite so quick to kick the door in. But, after no one answered the bell, what else was he going to do? Fuck off and try again later? Not likely. Not if there was any chance that the missing girl could be here. Rotating his ankle, he felt a sharp stab of pain. But his foot could stand it. He was reasonably sure that nothing was broken.

'It's empty,' a voice shouted from the top of the stairs. 'There's no one here. The whole place has been cleaned out, too.'

Shen appeared in the doorway, snapping on a pair of rubber gloves. 'Looks like we missed the party.' He looked glumly around the empty room. 'Or maybe your source sold you a bum steer.'

Carlyle grunted noncommittally. He hadn't told Shen about his conversation with Olga. That was something he had decided to keep to himself, for the moment at least. He had yet to make his mind up about the guys from Vice. Like a lot of coppers he had come across over the years, they made him feel uncomfortable. Maybe it was just him. Maybe it wasn't. Carlyle didn't really care either way. Over the years, he had learned to trust his own judgement. Right now he was wishing he had left them chasing hopeless masturbators round Soho, or whatever else it was that they did on wet Wednesday afternoons. He should have come up here on his own.

'Who owns this place?' Shen asked.

'I haven't checked that yet,' Carlyle replied almost absentmindedly. 'I was told that the girl was,' he corrected himself, 'that the girl *had been* here.'

'Recently?'

'Yeah, I think so. At least, since I originally found her. Maybe she was brought here after being snatched from Social Services. I thought it was worth checking out – just in case.'

'Of course,' Shen said, sounding unconvinced.

'She *could* have been here.'

'Well,' Shen sighed, 'she's not here now. Whoever was here has gone. And they've cleaned up after themselves pretty well, by the looks of things.' He poked at a loose floorboard with the toe of his boot. 'Did your source give you anything else?'

'No.'

'A wild-goose chase then.' Shen shot Carlyle a look that finally let his irritation show. 'Thanks for that.'

'Sorry.' Carlyle shrugged. 'But it was worth a look.'

'I suppose. These things happen.' Shen took a deep breath. 'Okay. Seeing as we're here, we might as well be thorough. I'll start at the back.' He stepped into the hall. 'This shouldn't take long.'

'I wouldn't have thought so.' Carlyle gazed vacantly at the ceiling. He was already finished. He had given up on Olga's tip. Clearly he had been chasing his tail.

'Which is probably just as well,' Shen grinned, 'seeing as you kicked the bloody front door in. We don't want one of the neighbours calling the police, do we?'

'Round here? Hardly likely.' Carlyle listened to Shen disappear into the kitchen and took another look around the dreary room. A torn bedsheet had been jammed into the top of the windowframe, in place of a curtain. A bare lightbulb hung from the ceiling. Tattered wallpaper covered the walls. A wide crack in the far corner suggested that there might be some kind of subsidence problem. Even the air he inhaled here felt dirty and tired.

The only piece of furniture was a small single bed with a metal frame; larger than a camp bed but a bit on the tight side for anyone much bigger than Carlyle. A child's bed? Maybe. Lying on the frame was a bare, striped mattress, which was stained in various places. There were no sheets and no pillows; nothing to indicate when it had last been slept in, or by whom.

What have I got for my time and my sore foot? Carlyle wondered. Sweet fuck-all, basically.

From the kitchen came the sound of breaking crockery, quickly followed by the sound of Shen cursing. 'Shit!'

Smiling, Carlyle dropped to the floor and adopted a press-up position. Lowering his chest even further, he turned his head to check under the bed. Amid the thick dust were tiny pellets of what looked like mouse droppings, but on the far side, by the wall, was a rag or a piece of clothing. Grunting with the effort, he pushed himself back up and wiped the dirt off his hands, reminding himself that a trip to the gym was overdue. Walking round to the far side of the bed, he knelt on the mattress and slid his hand down to recover the item. It was a child's T-shirt. He laid it out in front of him on the bed: the white cotton was grey with dirt, but you could still make out the legend *All you need is love* in flowery red script. Carlyle recognised it immediately, having taken it from Alice's wardrobe to give to the girl he had found in the park.

Hearing footsteps in the hallway, he quickly scrunched the T-shirt into a ball and stuffed it in his trouser pocket. Getting up from the bed, he turned to face Shen.

'Find anything?'

'Nope,' Shen replied, scratching his head.

'Okay,' said Carlyle. 'Sorry for wasting your time. Let's call it a day.'

ROSE SCRIPPS SAT in the windowless, airless video-review room, tightly gripping a Venti Gingerbread Latte in her left hand. The outsize cardboard cup was still more than half-full, but the coffee had long since gone cold. Rose now bitterly regretted spending £3.50 on it on her way in to the office. As a single mum living in one of the most expensive cities in the world, it was the kind of luxury that she couldn't afford – especially if she didn't actually drink the bloody thing. She took another sip and made a face. At least it was some sort of distraction from the appalling video material that she had been obliged to watch this morning.

Rose rolled her chair further away from the monitor, keeping her eyes focused on a spot eight inches above the screen on the wall behind it. That way, it looked as if she was still watching the footage, even though she wasn't. She had seen enough.

'Arrrghh . . .'

'Don't!'

'Yes . . .'

'Please . . .'

What Rose continued hearing, however, was another matter. She couldn't mute the sound and it was impossible to tune out, impossible to ignore. Even now, the incessant soundtrack of grunts, groans, cries and slaps affected her, got inside her head and messed with her brain. She could erase the images but not the sounds. They played in a loop inside her head until she could smell it, taste it, feel it.

She felt a hand on her shoulder. 'Want to take a break?' Detective Simon Merrett paused the video and dropped the remote on the desk nearby. 'This stuff is heavy going. It's okay for you to walk out if you want to.'

Rose nodded, biting her tongue in an attempt to stop the tears welling up. It wasn't professional; she should be beyond crying by now. She had been doing this for a long time: five years as a child protection social worker for the NSPCC – the National Society for the Prevention of Cruelty to Children – followed by two years on secondment to the Victim ID Team. There were still plenty of times like this, when she felt sick to her stomach, but it was a job that had to be done. Around 3,000 people a year were prosecuted for committing sex offences against children, including rape, assault and grooming. The people responsible for this morning's video nasty were just the latest on the list.

Grabbing her bag with her free hand, she quickly got up and headed out the door. In the ladies' toilet, she blew her nose and washed her face. Then she locked herself in one of the cubicles and sat down on the closed toilet lid and went through her coping routine. First, she got her breathing in order and cleared her head of all the images she had just seen, humming to herself to try and drown out those awful sounds as well. Then she went through the story of her day: Louise, her lovely, warm seven year old, jumping into bed with her at 6.32 a.m.; a rushed breakfast followed by the school run; then the journey to the office and her ridiculously decadent coffee purchase. Everything up to the moment she arrived at work. Everything, therefore, that reminded her that she was a normal person who did normal things; someone whose life wasn't all about wading through an ocean of other people's shit. Not *all* of her life, anyway.

Then she thought about the rest of her day.

After more than two hours in the video suite, Rose wondered how much more of it she could take today. She glanced at her watch, then pulled her mobile out of her bag. Hitting the most recently dialled number, she waited for a connection and listened to it ring.

'Hiya!' The chirpy voice of Sasha, the gormless but likeable Hungarian au pair that Rose shared with three other mums, came on the line. Some heavy beat thumped in the background; it sounded like Sasha was in a disco although it was probably just a shoe shop or something.

'Sasha, look, there's a change of plan at my end. I'll pick Louise up from school myself today.'

'Are you sure?' Sasha shouted back, over the music.

'Yeah, I'm going to work through lunch and then I can get away from the office later this afternoon. I'll do some more work at home tonight.' Setting this out for her own benefit rather than Sasha's, pre-empting any guilt she might feel at the thought of bunking off.

'Okay.'

'Are you still on for tomorrow?'

'Yes, of course.'

'Thanks. Speak then.'

'Okay. Bye.'

Rose ended the call and dropped the phone back in her bag. A couple of women had entered the toilets and started complaining about the latest collapse of the office IT system. After flushing for the sake of authenticity, Rose unlocked the stall and headed over to the washbasins. She didn't recognise the other two women and they ignored her. After washing her hands, she proceeded straight to her desk, giving the viewing room a wide berth.

About fifteen minutes later, Simon Merrett came and found her. He was a few years older than her, married, with two kids, one a couple of years older than Louise, and one a year younger. Merrett liked to hover by her desk, and Rose had the distinct impression that he was waiting for her to come on to him, but that was never going to happen. He was a good-looking guy but he was a colleague – and anyway, he was spoken for. Both of those were big red flags. Louise's father had done a runner three years before. Since then, Rose's 'private' life had been like a desert. But she could handle that. Apart from anything else, this job did nothing for your sex drive. If she got into another relationship, it would be with someone who had a boring job and could last the distance. That excluded any coppers and married men.

Coming closer, Merrett perched himself on the edge of her desk. In a pair of torn jeans and a Foo Fighters T-shirt, he looked thirty-five going on eighteen. Instinctively, she edged away from him slightly.

'Had enough for today?' he asked.

'Is there much more?'

'Nah, I've been through most of the rest of it.' He looked around the room, an open-plan office full of empty desks. 'Even by the standards of this place, it's really quite bizarre stuff.'

Rose fiddled with a Bic pen. 'At least we don't have to try and guess where that event took place.'

'No,' he nodded, 'we got lucky there. What kind of pervert has sex with a kid while on the London Eye?'

'What kind of pervert has sex with a kid, full stop?'

'Yes, but four hundred feet up in the air? In public?'

'One who doesn't have any concerns about getting caught,' Rose said in disgust. 'How many people complained?'

'Out of the eight hundred riding on it at the time?' Merrett scratched his head. 'Only two. A retired couple from Swansea who were in the next capsule.'

'Everyone else was looking at the view, I suppose. The House of Commons lit up at night is very nice.'

'And people are very good at ignoring things they don't want to see.'

Rose yawned. 'Tell me about it.'

'It was dark.'

'Not that dark.'

Merrett stood up. 'Anyway, we've got more than enough to start the interview. Want to watch it?' He grinned. 'It's your chance to see the master in action.'

'All right.' Rose felt her stomach rumbling but she wasn't hungry. She looked regretfully at her Venti Latte and grabbed a notebook from her desk. 'I'll be there in a minute.'

After reheating her coffee in the office kitchen microwave, Rose walked into the small dark room and nodded at the technician sitting behind a small editing desk, who was recording the proceedings in interview room number 2 next door. From behind the 6mm acrylic two-way mirror, Rose could watch the interview unobserved. Merrett was sitting at a table, head down, scribbling in a notebook. Next to him was a laptop. He was facing a fat, pasty-faced woman with dark rings under her eyes. She wore a navy-blue cardigan over a white T-shirt, and had a thin gold chain round her neck. Her long dark hair was badly dyed, with grey showing at the roots. It looked like she was in her mid to late forties, but Rose guessed that she could be considerably younger.

The woman sat forward in her chair, playing nervously with her hands. 'Can I have a smoke?'

Merrett finished what he was writing and looked up. 'No.' He pointed at the *No Smoking* sign on the wall, and the small red light that had just come on next to it. 'The light,' he explained, 'means that this conversation is now being recorded, and we are about to begin a formal interview. I am Detective Simon Merrett, based in West End Central. Please state your name.'

The woman thought about that for a moment, while Merrett waited patiently. Rose could see from the look on his face that he was in no particular hurry.

'Sandra,' the woman said finally. 'Sandra Scott.'

'And, Sandra, you can confirm that you have declined the offer of a lawyer?' Merrett said it softly but clearly, like it was a matter of no interest to him whatsoever.

'Yes, that's right.'

Next door, the technician let out a small chuckle. 'You really know how to find them,' he remarked.

Saying nothing, Rose took a sip of her coffee and winced. After ninety seconds in the microwave, it was still too hot to drink. Jesus, woman, she thought to herself, how difficult is it to get yourself a cup of coffee at the right temperature?

On the other side of the mirror, Merrett moved quickly through his remaining preliminaries. 'Your address is 135 Howard Road, E14 6XJ?'

'You know it is,' the woman said quietly. 'That's where you arrested me.'

'I'll take that as a "yes".' Merrett dropped his pen on the desk and leaned back in his chair, eyeing the woman carefully. 'Do you understand who we are?'

She frowned. 'You're the police.'

'We are the people who got the police to arrest you,' Merrett said, leaning forward. 'This is CEOP.'

Sandra Scott looked at him blankly.

'The Child Exploitation and Online Protection Centre. Ever heard of it?'

She shook her head.

'We protect kids from evil adults like you. We are the people who will be sending you to prison for many, many years.'

Rose smiled. Merrett liked to lay it on thick with suspects, sometimes. He joked that it was considerably less satisfying than smacking the shit out of them, but it generated less paperwork.

Scott let her eyes fall to the table. 'I did nothing!' she whined.

'Oh, yes?' Merrett hit a button on the laptop and a video started playing on the screen.

Not again, thought Rose, finally giving up on her coffee and dumping the cup in the bin.

Sandra Scott watched the images retrieved from the security camera inside the London Eye capsule while Merrett doodled on his pad. Rose closed her eyes, but those images were still playing on the inside of her eyelids. The man in the expensive suit; the tired and sullen-looking girl kneeling on the bench in the middle of the pod; the man grabbing the child by the hair; the man grinning for the camera . . .

Scott watched the clip with dead eyes. Rose got the impression that she had clearly seen it before. After about five minutes, Merrett paused the video. 'Well?'

The woman folded her arms and gave him a look intended to suggest defiance. 'That's nothing to do with me.'

Merrett paused, for effect, and then started laughing. 'Sandra, for fuck's sake – we found a dozen copies of this video burned onto DVDs in your flat. We have your emails sending it to your sick friends.'

Scott harrumphed vaguely but said nothing.

'You work in the security room at the London Eye,' Merrett continued, 'and we know that, after making these copies, you erased the original recording. You are therefore an accessory to child rape. A fucking sex-offender. It's jail for you.'

Don't overdo it, Simon, Rose thought. So far, all they had was this video. She wasn't at all sure what they would be able to end up charging Sandra Scott with.

'You are going to jail for a very long time,' Merrett repeated. 'Maybe for the rest of your shitty little life.'

Scott thought about that for a while. 'What do I get if I help you?'

Merrett made a face like the thought had never crossed his mind. 'That depends . . .'

For the first time, Rose thought she saw a spark of life in the woman's eyes, as she tried to calculate the odds. 'What do you want?'

'Who is the man in the video?'

'Dunno.'

'What about the kid?'

'Dunno.'

Merrett closed his notebook and placed the pen behind his ear. 'Well, then, Sandra, you are fucked. You are *totally* fucked.' He closed the laptop and stood up.

Sandra Scott spread her hands out on the table. 'But I do know *something*.'

'And what might that be?' Not rushing to take the bait, Merrett unplugged the laptop and stuck it under his arm.

Scott grinned nervously. 'I know when they'll be coming back.'

Chapter Twelve

ON THE THIRD floor of Charing Cross police station, Joe Szysz-kowski sat at his desk munching a bacon roll, making sure the brown sauce dripped on to the carpet, rather than on his jeans. He chewed slowly, while putting off writing up a report on the mugging of a Chinese tourist outside the National Gallery in Trafalgar Square, a report that he should have completed the day before. There was no real hurry. The clean-up rate for that type of crime was so low that the Home Office kept the numbers to themselves; in the official Recorded Crime Statistics they were included under the catch-all of 'robbery'. The Metropolitan Police defini-tion of mugging or 'street crime' was a combination of theft or attempted theft (or robbery) from the person plus assault against the person. The unlucky tourist had been hit over the head with a rolled-up newspaper and relieved of the £100 in his wallet. Sadder and wiser, he should be back in Shanghai by now; meanwhile the money itself would have immediately been spent on booze or dope; and the case was closed as far as everyone apart from the statisticians were concerned. There was no way that the sergeant was going to waste his day looking through dozens of different CCTV images in a futile attempt to identify the perpetrator. The report was a purely bureaucratic requirement – which somehow made it harder work.

Sticking the last of the roll in his mouth, Joe wiped his hands and mouth on a napkin and dropped it in the cardboard box that he used as a bin. All the waste bins in the station had been removed as part of an initiative to encourage recycling. Inspector Carlyle had responded by bringing in a couple of empty boxes from a nearby off-licence the next day – the cleaners still emptied them and everyone remained happy. Glancing over at the empty desk next to his, Joe wondered what his boss was up to. Carlyle had made himself scarce over the last few days, which presumably meant he was off chasing after the young girl he had found in the park. If he ever needed something he would call. Until then, Joe was more than happy to wait.

Letting out a loud burp, he looked around guiltily to see if anyone had heard. Happily, no one else on the floor at that time of the morning showed any indication of noticing. Joe stood up and stretched. He would make a cup of tea and then get down to his report. Definitely.

As he stepped towards the kitchen, the phone on Carlyle's desk started to ring. Joe looked at it warily. The phone kept ringing. Eventually, Joe picked it up. 'Inspector Carlyle's phone . . .'

'Carlyle?'

Joe didn't recognise the voice, but the woman sounded agitated. 'The inspector isn't here at the moment. I am one of his colleagues. Can I be of any assistance?'

'Who are you?' the woman asked suspiciously.

'Joe Szyszkowski.'

'And you work with Carlyle?'

'Yes,' said Joe, wishing now that he'd never picked the bloody thing up. 'I'm his sergeant.'

'Can you get a message to him?'

'Of course,' Joe replied testily. He was regretting that he hadn't bought a second bacon roll.

'It's urgent,' the woman hissed. 'He'll want to speak to me.'

'Okay.' Joe grabbed a pencil and a Post-it note from the desk. 'Fire away.'

'Tell him to call Alexa Matthews immediately.'

'Will he know what it's about?' Joe asked, in his best bureaucratic tone, but the line had already gone dead.

'YOU CAN TRUST Joe.'

'Why should I trust him? I sure as shit don't trust you.'

Carlyle glanced at Joe and grinned. 'Alexa is one of my favourite ex-colleagues.'

Joe Szyszkowski took a sip of his London Pride and said nothing.

Alexa Matthews didn't smile. She'd emptied her umpteenth double gin and tonic and wanted another. And also a smoke. 'Carlyle always was an annoying little shit,' she observed grimly, to no one in particular.

The three police officers were sitting in the snug bar of the Fitzroy Tavern on Charlotte Street, north of Soho. The Fitzroy was famous for having been a haunt of intellectuals like Dylan Thomas and George Orwell in the early to mid twentieth century. Now it was a generic, brewery-owned public house with more than its fair share of tourists and all the atmosphere of a bus station.

In short, it was a perfect location for their present rendezvous.

Matthews thrust her empty glass at the sergeant. 'Get me another drink, will ya?'

Reluctantly, Joe took the glass and stood up. He shot Carlyle a reproachful look and headed for the bar without enquiring if he, too, wanted a refill.

'Make it a double,' Matthews called to Joe's retreating back.

He pretended not to hear.

She turned to Carlyle. 'What did you bring him here for?'

Carlyle finished his Jameson, and felt the whiskey's warmth spread through his stomach. Hopefully Joe would do the decent thing and bring him another. 'I need the help,' he said. 'I can't do it all on my own.'

'I'm not sure I want him to know about this business.'

'Alexa,' Carlyle said firmly, 'Joe works with me. I've known him a long time. I came to you because I wanted to sort out the mess in SO14.' He stretched and yawned. 'I will do that – with Joe's help. And, of course, with your help as well.'

Matthews gave him a look. They both knew that to be a very ambitious statement.

'So, what do you want to tell me?'

Joe reappeared from behind a gaggle of students and carefully placed the fresh drinks on the table. Carlyle grabbed the Jameson gratefully. 'Thanks.'

'No problem.' Joe sat down on a stool and waited expectantly.

'Okay, okay.' Matthews took a swig of her gin. 'Things have recently gone to shit in a big way.'

WHEN MATTHEWS HAD finished explaining about her run-in with Tommy Dolan and her subsequent carpeting by Charlie Adam, she drained the rest of her gin.

Carlyle glanced at Joe, but neither man said anything.

'So . . .' Matthews said, staring into her glass, 'what are you going to do about it?'

What am I going to do about it? Carlyle asked himself.

'I'm worried that they'll kill me next time,' Matthews continued, 'or else hurt Heather.'

For the first time she seemed the worse for drink and Carlyle wondered how much she'd had before arriving at the Fitzroy. 'Nothing like that's going to happen,' he said soothingly. 'Adam might be a bit of a knob, but he's not going to do anything that stupid.'

'He's just a little shit,' Matthews mumbled. 'Anyway, it's not him I'm worried about.'

'Dolan,' said Joe quietly.

'Exactly,' said Matthews, waving her empty glass at him. 'Tommy *fucking* Dolan. Cunt-in-Chief.'

'I think you've had enough,' said Carlyle, taking the glass out of her hand and placing it carefully on the table. 'I remember Dolan from my time in the Unit. He's just a spiv who wants a quiet life. I'm surprised he had you beaten up, but he won't go any further than that.'

'I wouldn't be so sure of that.' Matthews sat back, closed her eyes and sighed deeply. 'There's too much money involved. People have died already.'

Carlyle gave her a quizzical look. 'What?'

'You know how it is in SO14. Everyone works for Dolan. Joe Dalton worked for him.'

Joe made a *so what?* face. 'The guy in the taxi? That was a clear suicide, no doubt at all.'

Matthews opened her eyes and started rubbing at her temples. 'Christ!' She turned to Carlyle. 'Does this one ever *catch* any crooks? *Why* did Joe Dalton feel the need to rip his own head off? That is the bloody question.'

'Which we have already asked ourselves,' Carlyle said evenly. He didn't like being talked down to by Alexa Matthews, but he needed her help now, so he would let it slide.

'But not yet answered,' Matthews shot back at him.

'No,' Carlyle admitted.

'Dolan runs an investment company called United 14,' Matthews said wearily. 'It takes money from their various different enterprises, in order to provide a pension "top-up" for the boys.'

'There's nothing new in that,' Carlyle remarked.

'No, but the economy is currently in the shit. It has been harder and harder for them to make a decent return.'

'Markets go down, they go up,' Carlyle said airily.

'Dolan can't sit around and wait. His glory days at SO14 may be coming to an end.'

'Why?' Joe asked.

'There is talk of bringing in another 150 armed protection officers to cut back on overtime. That means more than thirty grand a year to the likes of Dolan.'

Carlyle let out a low whistle. 'Bummer.'

'Dolan is steaming. He blames Princess Cheyenne.'

Joe and Carlyle exchanged quizzical looks. 'Who?' they asked in unison.

'The daughter of the Duke and Duchess of Colchester,' Matthews sneered. 'She's something like tenth or eleventh in line to the throne. She's at some crappy northern university studying the history of modern art, or some useless pile of wank like that. The annual protection bill for her alone is about four hundred grand.'

'A bargain,' Carlyle said sarcastically.

'That's nothing,' Matthews went on. 'The little genius now wants to go and study in America. That means two officers providing twenty-four-hour cover and a bill that could easily top a million. The papers are on to it and the top brass are running scared. They hope that if they can just get the overtime bill down, no one will notice that the overall bill keeps going up. The Commissioner has said the government already needs to find another twenty million a year to cover all the costs.'

'Royalty doesn't do belt-tightening,' Carlyle commented. 'Cuts, like taxes, are for the little people – people like us. Buckingham Palace has always refused to allow any cuts. They argue that the police and the state have a duty to protect both the Queen and the line of succession.'

Joe yawned, as he often did when his boss got on his soapbox. 'Coming back to Dolan,' he interjected.

'Dolan has had to diversify.'

'Into what?' Joe asked.

'Into things that some people can't live with,' Matthews said cryptically.

'Be more specific,' Carlyle demanded.

Matthews tried to stand up, wobbled, and fell back into her seat. 'That's all I'm going to say until I get myself out of there.'

Carlyle changed tack. 'Is Adam himself in on it?'

'He turns a blind eye. Can *you* get me out of there?'

'I'll speak to my boss,' Carlyle said. 'Why are you telling me all this now?'

'Because, annoying little shit though you are, you're my best bet for getting out of this whole mess and keeping my job.' This time Matthews made it successfully to her feet.

Carlyle tried one last time. 'What do they do?'

'Get me out and I'll give you more. Otherwise, that's your lot for now.'

'Dalton was in on it?' Joe persisted.

'Dalton couldn't take it any more. He couldn't hack it. He was a bit lame that way.' She brushed past Carlyle, and paused while trying to work out a path through the throng towards the door. 'Have you seen Allcock yet?'

'Who?'

'Dalton's girlfriend.'

Carlyle was embarrassed to admit that he hadn't got round to that yet. 'Not yet.'

Matthews gave him a crooked grin as she pushed her way past another group of drinkers. 'Better get on with it then, hadn't you?'

'HERE YOU GO.'

Helen tossed the brochure on to his lap and flopped down on the sofa.

'I thought it might bring back lots of happy memories,' she said with a smirk, picking up the remote control and switching on the television.

Carlyle looked down at the *Buckingham Palace: Official Souvenir Guide*, and made a face. 'Thanks a lot. When did you get that?'

'When we went on the tour there last year,' Helen said, flicking rapidly through a succession of channels in search of her nightly fix of audiovisual dross. 'Alice wanted it for a school project she had to do.'

Carlyle turned the thin volume over in his hands, looking for the price. 'How much did it cost?'

Helen shrugged. 'Dunno . . . eight quid, something like that.'

'So,' Carlyle felt a wave of parsimony wash over him, 'all in all, with the tickets and everything, the whole visit cost you what – fifty quid?'

'Easily.' Helen had just found an episode of *Argentina's Next Top Model* on some obscure satellite channel. Their time for talking was over.

'Talk about the rich getting even richer.'

Opening the brochure, Carlyle perused the text: *Buckingham Palace is furnished and decorated with priceless works of art from the Royal Collection.*

He glanced over at his wife, who was engrossed in watching some girl in a bikini and biker boots being abused by an overly butch photographer in the middle of some desert. 'Do they really need our money too?'

'What?' Helen didn't look up.

Sighing, he read on. *Buckingham Palace has 775 rooms, with 19 State Rooms, 52 Royal and guest bedrooms, 188 staff bedrooms and 78 bathrooms. More than 50,000 people visit each year as guests to banquets, receptions and Garden Parties.*

The inspector felt annoyed by the boundless silliness of it all. 'Have you got a decent hat? If I sort this mess out, maybe we'll get invited to a Garden Party.'

The girl on the TV was now in tears. She was being asked to pose naked – apart from the boots – in the desert with some kind of snake. It was a big beast, too, maybe a python. Tossing the *Official Souvenir Guide* on the floor, Carlyle cuddled up to his wife to enjoy the rest of the show.

Chapter Thirteen

UNLEASHING HIS INNER eight year old, Simon Merrett swivelled round in his chair to look at the bank of video screens ranged above the desk in front of him. 'This is like the Starship Enterprise,' he grinned. 'How do we get to Warp Factor Ten?'

Marshall Monk felt the pain in his stomach intensify. The General Manager of the London Eye tugged at the collar of his shirt and wondered if he should check the CEOP detective's ID again. 'I beg your pardon?'

Rose Scripps gave her colleague a dirty look.

'What I mean is,' Merrett said hastily, getting his chair back under control, 'how are we going to do this?'

Monk looked at the two uniformed policemen standing by the door of the control room, on either side of Sandra Scott. Scott looked her usual bovine self. The only thing that persuaded Monk that this wasn't some kind of a wind-up was the fact that she had turned up for the start of her shift wearing handcuffs. 'Well,' he said nervously, 'as I understand it, you are looking to apprehend—'

'Arrest,' Rose interrupted.

'Detain,' Merrett added unhelpfully.

Monk frowned, clearly not interested in their childish semantics. 'You want to get hold of the gentlemen who have booked a private capsule for the seven-thirty flight.'

Merrett glanced at the piece of paper with the booking details on the table in front of him. 'SEG Enterprises? Who are they?'

'I don't know,' Monk shrugged. 'But that was their second booking.'

'Payment?' Rose asked.

'Through a corporate credit card,' Monk replied. 'Amex, if I remember correctly.'

'The contact details are for a serviced office in Mayfair,' Merrett added, pleased to be able to show off that he had done some homework. 'SEG have rented space there for almost a year, but no one can ever remember anyone from the company actually turning up there.' He turned to Monk. 'So, what happens tonight?'

'One member of the group will need to check in at the priority check-in desk – the fast track booth – fifteen minutes before the scheduled flight time. Once the whole group is assembled, the capsule host will escort the group through the fast track entrance, thus bypassing the regular queue.'

'The capsule host?' Rose asked.

'Yes.' Monk smiled, happy to be speaking to this sensible-seeming woman, rather than her juvenile colleague. 'Every capsule has a host for the thirty-minute flight. The host is compulsory because there needs to be a minimum of three adults, over the age of eighteen, in each capsule.'

Rose looked at Merrett. 'But on that DVD . . .'

Merrett looked over at Sandra Scott, out of earshot, staring at the floor and not showing any apparent interest in their conversation.

Someone had doubtless been paid off, which made him wonder about Monk himself. Merrett turned back to Rose. 'We'll sort that out later.' He glanced at the clock above the screens, which showed 6.10 p.m. 'In the meantime, this is what we're going to do now . . .'

'MY DAUGHTER LOUISE is keen to go up on the Eye,' Rose said, looking up at the giant wheel in front of them. 'They went there on a school trip, and she's hassling me to take her again.' They were now standing in the standard queue, sandwiched between an aged French couple and a noisy hen party of middle-aged women dressed as cowgirls, and clearly the worse for drink.

'I'm sure Monk can sort it for you,' Merrett said, his eyes focused on the fast track check-in booth, twenty yards to his left.

Rose shook her head. 'No, thanks! I don't fancy it myself. I don't like heights at all.'

'It's not that high.' Merrett looked at his watch for the third time in as many minutes. It was 7.11. He wondered if they were going to be stood up. They were only three or four away from the front of the queue now. Behind them, the cowgirls were getting more excited. One of them cheekily pinched Merrett's backside. 'Hey!' He spun round angrily, to be confronted by a pair of bleach-blonde grannies collapsing into a fit of giggles.

'Look!' Rose grabbed Merrett's shoulder and turned him towards her. She was surprised to see that he was blushing. She gestured towards a tall, well-dressed man and a girl handing their fast track tickets over to a waiting host. The pair had their backs to Rose and Merrett and, given the distance, the girl could have been aged anything between eleven to sixteen. 'What about them?'

'Worth a look,' said Merrett, stepping out of the line and moving swiftly towards the newly arrived pair.

'What's the matter, love?' one of the grannies cackled. 'Worried what we'll do to you when we get you up in the air?'

'It isn't his bum he should be worried about,' another one shouted. 'Come back here, lover boy!'

Rose followed after Merrett, who was already five yards in front of her. Up ahead, she could see that the host was still checking their tickets and had not waved the man and the girl through. The Eye host said something into his walkie-talkie, and the well-dressed man turned round with a look of exasperation on his face. Rose stopped and studied his face. The crowds had thinned and, even at this distance, she was relatively sure that he was not the same man they had seen on the DVD. Before she could look away again, he caught her eye. She glanced over at Merrett, who had slowed his pace, trying to work out what was going on. The man followed her gaze and immediately turned back around. Grabbing the girl by the hand, he pulled her away from the booth, and started heading quickly in the direction of Westminster Bridge. The host looked surprised, but said nothing.

'Hey!' Merrett started running after the pair, and immediately went sprawling straight over a young boy who had appeared from nowhere, eating a large pink cloud of candyfloss. 'Shit!'

The boy started crying. Then he realised his candyfloss had landed in a puddle and he started screaming.

Merrett got up gingerly, holding his wrist. A large man with a shaven head and a Chelsea tattoo on his neck grabbed him by the arm. A small, nervous-looking woman, cigarette dangling from her mouth, hovered in the background. 'What the fuck do you think you're doing?' the man snarled. 'Why can't you watch where you're fucking going, you stupid wanker?'

'My arm,' Merrett winced.

'I don't care about your fucking arm,' the man shouted. 'You need to apologise to young Didier.' He gestured at the kid, who was still blubbing for all he was worth. 'And buy him some more candyfloss. Four bloody quid that cost.'

The boy had stopped crying by now, encouraged by the prospect of reparation. A small crowd had quickly gathered to see if Chelsea Man was going to beat the crap out of his son's tormentor.

Leaving Merrett to sort himself out, Rose hurried along the Embankment, scanning the horizon. For a second, she saw their quarry at the top of the steps leading to the bridge above. Upping her pace, she dodged through the tourist throng and headed after them.

Reaching the top of the steps, she was out of breath and panting. She couldn't remember the last time she had run anywhere, and the burning sensation in her chest was giving way to an urge to be sick. Looking over at Big Ben and the Houses of Parliament, she took a couple of deep breaths and waited for the nausea to subside. The sweat running down her back had gone cold, and she shivered. A cyclist flashed past her, inches away from being taken out by a number 12 bus. Two hundred feet up, the quarter bells in the belfry played the Westminster Quarters, signifying it was now 7.15. Of the man and the girl there was no sign.

ALLOWING HER FRUSTRATION to subside, Rose took her time returning to the Eye. When she finally got there, Chelsea Man and his family were gone. Merrett was sitting on the steps leading to the back entrance of City Hall, having his wrist bandaged by a paramedic from the Cycle Response Unit.

'Looks like it's broken,' Merrett groaned. 'I'll need to go and get it X-rayed at St Thomas's.' He didn't look at her or ask about their quarry.

'Did you get the kid a new stick of candyfloss?'

'Four bloody quid!' Merrett whined. 'I hope the little bugger chokes on it. Where did he come from anyway?' He ignored the grin on her face. 'What are you going to do now?'

Rose thought about it for a moment. 'I'll check the CCTV and have another word with Mr Monk,' she said. 'Then I'll get back to the office and write up a report.'

Merrett accepted a couple of painkillers from the paramedic and dropped them into his mouth. 'Leaving out the bit about the kid and the candyfloss.'

Rose patted him gently on the shoulder. 'Of course.'

Merrett took a swig from a bottle of water to wash the pills down. 'Thanks.' He offered her a drink.

Rose shook her head. 'No, thanks.'

'I appreciate it,' Merrett continued. 'No one likes looking like a dick.'

'No problem.' Rose gave him a reassuring smile. 'These things happen. You go and get your wrist seen to, and we can see where we are in the morning.'

She watched Merrett trudge off, feeling sorry for himself, and then she started off in the opposite direction, heading towards the footbridge over the Thames that would take her to Charing Cross on the north side. From there she could walk back to the office in about fifteen minutes. Approaching the Eye, she passed the fast track ticket booth, which was now empty. The last flight of the day had started and there would be no more customers this evening. On a whim, Rose stepped over to the booth and looked inside. It was empty, apart from a large black refuse sack that had been left, tied at the top, in the back, next to an open bin. She glanced around. There were a couple of staff tidying up litter, getting ready to usher the last visitors off the wheel and then go home for the night. But no one was paying any attention to her. Ducking into the booth, she opened her handbag and pulled out a large pair of tweezers and a small plastic bag that she'd saved from her last trip to Boots. Putting her handbag on the floor, she lifted up the sack, weighing it in her hand. It was full of used tickets, cardboard cups and empty plastic bottles; in short, a lot of crap to have to sort through. Rose sighed; she simply didn't have the time right now.

Carefully returning the sack to where she had found it, Rose peered into the bin itself. It was empty apart from a couple of tickets. Reaching inside, she pulled out both of them with the tweezers and placed them carefully on the ground. In the poor light, she picked up the first ticket and brought it close to her face. It was for the 7.30 flight, pod 12, in the name of Cunningham. On the back were the terms and conditions of use. Nothing else of any interest. Crumpling the ticket up, she tossed it back into the bin.

The second ticket was also for the 7.30 flight, this time for pod 8. It had the legend SEG Ent. typed in the bottom right-hand corner.

'Bingo!' said Rose under her breath.

Dropping the ticket into her plastic bag, she noticed that something had been scribbled on the back. Grabbing it again with the tweezers, she took another look. There was a name and a mobile number.

'Double bingo,' she whispered.

Chapter Fourteen

STANDING UNDER THE gloomy strip-lighting, Carlyle stared at the three corpses on the table and felt a bit queasy. He now wished that he had delayed his breakfast until after this visit to the East End. Pacing the concrete floor, he rubbed his hands together in a feeble attempt to keep warm. The room was cold, just as cold as it had been in the street outside. The weather had taken a turn for the worse and Carlyle reminded himself again that it was time to deploy the winter wardrobe. He cursed himself for not choosing a heavier overcoat. Through an open door, he could see several young assistants silently going about their business. All of them wore the same uniform of black jeans and a black fleece. None of them came into the room. None of them so much as glanced at him as they went past. Even more gallingly, no one had even offered him a cup of coffee.

Carlyle yawned, noisily.

'Inspector?'

'Yes.' He quickly finished his yawn and turned to face a smiling blonde woman, her hair tied back in a ponytail. About his height, in her late twenties or early thirties, she was wearing jeans and a heavy orange jumper over a grandpa shirt; a pair of thick, black-framed glasses were perched on the top of her head. 'John Carlyle, from the Charing Cross station.'

He extended a hand and she shook it limply.

'Fiona Allcock.'

'Thank you for seeing me.'

'Not a problem,' she smiled. 'Thank you for coming to the studio.' She gestured towards the table. 'Do you like my birds?'

'Well . . .' Carlyle forced himself not to take another peek. He didn't like dead things. And, as a London boy through and through, he thought animals were best suited to the countryside. 'What are they?'

'Sparrows.' Allcock stepped over to the table and picked up one of the birds, placing it face up in the palm of her hand. She lifted the bird towards Carlyle and two little dead eyes stared up at him. He swallowed uncomfortably. 'We got sent these little beauties from Lincolnshire only yesterday.'

'What will you do with them?' he asked, although he was not interested in the slightest.

'One of my assistants will skin the creatures today,' Allcock said, placing the dead bird back on the table along with its two chums. 'It's like removing the skin from a chicken before you cook it.'

'I see.' Carlyle, who had never skinned a chicken in his life, nodded wisely.

'Once that is done, the muscle fibres and bones are measured and posed,' she continued, reciting what was clearly a practised monologue. 'The carcass is then moulded in plaster and we make a final polyurethane mannequin. The skin is tanned and then fitted to the mannequin. Finally we add glass eyes and put it in a display.'

'Interesting.'

'These little ones are already sold.' Allcock perched herself on the edge of the table. 'They are going to a collector in Bristol.'

Despite himself, Carlyle was curious. 'And how much will they cost?'

'The final display will cost £8,500, plus vat.'

Eight grand? 'Interesting,' he repeated politely.

She gave him a suspicious look and slipped back into salesperson mode. 'Of course, what you've got to remember is that you are looking at weeks and weeks of work. It's a highly skilled professional job.'

'And you have many takers?'

'Oh, yes,' she beamed. 'Taxidermy is really fashionable at the moment. We're rushed off our feet.'

'I won't keep you long, then,' Carlyle said briskly. 'I wondered if I could have a quick word with you about Joe Dalton.'

'Ah yes, Joe.' She folded her arms and stared into the middle distance.

'I know that you already spoke to the officers who investigated his death,' he said gently, 'and I really don't want to go over old ground, but I was wondering if I could ask you a few questions.' He had read her statement in the original report; it had been perfunctory in the extreme.

'Of course,' she nodded. 'Are you reopening the investigation?'

'No, but there may be a connection with something else that I am looking into.'

'Oh?' She studied him carefully. 'How so?'

Carlyle smiled. 'That's what I'm trying to work out. Do you happen to know why Joe decided to kill himself?'

'No, not really.' She sighed, staring at the floor. 'Joe could always be a bit up and down. I saw him about a week before he died; I remember that he was rather gloomy but nothing off the scale.' She shrugged. 'I could put up with it, in small doses.'

'He was your boyfriend?'

She grinned. 'He was *a* boyfriend, Inspector. I liked Joe a lot, but he wasn't the love of my life or anything like that.'

Carlyle felt himself redden slightly, but kept going. 'Did he see your relationship differently? Is that what pushed him over the edge?'

She glanced at the dead birds, as if for inspiration. 'I don't think so. It was more than just a casual thing, but neither of us was prevented from seeing other people.'

'How did you meet?'

'At some party a few years ago. I remember he was quite a novelty. You don't meet many policemen in my social circle.'

'I suppose not.'

'No offence.'

'Of course not,' he smiled. 'I know exactly what you mean. I don't meet many taxidermists in *my* social circle. So . . .'

'Yes?'

'What was the connection? What was a copper like Joe Dalton doing hanging out with the beautiful people of the arts set?'

Allcock didn't rise to the bait. 'It's not so surprising really. We work—' she corrected herself, 'he *worked* for similar people.'

'What kind of people?'

'Some of my clients are royalty.'

Carlyle raised an eyebrow.

'Well, minor royalty.' She looked at him with an amused smile. 'Don't you read the papers?'

'Sometimes,' he grinned. 'But usually only the football pages.'

'Let me show you.' Allcock marched over to a pile of magazines in the corner, rising about four feet from the floor. Rooting through the stack, she found what she was looking for, five or six down from the top. Holding up an old copy of *ES Magazine*, she fetched it over. 'Here.' She opened the magazine at page 7 and handed it to Carlyle. Under the headline *Bright Nights, Big City* were a dozen or so photos of rich, successful, smug-looking people drinking champagne at an after-party celebrating the opening of an exhibition. Top right was a photo of Allcock herself, hair up, looking very glamorous in a black Chanel dress. She pointed to a hand that was just visible in the edge of the shot. 'Joe was standing next to me when this picture was taken, but he got cropped out.' Her index finger moved to the picture below. 'And that's the Earl of Falkirk.'

'The Earl of Falkirk.' Carlyle immediately recognised the arrogant-looking man wearing a dinner jacket, black tie undone.

'One of my clients. He's taken an ocellated turkey and a Japanese raccoon dog from me so far this year.'

'Did he know Joe Dalton?'

'Of course. Falkirk's twentieth to the throne or something. It was Joe who introduced us a couple of years ago. He worked as one of the guy's bodyguards.'

'He was a CPO?'

She looked at him blankly.

'A Close Protection Officer, CPO.'

Allcock frowned. 'Like I said, he was a bodyguard. It seemed like a cool gig. Joe liked the travel and the overtime. He said that some of the other bodyguards could be right sods, though.'

'How so?'

'Just, you know, annoying. He never really specified anything in particular.'

'Did he ever mention a guy called Dolan?'

Allcock thought about it for a moment.

'Tommy Dolan,' Carlyle repeated.

She shook her head. 'No. I don't think so.'

Carlyle closed the magazine and rolled it up. 'Can I keep this?'

She shrugged. 'Of course.'

'Thank you for your time.'

'No problem.' Allcock edged him towards the door. 'Can I interest you in an animal?'

Never in a million years, Carlyle thought. 'Out of my league, I'm afraid,' he mumbled, keen to leave the little dead birds behind and get out on to the street.

GORDON ELSTREE-ULLICK LAY on the bed in one of the guest rooms in Buckingham Palace, talking quietly into his mobile phone. After a while, he looked up and gestured towards his Protection Officer. 'Tommy, stick this on the corporate card, will you?'

Tommy Dolan looked at the outstretched mobile in Elstree-Ullick's hand and sighed. 'What is it this time?'

'Just a couple of plane tickets,' Elstree-Ullick told him. 'Let me know when the bill comes in.'

Dolan accepted the phone with as much enthusiasm as he would a steaming dog turd. Jamming it between his ear and his shoulder, he fished his Met-issue American Express corporate card out of his wallet. 'Hello?' he said grumpily.

Five minutes and fifteen grand later, he had paid for two first-class British Airways tickets from Heathrow to Jomo Kenyatta International airport in Nairobi. Gritting his teeth, Dolan told himself that this was just a cost of doing business. All the same, it took his current Amex bill to well over £20,000. That would mean more scrutiny from the SO14 Accounts Department. And that was the kind of attention that Dolan didn't like.

Sticking his card back in his pocket, he gave Elstree-Ullick a sharp look. The Earl of Falkirk, twenty-second in line to the British throne, just grinned in a way that let him know he had Dolan over a barrel. Everyone knew that royals borrowing funds from bodyguards was commonplace. According to the Unit Guidelines:

> *It is often inappropriate for the Royal Family to execute financial transactions due to 'confidentiality and security reasons'. Therefore, if the need arises, Protection Officers will incur expenditure on behalf of principals, which is then repaid.*

OF COURSE, WHEN that cash would actually get repaid was never specified.

Dolan tossed the phone back to Elstree-Ullick, who caught it clumsily. 'Off on a trip?'

'No, the tickets are for a couple of chums.'

'Nice,' Dolan remarked sarkily.

'Don't worry, Tommy,' Elstree-Ullick snapped back, 'it's not your money. Anyway, they might be of help with our operation.'

'Oh?'

'Yes, indeed.' Elstree-Ullick slipped the phone into an inside pocket of his jacket. 'We need to move on to pastures new. I'm thinking about Africa.'

'Is that such a great idea?' Dolan sniped. 'Doesn't everyone there have AIDS?'

'Don't be so prejudiced, man,' Elstree-Ullick drawled. Getting off the bed, he headed for the door. 'Anyway, I've got stuff to do now. We can discuss it at the party later.'

Chapter Fifteen

ALZBETHA WAS WOKEN by an almighty fart from the fat man in the bed beside her. Shivering, she realised that he had taken almost all of the duvet from her and she was left uncovered. Swinging her legs over the side of the bed, she sat up, listening to his calm, regular snoring. Her body ached all over, her head felt fuzzy and there was a strange foul taste in her mouth that she didn't recognise.

As the clock on the table flipped from 1:11 to 1:12, she stood up and tiptoed over to the small pile of clothes lying on the floor. Slowly, noiselessly, she pulled on her jeans and her pullover. Where were her trainers? She looked under the bed, but couldn't see much in the dark. The man coughed and pulled the duvet over his shoulders. Was he about to wake up? She decided that she could do without the shoes.

Padding out of the bedroom, she walked down the hallway to the front door of the flat. Holding her breath as it clicked open, she listened for any further signs of movement from the bedroom. Hearing nothing, she stepped out on to the landing. Leaving the door open, she ran down the stairs.

Two floors down, the night porter dozed fitfully at his desk on the ground floor, an almost empty half-bottle of Highland Park blended whisky resting snugly in the pocket of his jacket. A talk radio station burbled quietly in the background. Alzbetha surveyed the scene and walked briskly across the foyer, hitting the big green button that allowed you to exit the building. The glass door was heavy but, grunting with the effort, she managed to open it just enough to squeeze through. On the wet pavement outside, she turned left and started running.

After several minutes, Alzbetha began to feel safe. She slowed to a walking pace and started looking around. She had no idea where she was, but that was no surprise. Apart from the Palace, nothing in this city had ever looked familiar. The streets were empty of people, but there was still a steady stream of traffic moving past. Standing on the kerbside, she counted one, two, three cars go by. Waiting until a fourth was almost upon her, she walked resolutely out into the middle of the road, her eyes closed against the glare of its headlights.

ROSE SCRIPPS SAT on her couch with a large glass of Chardonnay and gazed vacantly at the television. Louise had finally gone to sleep and she now had some time to herself. Taking a sip of her wine, she tried to focus on the programme – yet another BBC costume drama but with extra shagging in an attempt to keep everyone interested. However, after a few minutes of watching women running around in bonnets, she could feel her eyes glazing over. With a sigh, she took the remote control from the arm of the sofa and switched off the television.

Getting up, she wandered over to the tiny dining-table. There, along with the wine bottle and her mobile, lay a small notebook open at the page where she had copied the name and number scribbled on the back of the London Eye ticket that she had rescued from the bin. The ticket itself had been logged at the station and filed along with her report. As she had promised, the latter contained a suitably sanitised version of the fiasco down by the river.

Rose wasn't sure how best they should proceed from here. She had arrived home assuming that it was something to be discussed with Merrett in the morning. Now, however, she didn't want to wait any longer.

After another mouthful of wine, she put her glass on the table and picked up the phone. Quickly, before she could change her mind, Rose dialled in the number from the ticket and waited for the ring tone. It seemed to take forever to get a connection. As she looked at the handset, checking that there was a signal, the number eventually started ringing. She could feel her heart beat faster, but still no one answered. After what seemed like an eternity, the voicemail kicked in: *This is Warren Shen's mobile. Please leave a message and a number that I can get back to you on.*

Warren What? Shed? Zen? Shen? What kind of a name was that? Without leaving a message, Rose ended the call and scribbled down the possible variants on this name. Placing the phone back on the table, she finished the last of her wine and refilled the glass. Then she took her laptop from the sideboard and powered it up.

After firing a few blanks on Google, she typed in *Warren Shen*. There were 795,000 results. Rose clicked on 'news': 12 results. Scanning down, she found *Police close Central London lap-dance bar*. Clicking on the link, she went to the short story on the *Daily Mirror*'s website:

> *A West End lap-dancing club used as a brothel where rich clients could buy sex and drugs has been shut down by police.*

Vice Squad detectives arrested seven people accused of help-
ing to run the basement Capricorn Club and seized cocaine
and cash. 'It is hard to believe that in the middle of a busy
neighbourhood, these shady dealings were blatantly going
on,' said Detective Inspector Warren Shen of the Metropoli-
tan Police. 'This type of criminal activity is a nuisance and a
blight on the community and we will continue to root it out
wherever it occurs.'

ROSE SAT STARING at the computer screen for a long time. If this
was the right Warren Shen – and it was an unusual name, so how
many of them could there actually be? – what did that mean for
the CEOP investigation? The only conclusion to be reached was
that she had no idea. Anyway, there was nothing more for her to
do tonight. The wine was now making her feel sleepy. Yawning,
she switched off the computer and headed for bed.

Chapter Sixteen

SITTING AT A table near the door, Gordon Elstree-Ullick sipped at his Potocki vodka and scanned the interior of Palermo, one of his favourite Mayfair drinking dens. The Gucci furnishings, Swarovski crystals, dark marbles, nutty-brown woods and abstract art above the long marble-topped bar gave Palermo the atmosphere of an American martini lounge in the late 1950s. If the Bond Street shoppers filling out the afternoon crowd didn't quite fit with that image, at least he could pretend.

'Why do you drink that Polish stuff?' Ihor Chepoyak finished his glass of Heineken and pointed at Elstree-Ullick's glass. 'Ukrainian vodka is much better.'

'Which is why you're drinking Dutch beer, I suppose,' Elstree-Ullick commented.

'When I drink vodka, I drink Ukrainian vodka!'

Elstree-Ullick inspected his glass. 'I like this stuff. Anyway, I don't think they serve any Ukrainian brands here.'

'They should,' Ihor grunted.

Elstree-Ullick took another dainty sip. 'Maybe you could make them an offer they can't refuse.'

Ihor looked confused. 'What?'

'Never mind.' Elstree-Ullick placed his glass carefully on the table. 'Anyway, that's not what we're here to talk about.'

Ihor smiled. 'No.'

Elstree-Ullick began: 'About the girl . . .'

'You are getting careless, my friend.'

'It was hardly my fault.' Elstree-Ullick looked to Ihor for some words of support or sympathy. When none were forthcoming, he went on: 'You've got to look at it positively. At least it solves that particular problem.'

'Solves it?' Ihor gave him a hard look. He again lifted his glass to his mouth, forgetting that it was empty. 'How does it solve it? The police have her back now.'

'Even if she is identified, it remains a dead end,' he grinned. 'So to speak.'

'Let's hope so, for your sake.'

'For *all* our sakes.' Elstree-Ullick finished his drink and signalled to the waitress, a horsey-looking girl with an unfortunate smile. 'Two more, please.' After the woman had retreated to the bar, he leaned over the table. 'We're in this together, remember?'

Ihor grunted noncommittally. As far as he was concerned, all business partnerships had a finite lifespan, and it looked like this one could soon be coming to an end.

'In the meantime,' Elstree-Ullick continued, 'there is a more pressing problem.'

'There is?' Ihor sat back in his chair and closed his eyes, allowing himself to imagine whipping out his Fort-12 CURZ pistol and putting a 9mm Kurz round between the eyes of the bastard Earl of Falkirk. He smiled to himself. It might very well come to that yet.

'I've made my last trip to the Ukraine. It's too much hassle to go back. And, rather more importantly, we need to find something new to keep the clients interested.'

Ihor opened his eyes. 'Like what?'

'I'm looking at some opportunities in East Africa,' Elstree-Ullick said. 'Kenya, to be precise.'

'I know nothing about Africa – neither do you.'

'No, but—'

Ihor yawned. 'The Ukraine is fine. You should be more worried about developments here in London.'

'What do you mean?'

'I hear that one of your customers nearly got arrested down by the river. Chased by some cops just as he was getting on to the London Eye.'

How the hell did you know about that? Elstree-Ullick wondered. 'No, no,' he said hastily, 'the guy just bottled it. There was no problem.'

'I see.'

'Yes, so – it is very much business as usual.'

'Maybe you should tell your clients to be a bit more low-key for a while,' Ihor said grumpily.

The waitress reappeared with their fresh drinks. She smiled widely and Elstree-Ullick wondered if she knew who he was. I'm so out of your league, sweetheart, he thought. He sat back in his chair and watched her buttocks shimmy inside her jeans, as she wandered off. Not a bad arse. Not bad at all. 'The thing is,' he drawled, still staring at the woman's rear end, 'the clients don't like being told what to do.' He eyed Ihor as if he was imparting some great wisdom. 'They want – they *need* – to be able to do whatever they want. Some of them are really quite competitive about it. If we cut down on the thrill factor, that's our USP out of the window.'

'A fuck is a fuck,' Ihor mumbled, sucking the head off his beer.

'But we are selling so much more than that,' Elstree-Ullick persisted. 'Plenty of people can supply a pretty girl. With us it's the whole experience.'

Keeping the glass near his lips, Ihor wondered just what the idiot was talking about. If you wanted an *experience* you went to Disneyland. What was wrong with good old-fashioned fucking behind closed doors? He looked at the boy in front of him, one of the most privileged people on the whole planet, yet a guy who knew nothing about the realities of life for normal people. He was a bloody Earl, for God's sake – so why was he getting involved in all this shit? And, more to the point, could he be relied on not to fuck things up? 'Just be careful,' he said finally.

'Of course,' Elstree-Ullick replied stiffly.

'Business is good,' Ihor went on, trying to ignore the fact that this boy would just not listen, 'which is all the more reason not to be complacent.'

'Never.'

Yeah, right, Ihor thought, as he drained his glass.

'Good afternoon, gentlemen.' The smell of perfume filled the air. Both men looked up to see Olga arrive at their table, a large glass of white wine in her hand.

She was dressed in a tight-fitting charcoal jacket with a matching skirt that fell to just below the knee; her powder-blue shirt had the top three buttons undone, giving a tantalising glimpse of décolletage.

As the woman sat down, crossing her legs, Elstree-Ullick felt a familiar tingling in his groin. Not for the first time, he felt angry at Ihor's insistence that he should not fuck the help. Did the idiot not realise that that was one of the basic perks of being a royal?

Reaching into her bag, she pulled out a tin of salve and deftly applied some to her lips. 'May I join you?'

'I thought that you already had,' Elstree-Ullick quipped, moving his chair closer to hers.

Ihor eyed her suspiciously. 'What are you doing here?'

Olga put the tin back in her bag and gently wiped her mouth with a napkin. After taking a sip of wine, she said, 'I have a business meeting at the Sheraton on Park Lane in forty-five minutes. I'm just killing a little time.'

Falkirk grinned lecherously. 'Maybe you could drop by and see me at the Palace later . . . have some champagne?'

Olga glanced at Ihor, then smiled slyly at Falkirk. 'Maybe. That could be fun.'

Ihor frowned. 'How did you know we were here?'

'I didn't,' Olga said sweetly. 'It's just a coincidence.' Turning to Elstree-Ullick, she upped the wattage on her smile. 'So – what are you two boys conspiring about here?' she asked.

'Just discussing business,' Elstree-Ullick said airily.

'Oh?' Glancing at Ihor, Olga arched an eyebrow. 'And is business good?'

'Not bad,' Ihor said quickly, giving Elstree-Ullick a look that said *Shut the fuck up*.

'Not bad?' Olga repeated slowly. 'That's good.'

'Yes,' Ihor nodded.

Olga made a show of thinking about things for a second. 'But what about the girl that died?'

'These things happen,' Ihor said stonily, his gaze now firmly fixed on the table.

'Yes,' said Olga brightly, 'I guess they do.' She emptied her glass in two gulps and stood up. 'Ihor, I will see you later.' Hands on hips, she fixed her eyes on Elstree-Ullick, her smile beginning to erode at the edges. 'Business must be extremely good if you can bring a child over from the Ukraine and just let her walk out in front of a car,' she said, not waiting for a response before sauntering to the door.

Gordon Elstree-Ullick watched her go, the grin still fixed on his face and the erection still in his trousers. Inhaling her lingering scent, he tried to make sense of what he had just heard.

ON THE SECOND floor of the Westminster Public Mortuary in Horseferry Road, the stern gaze of Barbara Enereich looked down upon the Forensic Suite that bore her name. Next to the portrait of the former President of the British Association in Forensic Medicine was a small plaque. The legend on it read: *Hic locus est ubi mors gaudet succurrere vitae.* Below, in a smaller script, for those like Carlyle whose Latin wasn't quite up to it, was the translation: *This is the place where death rejoices to help those who live.*

Bollocks, he mused, returning his gaze to the bank of four LCD monitors hanging from the ceiling. Three of them were blank; the fourth showed the scene inside Lab Number 2 – twenty yards further down the hallway. Biting his lip, he watched as the three forensic pathologists went calmly about their business, preparing for the autopsy of the young girl lying on the slab in the background.

Sticking his hands into his trouser pockets, Carlyle began pacing from one side of the cramped CCTV viewing room to the other. *Autopsy*, he remembered from somewhere, meant *see for yourself.* See for yourself? He would rather not, thank you very much. For Carlyle, this part of an investigation was something to be avoided whenever possible. He had been delighted when Westminster's new £1 million facility had opened, ending the need for him to be in the same room as the actual corpse. Watching the proceedings on television was far better than being in there along with her, but he still felt queasy. Nausea, mixed with the rage that had been bubbling through his guts in the days since the child had died, was creating a foul brew. Try as he might, he couldn't bring himself to believe that Alzbetha had now left them all behind while her body was still so shockingly present.

Looking over at Joe Szyszkowski, who was sitting on a plastic chair at the back of the room, eating yet another bacon sandwich, Carlyle felt his stomach do a double somersault. 'Let's go.'

Joe quickly finished chewing and gave him a funny look. 'But we've only just got here.'

Carlyle buttoned up his jacket and headed for the door. 'We know what happened, and we can read the report later. I don't feel any need to watch.' Without waiting for a reply, he pulled open the door and fled.

Out on the street, he gazed at the passing traffic and waited for the nausea to subside. His feelings of inadequacy would take a lot longer to pass. He had failed Alzbetha; failed her completely. There was no way around that – and there was nothing he could do to make amends.

Joe appeared a few minutes later and placed a careful hand on his boss's shoulder. 'We will circulate a picture,' he said quietly, 'and the fingerprints. Try to get an ID.'

Carlyle nodded.

Joe removed his hand and took a step back. 'We still have no real idea how she ended up on South Audley Street at one-thirty in the morning.'

'We know *exactly* how she got there,' Carlyle hissed.

'Well,' Joe said gently, 'what I mean is, we don't know where she came from. We have CCTV images showing the girl entering from South Street, but how she got there in the first place we don't know.'

Carlyle looked at him. 'There are quite a few blocks of flats around there ...'

'Yeah. And quite a few hotels. We have a couple of uniforms doing the rounds but they haven't come up with anything yet.'

'A couple?'

Joe shrugged. 'You know how it is. We've got two constables for the day. That's it.'

'Fuck's sake.' Carlyle kicked at a discarded cigarette packet on the pavement and missed. 'Anything else?'

Joe thought for a minute. 'We know that she had alcohol in her system, and zaleplon.'

Carlyle gave him a quizzical look.

'It's used in sleeping pills. And also she had been—'

Carlyle held up a hand. He didn't need any more details. 'You concentrate on trying to find her family. I'll go and have another word with Shen.' He watched Joe trudge off down the road, before disappearing into St James's Park tube station. Pulling his mobile out of his jacket, Carlyle found the number he was looking for and hit the call button.

'Hello?'

He was taken aback when Simpson answered immediately.

'Hello?' she repeated quickly, the irritation obvious in her voice.

'It's John Carlyle.'

'Yes?' Almost like she'd never spoken to him before.

'We've located the girl.'

'What girl?'

'The girl I found in Green Park.' He was regretting making this call now, just as she was probably regretting taking it. Still, he persevered. 'The Ukrainian girl who was snatched from Social Services.'

There was a pause while Simpson belatedly got herself on to the right page. 'Ah, yes. Good. Is she okay?'

'She's dead,' Carlyle replied matter-of-factly. 'She walked out in front of a car in Mayfair a couple of nights ago.'

'Oh.' The pause was longer this time. 'I'm sorry about that, John,' she said finally. 'I know that this was very important to you.'

'It still is,' he snapped.

'Yes, well, quite. Do you have anything to go on?'

'We are chasing a few things,' he said vaguely.

'You are working with Shen?'

'Yes, me and Shen . . . that's why I was ringing. How well do you know him?'

'Why do you ask?'

'I have my doubts.'

'John,' she said gently, 'you always have your doubts.'

'Maybe,' Carlyle said grudgingly, 'but I've seen him in action and—'

'And what?' she chided. 'He doesn't fit the John Carlyle template for the perfect copper?'

Ten yards down the road, a taxi driver almost mowed down a woman pushing a child in a buggy as she stepped on to a zebra crossing. The woman flipped the driver the finger and screamed abuse at the cab as it was driven hurriedly away. Carlyle returned to his conversation. 'I just want to know more about him.'

'All I know is that he is considered an up-and-comer in Vice,' Simpson said. 'But I will make some discreet enquiries.'

'Thank you.'

'In the meantime, remember what I told you.'

What was that exactly? Carlyle wondered 'Of course.'

'Keep going with it. But when you get to the end of the road, it's time to stop. I can't let you chase this forever.'

'I understand.'

'Good. Thank you for keeping me informed. Let's speak later.'

'Will do.' Carlyle ended the call and immediately pulled up a number for Warren Shen.

STANDING IN THE doorway of the former SNCF office on Piccadilly, CEOP Detective Simon Merrett watched Warren Shen as he stood on the kerbside ten yards away, obviously checking the number of an incoming call on his mobile. Deciding not to take it, Shen dropped the phone into the pocket of his jacket and crossed the road, heading north up Dover Street. Taking his life into his hands, Merrett danced across the four lanes of traffic, and followed at what he hoped was a discreet distance.

A couple of minutes later, Shen took a left down Hay Hill and stepped into an expensive-looking bar called Palermo. Standing on the corner, Merrett pondered what to do next. He was cold and tired, and the dull ache from his broken wrist was driving him mad. Scratching at it under the plaster cast, he cursed himself for giving up a day off to follow this guy around Central London, on the basis of what? A hunch? A desire to be seen to be doing *something* after the cock-up at the London Eye? Probably more the latter than the former. The truth was, he didn't really have much of a clue about what he was hoping to achieve.

After discussing the situation with Rose Scripps, they had decided that it would be premature to approach Shen directly until they had a better idea at least of what was going on. They had no evidence that Shen was bent but, by the same token, they had nothing to say that he wasn't. CEOP had experience of dealing with police officers who had got caught up in its investigations, most of it bad. It was hard enough getting a result with civilians; but dealing with people who knew how to hide behind the law, and could effortlessly play the system, made it well-nigh impossible. To protect their investigation, such as it was, they had to tread warily. Equally, to protect any investigation that Shen *might* be legitimately pursuing, they also had to tread warily. But there was a fine line between caution and inactivity, which was why Merrett had spent the last three hours walking the streets and hanging about in doorways.

It started to rain.

'Shit!' Zipping up his jacket, Merrett looked around for some shelter. Finding none, he jogged down the hill to the entrance of the Palermo bar. Arriving at the entrance, he was almost knocked over by a young guy in a suit and a tie on his way out.

'Hey!'

The man just ignored him and kept on going. Cursing under his breath, Merrett stepped inside. It took a moment for his eyes to adjust to the gloom. Looking casually around the room, he saw Shen sitting at a table near the bar with a large, shaven-headed guy. He caught the big guy's eye and quickly looked away. The rest of the place was fairly empty. There was a smattering of tourists and shoppers, but at least half the tables were unoccupied. Moving to the bar, he had to wait for a couple of minutes before the barman condescended to serve him. Trying not to wince at paying £4.50

for a bottle of Beck's beer, he took a seat at a table on the far side of the room, from where he could keep an eye on proceedings.

Pouring half of his beer into the glass provided, Merrett began surfing the net on his mobile, to give the impression of having something to do. Shen and his companion were still deep in conversation. Merrett resisted the temptation to try and take a photo of the pair, worried that it might attract the attention of the shaven-headed guy, whose gaze swept the room at regular intervals.

Finishing his beer, Merrett headed back to the bar for another Beck's. Just as he did so, Shen stood up, shook hands with his associate and walked towards the door. As casually as he could manage, Merrett did a U-turn, and followed him out. However, as he reached the door his exit was blocked by a short, stocky man stepping in front of him.

'Sorry,' said Merrett brusquely. 'Excuse me.'

The man placed a firm hand on his chest. 'Back,' he said, his English heavily accented.

'What?' Merrett took a step backwards, looking the man up and down, and did a double-take. He had the same shaved head and squat features as the man at Shen's table. Merrett glanced over his shoulder to check that there were, indeed, two of them.

'Yes,' said the voice, now behind him, pushing him towards the table just vacated by Shen. 'Over there.' He pointed to his colleague waiting patiently at the table, an amused grin on his face.

'I don't think so,' Merrett hissed. He looked around the bar. No one was showing any interest in his predicament, and the bartender had disappeared. What would happen if he kicked up a fuss?

The man gave him another shove. Then he stuck a hand into the pocket of his denim jacket and pulled out a switchblade. 'I could gut you with this and walk straight out of the door,' he said casually. 'You would bleed to death on the carpet before anyone even noticed.' He slipped the knife back in his pocket and gestured over to the table with his chin. 'Now, do as I tell you. Go and sit down.'

'Okay, okay.' Merrett's brain had frozen. He stepped quickly over to the table and sat down in front of the large smirking type, conscious of the man with the knife at his back, standing over him.

'Why were you watching me?' Ihor Chepoyak said by way of introduction.

Merrett tried to look nonchalant. 'I wasn't.'

Ihor looked at his empty glass and smiled. 'Don't lie to me. Are you a policeman? I can smell policemen from a mile away.'

'No.' The word was out of his mouth before Merrett realised it.

Ihor looked lazily up, past Merrett. 'Artem . . .'

Merrett felt a knee shoved into his back. As he leaned forward, an arm went round his neck. Before he could react, the man behind him had skilfully removed his wallet from the inside pocket of his jacket and dropped it on the table.

Rubbing his back, Merrett coughed as he watched Ihor pick up the wallet and slowly rifle through it until he found what he wanted. Tossing the wallet back to Merrett, he brought the ID card close to his face. 'CEOP,' he mumbled eventually. 'What is this?'

Sticking the wallet back in his pocket, Merrett said nothing.

Ihor's face broke into a broad smile, a gold tooth visible in the back of his mouth. 'So you are a kind of . . . pretend policeman, *Detective* Merrett?'

'Give me back my ID,' Merrett said, with all the authority of a bullied and beaten schoolboy.

'Certainly.' Standing up, Ihor pushed the card into the back pocket of his jeans. 'But first you come with us.'

'Like hell I—' Merrett felt a hand on his shoulder, quickly followed by the tip of the blade at his neck.

'Get up.' Ihor walked past him, heading for the door. 'I think you know the alternative.'

Mouth dry, legs weak, Merrett allowed himself to be hoisted to his feet. He looked round the bar for someone who could help. But, compared to when he had come in, the place seemed almost empty. He felt the beer churning in his stomach. 'I need to piss,' he said nervously.

'Piss in your pants,' said Artem grimly, as he ushered him towards the street.

Chapter Seventeen

THE CLOCK ON the wall showed that it was edging towards 5.31 p.m. Well past the time for her to be out of here. Sighing, Rose Scripps switched off her computer and dropped her purse into her bag. She would be late home again. Her commute normally took at least fifty minutes, assuming that the public transport system was working 'normally' – a leap of faith that was rarely justified when it came to London's antiquated tube network – and Sasha, her au pair, was due to clock off at six. Sasha wouldn't mind waiting, but Rose didn't like to go into overtime; she couldn't afford to pay for the extra help and felt guilty about leaving the girl to pick up the slack, even if it only meant twenty minutes here and there.

Scooping up her mobile, she felt it start vibrating in her hand. It was probably Sasha checking where she was. With a feeling of guilt bubbling up in her stomach, she hit the 'receive' button.

'Rose?' The anxious voice on the line wasn't Sasha at all.

Shit. Rose paused, wondering whether just to hang up. She could blame it on her service provider. Calls dropped off the

London network all the time. Her legs were telling her to get going. She glanced again at the clock: 5.32. *Shit, shit, shit.* 'Yes?'

'It's Claire.'

Rose recognised the voice. Simon Merrett's wife. 'Oh. Hi, Claire,' she said, belatedly trying to hide the complete lack of patience in her voice. She had met Mrs Merrett once, when Simon had organised a not particularly successful play-date for their respective kids in Hyde Park. The woman had seemed patronising and slightly aggressive, as if hanging out with single mothers was somehow beneath her. Or maybe she felt just threatened.

'Have you seen Simon today?' The question was laced with a mix of hostility and concern.

'No,' Rose said tartly, 'he's on a day off.'

'That's what I thought.'

You thought? She knew that Mrs Merrett – Ms Somebody-or-Other, using her maiden name – worked for some big law firm in the City. By all accounts, she wore the trousers in the Merrett household and Rose assumed that she kept Simon on a fairly short leash. Her colleague didn't seem to be the kind of guy who got a day off without his wife knowing exactly what he was going to do with it. But who could tell? Other people's marriages were rarely an open book.

'It's just that he was supposed to pick the kids up from gym class this afternoon,' the woman whined, 'and he hasn't showed up there.'

'Well . . .' It was now 5.36. Rose hopped from foot to foot, like a kid needing a wee. She simply had to get going. She had her own problems to sort, and the whereabouts of someone else's husband wasn't one of them.

'I've got to go and get them myself.'

'I don't know where he is.' Rose looked at her phone. Why couldn't she just hit the button to end the call? 'Have you tried his mobile?'

'Of course I've tried his mobile!' Claire Merrett snapped. 'It's just going to voicemail.'

'Yes. Of course. Sorry.' Why was she apologising to this bloody woman? Now 5.37. What was she supposed to do about it, anyway? Simon Merrett had always struck her as fairly reliable – at least, reliable enough to pick up his kids when he was supposed to. But with men you never really knew. 'I'll see if I can get hold of him,' Rose continued, switching her phone from one hand to the other as she struggled to get into her coat and hoist her bag on to her shoulder. 'I'll let you know if I manage to contact him.'

It was already 5.38. Checking she had her Oyster card in her pocket, Rose skipped towards the door. There was now only silence on the line. 'Hello?' But Claire Merrett had hung up or been cut off or whatever. 'Stupid woman!' Rose hissed as she reached the top of the stairs, in too much of a rush to wait for the lift. 'Find your bloody husband yourself.' Concentrating on not tripping up and flying arse over tit, she reached ground level and began the lengthy slog towards home.

IN THE END, it took more than an hour to get back home. Rose arrived at her flat frazzled and penitent, only to discover a scene of domestic serenity: Louise sprawled on the sofa, already fed and bathed, cuddled up to Sasha who was doing her homework.

'I didn't even notice the time,' Sasha smiled as Louise jumped up to give her mother a big kiss.

Rose had to resist the urge to burst into tears.

An hour later, with Louise tucked up in bed and Sasha sent home with an extra tenner in her pocket, Rose stood in the kitchen, sipping from a large glass of Oyster Bay Sauvignon Blanc, staring at her mobile, which lay lifeless on the table. She had texted Simon Merrett on her way into the tube station and left him a voicemail after she exited at the other end. Picking up the handset, she checked the missed-calls log, just in case. Seeing that no one had tried to call her since she had left work, she reluctantly hit Claire Merrett's number.

The phone barely had time to ring. 'Have you heard from him?' were the first words out of Claire Merrett's mouth.

'No. And you?'

'No, nothing. We were supposed to be going out tonight.' She sounded less in control than earlier, as if she'd been drinking. 'I can't understand it.'

Rose tried not to let her own concern show. 'Maybe something came up at work that I don't know about,' she said as soothingly as possible. 'A new case or something. Let me make a few more calls and see what I can find out.'

'Thank you.'

'Don't worry.' Rose grimaced at her reflection in the darkened window as soon as the words had left her mouth. It was a stupid thing to say, a kind of hopeless reflex. 'I'll phone you if I hear anything.' Ending the call, she sat down at the kitchen table, wondering exactly who to try first. She pulled up a number for Eric Babel, Head of CEOP Specialist Operations Support. Babel was their ultimate boss, but Rose had only met him twice, and even then only for a combined total of something like thirty-five seconds. She therefore didn't know him at all. Ringing him up with a false alarm would be a major embarrassment.

On the other hand . . .

Feeling relieved when Babel's number promptly went to voice-mail, Rose didn't leave a message. Putting down the handset, she tried to focus on her last conversation with Simon Merrett the day before. It had been fairly inconclusive. Still embarrassed by the débâcle at the London Eye, Merrett wanted to press ahead with the prosecution of the wretched Sandra Scott. That would give them at least something to show for their efforts. As for Shen, they still couldn't make up their minds what to do there. Yawning, Rose's thoughts turned to a bath, followed by bed. First, however, she pulled a notebook out of her bag and rifled through the pages until she found what she was looking for. Then, punching a new number into her handset, she made the call.

'YOU ARE THE guy from the London Eye.'

Simon Merrett shifted uneasily on the bare concrete floor. Squatting in front of him, Ihor held an expensive-looking Canon camera, slowly going through a series of digital images of Merrett receiving medical attention from the paramedic outside City Hall. He gestured to the cast on Merrett's broken wrist. 'Does it still hurt?'

Handcuffed to a metal ring set into the floor, Merrett said nothing. After they had bundled him out of the Palermo, he had been forced into the back of a silver Mercedes with tinted windows, and driven straight here. They had emptied his pockets, taken his mobile, his keys, his wallet and sat him down on the top floor of an unfinished office block somewhere in North London. Through the floor-to-ceiling window, he could see the transmission mast at Alexandra Palace blinking in the darkness. He was cold and hungry and his arse was numb. He wondered how he had managed to get himself into this mess. His guts spasmed as he realised that he had passed up his only chance of trying to make a break for freedom, when they had been in a public space. Now he was completely at their mercy.

'Of course,' Ihor Chepoyak smiled, 'now that we know who you are, we don't need the photos.' He began deleting the images, stopping at one showing Rose Scripps patting him on the arm. 'Who is the woman?'

Merrett bit down on his fear. 'Fuck off.'

The smaller man stepped forward, fists raised.

Ihor raised a hand. 'No, Artem. No need.' He deleted the image and stood up. 'We can find out easily enough. Why is Child Protection interested in all of this?'

Despite everything, Merrett laughed. 'Why do you think? You do what you do. We do what we do – which is to try and stop it.'

Ihor nodded at the reasonableness of it all. 'How did you find out about it?'

Merrett shrugged. Telling them the truth couldn't make much difference to anything. 'One of the Eye workers was selling the security tapes on the internet. She gave you up straight away.'

Ihor turned to Artem and said something Merrett didn't understand. Then he slipped back into English. 'Stupid woman. And Shen. Is he involved in this?'

Merrett gazed out of the window. 'Who?'

Ihor stepped forward and tapped his cast gently with the toe of his shoe. 'Don't lie,' he said gently. 'You weren't following me. You were following him.'

Merrett said nothing.

'Interesting. You are investigating a police officer.' Ihor stroked his chin in mock deliberation. 'You must think he is part of this. Corrupt.'

'Is he?' Merrett couldn't help himself.

'Come on, Detective.' Ihor smiled. 'I am not here to answer *your* questions, am I?' He tossed the camera to Artem and both men headed for the door. Switching off the lights, he turned to Merrett. 'We will be back later. Now is the time for you to make your peace with the world.'

Sitting in the darkness, Merrett had a half-hearted tug at the handcuffs and felt a sharp pain shoot through his broken wrist. He touched the cast where his daughter had drawn a little heart and scribbled *Silly Dad! Get well soon.* Silly, Merrett thought grimly, wasn't the half of it. Staring out at the orange glow of the North London night – so familiar, but so far away – he thought of Claire and the kids and wept like an infant.

'AND THIS IS the 1844 Room, decorated for the state visit of Tsar Nicholas I of Russia in, well, 1844.'

The Earl of Falkirk pointed to an oil painting of a sad, weak-looking man in military dress uniform. He had a bushy moustache and a very bad comb-over. The legend beneath the portrait read: *Emperor and Autocrat of All the Russias, King of Poland; Grand Duke of Finland.*

'He liked to keep the serfs in their place, apparently. Top man.'

Olga yawned. She wanted a drink, not a tour of these endless, dreary rooms. So it was a palace, big deal. There were plenty of palaces where she came from. Autocrat of All the Russias? Pah! Just another deluded man with a small cock and a big title. What did he achieve? Nothing. He was barely even a blip on the course of history.

Who would have thought this Englishman could be both a pervert *and* a history bore? Was it possible to come up with a worse combination in a man? Surely not.

The room was hot and stuffy. Olga felt sleepy and her feet ached. Unable to take any more, she dropped her bag on the carpet and flopped down on a nearby sofa. Closing her eyes, she leaned back and thought of a large, sparkling glass of Laurent Perrier Cuvée Brut Rosé.

Big mistake.

Within a second, he was upon her, pinning her to the red velvet, slobbering in her face. She could feel his erection against her leg as he tried to pull up her dress.

'Let go of me!'

She tried to kick him in the crotch but could get no leverage. One hand pinned her neck to the sofa while the other hiked her dress up around her waist.

'My, my,' Falkirk whispered, panting with the effort and the excitement. 'No panties.'

She watched in amused horror as he undid his trousers, pushing them down towards his knees.

'Hold on,' Olga gasped, trying to look impressed. 'Wait a second. I have protection.'

'I don't bother with that.'

'But I do,' she said sweetly, running her tongue across her top lip, hoping that she wasn't about to get a faceful. 'And you should see how I put it on.'

Quivering, Falkirk grunted his assent. Twisting away, she grabbed the handle of her bag, pulled it closer to her, before rummaging through the contents at the bottom of it.

Manoeuvring on the sofa to prise her legs apart, Falkirk made a noise like a puppy being strangled. 'Hurry up!'

'Got it!' Placing her hand around the grip, she pulled out the tiny Kevin ZP98 and pointed it at the spot where Falkirk's eyebrows met in the middle of his forehead.

'Whoa!' If anything, the gun seemed to make him more excited.

'This is Kevin,' she said quickly. 'It is a sub-compact semiautomatic pistol manufactured in the Czech Republic. My father gave it to me. It takes a 9mm Makarov cartridge.'

'A whore with a gun!' Falkirk laughed giddily. 'I'm in heaven. Heaven!'

Olga tried to ignore the stickiness around her belly button. 'The thing about Kevin,' she said calmly, 'is that it doesn't have a safety-catch. If you don't get off me this second, I pull the trigger and you die.'

Pointing the ZP98 just past his left ear, she fired. There was a loud bang and the Autocrat of All the Russias took one right in the kisser.

Olga turned the gun back on Falkirk. 'Off! Now!'

'Yes, ma'am!' With the grin still on his face, and his cock in his hand, Falkirk slowly slid off her and stood up.

Quickly getting to her feet, Olga pulled down her dress, keeping the gun trained on her host. She stepped away in disgust as he finished himself off and wiped his mess into the carpet.

A sour smell began to fill the room. Falkirk, the madness now gone from his eyes, buttoned himself up. 'Come on,' he said, heading for the door as if nothing had happened. 'Let's go and get that drink.'

ROSE ENDED HER latest call and checked her voicemail, just in case Merrett had phoned while she was on the line:

You have no new messages and eight old messages . . .

Rose hit the end button and dropped her phone on the table. She felt a gnawing in her stomach, but she had done what she could for tonight. *When he turns up, I'm going to bloody kill him,* she thought, as she stood up and turned out the light.

Chapter Eighteen

THEY WERE SITTING in the back booth of Il Buffone, a tiny 1950s-style Italian café on the north side of Macklin Street, just across the road from the flat. Alice had been coming here since she was born; Carlyle quite a bit longer. Today, it was just gone 4 p.m. and they were the only customers left in there. The owner, Marcello, had just flipped the *Closed* sign. Humming 'Cuore Matto' – 'Mad Heart' – an Italian pop song from the 1960s, he went about his end-of-day routine, in no hurry to usher them out.

Alice played with the straw in her orange juice and looked up from the table. 'You know, Dad, I'm not stupid.' She gave him a withering look.

Just like her mother, Carlyle thought. A familiar and not altogether unpleasant feeling of helplessness washed over him.

'Just because some of the girls in the class are behaving like idiots,' Alice continued, 'it doesn't mean that I'll behave like that too.'

Carlyle felt a stab of pain in his chest and forced himself to smile. 'I know, sweetheart.' This was his chance to raise the drugs issue, following Helen's tip-off about the latest problems at City School for Girls. His daughter seemed happy enough to talk about it, but Carlyle was painfully aware that he didn't really have much to say. After all, there was nothing that he could actually do to lessen the risks. He gripped his demitasse tightly. 'It's just that...' He glanced at the crumbling poster of the 1984 Juventus scudetto-winning squad on the wall above Alice's head. But even Trapattoni and Platini couldn't offer any practical assistance on this one. 'Well, your mother tells me a couple of girls were expelled.'

'Yeah, but that was a while ago now.' Alice finished her juice and pulled on her overcoat, signalling that she was ready to go home.

'One of them was in your class?' Carlyle observed, as casually as he could, conscious that he was slipping into policeman mode.

'Yeah, Susan Watts. But I never really hung out with her. I don't think she did anything, really.'

'What does that mean?'

Alice frowned. 'I don't think she actually *took* anything. Susan didn't do drugs herself. She always seemed manic enough without them.'

Carlyle raised an eyebrow. 'So what did she do then?'

'She just held some stuff for her boyfriend,' Alice replied, equally casually. 'That's what they found on her: five or six roll-ups with skunk in them.'

'Her boyfriend?'

'He goes to Central Foundation. Well,' Alice grinned, 'you know, he used to. He was expelled as well. He was a bit ugly. But he was sixteen.'

Sixteen? Carlyle thought. Jesus Christ. 'Oh,' he mumbled, trying to keep any trace of panic from his voice. What was more worrisome: drugs or boyfriends? Discuss. He took a deep breath. 'Do you—'

He was interrupted by Marcello, who appeared at the table with a couple of unsold pastries in a bag for Carlyle. He handed it to the inspector and smiled at Alice. 'How's school these days?'

'Fine, Marcello, thank you,' she said primly. 'Although I still have to submit to the occasional interrogation from my father.'

Marcello chuckled. 'You should listen to your father, young lady. He knows what he's talking about.'

If only, Carlyle thought. If only. His mobile started ringing in his pocket. He pulled it out and hit the receive button. 'Hello?'

'John? This is Warren Shen. You were trying to get hold of me?'

HE FOUND SHEN sitting in a dingy café off the Holloway Road, hunched over a mug of coffee. Facing him was a youngish woman, who looked pretty but tired and worried. Without saying anything, Carlyle pulled out a chair and sat down with them.

Shen nodded to the woman. 'Rose, this is Inspector John Carlyle. He's from the Charing Cross station. John, this is Rose Scripps. She's from—'

Carlyle cut across him brusquely. 'Have you heard anything from Ihor yet?'

Shen sat back in his chair and eyed Carlyle carefully. 'No. Not yet.'

'You know we found the girl.'

'I know,' Shen sighed. 'It's horrible.'

Carlyle glanced at the woman, who was watching them closely but said nothing. He turned back to Shen. 'So what are we going to do about it?'

The uncomfortable look drifting across Shen's face said *It's not really my problem*. He took a sip of his coffee and Carlyle noted the legend on the mug, celebrating Arsenal's *Invincibles* from 2003–4, the season when they didn't lose a single game. That did nothing to improve his mood. The inspector, a Fulham fan, hated Arsenal. The favoured club of the effete metrosexual media elite who understood nothing about football or its heritage, they were almost as bad as Chelsea.

'I will go and see Ihor again,' Shen said finally. 'And my boys have got the word out that we really want this one. We will keep at it.' His mobile started vibrating its way across the table and he grabbed it quickly. 'Hello? Yes . . .' Lifting up a finger to signify he would be back, Shen stood up and walked to the door.

Saved by the bell, Carlyle thought as he watched the superintendent standing out on the pavement, with his back to them, as he spoke on the phone. Suddenly he felt hungry. He looked at the woman, who was now checking messages on her BlackBerry. 'Would you like anything to eat?'

Without looking up, she shook her head.

CARLYLE WAS SIPPING a double espresso and waiting for his fried-egg sandwich when Shen finally reappeared. 'Sorry,' he said, holding out a hand. 'I've got to go.'

Carlyle shook it limply.

'I'll let you know when I get to speak to Ihor,' Shen continued. He looked over at the woman. 'Rose, keep me posted on your . . . problem.'

'I will,' she nodded.

'I hope your guy turns up.'

'Me too.'

'Okay,' said Shen, shuffling towards the door. 'See you later.'

As soon as Carlyle's sandwich appeared, he added some ketchup and took a large bite. The woman finally finished with her BlackBerry and dropped it into her bag. Fishing out a business card, she pushed it across the table towards Carlyle.

Taking a second bite out of the sandwich, Carlyle eyed the card: *Rose Scripps, Child Exploitation and Online Protection Centre.* 'What do you do there?' he asked.

'I'm a child protection social worker, on secondment to CEOP Victim ID Team from the NSPCC.'

'Mm.' Another bloody social worker, Carlyle reflected. That's just great. He was aware of CEOP, although he had never previously worked with anyone from there. An uncomfortable thought flitted through his brain: maybe he should have thought about contacting them earlier in his investigation. He looked Rose Scripps up and down. Could this child protection social worker be any use to him? 'And how do you know Shen?'

She studied him equally carefully. 'I don't, really. I was just hoping that he might be able to help me with a case I'm working on.'

'Good luck with that.'

Rose sat up in her chair and put her hands on the table. 'Why do you say that?'

Carlyle popped the last of the sandwich into his mouth and wiped his hands on a napkin; then he drained the last of his espresso. 'Well . . .'

THEY SPENT THE next twenty minutes drinking coffee and comparing notes. Carlyle was embarrassed to admit that Alzbetha had gone missing while she was supposed to have been in the care of Westminster Council but Rose showed no surprise. 'Last year, more than three hundred children arriving in the UK went missing from the care of local authorities,' she said.

'How many of them were being trafficked?' Carlyle wondered.

'Many are, for sure. I worked on Operation Pentameter a while back, and there's a market for children, just as there's a market for adults.'

'Pentameter?' Carlyle shook his head. 'Don't really know much about it.'

'We were targeting sex trafficking and forced labour. There were hundreds of raids, and hundreds of arrests. More than two hundred victims were recovered, including a dozen or so girls aged under eighteen.'

'You found twelve out of two hundred?' Carlyle made a face. 'That doesn't sound so good.'

'None of our statistics ever do.' She stared out the window, and for a moment he thought she might start to cry. When she turned back to him, however, there was a steely glint in her eye. 'Those children come from all over the place. Many of them are from West Africa, China and Vietnam, but also from places like the Ukraine in the old Soviet Bloc. Some come off their own bat, asking for asylum. Most are sent by traffickers. If they are picked up at the airport by the authorities, the traffickers know the likely places the children will be taken. Or they tell the children to run away once they get there. Local authorities just don't take the issue seriously enough.'

Carlyle grunted his agreement on that point.

'So, of course, when a child goes missing,' Rose continued, 'we have no records at all. No photographs, no real names and no documents. Vietnamese boys end up working in illegal cannabis factories. West African girls are forced into brothels or domestic service. The Chinese children work in restaurants or selling DVDs door to door.'

'Jesus.'

'Even the children staying in local authority homes can be abused. I was told of one case of four girls in care who were taken to work as prostitutes each day by their trafficker.'

'I suppose that makes good business sense,' Carlyle groaned, 'insofar as it cuts down on their costs.'

Rose frowned. 'Are you always this cynical, Inspector?'

'I try to be.' Carlyle smiled thinly. 'I like to think of it as a God-given talent.'

They sat in silence for a while longer. Finally, Rose stood up and announced that she had to go and collect her daughter.

'We should continue this later,' she said.

Carlyle nodded. 'Yes.' It seemed clear that there could be a connection between their respective cases. Signalling to the waitress for the bill, he watched Rose Scripps head off briskly down the road. Interesting woman, he thought. Maybe, just maybe, she can help me crack this.

Chapter Nineteen

IT WAS RIDICULOUS. There was nowhere you could smoke indoors these days. Out of uniform but on the clock, Tommy Dolan stepped on to the pavement on Cork Street, in the heart of Piccadilly, and lit a cigarette. Keeping one eye on the people inside the Block Gallery, noisily enjoying the Private View canapés and the Director's Cut Russian River Chardonnay (which he had to admit was very nice), he took a deep drag. *Ahh!* That was better. He exhaled in the direction of a poster displayed in the gallery window, advertising an exhibition by a young British sculptress named Henrietta Templeton.

'Hello, Tommy!'

Dolan wheeled round to see John Carlyle standing at the kerbside, next to a grinning fat bloke who, Dolan guessed, must be his sidekick.

'Fuck,' Dolan groaned, taking another puff. 'What do you want?'

'We're here to see your boss,' Carlyle said, the cheeriness in his voice belied by the hostility evident in his eyes.

'Huh?' Dolan took a final drag and flicked the cigarette in the direction of the gutter.

'Gordon Elstree-Ullick,' Carlyle said, looking past Dolan towards the throng inside. 'Also known as the Earl of Falkirk. Twenty-second in line to the British throne, I believe. The guy you're supposed to be protecting from whatever threat to his person may be lurking among those sculptures tonight.'

Dolan stepped in front of the door. He wasn't a particularly tall man, but he was still just about able to look down on Carlyle. 'He's hardly my boss. And I don't think he'd want to be disturbed at the moment – not when he's busy networking. Why don't you fuck off like a good little boy and I'll let him know you were wanting a word.'

Carlyle stepped closer. 'Now, now, Tommy. You don't want me to have to get Joe here to arrest you. Think of the embarrassment in front of your rich friends.'

A well-preserved woman in a fur coat of some description arrived at the door. Giving them a dirty look, she went inside.

'Arrest me?' Dolan snorted, once the door had closed behind her. 'For what? You're out of your fucking mind.'

'For assaulting Alexa Matthews, for a start.'

'I don't think so,' Dolan replied. 'I wouldn't touch that fat cow with a bargepole.'

'I've seen the mess she's in.'

Dolan grinned nastily. 'I think you'll find *she's* the one under investigation.'

Carlyle coughed. 'Then there's Dalton.'

'Joe?' Dolan's eyes narrowed. 'He committed suicide. What's that got to do with me?'

Carlyle leaned closer. 'We're on to you, Tommy. United 14 . . . the whole works. You've been pushing your luck for far too long.'

'Got a warrant?'

Carlyle said nothing.

'Thought not.' Dolan tut-tutted. 'It's just the same old snivelling bullshit from you, my friend. Now fuck off.' He put a hand on Carlyle's chest and shoved him away from the door. As Carlyle stumbled backwards, Joe Szyszkowski grabbed Dolan by the collar with his right hand and sank a meaty left hook into his stomach.

'Ooof!' A look of surprise spread across Dolan's face, as his legs buckled.

No one inside paid them any notice.

Half-marching, half-dragging Dolan away from the gallery entrance, the sergeant turned to Carlyle. 'I'll deal with this guy. You go on inside.'

THE TEMPERATURE INSIDE the gallery was at least ten degrees warmer than out on the street. Carlyle took off his overcoat and waited patiently for the girl on the reception desk to lift her head out of her book. Its title – *Bad Art for Bad People* – made him smile. Almost.

'Name?' With immense effort, the girl looked at him through her red-framed glasses and down her not inconsiderable nose. She was all blonde hair, Mummy's pearls and studied boredom. There were thousands just like her among London's well-heeled pretend professionals. He didn't let it get to him.

'Carlyle,' he said politely.

Putting down the book, she slowly scanned a sheet of names in front of her. A small smirk crept on to her lips. 'I'm sorry, but your name is not on the list.'

Carlyle dropped a card on the desk. 'That's because I'm a policeman and I'm here on business. It's nothing to do with the gallery.

I just need to speak to one of your guests. All very discreet.' He gestured towards the card. 'That's for your boss's information – a courtesy; so that you can let him know that I'm here.'

'A policeman?' Ignoring the card, the girl cocked her head to one side, as if she was trying to process this information.

'Yes. Take this.' Carlyle handed her his coat. 'I won't be long.' Stepping past the desk, he took a glass of wine from the tray held by a hovering waiter and scanned the main room. The gallery was a reasonable size, maybe 700 square feet, with a smaller room at the back. But, with easily 100-plus people in attendance, the place was very full. Everyone seemed to be chatting away, paying no attention to the art whatsoever, and the inspector's arrival passed unnoticed. Taking a mouthful of wine, Carlyle began moving slowly through the room, looking out for his man.

A couple of minutes later, he had located Falkirk talking animatedly to two blondes in a corner at the rear of the main gallery. They were standing behind a limestone sculpture called *Mindscape* that came with a price tag equivalent to almost three-quarters of Carlyle's annual inspector's salary. Finishing his wine, he carefully placed the empty glass on the tray of a passing waitress. Pulling his warrant card from his pocket, he stepped toward the trio.

'Hello? . . . Hell*oo* . . .' a voice boomed.

To his right, Carlyle saw a large, middle-aged man in a tweed jacket standing on a small platform raised six inches above the floor. He was holding a microphone which he tapped to see if it was working. The resulting feedback suggested that it was. The beam from an overhead spotlight reflected off his bald head as he stroked his prodigious handlebar moustache nervously. 'Good evening, ladies and gentlemen.'

Falkirk and his companions turned to face the speaker. As he did so, Carlyle caught his eye. Falkirk's face looked puffy; his expression glazed. He was clearly wasted. There was a flicker of recognition before the Earl looked away.

'As many of you will know, I am Laurence Block, owner of this gallery and host of this evening's event.'

Jettisoning the two women, Falkirk moved slowly but deliberately through the crowd, getting closer to the stage but also closer to the door.

'I would just like to say how delighted we are to be hosting this exhibition . . .'

Although he was only three or four yards behind Falkirk, Carlyle found it hard to keep up. People were listening to the speech and reluctant to let him through. One woman even kicked him on the shin as he tried to push past her.

'These works on display in the gallery tell tales of history and place, of isolation and hidden depths . . .'

By the time Carlyle reached the corner of the stage, Falkirk had disappeared from view. Had he managed to leave? The crowd was thinner here and the inspector could move more easily towards the door. Stepping outside, he looked up and down the street. There was no sign of Falkirk.

Fuck! Carlyle shivered in the cold, then remembered that he had left his overcoat behind. From inside came a smattering of applause as Block's speech came to an end, quickly replaced by the buzz of conversations being resumed. Pushing the door back open, he had one foot inside when he heard a voice from behind him.

'Boss!'

Turning, he saw Joe Szyszkowski frogmarching Falkirk across the road towards him.

'This is our guy?' Joe asked.

'Yes, indeed,' beamed Carlyle.

'Good,' the sergeant grinned. 'Otherwise we might have been facing a few civil liberties issues.'

Swaying on the tarmac, Falkirk tried his best to glare at the pair of them, saying nothing.

'What shall I do with him?' Joe asked.

'Where's Dolan?'

Joe gestured to the unmarked Volvo parked twenty yards up the road. 'In the car.'

'Okay. Stick this guy in there too and we'll go back to the station. I'll just collect my coat.'

SIMON MERRETT JERKED awake as he felt the toe of a boot in the small of his back. It took him a second to realise that he was still chained to the concrete floor of an empty office. His head was thick and there was a sour, metallic taste in his mouth. Before him stood the gangster's sidekick wearing an outsized Jack Bauer T-shirt, a blank expression on his face. In his right hand, hanging limply by his side, was a small black pistol. Merrett's eyes widened. Artem grinned, obviously revelling in the patent fear of the prisoner. Slowly, he made a show of clicking off the safety. Wincing, Merrett clenched both his teeth and his buttocks.

'Enough!' Ihor Chepoyak stepped out of the shadows and placed a hand on Artem's shoulder. Reluctantly, the smaller man put the safety-catch back on. Stuffing the gun into the back of his stonewashed jeans, he retreated to the far side of the room.

Gazing out of the window into the North London darkness, Ihor felt a terrible longing for home. It often came when he was in the presence of death. His greatest fear was that he would die in this shit-hole and never make it back to the Ukraine. His final resting place in Lychakiv Cemetery, in Lviv, had long since been chosen and paid for. A substantial crypt, close to the tomb of the poet Ivan Franko, had been secured with the help of a large bribe to a local official, who had overseen the removal and cremation of the remains of the Jewish merchant and his family who had resided there for the previous 120 years. Of course, someone could easily come along and do the same to Ihor himself in due course. But his mother had already been interred there, and Ihor took comfort in knowing that he would join her when his time came.

Finally, he looked down at Merrett. 'Don't worry,' he said quietly. 'Artem here is not going to kill you.'

Merrett's mouth went dry. Shivering against the cold, he tried and failed to think of something to say.

'But we have to do something,' Ihor continued.

'Let me go!' Merrett croaked.

Ihor smiled. 'I've been thinking about that. The problem is that you are a problem.' His expression hardened. 'And I have to deal with problems.'

Merrett's brain finally started working. 'People will be looking for me.'

'No one will find you here,' Ihor snorted.

'I am a policeman. There will be a massive search.'

Ihor made a face. 'Oh? So now you admit to being a policeman?' His laugh was harsh. 'Well, Mr Policeman, let them look.'

Merrett wiped his nose on the arm of his jacket. 'If you . . . harm me, what will Shen say?'

'Shen?' Ihor stepped closer to his captive. 'Shen doesn't even know that you exist. But I am sure that he will be delighted to know that you and your colleague Miss Scripps think that he is a corrupt officer.' Lifting his gaze to the ceiling, Ihor stroked his chin theatrically with his free hand. 'Yes, I wonder what he will think about that?'

Jesus, Merrett thought, how did he find out about Rose? There was nothing he could do about that right now. 'Shen?' he asked. 'Is he bent?'

'That is not your problem.' Moving behind Merrett, Ihor slipped a Fort-12 CURZ pistol out of his pocket. Bringing the barrel to the man's head he squeezed the trigger once . . . twice. By the time Merrett had pitched forward, his blood immediately pooling on the concrete alongside his corpse, the staccato whine of the gunshots had already dissipated through the empty building, to be replaced by the background hum of the traffic noise outside. Putting the gun back in his pocket, Ihor stepped round the body and headed for the door. He nodded to Artem, who was propped against the wall, looking bored. 'Let's go.'

LEANING UP AGAINST the front desk, Carlyle watched Falkirk and his lawyer scuttle out into the London night. It had taken the Earl less than an hour and a half to get legal representation down to Charing Cross police station. And it had taken his lawyer, an overly self-confident young blonde, less than ten minutes to have their interview terminated and her client released. Falkirk had said nothing and made no visible response when Carlyle had placed a series of photographs of Alzbetha's corpse in front of him.

'That went well, then,' said Joe Szyszkowski, appearing behind the desk with a mug of steaming tea in one hand.

The desk sergeant, catching the murderous glint in Carlyle's eye, shuffled off promptly in search of some paperwork that might need his attention.

Joe noisily slurped the tea. 'Dolan's Federation rep called as well. He says that they will be making a formal complaint.'

'Fuck him,' Carlyle growled. 'Is he still here?'

'No,' Joe sniffed. 'He walked out even quicker than his boss.'

'Great.' Carlyle felt rage and frustration bubbling in his guts, all the more corrosive because he wasn't sure what he realistically could have hoped for from tonight's little escapade. Patience wasn't his strong point, and he'd reached a place in this investigation where he just had to shake things up a bit.

'At least we've rattled their cage,' Joe remarked, more or less reading his thoughts, before placing his mug on a coaster on the desk. 'They'll have to move more carefully from now on.'

'Right.' Carlyle yawned. It was time to go home. They could work out what to do next in the morning. 'Oh, Christ!' Gazing across the waiting room, he saw Carole Simpson sweep through the front door. She looked tired but there was a grim determination in her eyes. He tried to remember the last time he had seen her here, at Charing Cross; it had to be the best part of six months. One thing was sure: she wasn't dropping in at almost ten o'clock at night for a social visit.

Simpson spotted Carlyle and her expression darkened further. Standing up straight, he waited for her to make her way over.

'John,' she said, nodding brusquely to Joe Szyszkowski, 'we need to talk.'

Chapter Twenty

GAVIN HEATH SAT behind the wheel of his Peugeot Bipper Pro, carefully nibbling on his Italian tuna sandwich. Mancini's café on Brecknock Road, 250 yards south of Tufnell Park tube station, was his usual stop-off, just over halfway through his eight-hour shift. Working for Column Security was boring but straightforward. Over the last three years, Gavin had worked his way up from a temporary summer job guarding a building site to becoming a supervisor on the North London circuit, touring a range of empty offices and shops between Kings Cross and Wembley. The job paid less than £12 an hour, plus he had to wear a stupid, fake uniform, but it helped pay for his Business Studies course at UEL – the University of East London.

Finishing his food, Gavin daintily wiped his mouth with a napkin and lifted his coffee from the passenger seat. Removing the lid, he blew on it gently before taking a cautious sip, as he watched the world go by. Tufnell Park was still lively at this time of night and he eyed a couple of pretty black girls laughing and joking as they waited at a bus stop.

When he'd stared at the girls for a few seconds too long, he let his gaze slip ten yards further along the road to Carleton House, which was his next port of call. Gavin studied the ugly, squat office block, stuck between a pawnbroker's and a discount supermarket, and wondered why anyone would build a speculative office block here. It was completely the wrong part of town even before the economy had gone tits up.

Unsurprisingly, there had been no takers for this 'premium' space, and the developer had gone bust. To date, Carleton House had never been occupied, and Gavin thought there was a fair-to-middling chance that it never would be. Inside, it had never even been fitted out. Even though it was less than three years old, the place already looked well on the way to becoming derelict.

The radio on the dashboard crackled. '*Gavin? How are things going?*'

The caller was Jessica in Despatch. She was a nice girl and, not for the first time, Gavin wondered if maybe she fancied him a bit. She'd even asked him out for a drink once, but he'd declined. He didn't want to get involved with anyone at Column other than doing his shift. Security was just a temporary thing. When he left it behind, he would leave it all behind.

'Everything's fine. I'm just at Carleton House in Tufnell Park.'

'*You haven't called in.*' Jessica dropped her voice. He could imagine her leaning across the desk, breathing into her microphone. '*That's not following protocol.*' She giggled, somehow making the word 'protocol' sound vaguely rude. '*And Clinton has gone off on one again.*'

Clinton Roache, the office manager, was always complaining about people not following the company's standard reporting procedures. Out on the road, you were supposed to check in with the office every hour.

Gavin checked the clock on the dashboard and sighed to himself. In truth, he had only checked in once in the course of his shift so far. 'Okay, sorry. It's all quiet but I'll definitely report back in during the next hour.'

'Thanks . . . I get off at eleven.'

Gavin smiled, realising that she'd checked his rota.

'I thought about getting a bite to eat . . .'

'I need to study tonight,' said Gavin firmly. 'I have a class in the morning.' It happened to be true, not that it mattered. He had to deliver 1,500 words on *The Causes of the Banking Crisis* to his course assessor by 10 a.m. – a piece of cake.

'Oh, fair enough.'

'Sorry.'

'No problem. Anyway, see you later.'

'Yeah, see you later.' The girl was a trier. *It's nice to be asked*, he told himself. *You should be kind to her.* Putting the lid back on his coffee, he placed it in the cup-holder on the dashboard and slipped out of his van.

Shivering against the cold, Gavin buttoned up his jacket, yawning as he did so. Waiting for a gap in the traffic, he glanced up at Carleton House. Frowning, he realised that the third-floor lights were on. The night before, the whole building had been in darkness; he was sure of that. Who had put the bloody lights on? It wouldn't be the first time someone had tried to see if there was anything inside – copper, wood, even carpet tiles – that they could nick. Vandals were another possibility. Less likely, an estate agent had taken someone round on a viewing and just forgot to switch the lights off.

'Shit!' If someone had indeed broken in, it would ruin Gavin's whole night; they would have to call the police and then he could be stuck here for hours. It would be a fight to claim the overtime, especially if Clinton made an issue of him not reporting in. Worse still, he could forget about getting his essay written in time for the morning.

Opening the van door, he planted one knee on the driver's seat and hit the call button on the radio. 'Jess, it's me.'

'*Hiya.*'

'There hasn't been anyone in to view Carleton House today, has there?'

'*I don't think so. Why?*'

'The lights are on.'

'*Hold on. Let me check.*'

Slipping back into his seat, he pulled the door closed as he waited.

A minute or so later, the radio crackled back into life. '*Gavin? I've checked the log. As far as I can tell, no one's been in there today.*'

Gavin scowled at his reflection in the windscreen. 'Okay. I'll go and check it out.'

'*Do you want me to call the police?*'

'No,' he said hastily. 'It's probably nothing at all. I'll call you from my mobile once I've taken a look.'

GAVIN STEPPED OUT of the lift on the third floor and punched the security code into the pad by the door. When he didn't hear the usual click of the lock releasing, he gently pulled on the handle. As the door opened, he tightened his grip on the aluminium casing of his Led Lenser P17 torch. Conscious of his elevated heartbeat, he stepped inside.

'Hello?' he shouted, trying to ignore the lack of confidence in his voice. 'This is Security.' No response. He scanned the room. The place looked pretty much as he remembered it from his last visit – bare floors, unfinished walls, a few cables hanging from holes in the ceiling where the polystyrene tiles were missing. More or less what you would expect from thirty square metres of unwanted office space in a shitty part of North London.

There was clearly nothing to report. He was glad they hadn't called in the police, and even more glad that the rest of his night hadn't been ruined. It was time to leave. The light switches were situated on the wall to his right. He stepped over to turn them off. Then, out of the corner of his eye, he saw a small dark shape scuttle across the floor ten yards away, where the space dog-legged to the right. Gavin grimaced: the rats were easily the worst part of his job. A second scuttled across the floor in front of him, and it was then that he noticed the smell. Some dosser had obviously used the place as his toilet.

'Hello? Is there anyone there?'

Caught in two minds, Gavin hovered by the lights. He urged himself to just switch them off and go, then he could finish his shift and get his paper written. On the other hand, what if the guy was still here, lying in his own shit after having downed a couple of litres of Double Diamond? The rats could have his toes off before he woke up. Maybe even his nose. He couldn't have that on his conscience.

Cursing under his breath, Gavin walked deeper into the empty office space, keeping his eyes glued on the floor for more rats. Turning the corner, he looked up, checking the familiar orange North London vista through the windows. He nearly jumped out of his skin as a third rat rushed past him and joined the other two as they excitedly scrabbled around the body. One by one the creatures skated through the blood pooled by the hook that had been set into the floor, their feet and bellies smearing the concrete.

Gavin stood mute as his brain tried to process what he was seeing – the hook, the handcuffs, the blood. He swallowed hard, twice, to stop his dinner from creeping back up his throat. Clamping his jaw shut, he concentrated on breathing through his mouth. Once he had that under control, he stepped close enough to the corpse to scare off the rats. 'Get out of here, you bastards!' he screamed, wafting a boot in the general direction of their fleeing backsides.

Pulling out his mobile, he called into Despatch. Jessica answered on the second ring.

'Jess,' he said, almost calm now, 'you need to get the police here ASAP.'

THE THREE OF them were sitting in the interview room that had been vacated by the Earl of Falkirk barely fifteen minutes earlier. Sipping his latest cup of tea daintily, Joe Szyszkowski eyed Carlyle with interest. Knowing what was coming, Carlyle thought that he should get his retaliation in first. 'What we've got,' he said, 'is—'

Simpson held up a hand. 'What we've got,' she said sharply, 'is another classic John Carlyle bull-in-a-china-shop episode. Do you know how many calls about you I've received this evening?'

Catching Joe's eye, Carlyle had to suppress a schoolboy smirk. It was like being thirteen again, staring at the prospect of double detention and a letter of reprimand.

Simpson counted them off on her fingers. 'I've had Singer from the Federation. Charlie Adam, of course, and Mazar Corrigan . . .'

Carlyle gave her a quizzical look.

'My oppo in SO14,' Simpson explained. 'Charlie Adam's boss. And those were just the calls about Dolan.'

Joe stared deeply into his cup.

'In terms of Falkirk—'

This time Carlyle held up his hand. 'Okay, okay, we get the picture.'

Clasping her hands together, Simpson bent across the table. 'So tell me what the bloody hell is going on here.'

Carlyle leaned back in his chair and stuffed his hands in his pockets. 'Falkirk is the guy who was in Green Park when I found the girl.'

Simpson's eyes narrowed. 'Are you sure?'

'Absolutely. He recognised me tonight. Which is why he tried to do a runner.'

Joe nodded in agreement. 'That's right.'

'But,' Simpson said slowly, 'so far, you have no evidence linking him to child trafficking.'

'There is a Child Exploitation and Online Protection investigation currently ongoing,' Carlyle countered, deflecting the question, 'that we think is chasing down the same group.'

'Why is it,' Simpson sighed, raising her eyes to the ceiling, 'that you spend all your life chasing investigations that are the responsibility of other people?'

'But . . .' Carlyle protested.

Simpson forced herself to make proper eye-contact with the troublesome inspector. 'It is time,' she said slowly, 'to put this business aside.'

Holding Simpson's gaze, Carlyle told himself to stay calm. *Don't raise your voice. Just talk your way out of this.* His mind, however, was suddenly blank. When his phone started buzzing in his pocket, he took it out, playing for time. 'Hello?'

'Carlyle? It's Rose.' The voice on the line was tremulous.

'Who?'

'Rose – Rose Scripps, from CEOP.'

'Yes, yes?' Carlyle ignored Simpson's impatient glare.

'They've found Simon,' Rose cried.

'Who?' Carlyle snapped.

There was nothing but a sob on the line.

'Hello?'

'They've found Simon,' she said eventually. 'Simon Merrett.'

'Yes?' Carlyle said, but gently this time. Realising where this was going, he was annoyed by his earlier churlishness.

'He's dead.' She fought for a breath. 'He was shot in the head.'

Chapter Twenty-one

STEPPING PAST ONE of the forensics crew, he took in the rodent footprints in the congealing blood, the chains and the smell of piss. Then he looked at the victim's face. It came to him almost immediately. Without a doubt, he had seen this guy before. Even the where and when popped into his head without a moment's further thought. He closed his eyes and saw the same guy sitting in that bar, sipping his beer, playing with his mobile phone. It was just like watching a video.

Why had he been there?

Why was he here?

And why had he been executed?

Warren Shen moved out of the way and let the ambulance crew lift the corpse onto the stretcher. Adopting the air of a curious onlooker, he watched the forensics team packing up before they headed back to the West Hampstead station. One of the bullets had been recovered, lodged in the wall by the door. The other, as far as anyone could tell, was still in Merrett's brain. Shen had a pretty good idea who had put it there. Wandering over to the window, he gazed down on the ambulance waiting by the kerb.

'That's him.'

Shen turned to see the victim's colleague, Rose Scripps, identify the body with a nod. Standing with arms crossed, she watched as Merrett was quickly covered with a sheet and carried off. Shen waited for her to notice him and come over. She looked deathly tired, and had clearly been crying, but now she was all business. 'What are *you* doing here?' she asked, her voice cracking round the edges.

'I'm very sorry,' he said, placing a hand on her shoulder. 'I've never lost a colleague like this, and I can't imagine how terrible it must be.'

She took a step back from his touch, her eyes dropping to the floor. 'It will be a lot worse for his wife . . . and for the kids.'

Shen stared at his trainers. 'Yes, quite.'

'At least I was able to identify the body, so I could spare her that.'

'I heard it on the radio,' Shen said, finally addressing her original question. 'I recognised his name. I told them to call you.'

'How did they know it was Simon?' she asked.

'He still had his wallet on him. They identified him from his credit cards.'

'No evidence of robbery?'

'I don't know,' Shen said vaguely. 'His CEOP ID is missing apparently, but you'd have to speak to the investigating officer.' He gestured to a portly, middle-aged man talking quietly into a mobile on the far side of the floor. 'Kevin Ellington, over there. I know him a little. He's a decent bloke.'

Rose nodded silently.

Shen glanced out of the window as the ambulance pulled away. 'What was Simon working on?' he asked, as casually as he could manage.

Rose thought about that for a second. Turning to face her, he could see that she was torn about what to reply. 'I don't know,' she said finally.

You don't want to play then? Fair enough, Shen thought. In that case, we won't play. But you sought me out, remember? He felt a stab of resentment towards this woman who had asked for his help but who clearly didn't trust him.

'I don't actually know what he was doing when he went missing.'

I do, thought Shen, up to a point. 'Well,' he said, 'I'm sure Ellington will get to the bottom of it. Let me know if there's anything I can do.' Without waiting for a reply, he headed for the door, his mind already focused on what he had to do next.

Slowing to walking pace, Alice started looking around her. She had no idea where she was. The streets were empty of people, but there was still a steady stream of traffic on the road. Standing on the kerbside, she counted one, two, three cars go past. Waiting until a fourth was almost upon her, she walked out into the road, her eyes closed against the glare of the headlights.

Shit!

Carlyle woke with a start. Rolling on to his back he blinked once, twice. He had been drooling on to his pillow and felt the damp coldness of his saliva behind his ear. Helen, her back to him, snored quietly beside him. The pale green numbers of the alarm clock by the bed read 3.23. He knew that further sleep was unlikely and he needed to piss. Even so, he was reluctant to get up for fear of waking his wife.

He was not the kind of man to dream. In the grainy, orange darkness, he stared at the ceiling and thought about his nightmare. From some nearby street, Kingsway perhaps, or Shaftesbury Avenue, he heard the rise and fall of a siren – maybe an ambulance, maybe a police car – on its way to try and clean up someone's late-night mess. Whatever it was, he was glad that it did not involve him.

Chapter Twenty-two

THE WEATHER WAS foul, in keeping with his mood. With his right shoulderblade leaning against the cold windowpane, Carlyle felt the rain lash against the glass and listened to the wind whining as it whipped down William IV Street. He had been standing here in one of the larger meeting rooms on the second floor of Charing Cross police station for almost an hour, effectively doing nothing. Now he sullenly sipped his cold coffee and glanced up from the screen of his mobile to watch Rose Scripps and Joe Szyszkowski as they rearranged a series of photographs and documents that were laid out on the table. The combined efforts of their respective investigations were there in front of them. The display featured all the major players, known and unknown, with a picture of a grinning Falkirk, clipped from a glossy magazine, at its centre. All three of them now stared intently at the installation, as the seconds ticked past. Nothing jumped out at them.

The energy levels in the room were sinking fast. Not for the first time that morning, Carlyle wondered about Shen. He had called him twice since last night; but with no reply. Carlyle's mobile showed no missed calls, no messages. The superintendent was clearly ignoring him. He shoved the phone back in his pocket and stifled a yawn. 'So what do we have?'

Rose stepped back from the table. She looked completely exhausted, like she hadn't slept at all. Her mouth opened but she said nothing.

Joe scratched his head, focusing his gaze on a patch of wall above Carlyle's head. 'Is Simpson happy for us to be doing this?'

Carlyle shrugged. He hadn't spoken to the commander since she had left the station the night before. He didn't want to speak to her about Merrett until he knew if his death was relevant to Alzbetha. The last thing he needed was Simpson thinking that his wild-goose chase had taken yet another diversion.

The fixed-line telephone sitting on the windowsill next to Carlyle started ringing, causing them all to jump. He leaned over and picked up the receiver. 'Yes?' he demanded.

'John?'

'Yes.'

'It's George Patrick. We've got a delivery down here for you at the desk.'

'Yeah?' Carlyle asked, surprised. The front desk never took deliveries.

'Yeah,' the desk sergeant replied, 'a large box from Candy Cakes. Looks good.'

'Cakes?' Carlyle felt his stomach rumble.

'It's kosher,' Patrick confirmed. 'We've run it through the X-ray machine. There's a note as well.'

'Okay.' Carlyle glanced at Joe who, perking up at the mention of food, gave him a hungry look. 'I'll be down in a minute.'

STANDING AT THE front desk of the station, Carlyle looked at the dozen cupcakes in the box, each one topped with a different, brightly coloured icing, and smiled. He picked up an electric-blue one and took a bite. It was delicious and he finished it off in two quick mouthfuls under the wistful gaze of George Patrick and a loitering PCSO. Carlyle gestured towards the box. 'Help yourself.' After they had chosen, he picked out another three (one for Joe, one for Rose and another one for himself) and headed back towards the stairs.

'Don't forget the note,' Patrick reminded him through a mouthful of bun.

'Oh, yes.' Carlyle did a quick U-turn. Careful not to drop any of his collection of cakes, he grabbed the small envelope that had been taped to the lid of the box, and stuffed it into his pocket.

Five minutes later, he had finished a second cake and was sitting back at his desk with a fresh cup of coffee. Joe and Rose could be left to their own devices; it was time for him to catch up with some of the paperwork he'd let slide in the last few weeks. Waiting for his computer to power up, he remembered the envelope in his pocket. On the front, it simply read *Inspector Carlyle*, carefully handwritten in black ink. Ripping it open, he pulled out a small piece of card, slightly bigger than the size of a cigarette packet. At the top was printed the Candy Cakes logo, a pink cake with a heart on it, along with their company's website address and phone number. Written on the card, in the same script as the envelope, was a simple message: *Check out the AUFS.*

AUFS? Carlyle didn't like puzzles. He didn't like the sense that people were toying with him. *If you have something to say, just fucking say it*: that was his motto. Drumming his fingers on the desk, he watched the somersaulting hourglass on his screen, as the computer continued its struggle towards life. While he waited, he picked up the receiver on his desk phone and dialled the number printed on the card.

A cheery young female voice answered immediately. 'Candy Cakes, Sarah speaking. How may I help you?'

Carlyle slowly and carefully explained who he was and the nature of his enquiry.

The cheeriness in the girl's voice was immediately replaced by wariness. 'Hold on, please.'

For almost a minute, he listened to the happy hubbub from the shop. Finding himself craving a third cake, he tried to think of something other than food.

Finally, a different voice came on the line. Older. Sterner. 'Mr Carlyle?'

'Inspector.'

'Yes, of course. I am Julia Greene, the company's owner. How can I help you?'

Hadn't the girl who answered the phone – he had already forgotten her name – explained that? Carlyle gritted his teeth and repeated his query.

'A lady came in this morning,' said Greene smoothly, once he had finished, 'and asked us to deliver the box to you. I hope you liked them?'

'They were delicious.' Carlyle smiled despite himself. 'However, I forced myself to stop at two.'

'Aha! I like a man who can show some discipline.'

Was she flirting with him? 'What else can you tell me about the customer?'

'A secret admirer, eh?'

Carlyle felt embarrassed. 'Hardly.'

'Well, she was tall, elegantly dressed, wore large sunglasses. Maybe in her early to mid thirties.'

Carlyle thought back to his meeting with Olga in the Garden Hotel. 'Did she use a credit card?'

'She paid cash, and she paid a tip in advance for the delivery girl, which was nice. Quite a few people don't even bother these days. You'd be surprised.'

'Was she English?'

'No,' Greene said firmly, 'definitely not. Her English was good, but she had a strong accent. I assumed that she was Eastern European.'

Close enough, Carlyle thought. 'That's been very helpful, thank you. And thanks again for the cakes.'

'It was our pleasure,' Greene purred. 'Come and visit us some time, Inspector. We'd be delighted to see you.'

'I will, thank you.' He put down the receiver just as the welcome screen finally appeared on his computer. Typing in his log-in and password, he went straight to Google. As someone who had struggled with a typewriter in his early years at work, Carlyle knew that he would always retain a small sense of wonder when it came to computers; even more so with the internet. The amount of useful information that was out there, just waiting to be grasped, was truly miraculous. All you had to do was type in the right things in the little search box.

Carlyle typed in 'AUFS'.

50,300,000 results in 0.15 seconds.

Adelaide University Film Society.

Another Union File System.

Linux patch aufs package.

He scrolled down the first five or six pages of search results, finding nothing that seemed remotely relevant. He went back to the top of the page and hit the Advanced Search button.

Find web pages that have all these words. Slowly he typed in 'AUFS and Falkirk and orphanage'.

74 results in 0.3 seconds.

That was more like it.

The first two, in Cyrillic script, he ignored. The third one down was a website for the Anglo-Ukrainian Friendship Society – AUFS. Carlyle clicked on the link. The front page displayed the Union Jack alongside the yellow and blue Ukrainian flag. Looking along the top, he hit the Directors button. In front of him suddenly appeared the smiling face of the Rt Hon. Gordon Elstree-Ullick, Earl of Falkirk, the society's chairman. Carlyle sat back in his chair and pondered how much further this took him. Noticing a button called 'Photos', he clicked on that and scrolled down through a selection of events, including one entitled *Sandokan International Children's Camp.*

On 7 September, Gordon Elstree-Ullick, Chairman, led an aid delegation to visit the camp . . . Carlyle looked through multiple pictures of sad, pale-looking children receiving boxes of clothes and toys out of the back of an AUFS-branded lorry. At the bottom was a group photo of maybe seventy or eighty kids posed, along with the aid workers. In the middle, smiling for the camera, was Falkirk himself. Carlyle increased the size of the photo so that it filled the whole screen.

Peering at the computer, he tried to make out each child individually. However, it was a low-resolution image and therefore hard to focus on. I need to get glasses, he thought glumly. My eyesight is going. Leaning closer, he studied each face individually.

Reaching the end, he went back to carefully study each one again. There were a couple of girls who maybe looked like Alzbetha, but he couldn't be sure. He wondered if this Sandokan place would have proper records and whether he would be able to get hold of them. But that wasn't the kind of information he could hope to access without Simpson's help.

After sending a copy of the photo to a nearby printer, he looked along the line of adults on the back row. Three from the end, over on the right, he spotted someone who looked familiar.

A hungry-looking Joe Szyszkowski appeared at his side. 'Got any more of those cakes?'

Ignoring the question, Carlyle pointed at the man in the picture. 'Who does that look like to you?'

Joe peered at the screen for a couple of seconds. 'No idea.'

'That,' said Carlyle, tapping the screen, 'is Ihor Chepoyak. I'm sure of it.'

'Shen's mate?'

'The very same.' Pushing back his chair, he jumped up. 'Let's go.'

IGNORING AN OFFER of coffee, Warren Shen stood facing Ihor Chepoyak in the back room of Janik's café and wondered about the wisdom of coming up to Kentish Town on his own. There were two messages from that funny, distracted policeman from Charing Cross on his mobile, neither of which he'd responded to. Carlyle had stirred up this hornet's nest, so maybe he should have brought him along. Whatever, it was too late now. 'Where's the gun?'

Ihor stubbed out his cigarette and exhaled a long line of smoke in the direction of a poster, advertising a Christina Aguilera concert in Kiev, which had been stuck on the wall since his last visit. 'What gun?'

'The gun you used to kill that policeman,' Shen said, as casually as he could manage.

'What policeman?'

'Merrett. Simon Merrett. The guy we found chained to the floor in that empty office block in North London.'

Ihor made a face as he slurped his espresso. 'That was quick.'

Shen stiffened at this confession of sorts. 'You left a bullet in his brain.'

'Two.'

'One entered the back of his head,' Shen said mechanically, 'and exited through the front. One of them did not exit.'

Ihor shrugged. 'Does it make a difference?'

'Not really. The point is that you've overstepped the mark. This will have to be dealt with. You can't kill policemen in this country.'

Ihor emptied his demitasse. 'He wasn't a policeman; he was just some kind of social worker.'

'He was CEOP,' Shen said wearily, clearly bored by the semantics, 'part of the team. Anyway, why was he investigating you? Was it because of this girl?'

'Me?' Ihor laughed. 'He wasn't investigating *me*. He was investigating *you*. They think you are corrupt.'

Shen thought about that for a moment, then decided it was irrelevant to the matter in hand. 'Have you got the gun?'

Ihor pulled the Fort-12 CURZ pistol out of his pocket and aimed it at Shen. 'Of course I have.'

'THERE – THAT ONE! Down at the far end.'

Joe Szyszkowski steered the unmarked Ford Focus between the potholes on Arkan Street, until Carlyle pointed to a space opposite the shabby café. 'Park it there.'

'Shit!' said Rose Scripps, sitting in the back. 'I've lost my signal. My au pair's going to kill me.'

Joe glanced at Carlyle, who shrugged. Rose had insisted in coming along for the ride and he couldn't be bothered to argue with her. Getting out of the car, he crossed the road. The café looked empty of customers, just like the last time he was here. It was late in the day. He wondered if there was any *babka* left.

Reaching out to open the front door, he heard the shot. For a moment he paused, his hand on the door handle, signalling to Joe that he should call for back-up. Then he stepped cautiously inside. There was no one behind the counter and, Carlyle noted sadly, no cake either. *Matter in hand*, he told himself, *matter in hand*.

'Police!' he shouted. The silence grew louder. Gliding across the linoleum floor to the back room, he thought he heard something – a groan. Joe had arrived at his shoulder. Wisely, Rose had stayed on the street outside.

'Reinforcements?' Carlyle whispered, waiting for the welcome sound of sirens approaching.

Joe nodded.

This time the noise from behind the door was louder. It definitely sounded like someone in pain.

Still no sirens.

'Fuck it!' Carlyle turned the handle and burst inside, Joe following behind. The pair of them walked straight through the pool of blood spreading on the floor.

'Fuck!'

Shen sat slumped, dazed, in a chair. He had been shot in the stomach. With some effort, he raised his chin and looked at Carlyle. 'Get me an ambulance,' he rasped.

'It's on its way,' Carlyle said, leaving Joe to check Shen's pulse and make him more comfortable.

'I'll be okay,' Shen continued. 'He didn't want to kill me, just slow me down.'

'Ihor?' Carlyle asked.

'Yeah.' Shen tried to nod. 'It was the same weapon he used to shoot Merrett. He legged it out the back.'

Conscious that he was trailing blood all over the place, Carlyle quickly slipped off his shoes and checked the alley behind the café. By now, of course, Ihor was long gone. The inspector went back inside and – still in his stockinged feet – looked through the two rooms upstairs, without finding anything of interest.

By the time he came back down to recover his footwear, Shen was being wheeled out to a waiting ambulance, while Joe and Rose were talking to a couple of the dozen or so uniformed officers who had arrived on the scene in response to reports of an officer down.

Once they had been abused for trashing the crime scene, given their statements and extricated their car from behind the police cordon, Carlyle insisted that the sergeant drive Rose home. 'Drop me at the nearest tube,' he told Joe. 'We'll call it a day.'

'What are our next steps?' Rose asked.

'I don't know that we have any,' Carlyle said wearily. 'Simpson will be mad when she hears about these latest developments, so it's doubtless back to the day job for me. Ihor is probably on his way out of the country by now. The Border Agency may or may not be able to stop him disappearing. He could be on the Eurostar already. If he gets to Paris or Brussels, forget it.'

'We have the link to Falkirk,' Joe reminded him.

'We do, but that's not enough.' They turned a corner and Kentish Town underground station appeared before them. 'Let me out here.'

With Joe idling in traffic, Carlyle jumped out of the car. Not realising that his shoes were still leaving faint prints of Shen's blood on the pavement, he picked up a copy of the *Evening Standard*. Reluctant to join the crowds heading into the tube station, he walked into a pub and ordered a double Jameson. Sitting with his drink and his paper, watching normal people going about their business, he savoured a feeling of relief at rejoining the real world, if only for a little while.

Chapter Twenty-three

CARLYLE SAT ON the front pew close to the central aisle in the chapel at the West London Crematorium, in Kensal Green Cemetery. The chapel could accommodate up to 100 people, but he was alone and no one else would be turning up. It was just him and the apologetic piped music. In front of him, Alzbetha's oak casket sat on the catafalque beneath a high, navy canopy, with floor-toceiling curtains descending on either side. Feeling tense, he glanced at his watch and read through the General Cemetery Company's leaflet on 'committal procedures' for the third time.

Shivering in the cold, he wondered why they couldn't just press the start button and get on with it, considering that there was to be no service. They were still trying to track down any family that the girl might have back in the Ukraine. It might be a lost cause, but Carlyle had decided to collect her ashes, just in case. If he hadn't been able to look after her in life, he thought, at least he could do it in death.

He had insisted that the Local Authority should not be allowed to bury the child in a 'pauper's grave' – which was just a pit containing up to thirty bodies. Most people assumed that mass graves had gone out with Charles Dickens, but sadly it was not so. Only a week or so earlier, a fox had taken a baby from another pauper's grave in Battersea New Cemetery. The grave had not been properly sealed. That was London: all human life was here – all human death as well.

The arrangements had been handled by B. German & Son of Lamb's Conduit Street and the cost covered by Westminster Social Services. Carlyle had tried to speak to Hilary Green, the social worker he blamed for 'losing' Alzbetha, but she was still off on sick leave. He had, however, met the funeral director, politely declined a Rowan Garden Ashes Plot (£1,575) and confirmed that he wanted to have custody of Alzbetha's ashes at the end of the cremation. 'Not mixed up with anyone else's,' he had insisted grumpily, as he stood in the shop watching another customer being loaded into the back of a hearse.

The director smiled wearily. 'The cremator has to provide a separate tray for each cremation, sir,' he said, 'so it's impossible that the remains of two bodies could be mixed up.'

'I see.' Carlyle wasn't exactly convinced, but he couldn't really argue the point.

That had been a week ago. Now he sat waiting on the uncomfortable oak pew. A door squeaked behind him and he heard light footsteps cross the stone floor, but he didn't look round. Why couldn't they just get on with it? Carlyle looked again at his watch. It was almost 11.15. It should have been finished by now.

There was suddenly a hand on his shoulder. He looked up. 'What are you doing here?'

Helen bent over and kissed the top of his head. Unbuttoning her overcoat, she sat down beside him. 'I wanted to come,' she said quietly, taking his hand. 'I know this is important to you.' She nodded at the coffin. 'Imagine if . . .'

He squeezed her hand. 'Don't.' He had already imagined it – a lot – and he didn't want to give the fear and paranoia about his daughter currently bouncing around his head any credibility by talking about it. 'What about work?'

She shrugged. 'I told them that I had a funeral to go to.'

The music stopped, replaced by a sudden mechanical rumbling as the coffin began to move. The curtains closed in front of the coffin and they sat in silence, listening to the box trundling towards the two small doors in the rear wall.

IMMEDIATELY AFTER THE cremation, Helen had to go back to work. Carlyle, unable to summon the energy to do likewise, offered to go and pick Alice up from school.

Standing in the crematorium forecourt, Helen put her arm through his and began marching him steadily towards the main road. 'You can't,' she scolded gently. 'She'd be mortified. She's too old for that now.'

Carlyle felt a pang of nostalgia for his daughter's rapidly disappearing childhood. 'Yes,' he said slowly, 'of course.' He felt a raindrop on his head and quickened the pace. 'Speaking of school, any more news on the drugs front?'

'Nothing, thank God.' Helen matched his stride. 'I think the school has managed to sort the problem out.'

'For now.'

'Hopefully, for good. At least, as far as Alice and her friends are concerned. They're all nice, sensible girls.'

'Yeah,' Carlyle nodded. But he remained unconvinced.

'What are you going to do with that?' she asked, nodding in the direction of the small brushed pewter urn he carried in his free hand.

'I don't know.' He shrugged. 'We're still trying to find the parents. If they don't turn up, I reckon we should scatter them somewhere.'

'Where?'

'Somewhere nice, I suppose.'

'Do you have anywhere particular in mind?'

'No, I haven't thought that far ahead.'

'I'm sure we can think of somewhere.'

He leaned down and kissed her tenderly on the cheek. 'Thank you for coming.'

She reddened slightly, and he wondered when was the last time he had seen his wife blush. She kissed him back. 'You did a good thing; making sure that this was done properly.'

Carlyle listened to the background hum of the city traffic getting closer. Arm-in-arm, they walked back towards daily life in comfortable silence.

SITTING IN THE back booth of Il Buffone, Carlyle finished his omelette and pushed the empty plate away from him, right up to the urn at the far end of the table. Marcello clearly wasn't happy about having Alzbetha's ashes in his café but, other than crossing himself theatrically and muttering a few things in Italian under his breath, he kept his own counsel.

As Marcello cleared away his plate, Carlyle ordered a double macchiato and an apple Danish for dessert. While he waited, he watched an elderly gentleman on a rickety old bicycle turn into

Macklin Street and come to a stop outside the café. After locking his bike to a lamp post and removing his crash helmet, he came inside and sat down opposite the inspector.

'Mr Carlyle?' he asked, with a mischievous twinkle in his pale blue eyes. He had the cheeky demeanour of an eight-year-old boy in a sixty-five-year-old body.

'*Inspector* Carlyle,' Marcello shouted from behind the counter.

'Of course,' the man beamed. 'I do apologise, Inspector.' He held out a hand. 'Ewen Mayflower.'

Carlyle shook it. 'Can I help you?'

Mayflower ran a hand through his cropped silver hair. 'It's me who can help you, I think.'

Just then, Marcello arrived with Carlyle's macchiato and pastry. Placing them on the table, he hovered expectantly.

'Ah, yes,' said Carlyle's new dining companion, picking up a menu and peering at it over the top of his glasses. 'Could I please have a cup of tea and two slices of brown toast, with no butter. Thank you.'

Marcello repeated the order and retreated behind the counter.

Munching on his pastry, Carlyle watched the other man remove his reflective yellow vest, under which he was wearing a brown jacket and a white shirt, topped off with a blue cravat. Mayflower adjusted the handkerchief in his breast pocket. 'A bit casual in the wardrobe department today. I've got the day off, you see.'

Declining to point out that, however casual he felt, Mayflower was still rather overdressed for Il Buffone, Carlyle sat back on his bench. 'And what is it that you do, Mr Mayflower?'

'Sir Ewen, please.'

Carlyle's heart sank. How had this nutter arrived at his door?

Marcello quickly arrived with the tea and toast. Mayflower declined milk. Blowing on his tea, he smiled. 'Only joking.'

Carlyle frowned.

'My full title,' the fellow continued, 'if you're the type of person for whom these things matter . . .'

I'm not, thought Carlyle sharply. But he let it slide.

'. . . is Sir Ewen Mayflower, GCVO – which stands for Grand Cross of the Royal Victorian Order.'

'Interesting,' Carlyle said, already wondering how he was going to make his escape.

'But you can call me Ewen.'

'Thank you.'

'According to my job title, I am the Lord Chamberlain.'

Carlyle looked confused.

'Head of the Royal Household.'

'As in the guy in charge of Buckingham Palace?'

'You could say so, yes.'

'And what does that involve?' Carlyle asked, his interest now piqued.

'Well,' Mayflower finished munching on a piece of toast, 'the Royal Household aims to provide exceptional advice and support to the Queen, enabling her to serve the nation and its people.'

Spare me the pitch, Carlyle thought. 'Which means what?' he cut in. 'In layman's terms?'

'I was warned that you were . . . direct.' Mayflower smiled politely. 'In layman's terms, I am the operational head of the "below stairs" elements of the royal palaces. I am responsible for the domestic staff, from the royal kitchens, the pages and foot-men, to the housekeeper and her staff.'

'How very Victorian.' Carlyle let his gaze wander. Out in the street, Trevor, a local pre-op transsexual, was shouting at a couple of the dossers from the nearby halfway house, his oversized Adam's apple bobbing up and down thirteen to the dozen.

'It's a very big operation,' Mayflower continued, determined not to be put off by Carlyle's snide response. 'We employ something like a thousand staff, give or take, across a wide range of professions, whose varied skills include catering, gardening and furniture restoration. There are even two employees whose job it is to look after the three hundred clocks.'

'I see.' Outside, Trevor had flounced off and the drunks were now arguing among themselves.

Mayflower was on a roll: 'There are five departments in the Royal Household. There is the Private Secretary's Office, the Master of the Household's Department, the Privy Purse and Treasurer's Office, the Lord Chamberlain's Office, and the Royal Collection Department.'

A thought belatedly popped into Carlyle's head. 'So you work with SO14?'

'Yes!' Mayflower's eyes danced with glee, like a teacher who had just got through to a particularly slow pupil. 'The Royal Household appointed a Director of Security Liaison a few years ago. I believe we have a number of acquaintances in common, such as Mr Adam and Mr Dolan.'

Slowly Carlyle re-established eye-contact. 'Why are you here?'

Mayflower picked up the second slice of toast. 'Carole Simpson asked me if I could be of assistance.'

'You know Commander Simpson?'

'Oh, yes!' Mayflower waved his piece of toast in front of his face. 'I've known Carole for a very long time. She is a wonderful woman.'

Carlyle said nothing.

Mayflower nibbled again on his toast. 'Such a shame, what happened to her husband.'

'Yes.'

'And for this latest . . . upset to happen to her, just when it looked as if she was getting things back on an even keel.'

Carlyle's eyes narrowed. He knew he was being toyed with. 'What happened?'

'Didn't you know?' Mayflower asked, as if amused. 'Joshua was beaten up last month by one of the other inmates. Nothing too serious, but he was in hospital for a few days. The prison authorities then insisted on having him handcuffed to his bed – outrageous! Carole was mortified, and rightly so.'

'Oh.' Carlyle felt a slight pang of guilt. All the extra aggravation he'd caused Simpson in the last few weeks, while she'd had this stuff on her plate.

'He was teaching a maths class,' Mayflower said cheerily, 'and apparently he shouted at one of the more stupid pupils, who took offence. He's always been too arrogant for his own good, that fellow. But, even so . . . Carole has been in quite a state about it all.'

'I can imagine.'

Mayflower put a tactful hand on Carlyle's forearm. 'Don't say I mentioned it.'

'No.'

'I don't suppose she'd want many people to hear about it.'

'No.'

'And,' Mayflower removed his hand and took a sip of his tea, 'she's worried about you too, you know.'

The inspector was genuinely surprised. 'She is?'

Mayflower placed his cup back on its saucer. He glanced at the urn, but said nothing. 'This case of yours – very nasty.'

'She told you about it?'

'She mentioned some of the details.' The sparkle went out of Mayflower's eyes and he was all business now. 'Obviously, anything to do with the Palace is of interest to me.'

'Simpson doesn't seem to think it has anything to do with the Palace,' Carlyle said, aware of sounding churlish.

'Carole is a very open-minded and fair person,' Mayflower said evenly. 'She also has a great deal of faith in you, and respect for your judgement.'

Feeling himself redden slightly, Carlyle said nothing.

'At the same time,' Mayflower continued, 'she told me that you can be a bit of a bull in a china shop.' Carlyle started to protest, but the other man held up a hand. 'You simply can't take that approach at the Palace. You will get nowhere.'

'I used to work there.'

'I know.' Mayflower crossed his arms and sat back on his bench, his point made as far as he was concerned. 'And look how that ended. A particularly unhappy chapter of your career, as I understand it.'

'That would be a fair description of it,' Carlyle sighed.

'So, this is where I come in. I can help you satisfactorily pursue your investigation, while ensuring that the interests of the Royal Household are also properly looked after.'

'And what if the two collide?'

'Inspector,' Mayflower said firmly, 'I can assure you that if there is anything at all to your suspicions regarding Thomas Dolan and the Earl of Falkirk, you will have my full support and assistance in ensuring that they are brought to justice.'

'Falkirk?' Carlyle asked, fully engaged now.

'Carole says that you have some serious concerns about our Mr Elstree-Ullick.' Mayflower looked around theatrically. 'Between us, I too have concerns. They may be the same concerns, or they may be different, but the basic point is that Gordon and his cronies could end up doing a great deal of damage to the Royal Household.'

That's hardly my primary concern, Carlyle thought. But he bit his tongue. 'Do you have any evidence?'

'I like to think that I operate with a light hand on the tiller,' Mayflower replied, 'but I hear things and I have seen things.'

'What kind of things?'

'Well . . . he treats the staff terribly. He ran over one of the bodyguards in his Aston Martin a few months ago, broke the poor man's leg. Did he apologise? No. Did he agree to be interviewed about it by the police? Hardly. He acts as if he is above the law.'

'Isn't he?' Carlyle asked. 'That's exactly what it sounds like.'

'He most certainly should *not* be!' Mayflower banged his fist on the table. 'It is crucial that justice is seen to be done. The Earl is no different from the rest of us in that regard. Only the Queen herself is immune from prosecution.'

The inspector raised an eyebrow. 'The Queen is immune from prosecution?'

'Yes. British justice is administered in the name of the monarch. The sovereign not only has immunity from prosecution, but it has also become accepted that he or she cannot be required to give evidence in court. Historic precedent and tradition aim to protect the dignity of the monarch, and therefore the process that dispenses justice in her name.'

Carlyle frowned. 'So if the old girl lost it one day and started down The Mall taking out tourists with an Uzi, she would be able to get away with it.'

Mayflower smiled indulgently. Simpson had already warned him that the inspector could be most trying, and he was determined not to be riled by Carlyle's childishness. 'An arresting image, Inspector, but it's hardly a plausible scenario, is it?'

Carlyle's frown deepened. 'But what about the principle?'

Mayflower laughed. 'What a strange policeman you are, Inspector!'

'What else does Falkirk get up to?' Carlyle asked, trying to get the conversation back on track.

'He is a very colourful character. There are lots of unaccredited guests, drinking parties, young girls . . .'

'How young?'

A pained expression crossed Mayflower's face. 'Younger than you would have thought necessary, by all accounts.'

Having no time for the cryptic, Carlyle changed tack. 'I've spoken to Falkirk,' he said abruptly. 'And he did not cooperate in any way.'

'So I heard.' Mayflower pursed his lips and steepled his fingers in prayer. 'Maybe we could talk to him together?'

'How would that help with my investigation?'

'You have no leverage over him. I, on the other hand, can realistically hope to have some influence on his access to the Palace and on the privileges he enjoys there. Maybe, together, we can have a different type of conversation with him.'

'What type of conversation?'

'Well . . . Gordon has a self-pitying approach to life, something which is surprisingly common among the royals. Maybe we could give him something more tangible to worry about than his usual concerns.'

Not very likely, Carlyle thought. On the other hand, it would be stupid to turn Simpson's emissary away. He signalled to Marcello for the bill. Turning back to Mayflower, he tried his best to give a look that might just be considered an approximation of gratitude.

'Okay,' he said, 'when did you have in mind?'

Chapter Twenty-four

ALEXA MATTHEWS SAT up in bed and yawned, idly scratching her left breast through the thin cotton of her T-shirt as she watched Heather who was curled up beside her, dead to the world. It was 2.10 a.m., which meant that her disciplinary hearing was due to start in just under eight hours.

At the hearing, she would be represented by her Federation rep, but the guy was so totally useless that she was seriously thinking about doing it herself. The whole situation was a complete nightmare: her transfer out of SO14 had collapsed and Charlie Adam's threat to have her thrown off the Force completely was not something that the union had been able to have lifted. By tea-time, Alexa thought, she might no longer be a policewoman. No job was bad enough, but it also meant no pension. Last time she looked, there was just over £56 in her savings account. She would be totally screwed.

Sitting there in the dark, she wondered what she could do for a living if she left the police force. Nothing sprang to mind. A shiver of fear went through her. She desperately wanted a fag. Heather had always insisted on a strict no-smoking policy in the bedroom, but tonight, surely, she should be allowed. She gave Heather a gentle poke to see if she was really asleep. There was no response, so Alexa decided she would risk it. Reaching down alongside the bed, she heaved her bag on to her lap and began rummaging around for a packet of Lambert & Butler's and her lighter. Underneath the cigarettes, she noticed her mobile was flashing. Someone had sent her a message. Sticking a cigarette in her mouth, she opened it.

Wakey, wakey!

She looked at the time of the weird message: 2.06. Some tosser had obviously texted the wrong mobile number. Grunting, she tossed the phone back into her bag and pulled out her lighter. There was the sound of footsteps on the street outside, then the door to their building opened. The couple downstairs had been out partying again, Alexa assumed, lucky buggers. Lighting her cigarette, she took a deep drag. 'Ahh!' As soon as the nicotine entered her bloodstream, the world suddenly seemed a less scary place.

She was carefully blowing the smoke away from the bed, when the door was kicked in. In the doorway stood two men with balaclavas covering their heads. One carried a small wooden rounders bat, like a half-sized baseball bat. The other was carrying two large plastic bottles filled with liquid, one in each hand.

Alexa stared at them dumbly. Was she dreaming?

Heather grunted and pulled a pillow over her head.

Alexa snapped out of her stupor. 'Get up, you stupid bitch!' she hissed, struggling out from under the duvet.

She had barely got her feet on the floor when the man with the bat stepped forward and smashed a fist into her face. 'Back on the fucking bed!'

Holding her broken nose, Alexa moaned as the other man unscrewed the cap from one of the bottles. She could smell the petrol even as he began pouring it over the bedcovers.

'Hey!' Belatedly coming to life, Heather sat bolt upright. Dropping one of the bottles on the bed, her attacker grabbed her by the throat and started pouring petrol from the other over her head. She tried to cry out but the fuel flowed into her mouth and she began to gag.

'No! Please!' Alexa tried to push herself up again, but her legs had turned to jelly. Then she saw the spark of the lighter. Her bowels loosened, and then gave way completely, the stench mixing with the smell of the petrol. She looked at Heather trying desperately to clean the petrol from her eyes, and started to cry. 'There's no need,' she sobbed. 'I'll go quietly. I'll say nothing.'

The men emptied the last of the petrol from the bottles and stepped away from the bed. 'You were told to keep your mouth shut,' one of them replied flatly. 'But you didn't, did ya?'

'I won't tell,' Alexa moaned.

'We know you won't,' he sneered, tossing the lighter towards her. For a moment, there was silence, then a *whoosh* and the smell of burning. The last thing she heard was Heather's screams.

ROSE SCRIPPS LOOKED up at the arrivals board located in the middle of the tiny terminal of City Airport in East London. It indicated that SwissAir LX462 had arrived on time. Standing to her left, a cluster of taxi drivers were waiting by the gate, holding up name-boards for their passengers. As casually as she could manage, Rose strolled past them, glancing at each one in turn. None of the boards had the name Boyko scrawled on it. That, in itself, was of no particular significance but it did nothing to quell the gnawing worry in her stomach. This operation would end up costing thousands of pounds. Had their intelligence been wrong? It wouldn't be the first time.

A disembodied voice reporting from airside gave her the answer. '*Here we go. The girl is moving through customs now. Just like her picture. Stick-thin, short blonde hair, dark eyes.*' Rose pushed the Bluetooth Headset deeper into her ear. The ubiquitous technology wouldn't draw any unwanted attention from civilians but she didn't want the bloody thing falling out once it all kicked off. She glanced over at Colin Haddon, the liaison from the UK Border Agency. Haddon was part of the Agency's Operation Paladin, responsible for unaccompanied children arriving at British ports and airports. He was in charge of the operation so long as they remained on airport property.

'*She's wearing a denim jacket and red trousers. Carrying a small red holdall. Easy to spot.*'

Standing at a news kiosk, flicking through a driving magazine, Haddon made eye-contact but didn't otherwise acknowledge her. He had been less than pleased at being dragged out on this foul night, moaning about having to go on 'another wild-goose chase'. Rose had been sympathetic but had stood her ground. They'd had precise intelligence for once and now the thirteen-year-old runaway from an orphanage in the Crimea had turned up just as anticipated. They were on to something here, just as long as they didn't lose the girl.

Rose wondered if she should have argued harder for more bodies for her team. There was no one else from CEOP. Simon Merrett hadn't been replaced yet and the rest of the team were thinly spread. Rose wasn't exactly thrilled to be here herself; paying Sasha, her au pair, £10 an hour that she didn't have, to look after her daughter, while she was hanging around on the other side of London. Rose began fretting as she wondered whether Louise had gone to bed yet.

In addition to Haddon, she'd been given three Armed Response Officers: little more than teenagers with guns, who were hovering in the darkness outside. Should she have called Inspector Carlyle? Then again, what could he do that three strapping young men kitted out with Heckler & Koch G36s couldn't? Would he have even agreed to come all the way out here, if she'd asked? She knew that she wasn't the only one with family commitments.

Rose turned away from the arrivals gate and took a few steps towards the only restaurant in the terminal that was still open. 'Remember,' she said quietly into the microphone boom, 'let her come all the way through. She's bound to be picked up. We want *both* of them.'

'Yes, Mother,' Haddon teased.

She turned back to the arrivals gate. Passengers had started appearing, and Rose felt her heartbeat accelerate till she was conscious of the pulse in her neck. She had a sudden need to pee and grimaced – that would just have to wait.

'She's here.'

Rose spotted the girl immediately among the grey morass of business travellers. Her name was Yulia Boyko. Looking older than thirteen, but not by much, she was travelling on a fake Italian passport in the name of Camilla Gaggioli. Left Simferopol at 7 a.m. this morning, travelling to Milan and on to Basel before catching the SwissAir flight into City.

Welcome to the East End of London, thought the CEOP officer. You think you're coming here to work as an au pair and study English. She shook her head sadly. Don't they all . . .

Yulia was pretty, if tired-looking and a little thin. Moving slowly, she tried to look like she knew where she was going and who she would be meeting. Passing barely five feet in front of Rose, she walked tentatively to the front entrance of the terminal building and looked out into the grubby darkness. Seeing nothing to comfort her, the girl turned and headed back in Rose's direction. Rose wanted to reach out and stop the girl, and give her a hug. But she knew that she couldn't do that now; she couldn't do that ever. What was she going to give her? A one-way ticket back to the Ukraine, and to God knows what problems back home. Just make her someone else's problem. That was all that mattered.

Out of the corner of her eye she saw a man in his twenties walk up to the girl. He had curly black hair, and wore a dark suit with a pale blue shirt open at the neck.

'He's here.' Rose watched as he took Yulia Boyko by the arm, leaning towards her to say something. The girl nodded.

'Let's go.'

Haddon walked casually over to join Rose. Together they watched the man validate his parking ticket and lead the girl out of the terminal.

'He's heading for the short-stay car park. We are fifteen feet behind him. We will be there in two minutes.'

A reassuring voice came out of the darkness: 'Understood.'

Rose winced as they stepped outside into a sharp wind. She zipped up her parka as she moved forward. Looking up, she realised that there was no one else on the pathway between them and their quarry. For no apparent reason, the man looked round and stared directly at them. Rose fought to avoid making eye-contact. Haddon quickly slipped his hand into hers. 'Keep walking,' he said quietly, a casual grin plastered over his face. 'If we walk past them it's not a problem.'

Clasping her fingers in his, she felt the ring on his wedding finger. Embarrassed, she tried to remember the last time she had held the hand of anyone other than her daughter. The man turned away from them and took the girl by the arm. Haddon let Rose's hand drop as he whispered into his microphone. 'Almost there . . .'

'We have you covered. We will follow your lead.'

Reaching the car park, the man ducked in between two vehicles, and the girl followed. Just then, Haddon broke into a jog. Falling in step behind him, Rose realised that he had unholstered his Glock 17. Suddenly she felt extremely vulnerable. They slipped behind a green Toyota and watched the man walk across the car park, the girl in tow, towards a large black BMW SUV parked next to the perimeter fence. The scene was illuminated by floodlights from the sugar refinery next door. Rose peered into the shadows. Where were those Armed Response guys?

'It's the BMW,' Haddon hissed.

'Got it.'

As Rose and Haddon began to walk across the car park, they heard the beep of the SUV's doors unlocking. The young man hustled the girl into the front passenger seat and slammed the door behind her. Walking around the front of the car, he opened the driver's door and slipped inside. The two officers were about five yards away when they heard the engine purr into life and the BMW started edging out of its parking space. Without waiting for Haddon, Rose ran up to the back and hammered on the rear door. 'Hey!'

The brake-lights came on and the BMW stopped.

'Watch where you're going!' Rose shouted into the wind. Haddon stepped round behind her, keeping on the driver's blind side.

'*Moving in . . .*'

The driver rolled down the window and craned his neck to look back at Rose.

She gave him a pained expression. 'You could have run me over here!'

'Get out of the way,' he snarled. The BMW started rolling backwards again.

Rose stepped out of its path just in time to see one of the Armed Response Unit step up to the driver's door and stick the barrel of his G36 through the window. 'Turn the engine off NOW!'

Another armed officer appeared on the passenger side.

The driver did a double-take and slowly did as he was told.

The tension drained out of the scene.

'Step out of the vehicle.'

Slowly, the young man got out of the car and allowed himself to be placed face-down on the tarmac and cuffed.

Yulia Boyko sat silently in the passenger seat, tears rolling down her face.

Rose smiled at Haddon, who looked relieved to be reholstering his Glock. 'Thanks.'

'Our pleasure.' He smiled weakly. 'It's nice when it all works.'

'Tell me about it.' Rose gestured towards the SUV. 'I'll get these two back to CEOP.'

'Let me know how it goes.'

'Will do.' But she was talking to the back of his head. Haddon was already heading back to the terminal, this messy little scene in the airport car park no longer his problem.

'SIT DOWN, PLEASE.'

Keeping his gaze focused on a spot somewhere outside the window, Carlyle took the spare chair in front of Simpson's desk and waited to be introduced to the fat, thirty-something man with the receding hairline sitting next to him.

Tapping at the keys on her mobile, Simpson studiously ignored them both.

After ten or so seconds had crept past, the man let out a large sigh and turned to introduce himself. 'Ambrose Watson.'

Carlyle stared at the outstretched hand and, after a moment's hesitation, shook it limply.

'IIC,' Watson explained. Loosening his tie, he wiped a bead of sweat from his pink brow.

Carlyle grunted noncommittally. In the wake of Alexa Matthews and her girlfriend getting barbecued, it was no surprise that he'd been called in for a chat with Internal Investigations Command.

Still not looking up, Simpson cursed under her breath as she struggled to complete her text message.

Watson glanced at his watch and sighed again. 'I'm looking into the Matthews killing,' he remarked, to no one in particular, 'and I was wondering where the inspector was on the night in question?'

Berk, Carlyle thought. Why would I ever do anything to Matthews? He tried to look nonplussed. 'I was at home.'

Watson coughed. 'Alone?'

Simpson finally completed her message and hit the send button. 'Ambrose,' she said, suddenly looking up, 'for goodness' sake, we don't have time for this nonsense.'

Carlyle, taken aback by this evidence of his boss's clear support, suppressed a smirk and said nothing. Indeed, he felt a small stab of affection for the commander that, until recently, he wouldn't have thought possible.

'But,' Ambrose huffed, going even pinker in the face, 'I have to—'

'You have to deal with a difficult situation,' Simpson cut him off, 'and we understand that. The reason why we are all here is not because the inspector might be a suspect,' she gave Carlyle the briefest of looks, 'but because he might be able to assist you in getting to the bottom of this.' She placed her mobile carefully on the desk. 'Don't burn your bridges before you've even started.'

Failing to hide his annoyance, Watson dropped his eyes to his lap.

'It's not like the IIC are ever particularly popular.' Simpson grinned.

Fuck me, Carlyle thought, she's even taking the piss. Seeing the glint in her eye, he wondered if she might have found a boyfriend while her old man was inside. That might explain her good mood.

Watson started chewing his lower lip, and Carlyle almost felt sorry for him. The reality was that he didn't really have any particular views of the Internal Affairs guys. He took coppers – from traffic cops to the commissioner himself – like he took criminals: in other words, just as he found them. One of the biggest mistakes you could make was to mark someone's card just because of their job. For Carlyle, it was a basic fact of life that any group of individuals, whether collected together by profession, religion or, rather more importantly, allegiance to a particular football team, would provide a mixed bunch: good, bad and indifferent. 'All things are relative,' his father would always say, 'and all people, too.' Alexander Carlyle had arrived in London from Glasgow in the 1950s, escaping de-industrialisation and relentless economic decline at home. Pragmatic to the core, he had taken a variety of jobs to keep the family unit together. 'Don't judge a book by its cover,' he would also tell his son over the dinner-table, 'and don't cut off your nose to spite your face.' It was sound advice that the inspector had often taken to heart. That, as much as anything else, made him happy to be his father's son.

Watson hadn't made a great first impression, but Carlyle realised that he had to give him a chance to redeem himself. 'This is down to Dolan,' he declared evenly. 'There have now been two violent deaths in SO14, and Tommy Dolan is the connection between them.'

'But PC Dalton was suicide,' Watson argued.

'Yes,' Carlyle agreed, 'but why did he kill himself? Dolan was involved in something that Dalton couldn't stomach being caught up in any longer.'

Watson made a face like he was constipated. 'So he decapitated himself with some nylon rope?'

'I think . . .' Carlyle looked at Simpson who gave a slight nod, signalling that he should proceed, 'that Dolan is running some kind of prostitution service. Working with various colleagues, he is providing a range of girls to top-end clients. He may even be using some of the rooms at Buckingham Palace for such entertaining. The income goes into an investment company called United 14, which is a secret pension fund for Tommy himself and his cronies.'

Watson sat in silence for some moments, looking like a hungry man who had missed his lunch. 'Do you,' he said finally, his voice weak, 'have any . . . *evidence*?'

'Nothing that we are in a position to share at this time,' Carlyle said quickly, while avoiding Simpson's gaze.

Relieved that this was just a kite-flying exercise, Watson perked up a bit. 'How could Dolan have done all this?' he asked.

'He's been there a long time.' Carlyle shrugged. 'He knows everybody who works in the Palace, and knows everything that goes on there. He has an eye for a fast buck. Also he's no fool.'

'But still,' Watson pushed back, 'what about his commanding officer? Surely this type of thing couldn't be going on behind his back.'

'Charlie Adam is a fool,' Carlyle said. 'I don't think he's involved but, whether he knows about it or not, I don't think he could actually do anything to stop it.'

'Have you spoken to Dolan?'

'He's hiding behind his union rep,' Carlyle said, 'and saying nothing. I don't suppose he personally torched Matthews and her girlfriend. Someone else will have done the dirty work.'

How had this meeting gone so badly wrong? Watson wondered. He shifted in his seat, keen to get out of the room.

'How do you suggest we proceed?' Simpson said swiftly, before he could bolt.

Carlyle nodded at the unhappy fat man. 'Ambrose needs to speak to Dolan. Make it known to him that he's being investigated. That will help undermine any union investigation into Joe and me.'

'But . . .'

Carlyle stood up and gave Watson a comforting pat on the shoulder. 'Look into United 14. Then give me a call when you've got something. But keep it discreet. I don't want it known that we're working together.'

'We are?' Watson looked at Simpson pleadingly. All he got in return was a smile.

'Keep that to yourself,' Carlyle joked. 'I have enough image problems as it is without people knowing that I'm working alongside internal affairs.'

'What will you be up to now?' Watson asked wearily, ready to play along in order to get this conversation over with.

Carlyle was already at the door. 'I've got a few ideas,' he said over his shoulder, grinning at the back of the IIC man's head. 'Don't forget to keep me in the loop.'

FIVE MINUTES AFTER leaving Simpson and Watson, Carlyle crossed Praed Street and made his way under the arch leading to the old section of St Mary's Hospital. Letting his mind wander, the inspector contemplated the three things he knew about St Mary's. Charles Romley Alder Wright, an English chemist, first synthesised heroin there in 1874; Alexander Fleming discovered penicillin there in 1928; and, in 1954, Elvis Costello was born there. Two of those three things he felt very grateful for; as another singer once said, two out of three ain't bad.

Stepping inside the main hospital building, however, he immediately felt oppressed by the sense of gloom and despair that he always associated with hospitals: patients and family members shuffling about as if they had the world on their shoulders, which they probably had; or members of staff rushing around as if they were trying to juggle impossible workloads, which they probably were.

Being both squeamish *and* morbid, it took a lot to get the inspector inside one of these places. Today, driven by more than a little guilt, he took the elevator to the third floor, where Warren Shen was enjoying the delights of a small private room, paid for by the Police Federation.

When he arrived at Shen's door, Carlyle was pleased to see the superintendent propped up in bed, talking happily to a petite dark woman who was sitting beside the bed. Appearing tired and drawn, she looked far more in need of a lie-down than Shen himself. Or, at least, she would have done if it wasn't for the various tubes coming out of Shen's arm, and the large swathes of bandages visible under his pyjama jacket.

As Carlyle gave a gentle knock on the door, the woman whispered something in Shen's ear, then shuffled out of the room without acknowledging Carlyle's presence.

Shen smiled weakly. 'John,' he croaked, 'come in.'

Carlyle took the vacated seat, and watched the woman give him another dirty look before stalking down the corridor. He turned to Shen. 'Sorry to interrupt.'

'Don't worry, it's nothing personal. My wife isn't very fond of policemen at the moment.'

Carlyle unbuttoned his jacket. 'That's understandable.'

Shen slowly lifted a plastic mug from his bedside table and sucked some water through a straw. 'Yes, it is.' His gaze darkened. 'I think Maria's going through some form of post-traumatic stress about what happened. Thank God for her mother – and that's something I never thought I'd hear myself say – looking after the kids.'

'Mm . . .' Carlyle didn't know what else to say.

'She wants me to quit.'

'The mother-in-law?'

'No.' Shen half-laughed, half-coughed. 'Well maybe her, too, but Maria is hassling me to pack it in.'

Carlyle watched an attractive young nurse walk past the door. 'Will you?'

'No, of course not. What else could I do? I could get some kind of pension but it wouldn't be anywhere near enough to get the kids through university, assuming that they want to go. Besides, I'm too young. Anyway, I've told her that I'm not likely to run into Ihor Chepoyak again, so what's the problem?'

Carlyle thought about the nurse – very blonde, very pretty. 'I'm sorry . . .'

'Ah!' Shen held up a hand. 'These things happen. It was my own fault. Maria knows that. I think that's why she's so freaked about the whole thing.'

'What about your friend Ihor?' Carlyle asked.

Shen let out a long breath. 'I would assume he'd made it back to Kiev about the time I was coming out of surgery. He'll never be caught.'

'No.'

'But look on the bright side. That probably means he'll eventually end up face-down in a muddy field somewhere minus the back of his head.' Shen took another sip of water. 'At least, that's what I hope happens to the bastard.'

'And what's happening on your patch?'

Shen grimaced. 'Ah, well, it's a good time to be off sick. That will be a mess for a while. Lots of arguments, lots of violence until the next alpha male scumbag emerges, just like Ihor did a few years ago.'

'And the girl . . . Olga?'

'No idea.' Shen yawned. 'Look, John, thanks for coming, but Maria will be back in a minute and—'

'No problem.' Carlyle stood up. For a moment he hesitated, wanting to ask Shen why one of Falkirk's clients had his phone number written on the back of a ticket for the London Eye. After all, that same phone number had got Simon Merrett killed. He looked down at Shen happily playing the victim in his hospital bed. What were the chances of getting a straight answer? The inspector turned to the door. 'See you later. And you let me know if there's anything I can do.'

'Thanks. Let me know how you get on with the investigation.'

'I will.' As the words came out, Carlyle was already halfway through the door, happy to avoid another encounter with the formidable-looking Mrs Shen.

Chapter Twenty-five

'AND THE LORD God planted a garden eastward in Eden; and there He put the man whom He had formed.'

Sitting on the otherwise empty terrace of the Grand Restaurant, located within the Central Botanical Gardens of the Academy of Sciences of Ukraine, Ihor Chepoyak drank deeply from his bottle of Lvivske Premium beer and gazed north, past the domes of the Mikhailovsky Cathedral, towards the city. Although the cold wind made his eyes water, Ihor had no desire to go inside. It was good to be home.

The nature of his trip back from London had been a little improvised – ferry to Zeebrugge, train to Munich, flight to Kiev – but his Czech passport had been up to the job and, although slow, the journey had proceeded without drama. Sitting here, in the calm beauty of the carefully tended gardens, it was almost as if the grime and violence of London had never existed. Such a horrible city! He was more than pleased that he would never be going back there again.

At the same time, Ihor knew that he would not be staying in Kiev for long. The investigation into the Sandokan International

Children's Camp had been completed, and the Prosecutor General's Office had called for arrests to be made. Deputy Prosecutor General Dmytro Gazizulin would now have to throw Parliament and the media a bone or two. Ihor knew that Falkirk might be untouchable, but he himself wasn't. He would have to work hard to prove his continuing usefulness or face a bullet or, at least, a prison sentence. Ihor wasn't sure which was worse. Going back on the road would be a small price to pay to avoid either.

Draining the last of his beer, he watched the woman's slow, steady progress up the path towards him. As she got closer, he noticed that she wore no make-up. Her hair was pulled back into a simple ponytail, and she was dressed plainly, in jeans and a red fleece jacket, with a pair of black slip-on, flat shoes. My God, she is beautiful, he thought, in the detached way of a man aware that he has the intelligence and the strength to keep his thoughts to himself.

As she approached his table, he stood up.

'Let's go inside,' she said, not breaking her stride.

THE DINING ROOM of the Grand Restaurant was as empty as the terrace had been. A couple of waiters hovered around anxiously, possibly wondering if they'd ever see another customer. Choosing a table by the window, the woman ordered a mint tea. Ihor asked for another beer. 'How are you, Olga?' he asked, once the waiters had scurried away.

She frowned. Up close, he could see that she looked tired. 'We're not in London now,' she said. 'You don't have to call me that any more.'

Ihor bowed slightly. 'Of course, Ms Gazizulin.'

'For God's sake, Ihor.' Pulling a packet of Marlboros out of her bag, she gestured through the window, towards the city. 'Here, in the real world, Alexandra is my name.' She offered him a cigarette. 'But you know I'm not into formality or hierarchies, like my father. Alex is fine.'

'Okay, *Alex*.' Ihor accepted the cigarette, lighting it from a book of matches taken from the table. He lit her cigarette next and dropped the match in an ashtray, before sitting back in his chair, waiting for the lecture to begin.

The waiter arrived and placed their drinks on the table. Alexandra Gazizulin stirred her tea at length, then took a drag on her cigarette and exhaled vigorously. 'Ah! It's so nice to be able to smoke where you like.'

'Yes.'

She flicked some ash into the saucer of her cup. 'My father is not happy.'

Ihor fingered the full bottle of Lvivske Premium but did not lift it from the table. 'I can understand that. But there was no real alternative.'

She cut him off with a sharp look. 'There is always an alternative. You have destroyed a valuable business.'

'We were going to have to get out of London anyway,' he said, as casually as he could manage, the relaxed mood he'd been enjoying since his return ebbing away. 'Your English friend had already had enough.'

'Falkirk?' she scowled. 'He was just being melodramatic.'

Ihor said nothing.

'He's confused,' she continued, a sneer draining the beauty from her face. 'He thinks he is some kind of entrepreneur, rather than what he really is.' She stubbed her cigarette out violently in the ashtray.

'Which is what?' Ihor asked.

'A rich pig.'

One of the waiters reappeared with menus in hand. Alex waved him away.

'So what do we do now?' Ihor asked, finishing his own cigarette. 'Any ideas?'

Ihor knew better than to suggest anything. 'No.'

'I didn't think you would.' She pulled another cigarette from the packet and stuck it in her mouth, this time not offering him one. 'Finish your beer quickly,' she said, pulling a match from the book while glancing over his shoulder. 'We have to go and see my father.'

Ihor felt a dull pain in his stomach. Turning in his seat, he saw the two men standing by the door. Suited, shaven-headed, expressionless, they were facsimiles of himself from fifteen years ago. Faces like granite, while smiling on the inside. Slowly he forced himself to finish the beer. Who knows? It might be his last in this life. Placing the empty bottle on the table, he fished a couple of notes from his pocket and let out a small burp.

'Urgh!' Alex grimaced. 'Let's go.'

ANOTHER NIGHT, ANOTHER drinks reception. It was all so tiring. This time it was abstract paintings by a famous actor. All well and good, but if the old bugger hadn't won a couple of Oscars, no one would give a hoot. Tiring of the gallery owner's attempt to sell him one of the canvases for a ridiculous price, Gordon Elstree-Ullick stepped into the street to bum a cigarette from his protection officer.

'Got a fag, Tommy?'

Stepping out of the shadows, Dolan pulled a packet of Rothmans King Size from the breast pocket of his jacket and tossed it to Falkirk.

Falkirk removed a cigarette, stuck it in his mouth and handed back the packet. 'Got a light?'

'Here you go.' Dolan handed him a lighter, waited for him to light up, and then decided to have a cigarette himself.

For a few moments, both men stood smoking on the pavement eyeing each other carefully. This was the first time in almost a week that the SO14 man had turned up for work. Something was going on but, so far, Dolan hadn't said a thing about what he had been up to. If there was one thing that Falkirk hated above all else, it was the help being unreliable. Unreliable and secretive.

At the same time, however, the Earl realised that things with Tommy Dolan were considerably more complicated than the traditional master–servant relationship. Taking a final couple of puffs, he ground out the remains of his cigarette beneath his Lobb shoes. 'How's it going?'

Dolan grunted noncommittally.

Falkirk watched a pretty girl walking down the other side of the road. 'I hear you've lost another colleague.'

'Messy,' was Dolan's only reply.

Falkirk half-turned to re-open the door to the gallery. 'Tommy,' he said almost casually, as if it was an afterthought, 'if you had anything to do with that, anything at all, it will have a . . . significant impact on our working relationship.' Without waiting for a reply, he stepped back inside. Maybe he should spring for one of the limited-edition prints. It might make a nice Christmas present for the Queen.

'Plonker!' Dolan hissed, before retreating to the shadows.

SITTING IN HIS ramshackle office, in front of a poster proclaiming the 1997 NATO-Ukraine Commission, General Dmytro

Gazizulin puffed on his Montecristo No 2. Through a cloud of cigar smoke, he gazed across the desk at Ihor, his expression an uncomfortable mix of displeasure and resignation. 'Alexandra tells me that the situation in London is irredeemable.'

Ihor shrugged. He looked at the bottle of Nemiroff Black Label on the desk. Beside it lay a Makarov PM semi-automatic, with the safety-catch on. Behind that was a framed photo of the general in his younger, Red Army days, his head popping out from the top of a T55 tank. Back then, Gazizulin was heading off to Afghanistan, fighting for the Motherland. Now all he wanted was to suck up to NATO and squeeze out whatever was on offer from the European Union.

The general was the ultimate pragmatist. Ihor liked him like that, since it gave him hope for his own future – over the next few minutes and beyond.

Normally, the vodka would have been flowing by now. Not today, however. That was fair enough. Ihor knew that he was not going to be considered Employee of the Month this time around.

The question was: just exactly how deep in the shit was he?

The fact that he had been brought to the Kirichenko barracks, thirty kilometres outside Kiev, gave Ihor confidence. He had relaxed as soon as Alex's black BMW X5, with the four of them inside, had turned on to the H-08, heading south towards Cherkasy. Driving down the familiar four-lane highway the general's daughter had even slipped the latest Sade CD on to the stereo. To Ihor's mind, it was not as good as the old stuff, but still not bad. Soon Alex was singing along quietly, apparently oblivious to her travelling companions. Leaning back, closing his eyes, Ihor was able to ignore the goons in the back and enjoy the smooth tunes of *Lovers Rock* for the rest of their short journey.

Those same goons were now standing outside the general's office, awaiting further instructions. If they were going to kill him, they would not kill him here. That at least gave him a chance of escape. And, anyway, maybe things hadn't come to that, not yet at least. He knew better than to give the impression of being a condemned man. The Ukraine was not like London; people here could smell the fear. And they would act on it in an instant. He flicked a glance at Alex standing to his right, just at the edge of his vision, with a blank expression on her face. She had not said a single word since they had arrived at the Kirichenko.

The comforting sound of boots on the parade ground reminded Ihor that here he was on home territory. He felt a pang of nostalgia for the simplicity of the old days. He remembered hours spent on the square outside; in the snow in only a vest, his skin turning blue; the crunch of gravel underfoot; the cold air in his lungs.

That had been before things had gone out of control: before his discharge, before his move into the private sector, working abroad to avoid jail, and making money. Good money. The money had always been good. Ihor was not greedy; he had made money for the general and had never taken more than his own due. There was surely no reason why it should end now.

Inside the office the general had the heating turned up high, till Ihor felt the sweat beading on his brow. He felt drowsy. Maybe it would be better to be outside. He stifled a yawn. The general pulled a pile of papers out of a drawer and dropped them on his desk. 'My final report.'

'What does it say?' Alex asked.

The general shrugged. 'What do you expect? It concludes that the rumours about children being sold to Western countries have been grossly exaggerated. However, some people have a case to answer. By the time it goes to Parliament next week, the Director of the Sandokan International Children's Camp will be in jail.'

'But,' Ihor frowned, 'if he talks . . .'

'He will not talk,' the general said, with quiet finality. 'Parliament will accept the report, return to hurling insults at each other, and we will get back to business as usual.'

'Assuming that we can still operate in London,' Alex chipped in, giving Ihor a sour glance.

'Quite.' The general poked his half-finished cigar towards Ihor. 'So?'

'So?' Ihor repeated vaguely.

'Is it irretrievable or not?' the general asked, clearly irritated, before clamping the cigar back between his teeth.

'I can't go back,' Ihor said evenly.

The general picked up the gun. 'Shooting two policemen,' he said slowly, 'that was a fairly stupid thing to do.'

Alex grunted her assent.

'Only one of them was a policeman,' Ihor protested, careful to keep a straight face, 'and he's not dead.'

The general looked over at his daughter for confirmation.

'He was discharged from hospital in London yesterday,' Alex confirmed. 'He should be able to go back to work.'

'Not that it makes any difference to our situation,' the general complained. 'We have invested a lot of time and effort in England.'

'And made a lot of money,' Ihor chipped in.

'Which is just as well for you, or you'd already be pig food.'

Ihor bowed his head in penitent understanding.

'There is also the question of the girls,' Alex said quietly.

The general gave her a quizzical look.

'The children,' she added.

'Ach!' The general waved away the smoke around his head. 'You are too soft. I have said so many times.'

'There are some that are just too young to be sent over there,' Alex persisted.

'That is not our decision,' the general snapped. 'I have already told you – that is a matter for our English friends.' He looked at Ihor. 'That is how the free market works, is it not? The buyer is always right!'

'Always!' Seizing the chance for some male bonding in the face of the woman's weakness, Ihor risked a grin. 'It has always been the Englishman's decision. He said that the young ones were his USP.'

'His what?'

'Unique Selling Point,' Alex translated, with a sigh. 'He is a sick bastard, that one. He wanted to fuck me as well.'

'I would have thought you were too old for him,' the general sneered, 'by quite some margin.' Reaching behind his chair, he opened the bottom drawer of a filing cabinet and pulled out three glasses, before finally uncorking the bottle of vodka.

Ihor laughed, ignoring her dirty look.

'The man is a degenerate pervert,' Alex complained.

'Which is why we are doing business with him.' The general smiled mirthlessly, pouring half an inch of vodka into each glass.

'He was planning to go elsewhere already,' Ihor declared. 'He was finished with the Ukraine. Said he was worried that things were getting too difficult.'

'Is that so,' said the general, handing out the glasses. 'Maybe if you explained to our royal friend about *my* role in all of this,' he continued, 'his concerns would be alleviated.' He raised his glass.

'Drink!' The general downed his vodka in one, and signalled for the others to do the same.

Ihor enjoyed the warm feeling on the back of his throat, then spreading through his body.

Alex emptied her glass and placed it back on the table. Leaning over the desk, she kissed her father on the forehead. 'Falkirk doesn't know the truth about me,' she said, 'never mind about you. That is as it should be. He is capricious and weak. One day he will give up his associates to the police – for all we know, he may have done so already.' She nodded at Ihor. 'They won't find him. But they *would* find us.'

The general nodded as she stepped away from the table. 'Ihor?'

'Yes?'

'We are in business, are we not?'

'Yes, of course.'

'Good.' The general slowly, carefully, refilled the three glasses. 'In business,' he said softly, 'you have to plan for different scenarios.' He handed over two of the glasses, before sipping with evident pleasure from his own. 'So, let us assume that we have two basic scenarios here. One – we stay in London. Two – we leave. Alex will go back there to work out which strategy is the most practical.'

'But . . .' Ihor glanced at the devilishly handsome woman beside him who said nothing, gave nothing away.

'Either way,' the general continued, 'there will have to be changes. There is more than enough scrutiny of our affairs as it is. We have to make sure that nothing comes back to our door.'

'How do we do that?' Ihor nervously chucked the vodka down his throat.

'We do that,' the general said gently, 'by you taking care of the royal pervert.'

Chapter Twenty-six

It was a heartbreakingly beautiful North London day, the sense of wonder and anticipation enhanced by the presence of early death. Carlyle stood under an oak tree in Stoke Newington's Abney Park Cemetery, drinking a bitter flat white from a paper cup and imagining his own funeral.

When his time came, he wanted to take his leave on a dark, gloomy day, just to help get everyone into the right mood. Blue skies, sunshine and a friendly nip in the air made you celebrate life, rather than embrace death.

Celebrating life: that was probably what the priest was now telling the mourners this was all about. But that was what priests were for, talking crap at every opportunity.

As he watched Simon Merrett's coffin being lowered into the ground, he thought back on Alzbetha. He still hadn't worked out what to do with her ashes, which were sitting in the Covent Garden flat, on top of the microwave in the kitchen. Alice thought it was 'sick' to hold on to them, but Helen was sanguine. 'No one's in any rush,' she told him, when he had fretted about his daughter's reaction, 'certainly not Alzbetha. Anyway, before we do anything, we need to be sure that the girl's parents are not going to suddenly turn up.'

'Not much chance of that,' Carlyle observed.

'Anyway.' She kissed him gently on the lips. 'We'll think of something.'

Not for the first time he was grateful for his wife's level-headedness. She knew how much this case had troubled him, and he was deeply grateful for her calm support.

The only funeral that really troubled Carlyle was his own. As a child, he had dreamed of travelling through space in a coffin, on a serene journey that would go on for ever. How he got into space in the first place was never made clear, but the idea appealed. Even now it seemed far preferable to any of the earth-bound options. Carlyle felt a fear of being buried; nor did he much fancy being incinerated. Assuming he couldn't eventually make it into orbit, he had decided that he would prefer being interred in his own crypt – situated somewhere windswept, but with a nice view.

Over the years, he had given this considerable thought. When he tried to discuss it with them, however, Helen and Alice just laughed. He knew that, when the time came, he would be dead and therefore past caring, but still . . . The idea that he should get it properly written into a will gnawed away at the back of his mind.

After experiencing two in quick succession, he wondered how many funerals he would attend before his own. Not all of them would be work-related, of course. His grandmother, well into her nineties now and living in a care home in Glasgow, would go in due course. His parents, Helen's mother, a couple of aunts . . . they all added up.

At least Simon Merrett had commanded a decent turnout. Carlyle counted thirty-seven people graveside, excluding the priest, the staff from the funeral parlour, and the two gravediggers sitting in their van a discreet distance down the road. He hoped that this would be some kind of comfort to Merrett's wife, but suspected it would not.

The inspector glanced at his watch – 11.18 a.m. – and had a sudden hankering for a glass of Jameson. But that was never a good sign at this time of day, and he pushed the thought away. Feeling self-conscious, he did a small jig under the tree, shifting from foot to foot, impatient to be on his way.

Finally, the service was over. Slowly, the group began to disperse, breaking up into twos and threes as they made their way back to the car park. Carlyle watched Rose Scripps briefly hug the wife and step away, dabbing at her eyes. As Rose headed towards him, he took in the bleak expression on her face. In black trousers and a black overcoat, her hair cut shorter than previously and wearing minimal make-up, she looked older than before.

Carlyle smiled weakly, by way of greeting.

Rose nodded.

'I didn't know Merrett was a Catholic,' Carlyle remarked, watching the priest in deep conversation with one of the mourners.

'Neither did I,' Rose replied, her voice sounding a little shaky. 'It's amazing how little you know about the people you work with.'

Not really, Carlyle thought.

'I've probably spent more time with Simon over the last year than his wife did,' she continued. 'In fact, I know I have. But I still know very little about him.' She let out a brittle laugh. 'In fact, I didn't even know which football team he supported.'

'Oh? Which one was that?'

'Chelsea. He even had a season ticket there, apparently.'

'Mm.' A grossly crass and uncharitable thought popped into Carlyle's head. He slapped it away. 'Shall we get going?'

'Yes.' Rose fell into step beside him, slipping her arm through his as they headed for the gate. Taken by surprise, Carlyle felt himself go tense. Unsure how to react, he kept walking and said nothing.

DRESSED IN A pair of jeans, New Balance trainers and a Hannah Montana sweatshirt, Yulia Boyko looked relaxed and happy. Ensconced in one of the meeting rooms at CEOP, she daintily sipped a can of Coke Light while flipping through the pages of a celebrity magazine. Looking up, she saw Rose standing in the corridor outside and smiled.

'She seems like a sweet kid,' Rose mused. Gently pulling the door closed, she looked up at the inspector. 'I think that she understands that she's had a lucky escape.'

'*Very* lucky,' Carlyle quipped, thinking about her impending deportation.

'I did some research,' she continued, ignoring his sarcasm. 'Apparently, there are about 100,000 kids in the Ukraine who are either homeless or have been abandoned by their parents, for one reason or another. Yulia lived with her father, stepmother and three sisters until she was six. When the father did a runner, she was sent to a grandmother, but the old woman died when Yulia was nine. That's when she ended up in an institution.'

'Jesus.' Carlyle hated these kinds of stories. The shit that some people – some *children*, for fuck's sake – had to put up with was just too horrifying. Poverty porn wasn't his thing; not when he could do sweet fuck-all about it.

Rose ploughed on, not picking up on his discomfort. 'Children dumped in orphanages normally grow up lacking the most basic social skills. But this is one smart kid. She hasn't had much in the way of formal education, but she can still read and write. She says she picked up English from watching TV shows. When the traffickers told her she was going to London, she jumped at the chance.'

'What's going to happen to her now?' Carlyle asked, trying to move the conversation along.

'She's going back there in two days.'

'Very lucky.'

'At least she's still alive.'

'Good point.'

'I know we're not doing much to help her,' Rose shrugged, 'but there's no way she's going to be allowed to stay.' She looked down at her hands. 'What I have done though, is to contact the British Embassy in Kiev.'

'And?'

'They put me in touch with the British Council. They are sponsoring some educational programmes over there, and I think we can get Yulia enrolled on one of those.'

'Great.'

She punched him gently on the arm. 'It *is* great. From there she can go on to be a peer educator within a UNICEF-supported Life Skills Education for the Prevention of Trafficking and Unemployment Project . . .'

'Mm.'

Rose didn't let his cynicism interrupt her flow '. . . which tries to help social orphans to understand and exercise their rights.'

'You're right,' said Carlyle, actually impressed, 'it's a real start. Well done.'

Rose blushed ever so slightly. 'Let's see what happens,' she said, smiling. 'In the meantime, she has been very cooperative.'

'Isn't that unusual?'

'Very. But the traffickers have no real leverage over her.'

'Because she's an orphan? With no family for them to threaten?'

'Because she's a smart kid who realises that she will have to fight for everything she gets in this life. And because we can offer her a decent alternative.'

CARLYLE HELD OUT a hand, and Yulia shook it politely. He nodded towards Rose, who smiled brightly. 'Thank you for talking to us.'

'No problem,' the girl said quietly, her eyes lowering to focus on the pages of her magazine.

'Yulia . . .' Rose placed a gentle hand on the girl's forearm, causing her to look up again. 'This is the policeman I told you about. Inspector Carlyle.'

The young girl glanced at Carlyle and nodded.

'It would be great,' Rose continued, 'if you could tell him what you already told me – so that he can understand how you came to England.'

'Okay.' She took a deep breath and launched into a short monologue that had obviously been perfected during various conversations with Rose: 'I spent the last four years at the Sandokan International Children's Camp. Three times I run away. This time, the Director tells me to go with the Englishman who comes to our camp. His name was Gordon.'

Carlyle looked at Rose. 'Falkirk?'

Rose nodded. 'She identified him from a photograph yesterday. We now have a full statement, signed in the presence of a lawyer.'

'Did you speak to this man?' Carlyle asked the girl.

'No.' The girl toyed with a page of her magazine. 'He was too important to speak to any of us. Anyway, he didn't know that I understood English.'

'What happened next?'

'They took us to a hotel.'

The girl's composure was slipping. Carlyle wondered how hard he should push. 'How many girls?'

'There were four of us. They split us up. I was given my tickets and told to meet the man at the airport.'

'And the others?'

Yulia's eyes glistened with tears. 'I don't know.'

Carlyle looked over at Rose, who just shrugged. He stood up and said, 'Thank you, Yulia. You have done very well talking to us. We are very grateful.'

The girl smiled shakily. Carlyle had one more question for her, but he wanted to let the child regain her composure. Turning to Rose, he asked: 'Have we spoken to the Ukrainian authorities?'

'I spoke to someone in the Ministry of Internal Affairs. Apparently there is a big investigation going on into the children's camp being run by the Kiev Deputy Prosecutor – some general or other.'

'A general?' Carlyle laughed. 'We could do with some of that over here – I mean the smack of firm leadership.'

Rose flicked through the pages of her notebook, looking for the name. 'General Dmy-tro Gaziz . . . ulin.'

'General Gazizulin is a big man in Ukraine,' Yulia chipped in.

'Yes.' Rose nodded. 'I spoke to one of his assistant assistants or something. They are sending me over some files.'

'Are they investigating Falkirk?'

'I didn't ask.'

'Let's find out.' He turned back to the girl. 'Is it okay if I ask you one final question?'

The girl nodded.

'Do you know a girl called Alzbetha? She is maybe eight or nine years old. I think she may have been at the same camp as you.'

Yulia thought about it for a second, before making a face. 'No, I don't think so. I am older than that and they kept the younger children separate.'

'Fine. Thank you again for talking to me.' Carlyle stuck a hand in his pocket and pulled out a £10 note and some change. He placed the money on the desk next to the girl. 'Get yourself something to read on the flight home.'

The girl flashed him a small smile. 'Thank you.'

He was saved from a feeling of utter uselessness by the mobile phone vibrating in his pocket.

'Carlyle.' He smiled weakly at the girl and fled the room.

'Inspector, this is Alex the concierge from the Garden Hotel.'

'Yes?' said Carlyle warily, expecting that he was about to be asked a favour.

'The girl's back.'

'Eh?' Relief at being out of the interview room was now mingled with irritation at the concierge's cryptic statement.

'The girl you were with last time,' Miles explained. 'She's booked the penthouse suite. Paid for it this time, as well.'

Fuck. He was about fifteen minutes away by foot; maybe something less than that if he jumped in a taxi. Or maybe not. 'Is she there now?'

'She went up about ten minutes ago,' Miles replied with the enthusiasm of a man making a big inroad into his debt at the Bank of J. Carlyle.

'Alone?'

'As far as I know.'

Carlyle thought for a second. 'Okay, get me her booking details, including the credit card she used. And call me if she makes a move. I'll be there in ten minutes.'

'AH, INSPECTOR. I was wondering when you would manage to get here.'

Standing in the doorway of the hotel's penthouse suite, feeling rather sweaty and dishevelled after jogging across Soho, Carlyle looked Olga up and down as he caught his breath. She wore a white dress shirt with the top two buttons undone, over a pair of expensive-looking jeans. Barefoot, sipping from a small bottle of Evian, she was looking good. More than good, just like an expensive hooker should.

'I didn't think we'd see you again,' he said, once he was confident that he could open his mouth without his tongue falling to the floor.

'Why not?' A look of mock surprise moved carefully across her face. 'Because the unfortunate Mr Ihor Chepoyak happened to go a little bit crazy?'

Carlyle sat himself on the bed. The lady clearly had an agenda, and he might as well hear it sitting down. 'I thought you worked for him?'

'Are you responsible for the actions of *your* boss?' she asked, not confirming or denying anything.

Carlyle smiled. He was more than capable of answering a question with a question himself. 'Do you know where he is?'

'Not any more.' She sipped her water and grinned, enjoying the game.

'So what are we talking about?' Carlyle asked.

The woman gave him a serious look. 'I heard about the girl.'

Which one? Carlyle wondered. She knew about Alzbetha, but did she know about Yulia as well? He steeled himself, so as not to give anything away. Attractive women were the worst for getting you to say too much. 'Alzbetha? I still have her ashes.'

'Urgh.' Olga shivered.

'She had to be cremated,' Carlyle said evenly. 'If we don't find her family soon, we will have to do something with them.'

'Are you still investigating her death?'

Carlyle stood up and gave her a stern look. 'A young girl is trafficked and killed – that is not the kind of case that you just walk away from.'

'No.' The woman's face darkened. 'I understand.' She carefully screwed the top back on the water bottle and let it fall on to the bed. 'Did you find anything at the house?'

Carlyle wondered if he should try and nab the bottle for fingerprints. Was it worth the cost – spending another couple of hundred quid that the Met didn't have on forensics services? Probably not. 'Which house?'

'Ihor's safe house,' she pouted. 'The one I told you about. Thane Villas.'

'Nothing. It was empty.' He paced in a small circle, hands in pockets, trying to wear out the carpet just to annoy Alex the concierge. 'That address cost me a lot of money, as I remember.'

'Okay, okay. Let me make it up to you.' Olga lifted a large shoulder bag on to the bed and pulled out a number of A4 sheets of paper.

'What are these?' Carlyle asked.

'These documents show that 75 Thane Villas is ultimately owned by a company called . . . United 14.'

Good to know, thought Carlyle. That's another nail in Tommy Dolan's coffin.

'I believe,' Olga said archly, 'that this is a company owned by the police.'

'It is privately owned by a group of policemen,' Carlyle said stiffly. 'That is not the same thing.'

'Whatever,' said Olga, handing over the papers. 'But the mortgage is paid by a second company . . .'

'You wouldn't have thought that these guys would have needed a mortgage.'

'It's all about leverage,' Olga said breezily, having satisfied herself that she was dealing with a financial idiot. 'The mortgage is paid by a company called Black Prince Elite Enterprise Holdings.'

Ho, bloody ho, thought Carlyle, seeing now where this was going.

'Which is owned by . . .'

Don't jump in.

'A very important man . . .'

Giving her good eye-contact, Carlyle nodded to show he was listening.

'Called Gordon Elstree-Ullick, who is . . .'

Don't smirk. Let her tell it.

'The Earl of Falkirk.'

'I see.'

'He knows the Queen!' she squealed. 'He is something close to the English throne!'

'Do you know him yourself?'

'Yes,' she grinned. 'As a matter of fact, I do.'

CARLYLE FOUND ALEX the concierge in the gloom of the otherwise empty Light Bar on the ground floor of the Garden Hotel. He was sitting in a booth at the back, drinking a cranberry juice and catching up with his paperwork. 'I hope you two didn't mess the sheets,' he said, stabbing at the keys of a outsized calculator and not looking up.

Ignoring the barb, Carlyle took a seat nearby. 'What have you got?' Feeling the need for a £6 fruit juice himself, he tried to catch the eye of the bartender, but the guy studiously ignored him as he went on drying glasses and placing them under the bar. Berk, Carlyle thought, returning to the matter in hand.

Miles pulled a sheet of paper from the bottom of a pile and placed it in front of the inspector. 'This has come from a contact at the credit-card company.' He jabbed at the document with his index finger. 'It's confidential information, so I'm not supposed to have it. And *you* are certainly not supposed to have it.'

Carlyle adopted a look of inscrutable officialdom.

'You cannot use this in court,' Miles said firmly, 'and it doesn't go any further than us.'

'You have a contact?' Carlyle asked. 'What kind of contact?'

'One that you don't need to know about in any kind of detail,' Miles replied sharply, before sipping at his juice through a pair of straws, like an overgrown schoolboy. 'Fraud is a big issue – both for us and for them. It can easily cost us tens if not hundreds of thousands of pounds, if we don't keep on top of things. We don't want that to happen, neither do they. A free flow of information helps us both.'

Not wanting to annoy his source any further, Carlyle nodded as he scanned the list of names and numbers. 'Understood.'

'So,' Miles said, jabbing at the paper again, 'what this shows you is that the card used to pay for the penthouse suite is registered, in the name of Olga Gladkyy, to an address – a very expensive address – in Highgate.'

'Okay.' Carlyle was interested, but not that interested. Olga knew how to play him. By his way of thinking, she must have known that they would get to this, which meant it must be fairly useless information. Otherwise, she wouldn't have used the card.

'There are three other names with cards registered to that address,' Miles continued, 'all women. Daria Khudzamov, Anichka Ischenko and Alexandra Gazizulin.'

Alexandra Gazizulin.

Carlyle stared at the name on the sheet of paper for several moments.

Gazizulin.

'Thanks for this.' Carlyle grabbed the piece of paper, folded it in three and placed it in the inside pocket of his jacket. He stood up and offered Alex the concierge his hand. 'Keep me posted on any comings and goings at the penthouse.'

'Will do,' Miles nodded, shaking Carlyle's hand, not getting up from his seat. 'She is booked in for just the one night.'

'Anything of interest, I want to know.'

'Of course.' Miles was already tapping on his calculator again and scribbling some numbers on his papers.

With a spring in his step, Carlyle headed through the lobby and out into the street. Alexandra Gazizulin, he thought happily, maybe you're not that bloody smart after all.

Chapter Twenty-seven

TOMMY DOLAN STOOD in a corner of the upstairs bar in the Star and Garter on Poland Street, sipping a pint of Copper Dragon Best with a doleful expression on his face.

'The Federation has dropped my case.'

'That would be because the murder of a policewoman has given them something else to worry about,' Joe Szyszkowski replied sharply.

'They told me to walk away quietly,' Dolan grumbled, 'or I could be in some really deep shit.'

Carlyle glanced at Joe, eyebrows raised slightly. 'I'm not surprised.'

'It was a bloody liberty, in the first place,' Joe chipped in, gripping his bottle of Peroni tightly and leaning in towards Dolan in a vaguely threatening manner.

'My rep was a useless little shit,' Dolan moaned into his beer glass, oblivious to the lack of sympathy he was receiving. He looked up. 'But, hey, at least you guys are in the clear.'

It's just one big game to you, Tommy, isn't it, Carlyle thought. He took another nip of his Jameson and felt his stomach rumble. He wanted to be home, sitting on the sofa with Helen and Alice, not standing in a crowded pub having to listen to this whining wanker. 'What about Alexa Matthews?' he asked.

'Don't know about that,' Dolan sniffed. 'Maybe someone got carried away.'

'That's why we're here, Dolan,' snapped Joe, lifting the bottle to his mouth but not taking a swig. 'You said that you had something for us.'

'All I want,' said Dolan, once again displaying the self-awareness of a flea, 'is to retire with my pension.'

Taking a final gulp of whiskey, the inspector placed his empty glass on the bar. 'Okay, Tommy,' he said, 'I'm off in one minute. Time to put up or shut up.'

Dolan cradled his pint thoughtfully, eyes lowered, looking like the crafty little shit he was. 'I can give you Adam,' he said finally.

'Charlie Adam!' Carlyle attempted a snort of derision. 'Why should I give a fuck about Charlie Adam? He's too stupid to be bent.'

'I wouldn't be so sure.'

Carlyle put a hand on Dolan's shoulder. 'For the avoidance of any doubt, Tommy, I do not give a flying fuck about Charlie fucking Adam. Not least because I hear that the little muppet is resigning next week.'

Dolan stared at Carlyle.

So did Joe.

Both of them thought he was making it up.

Both of them *knew* that he was making it up.

Neither of them challenged him on it, however.

'Time's up,' Carlyle said. 'Give me Falkirk or fuck off.'

Dolan made a face. 'Do we have a deal?'

'Cheeky cunt,' said Joe, grinning.

'You know how it works, Tommy,' said Carlyle, glaring at his sergeant, and trying to get him to calm down. 'There can be no promises.'

Dolan fixed him with a look that said *I might get fucked here, but I'm not going to get fucked stupid.* 'I understand that,' he said slowly, 'but *we've* got a gentleman's agreement, don't we?'

'None of us are gentlemen, Tommy,' Carlyle replied haughtily. 'But for my part, assuming that you personally didn't have anything to do with torching Alexa and her girlfriend, I will limit my interest to Falkirk. And I will speak to Simpson to see if that will hold true for the rest of the investigation. Then it will be down to you and your union rep.'

'Great,' said Dolan, without any enthusiasm. 'The little twat is about twelve years old. He doesn't have a fucking clue.'

'That's the thing, Tommy,' Carlyle grinned. 'Even the Police Force reps are looking younger and younger these days.'

Dolan stared at him blankly.

'You have to give a statement to IIC,' Carlyle continued. 'Go and speak to a guy called Ambrose Watson. He seems okay.'

'If he's IIC,' Dolan hissed, 'he's bound to be a git.'

Whatever, Carlyle thought. 'Anyway,' he said, 'you have to talk to him. I'll see what I can do in the meantime.'

'What are your next steps?' Dolan asked, failing to recognise that he was now a policeman in name only.

'That's my problem, Tommy,' Carlyle replied, finally heading for the door. 'You'll have to leave it to me.'

Chapter Twenty-eight

'WHAT'S HE DOING here?' Gordon Elstree-Ullick turned in his seat, eyeing Carlyle up and down.

Sitting behind the gilded cherrywood desk in his spacious office on the ground floor of the west wing of Buckingham Palace, looking out on to the central quadrangle, Sir Ewen Mayflower spread his hands wide. 'I asked the inspector to come,' he said evenly, 'because I thought that he might assist in our conversation.'

Falkirk couldn't have looked any more disgusted. 'This *po-liceman*,' he hissed, in his best Eton-meets-Harlem accent, 'tried to arrest me.'

Carlyle glanced at Mayflower and said nothing.

'The point is—' Mayflower persevered.

'The point is,' Falkirk interrupted sharply, but in a voice tinged with fear, 'that you have got me here under false pretences.' He stood up and stared Carlyle in the eye. 'This is the second time this . . . incompetent officer has harassed me.'

Carlyle couldn't resist the slightest of grins. 'Dolan has given you up, Gordon,' he said quietly. He then looked theatrically at his watch, hoping that Ambrose Watson had completed the interview by now. 'It's all over.'

'Damn you,' said Falkirk, pushing past Carlyle and heading for the door. 'I will be speaking to my lawyer about this, once again.'

Enjoying the show, Mayflower raised his eyes to the ceiling.

'Yes, you will,' Carlyle agreed, placing a hand on Falkirk's shoulder. 'However, that will be after I have arrested you and charged you with people-trafficking, controlling prostitution – and murder.'

Mayflower let out a tiny gasp.

Falkirk shrugged off the inspector's grasp, before jumping towards the door. Pulling it open, he bolted down the corridor.

Sighing, Carlyle headed after him.

'Be careful with the antiques,' Mayflower yelled after him.

In no particular hurry, Carlyle followed Falkirk down a corridor into the Blue Drawing Room, a cavernous space with chandeliers hanging from the ceiling like distended jellyfish. Trying desperately to place a call on his mobile, Falkirk tripped on the thick red carpet and went sprawling, dropping the handset as he did so.

Stepping past the Earl, Carlyle stomped on the mobile several times. 'That's the one phone call you're allowed,' he growled, trying not to enjoy himself too much.

Falkirk staggered to his feet and swung a kick at Carlyle, catching him right on the thigh.

'You fucking bastard,' Carlyle snarled, reaching out and grabbing a vase from a table just to his left. Fitting his grasp perfectly, the blue and white vase was about twelve inches tall, thin at the neck and round at the bottom. In one fluid, elegant movement, he smashed it down on Falkirk's head, sending him back to the carpet in a haze of fragmenting porcelain and blood.

'Oh my!' Mayflower panted. 'Oh my, oh my, oh my.'

Waiting for his adrenaline rush to wear off, Carlyle looked at the Head of the Royal Household, who was on his knees picking pieces of vase off the carpet. 'Chinese,' he mumbled. 'Seventeenth-century . . . Qing Dynasty.'

'Take it out of their Civil List money,' Carlyle quipped.

Blood oozing from his scalp, Falkirk groaned as he tried to get up. 'Stay still!' Mayflower slapped him sharply on the top of his head. 'Don't move!' He gestured for Carlyle to help. 'We have to keep all the fragments.'

Carlyle stood exactly where he was, saying nothing.

With both hands now full of shards, Mayflower looked up. 'You can't arrest him until we're sure that we've recovered all the pieces. I need to call in the specialist restorers.'

'I suppose you've got them available on speed dial,' Carlyle grinned.

Mayflower fixed him with a hard stare. 'Don't be flip, Inspector, that vase was priceless.'

'Bill me,' said Carlyle, suddenly feeling weary of being in the presence of all this wealth.

But Mayflower was talking to himself. 'We will have to get another from storage while we glue this one back together.'

'Storage?' Carlyle asked.

Falkirk emitted another groan. Carlyle took a half-step closer and gave him a sly kick.

Busy building a pile of his precious vase fragments on the carpet, Mayflower pretended not to notice. 'We have plenty more works in storage,' he explained. 'There is far too much to put on display.'

'Why don't you sell some of it?' Carlyle asked. 'It could help pay down the national debt or something?'

'Oh, no! That would never do.' Mayflower looked at Carlyle as if he was even more stupid than a policeman should be. 'The family would never stand for that.'

'I suppose not.' Carlyle fell to his knees and handcuffed Falkirk. 'Hoarding loads of expensive shit in the basement makes so much sense, after all.'

'I think that maybe it does,' Mayflower grinned cheekily, 'if it happens to be *your shit*, Inspector.'

CARLYLE BUNDLED FALKIRK into the back of the police BMW already waiting in the quadrangle, taking care to bounce his head firmly off the frame of the door as he did so. Falkirk grunted, but did not complain. The driver gave him a questioning look, but Carlyle just glared back at him and the man said nothing.

Joe Szyszkowski sat impassively in the front passenger seat. Walking round, Carlyle bent down to the window: 'Get him back to the station and make sure to leave him in a cell for an hour. Then we'll go and talk to him. He sees *nobody*. And he's already had his one phone call.'

Joe gazed through the windscreen at a young woman walking a gaggle of Corgis. 'Understood.'

'Good. I want as few people as possible to know that he's in custody.'

Joe gestured at the bloodied, sullen figure visible in the rear-view mirror. 'Shall I get him cleaned up?'

'Leave him.'

'Are you sure, boss? It could become an issue.'

'Okay,' Carlyle sighed, 'whatever you think. I'll be back in an hour or so.'

'See you then.' Joe buckled up his seat belt and turned to the driver. 'Let's go.'

Carlyle stepped back from the car and watched it pull away. He then turned to Mayflower, who had been hovering at a discreet distance. 'Thank you for your help.'

'My pleasure, Inspector.' The Head of the Royal Household held out his hand, and they shook. 'I just hope this matter can be concluded speedily, and with a measure of discretion.'

'I think that there is relatively little chance of that,' Carlyle replied, wiping cold sweat from his brow. 'However, I assure you that I will make every effort to see that you are not inconvenienced unnecessarily, and that the Royal Household is embarrassed by any forthcoming revelations as little as possible.'

Mayflower's eyes sparkled. 'My, what a very diplomatic answer!'

Carlyle shrugged. 'I promise that I will do my best.'

'Don't worry, Inspector. There are always some things that are beyond our power and control. In such circumstances, all one can do is try to do one's job. The really bad apples have to be dealt with, and if it all gets a bit messy, well . . .' he gestured back inside the Palace, 'it's not as if these good people don't know a thing or two about scandal.'

'I suppose not,' Carlyle laughed. 'And sorry again about the vase.'

'These things happen.' Mayflower patted him gently on the arm and began guiding him across the quad. 'It will take many months and quite a bit of superglue, but that artefact will be back on display by this time next year.' He gave Carlyle a searching look. 'Of course, I'll have to tell the Queen about what happened.'

'Really?'

'No,' Mayflower chuckled, 'she'll never notice. Why should she? She owns hundreds of the damn things.'

At the North Centre Gate, they parted company. Mayflower was already on his way back inside when Carlyle had a further thought. 'Sir Ewen!'

Mayflower stopped and turned. 'Yes?'

'One final thing.' Carlyle jogged over to explain his request.

Mayflower considered it for a second. 'That is something that I would definitely have to check with Her Majesty.'

'Is it . . . do-able?' Carlyle asked.

'I can at least ask,' Mayflower said thoughtfully. 'I *will* ask. I don't know if such a thing has ever been done before, but under the circumstances, I think it is a very reasonable request. And it is a very good idea on your part. I myself will support it and suggest it is the very least we can do.'

'It would be a very private thing.'

'I understand,' Mayflower nodded. 'Let me see what I can do. I am sure that we can sort something out.'

ON HIS WAY back to the station, Carlyle took a detour into St James's Park, sitting himself on an empty bench. Watching the tourists feeding the ducks, he let his mind wander. The skies were leaden and he shivered in the cold. St James's was by no means his favourite park, but with the Palace to his left and the London Eye rising over the Downing Street skyline to his right, it was one of the places where he felt most conscious of being in London with a capital 'L'. He was in the heart of his city, his home – the place where bad things were not supposed to happen; where it was his job to make sure that those responsible were punished.

Chapter Twenty-nine

FALKIRK HAD FOUND himself a new lawyer. Sasha Stuart, six foot two, all blonde hair and A-line skirt, stood in front of the desk sergeant, hands on hips, looking to rip someone's head off.

'My apologies for keeping you waiting, Ms Stuart,' the inspector said politely, ushering her past the desk and into the station proper.

'Your apologies are not going to be good enough, Inspector,' she replied haughtily, 'especially given your track record when it comes to harassing my client.'

'I assume that you've seen the charges against him,' Carlyle continued evenly. 'And don't forget that we will be throwing in resisting arrest, assaulting a police officer and,' he failed to avoid a smirk, 'criminal damage as well. He's turned into a right little one-man crime wave, your client.'

Stuart sighed. 'Criminal damage? What criminal damage?'

'He destroyed a priceless vase,' Carlyle said through pursed lips, 'while trying to evade arrest. It belonged to the Queen. I don't think Gordon will be getting his invitation to Balmoral this Christmas.'

'As far as I am aware, my client likes to spend the winter months in the Bahamas,' Stuart said icily.

'I'm not surprised,' Carlyle quipped. 'Does he like to take a few little girls along with him?'

She gave him a flinty stare. 'Not only will we be taking this matter up at the highest level within the Metropolitan Police Force,' she said grimly, 'but we will also be making a complaint to the Independent Police Complaints Commission.'

'That's very interesting,' Carlyle replied, trying to sound as nonchalant as possible. 'But I would have thought you would want to avoid the publicity.'

'Hardly,' she snorted. 'This is by far the worst case of harassment I have ever encountered.' She looked him up and down. 'The average policeman makes only nine arrests a year – and that includes drunks, fare dodgers, television licence fee evaders, people like that. Assuming that you are indeed *average* . . . almost a quarter of your arrests for this year as a whole have involved my client.'

'Your point being?'

'My point being,' she extended a carefully manicured index finger to within half an inch of his nose, 'that you do *not* arrest people like the man who is sitting – once again – in your police station. *No one* arrests people like him.'

Carlyle fought to keep his temper in check. 'No one is above the law.'

The finger veered away from his face and poked him on the shoulder. 'Grow up, Inspector. Just grow up!' Turning away, she headed briskly towards the interview room. 'Of course, once this matter has been sorted out, we will be pushing for your immediate dismissal.'

'You know that is never going to happen.' Carlyle skipped after her, hoping that he was right.

AMBROSE WATSON WAS flushed bright red, and sweating heavily as if he'd just run a half-marathon. 'Dolan had a heart attack,' he said sheepishly, 'while he was being interviewed.'

'Fatal?' Joe asked.

'Yes,' Watson admitted reluctantly. 'The paramedics say he was dead before his head hit the desk.'

'Shit happens,' said Carlyle, trying not to look too pleased about it.

'It's just a shame he couldn't have lived another twenty minutes,' Ambrose lamented. 'He died before he could sign his confession. It was being typed up when it happened.'

'That,' said Joe, 'is not good.'

'For fuck's sake, Ambrose,' Carlyle complained, 'couldn't you have stuck a pen in Dolan's hand and approximated his scrawl?'

Watson stared at Carlyle in horror. His mouth opened but no words emerged.

'He's only joking,' Joe said limply. He glared at Carlyle and then smiled at Watson. 'The inspector's sense of humour can be a bit off at times,' he added quickly. 'They've sent him to see a police psychologist about it several times. Basically, stress seems to short-circuit some of the synapses in his brain. It's like he's got a kind of mild version of Tourette's Syndrome, or something.'

Fuck off, thought Carlyle.

Watson kept his own counsel.

'What did Dolan's statement say?' Joe asked, trying to move the conversation on.

'Basically,' Watson explained, 'he blamed everything on the Earl of Falkirk. He admitted being party to conversations about Matthews, but denied plotting to kill her. According to Dolan, the incidents involving Merrett and Shen were down to Ihor Chepoyak. Rather convenient, given that the Ukrainian gentleman has gone to ground somewhere, but there you go.'

'So where does that leave us?' the inspector asked.

'Well,' said Watson, mopping his brow with a ragged paper tissue that he had fished out of his pocket, 'the statement is obviously no longer usable in court. You'll have to find other evidence you can use against Mr Elstree-Ullick.'

'No problem,' said Carlyle, suddenly energised. Ignoring the funny look that Joe was giving him, he shook Watson by the hand. 'Thanks for letting us know about Dolan. But don't bother to tell us about the funeral arrangements. We won't be sending flowers.'

CARLYLE AND JOE patrolled the lobby of Horseferry Road Magistrates' Court in Victoria, situated close to New Scotland Yard. For more than two hours, they had been waiting for a judge to make an initial ruling on the charges against the Earl of Falkirk. It was now well past normal business hours for the court. While Joe mumbled into his phone, explaining to his wife why he would be home late, Carlyle paced about nervously.

In the normal way of things, getting a judge to hear anything after four o'clock in the afternoon was well-nigh impossible. The inspector would have happily let Falkirk spend a night in the cells, but the Earl and his lawyer had enough clout to persuade a Crown Court Recorder by the name of Harold Stephenson to hear their request for bail the same evening. Stephenson, known among the tabloid press as the Hanging Judge of Horseferry, because of his no-nonsense approach towards dealing with miscreants, was very much a nine to five or, rather, a ten to four man. Being prepared to turn up outside of normal working hours was not a courtesy that would have been extended to any regular member of the public. And if he would sit late for the Earl, who knew what other favours might be granted? Unbelievably, Falkirk might actually be allowed to walk free while awaiting trial.

It crossed Carlyle's mind that Stephenson might even be one of Falkirk's clients. The idea made the acid in the inspector's stomach bubble, but it was complete speculation and he forced himself to drop such a thought.

As Joe finished his call, the look on his face suggested that his wife, Anita, had shown only a limited understanding of his circumstances. He slumped on a nearby bench and yawned. Carlyle sat down next to him. All they could do now was wait.

Ten minutes later, the click-clack of heels on the stone floor caused both of them to look up. Out of uniform, Commander Carole Simpson looked like she was heading off for a night on the town. As she approached them, however, even the make-up could not hide the ashen look on her face.

The pain in Carlyle's stomach intensified. 'What's going on?' he asked by way of greeting.

Simpson signalled for Joe to come closer, then looked around to make sure no one was within earshot. 'The judge has granted bail,' she said quietly.

'That's not possible,' said the two policemen in angry unison.

'Keep your voices down!' she hissed, stepping even closer. 'You know very well that it is.'

'We've been hanging around here for ages, waiting for the hearing to be called,' Joe objected.

'The judge didn't ask to hear from you. The Crown Prosecution Service vigorously opposed bail, but his lawyer gave the necessary assurances.'

'Necessary assurances, my arse,' Carlyle snorted. 'The bloody CPS have fucked us.' All of them knew that the track record of the Crown Prosecution Service in London was extremely poor. Mismanagement of cases meant criminals were far more likely to skate before or during a trial than anywhere else in England and Wales. Cases were poorly prepared, and results were generally so bad that defendants had more chance of having their cases dropped than of being found Not Guilty by a jury.

'That's it,' said Joe, shaking his head. 'He'll be off.'

'He's going into a clinic,' Simpson explained. 'His lawyer claims he has suffered from a mental and physical breakdown as a result of police harassment, and therefore needs to go into rehab.'

'Rubbish!' said Joe. 'What that little arsehole needs is a good thrashing.'

'It might have helped if you had got a police doctor to see him,' Simpson rebuked them.

'There wasn't time,' Carlyle said. 'Did they make him surrender his passport?'

'No.'

'For fuck's sake!' Carlyle stamped his foot on the floor in frustration. 'He'll do a runner.'

'He left along with his lawyer fifteen minutes ago,' Simpson said matter-of-factly. 'For us it's now over.'

'Bollocks,' Carlyle raged.

Again, Simpson ignored his petulance. 'You've done a good job,' she said, 'and more than a good job. I'm proud of you both.'

Carlyle felt a frisson of embarrassment slither down his spine. Never good at accepting compliments, particularly in the face of abject failure, he stared at the floor.

'That's the truth.' Simpson smiled weakly. 'I know you boys don't do all that touchy-feely stuff, but I am truly proud of the way in which you haven't let this one go, but pursued it all the way to the end. You did the right thing.'

'It's not the end,' Carlyle protested.

'It is for us,' Simpson said firmly. 'It's down to the CPS now and you have to leave it to the lawyers. This guy will not get a free ride just because of who he is. This whole thing has gone too far, way too far. No one is forgetting that a policewoman died here. Or that Merrett was tortured to death. Or that Shen was seriously injured.'

'The fucker has just walked!' Carlyle looked around helplessly, as if for something to kick.

'The judge also granted a media-gagging order,' Simpson stood her ground, giving Carlyle a knowing look, 'so no running off to your friends at the bloody BBC.'

Trying to look inscrutable, Carlyle said nothing.

'I will speak to you later in the week,' Simpson concluded, buttoning up her coat. 'I am sure you have plenty of other things to be getting on with. There always comes a time when you have to leave a case behind. This is such a time.'

Carlyle kept his eyes to the ground as he listened to her footsteps receding across the stone floor. The only thought filling his head was how he continued to fail that little girl he had found in the park.

Joe gave him a consoling pat on the shoulder. 'Drink?'

Carlyle pondered the offer for a moment. 'Won't Anita be pissed off if you don't get home?'

'Fuck it,' said Joe. 'Just a quick drink . . . or maybe two.' He grinned. 'We need it. She'll understand.'

'Good woman,' Carlyle said, trying to smile.

'Yes,' said Joe happily. 'Yes, she is.'

Chapter Thirty

WITH HIS FINGER hovering over the send button, Carlyle scanned his report one last time. *In conclusion*, it read, *it appears that the victim died as a result of asphyxiation while indulging in a sex act on his own.* Nice word 'indulging', Carlyle thought. The silly little sod had accidentally hanged himself with a pair of women's knickers. According to the pathologist's report, he hadn't even climaxed. He shook his head. 'What a way to go!'

The fact that the victim had been some mini-television celebrity had got the papers interested, and the story had lasted for a couple of days. If nothing else, it had provided the inspector with an amusing interlude in the slow, boring weeks since Falkirk had escaped his grasp.

As expected, the Earl had disappeared. Having been due in court two days ago, Carlyle was not in the least surprised when the man failed to turn up. His lawyer – the statuesque Ms Stuart – had explained to the judge that her client was being treated for depression 'at an unknown location'. Happily, the judge was not Harold Stephenson this time round, but a low-key and sensible magistrate called Joe Davies. Having examined the paperwork, Davies issued a warrant for Falkirk's immediate arrest, with a minimum of fuss.

However, that was a warrant that no one expected would be served any time soon.

AS HE PUSHED his latest report into police cyberspace, the inspector's mobile started vibrating on his desk. He picked it up: no number identified. Did he want to answer it? Probably not. He hit the receive button. 'John Carlyle . . .'

'John?'

Didn't I just say that? he thought crossly. 'Yes.'

'It's Rose – Rose Scripps from CEOP.'

'Of course,' he said, his mood instantly softening. 'How are you?'

'I've found Falkirk!'

Carlyle took the phone from his ear and held it in front of his face, looking at it in quiet bemusement.

'John?'

He returned it to his ear. 'Yes?'

'I said, I've—'

'How?'

'He's in *Paris Match*.'

'What?'

'Last week's *Paris Match* – it's like a French version of *Hello*.'

'Yes, yes.' He knew what the damn magazine was. Helen would bring home an occasional copy, and Carlyle wasn't averse to taking a sneaky peek at the photos of the topless actresses.

'Someone left a copy on the tube, and I picked it up and started leafing though it. There's a small picture and story on page seven – *Royal bad boy drying out at Swiss clinic* . . . yada, yada . . . then a quote from a "friend" saying that he's trying to turn over a new leaf.'

'So he's in Switzerland?' Carlyle asked, more than interested now.

'Yes. Or at least he was recently. Some place called the Kippe Clinic.' She spelt out the name. 'Does this mean we can get him now?'

'It means that we can bloody well try!'

Chapter Thirty-one

'Okay, Mum, no problem. I'll definitely be back by then. Of course I understand. Bye.'

Rose Scripps tossed the mobile onto the dashboard of their unmarked Peugeot, the cheapest rental they could find at Geneva Airport. After drumming her fingers on the steering wheel for several moments, she turned to Carlyle and sighed. 'I've got to be back home by tomorrow morning.'

Sitting in the passenger seat, a mute Carlyle stared through the windscreen at the almost empty car park. Less than a quarter of a mile away, the Kippe Clinic glinted in the weak sunshine. Nothing had travelled along the narrow tarmac road leading down to the single-storey glass building for more than an hour.

'My mother's off on holiday,' Rose explained apologetically, 'so she can't look after Louise any longer.'

'Where's she going?'

'Devon.'

'A bit cold there at this time of year?'

'She has a sister down there, near Totnes. We've visited a few times. It's nice.'

Carlyle grunted. He'd never been to Devon in his life and didn't feel like he was missing anything.

'Anyway, I'll have to pick up my daughter.'

'Of course.' Carlyle felt embarrassed by the amateurishness of their set-up: the fight against international crime laid low by a lack of childcare. He was unhappy with Joe for putting him in this position; unhappier with *himself* for putting him in this position. Joe had half-heartedly volunteered to come along, but he had family problems too. Come to think of it, so did Carlyle. Helen's patience regarding this case was wearing mighty thin. And when he explained he'd be heading for Switzerland with Rose Scripps in tow, his wife had become decidedly frosty. 'Do what you have to do,' had been her final comment.

'I'm sorry,' Rose continued, 'but it has been three days already, and I didn't know how long you were thinking of waiting here.'

'No problem,' he said.

'Anyway,' she went on, 'this is looking like a wild-goose chase.'

'Yeah,' he agreed reluctantly.

'Even if Falkirk turns up,' Rose persisted, already talking herself on to the flight home, 'and we get him, he'll try and stay here in Switzerland.'

'We have a warrant.'

'Mm.' She glanced at the clock on the dashboard. It read 10.53 a.m. 'The afternoon flight is at five-thirty.'

'I know,' Carlyle nodded, admitting defeat. If Rose was heading back home, there was no point in him staying either. Apart from anything else, he needed her to get him around, as he couldn't drive. 'We'll call it a day at two o'clock, get something to eat, and be at the airport by four. Plenty of time.' Gazing down over the town of Villeneuve, past the Grangette Nature Reserve and across Lake Geneva, he felt a very long way from Charing Cross. 'It must be tough,' he said diplomatically, 'being a single parent.'

'You just get on with it.' Rose shrugged. 'Most of the time it's fine. It's not like I have to worry about juggling trips abroad too often.'

Carlyle smiled. 'Me neither.'

'What about your wife?'

Carlyle tensed. 'What about her?'

'Doesn't she mind you being here?' Meaning: *being here with me?*

Carlyle chose his next words carefully. 'She understands that sometimes I don't have control over where my job takes me – although I work very hard at making sure I'm not away from home any more than is absolutely necessary.' Meaning: *subject closed.* Bored, he flipped through the glossy brochure for the Kippe Clinic resting on his lap. 'How much is 30,000 Swiss Francs?'

'About . . .' Rose Scripps did the calculation in her head, 'almost twenty thousand pounds – something like that.'

'Fucking hell!' Carlyle let out a low whistle. 'Imagine spending twenty grand on two weeks of revitalisation and regeneration stress reduction therapies.'

'Is that what Falkirk is doing?'

'No idea.' Carlyle flipped the page. 'Listen to this: *We are leading international experts in illnesses common in the global, de-industrialised, post post-modern society in which we live – disorders and illness related to an individual's capability of coping with factors such as stress, daily frustrations, highly competitive work environments, anxiety and unsorted anger.*

'Stress is for rich people,' Rose mused. 'The term itself was only invented in the 1930s.'

'What is it, anyway?' Carlyle asked, though not interested in the slightest.

'Technically it is defined as a non-specific response of the body to a demand for change.'

'Sounds like crap to me.'

'What a sensitive soul you are!' Rose laughed.

'That's me.' Carlyle tossed the brochure into the back and grabbed a pair of binoculars from under his seat, bought specially for their trip at Field & Trek on Maiden Lane in Covent Garden. Getting out of the car, he scanned the vista with the practised incompetence of the occasional tourist. The clinic lay off to his left, maybe 300 feet further down the mountain. On one side extended lush green fields, on the other a small forest. A small group of gardeners was tending flower beds at the front of the building, and a couple of cleaning staff stood enjoying a cigarette and a natter by a side door.

Switching his attention to the spa centre on the far side of the clinic, he could make out the half-Olympic-size pool, surrounded by recliners, through the floor-to-ceiling windows. The pool itself was empty but, in the far corner, Carlyle could discern a blonde masseuse vigorously working on a guest on a massage table. Readjusting his towel, the man sat up as she handed him a small bottle of water.

'At last.' Plonking the binoculars down on the car roof, Carlyle slipped round the bonnet of the car and headed rapidly across the car park.

'Where are you going?' Rose yelled after him, struggling to get out of the vehicle.

'It's him. Hurry up!'

'John . . . here!'

He half-turned, just in time to catch the small canister as it flew towards him. He looked at it nestling in his hand: it was about as tall as a Coke can, and half as wide. It could have been a small container of shaving foam, or maybe an asthma inhaler.

'Pepper spray,' Rose explained. 'If he gives you any trouble, aim for the face.'

'Nice one,' he grinned, shooting off a little burst downwind. 'Thanks.'

'I brought it specially from London.'

'Excellent!' Another gold star for Heathrow airport security. 'Not necessarily legal, but just the job.' He began moving again.

'What are you going to do?' she called.

That, Carlyle thought, is a very stupid question. Lengthening his stride, he hit the grass beyond the tarmac and began running downhill towards the building.

Chapter Thirty-two

By the time Carlyle reached the clinic, he was out of breath. A kitchen helper was standing by an open door, an unlit cigarette in her mouth. The woman nodded at Carlyle and began fiddling in her pocket for a box of matches. Nodding back, Carlyle slipped past and stepped inside, moving into a long corridor which, he guessed, led towards the back of the building. Ten yards down, on his left, was a set of doors leading to the swimming pool. Pushing them open, he found Falkirk standing in front of him, dressed in jeans, T-shirt and a pair of loafers.

'Inspector.' Falkirk frowned. 'What are you doing here?'

'I'm here for you.' Stepping closer, Carlyle could see that his quarry's pupils were hugely dilated, a clear indication of drug use, and he looked unsteady on his feet. There were dark rings round the eyes and his face was puffy. He looked exhausted. All in all, the man was hardly an advert for two weeks' R&R in the Alps.

'Me?' Falkirk made a half-hearted attempt at a smile.

Carlyle's smile was equally false. 'I have a warrant for your arrest,' he said stiffly, patting his jacket pocket. After the cold outside, the heat of the spa made him feel suddenly drowsy. He stifled a yawn, the strong smell of chlorine reminding him of the days – more than thirty years before – when his dad had made him train with the Hammersmith Penguin Swimming Club at the Fulham Baths.

'A warrant? I don't think so,' said Falkirk warily, not coming any closer.

Snapping from his reverie, Carlyle pulled the envelope out of his pocket and held it up for the Earl to see. 'It's all over, Gordon,' he said. 'Now we have to go back to London.'

'No one calls me that.' Falkirk took a couple of steps backwards. 'And no one tells me what to do.'

Carlyle moved towards him. 'We have to go now. We have a flight to catch.'

Falkirk grinned as he looked past Carlyle. 'I don't think so.'

Carlyle half-turned to see two security guards take up position on either side of him. Each man had a 9mm SIG-Sauer P220 semi-automatic pistol holstered at his side, standard Swiss Army issue.

'Police,' proclaimed Carlyle, holding up a hand.

'Do they look like they give a toss?' Falkirk snorted.

Not in the slightest, Carlyle thought, girding his loins for the trouble ahead.

As the first man reached for his gun, the inspector gave him three seconds of the pepper spray. Just like in the training video, the guy dropped his gun, fell to his knees and began clawing at his face. Carlyle then turned to his colleague, who backed away rapidly, tripping over a handily placed float and stumbling into the swimming pool. Ignoring Falkirk's hysterical laughter, Carlyle waited for the guy's head to pop back up to the surface, and gave him a spray too. With the security guards now engaged in synchronised screaming, Carlyle regarded the tube in his hand with barely concealed admiration. This is great stuff, he thought. I must remember to get some of my own once I get home. Stepping back, he gave the kneeling man a satisfying kick in the ribs that sent him tumbling into the water after his colleague. Carlyle booted the SIG-Sauer into the pool for good measure, and looked up.

Falkirk was gone.

IT TOOK THE inspector a couple of seconds to spot the Earl, who was now sprinting across the lawn outside, heading for the nearest trees, which were maybe 300 metres further up the mountain. Carlyle shook his head. 'Where the hell are you going?' he said to himself, wondering if he had the stamina to catch the younger man.

Outside, the air had darkened. Vicious-looking black clouds scudded across the sky and Carlyle could smell rain in the air. A fat droplet of water exploded on the gravel right in front of his feet, with the promise of much more to come. Head down, blood pumping, he took a deep breath and charged ahead – running straight into Rose, who had suddenly appeared in front of the clinic.

'Falkirk!' she gasped, as he bounced off her.

'I know,' said Carlyle, hopping from foot to foot, reluctant to stop moving as he eyed the fleeing figure in front of them. Belatedly, he realised that she was clutching her face. Pulling her hand away, he saw a nasty cut under her right eye, which was already half-closed. 'Did he hit you?'

'I tried to stop him.'

'Are you okay?'

'Yeah. Can you catch him?'

'Sure,' Carlyle quipped, despite the fact that Falkirk now had a lead of about 150 metres as he headed for the treeline. He handed the pepper spray back to Rose. 'Get inside. Make sure the security goons don't do a runner. Give them another blast of the spray if necessary. And get someone to call the local police.'

SETTING A STEADY pace, Carlyle tried to ignore the burning sensation in his chest. Not for the first time recently, he wished that he'd spent more time in the gym. The adrenaline rush gained from clobbering those two security guys was wearing off, and he began to feel a creeping heaviness in his legs. The fact that he wasn't exactly dressed for the occasion didn't help either.

Not wishing to completely knacker himself before he caught up with his quarry, he let Falkirk stretch his lead slightly, confident that ultimately the man had nowhere to go. As far as the inspector could tell, the Earl had left the clinic with nothing that might help him evade capture for any length of time. Maybe he had a little cash in the pockets of his trousers but without a credit card, mobile phone or passport, he was well and truly fucked. That thought made Carlyle smile. Despite his own discomfort, he was perfectly happy to let the bastard continue spending his day running round a Swiss mountain in the cold and rain – with a bit of luck the blue-blooded bastard might even catch pneumonia.

As Falkirk disappeared among the trees, Carlyle slowed his pace even further. It took him another couple of minutes to reach the edge of the forest. Peering into the gloom, he could see that it was composed of a mix of pine and spruce trees, planted closely together in precise rows. Hesitating, he looked back the way he had come. Rose had disappeared inside the building. Surely, someone must have called the gendarmerie by now. Assuming that the cavalry would be coming from Villeneuve, situated just down the mountain by the side of the lake, or maybe from Montreux next door, the police should be able to reach the clinic in ten minutes or so. But when he listened for the sound of sirens, there was nothing.

Bloody cops, Carlyle thought. They are all the same the world over; always taking their own sweet time; never around when you need them.

He tried to imagine what Falkirk's plan of action might be. To his right was a narrow, muddy path leading deeper into the forest. Carlyle could make out a number of footprints, although he had no idea whether any of them belonged to Falkirk. Careful not to lose his footing, he set off again.

Less than twenty yards into the trees, he could no longer see back to the open ground at the edge of the forest. Apart from the path he was following, the inspector had no sense of where he had come from: it was just trees, trees and more trees. They all looked the same to him. Surrounded by nature, he suddenly felt rather sorry for himself.

Any feelings of self-pity were cut short when a lump of wood was smashed across the back of his head. Carlyle staggered forward. A second blow sent him to his knees and he felt cold mud seeping through the fabric of his trousers. He stretched his hands out in front of him to halt his fall, but a third blow sent him down fully. The last thought to pop into his head, before the lights went out, was, *Oh shit!*

A BOOT IN the ribs brought him back out of the blackness. As he came to, Carlyle realised that he had mud in his mouth, a piece of twig up his nose, and the mother of all headaches. Blinking, he waited for another kick. When it did not come he lay still, trying to clear his head. He listened as hard as he could, but still there were no sirens. A bird squawked overhead and he heard footsteps approaching from somewhere behind him.

'On your feet!' Falkirk grabbed him by the hair and, with a grunt, pulled him upright. Feeling a serrated blade against his neck, Carlyle found his feet. Looking down along the end of his nose, he recognised the familiar red handle of an outsize Swiss Army knife.

'Rather appropriate, don't you think?' Falkirk remarked grimly. His pupils seemed as big as pennies. For the first time, it occurred to Carlyle that he might have a real problem on his hands.

'You are about to be done in by the finest technology that the Swiss have to offer,' Falkirk continued. He pulled the knife from Carlyle's neck and waved it airily above his head. 'It was either that or drowning you in chocolate.'

'There are worse ways to go, I suppose.' The inspector gingerly felt the back of his head. Even more gingerly, he gave it a gentle shake. The pain bounced around his brain for a few seconds, then resumed its residency in the base of his skull. He tried to step away casually from his drugged-up captor, but Falkirk skipped forward, pressing the knife firmly against his windpipe.

'This is getting out of hand,' Carlyle coughed.

'You should have left me alone,' Falkirk snarled.

'What are you on?' Carlyle asked, injecting as much reasonableness into his voice as he could manage. 'Crystal meth? Speed? Cocaine?'

'Poppers,' Falkirk replied casually.

Poppers, okay. Carlyle struggled to sift through what he knew about poppers – amyl nitrite, used to enhance sexual pleasure. As far as he could recall, they weren't supposed to make you violent. 'Look,' he said quietly, taking each word slowly in case he had called it wrong and Falkirk tried to chop out his Adam's apple, 'we have to go back. This needs to get sorted out. It *will* get sorted out, but we have to go to London to do that.'

'No!' A look of panic flashed through Falkirk's eyes as he flicked the blade away from Carlyle's chin and thrust it twice into the inspector's stomach, sawing at his ribcage.

'Fuck!' Carlyle staggered back, holding his gut.

He looked down, expecting to see his own entrails spilling through his fingers. Almost disappointingly, there wasn't that much to see – and only a little blood. The pain, however, was intense.

Am I dying? he wondered.

How fucking banal.

Is this really it?

Chapter Thirty-three

TRIPPING OVER AN exposed root, Carlyle fell backwards. Looking up, he focused on a patch of grey sky between two trees. I need to see blue sky, he thought, spitting out a lump of phlegm. I need to see blue sky again before I die.

Falkirk fell on top of him before the inspector could move. With one hand on Carlyle's neck, he brandished the knife in front of the policeman's face. 'You should have done what you were told and left well alone,' he hissed. 'Because now you will die.'

Feeling all the energy drain from his body, Carlyle closed his eyes and waited. Still there was no sign of sirens coming to his aid.

What he did hear was the click of the safety-catch on a semi-automatic being released.

'Get up!'

Carlyle opened his eyes to see Ihor Chepoyak pulling Falkirk up by the collar of his T-shirt. Dressed in full combat gear, complete with green and black face-paint, Ihor had the barrel of a Fort-12 CURZ pistol gently caressing the Earl's temple.

'Throw away the knife.'

Doing what he was told, Falkirk threw the Swiss Army knife into a muddy puddle about three feet away. 'What are *you* doing here?' he asked, a nervous quaver betraying any attempt to sound indignant.

'I'm here to kill you,' Ihor said, almost apologetically.

'Why?' Falkirk asked, his bottom lip visibly trembling now.

'Why? Why?' Ihor made a face. 'This is not like one of those movies where you have to explain everything just to give the victim time to escape. What does it matter anyway? Your life has less than a minute left to run. Less than ten seconds, in fact.'

'But—'

'But nothing.' Ihor pulled the trigger, and the crack of the 9mm Kurz round sent the birds flying from the surrounding trees. Slowly, Falkirk keeled over into the undergrowth, a surprised look on his face.

Ihor turned to Carlyle. 'Not at all like the movies, huh?'

'No.' Thinking of Shen and Merrett, Carlyle remembered rule number one – always humour the man with the gun. 'When it comes to the cinema, I've always been a fan of more violence and less dialogue myself,' he said.

'Me also,' said Ihor.

Now AT LAST he could hear the fucking sirens. This had been a truly outstanding effort by the Swiss police.

'Time for me to go,' Ihor declared. He saw Carlyle eyeing the Fort-12 nervously. 'Don't worry,' he grinned, 'I'm not going to pop you. Olga gave me strictest instructions that you were not to be hurt.'

Feebly trying to massage away his headache, Carlyle rubbed the back of his neck. Not hurt was stretching it a bit, but at least he was still alive. 'Olga?'

The sirens grew louder.

'She likes you,' Ihor smirked. 'It is your good fortune that you are already married!'

The sirens suddenly stopped and were soon replaced by shouting and a general commotion somewhere in the middle distance. Presumably the gendarmes would be here within a few minutes.

Ihor helped Carlyle to his feet. 'You didn't see me.'

Carlyle looked down at Falkirk sprawled on the ground with a bullet in his brain, and liked what he saw. He shook his head.

Ihor tapped the handle of the pistol. 'Also, this is the same weapon as the one used in London, so no ballistics comparisons.'

Carlyle thought about Merrett and Shen. What about justice for them? Surely he owed them better than this shabby deal?

Seeing how the inspector's mind was now working, Ihor gripped the pistol tightly. 'I gave you Falkirk,' he said slowly. 'He was the main man. Either we are even, or there is a problem . . .'

Carlyle stared at the gun. Under the circumstances, 'even' sounded good. He nodded. 'Understood.'

'Good!' Ihor stuck the pistol in the waistband of his combat trousers and extended a hand.

Carlyle shook it. 'Thank you.'

'It's nothing.' Ihor shrugged. 'You were lucky. If you want my advice, maybe being a policeman is not right for you.' He spat in the direction of Falkirk's corpse. 'Not if a guy like that can get the better of you. You should really think about doing something else.'

Carlyle laughed weakly. 'Maybe you're right.'

The shouting was louder now. Carlyle reckoned that they must be almost into the forest, perhaps less than a 100 metres away.

'I'd better get going,' Ihor said. He turned and began jogging away, heading along the trail. In less than ten seconds, he was out of sight. Wearily taking a seat on a fallen tree, the inspector waited for his rescuers to arrive.

Chapter Thirty-four

No question, if you had to go to jail, Switzerland was a good place to do so. The Service de Police holding cell on Rue du Lac 118 was cool, quiet and spotlessly clean. Sitting on a tiled bench, his back resting against the wall, Carlyle rather liked it. His wounds were far less serious than Carlyle had originally feared and a generous supply of painkillers left him feeling quite mellow as he dined on takeaway pizza. The coffee left a little to be desired but, happy to be alive, he didn't feel the need to be too picky.

After a couple of hours, he was brought to an interview room and ushered inside. Cleaner and airier than the interview rooms at Charing Cross, it still retained the air of disappointment and despair that infused police stations the world over.

'Any chance of another cup of coffee?' Carlyle asked, as he sat down at the empty desk.

'Someone will be here to interview you soon, Mr Carlyle,' said the young officer who had delivered him here, his English angular and precise.

'It's *Inspector* Carlyle,' Carlyle mumbled. He forced a smile on to his weary face. 'Look, son,' he said, trying to keep the exasperation from his voice, 'I'm a police officer, too.'

The policeman looked at him blankly. 'You are here,' he said stiffly, 'under suspicion of committing a crime.'

'I know, but—'

'In Switzerland, no one is above the law, *Mr* Carlyle,' he said earnestly, 'not even police officers.' Turning, he left the room without another word.

'INSPECTOR CARLYLE?'

He must have dozed off. Slowly coming to, he focused on the small paper cup that had been placed on the table in front of him. Grabbing it, he downed the espresso in two gulps and sat back, waiting for the caffeine to do its job. 'Thank you.'

The man in front of him nodded. Not in uniform, Carlyle guessed he must be in his late thirties. He had short, salt-and-pepper hair and a day's stubble, which suggested to Carlyle that this little incident had interrupted the man's day off. That would help explain his pissed-off expression.

Dropping a thin folder on the desk, the new arrival sat down on the opposite side of the table. 'I am Jonas Chauzy,' he said quietly, in accentless English, 'First Deputy Chief at Fedpol.'

Carlyle looked at him blankly.

'*Office fédéral de la police*,' Chauzy explained. 'We are part of the Federal Department of Justice and Police. I deal with socio-political issues such as the co-existence of Swiss and foreign nationals and the fight against crime.' He gave Carlyle a hard look. 'Normally it is a fairly straightforward job, but today . . .'

Carlyle shrugged. 'Sorry about any inconvenience.'

'Inconvenience?' Leaning back in his chair, the look on Chauzy's face was part-smile, part-grimace. 'Inspector, I have one man dead and two more in hospital.'

'The dead man was nothing to do with me,' Carlyle said evenly.

Chauzy opened the file to look at his notes. 'Just before he died, you were pursuing him . . .'

Carlyle had already given an initial statement and he knew his lines well. The key to getting out of here quickly was to keep it simple and not worry about any repetition. 'Someone hit me from behind. When I woke up again, Falkirk was lying dead on the ground and your guys were just arriving.'

Chauzy studied him doubtfully.

'The forensics will back that up,' Carlyle continued evenly.

Chauzy glanced at his folder, but still said nothing.

After a few moments, Carlyle decided to cut to the chase. 'Am I going to be charged with anything?'

Chauzy closed the folder and rubbed his temples. 'There is also the question of the assault on Frank Furrer and Marcus Voney at the Kippe Clinic.'

'That was a simple matter of self-defence,' Carlyle said quickly. 'They were threatening to shoot me.'

The First Deputy Chief stood up and leaned across the table, his jaw clenched. A black look passed across his face and, for a moment, Carlyle wondered if he was about to become a victim of police brutality. However, whatever violence may have been in his heart, Chauzy quickly thought better of it. Taking a step backwards, he stuck the file back under his arm and placed a hand against the door. 'You are free to go, Inspector. Your colleague is waiting for you at the airport.' He looked at his watch. 'There is still a flight that you can catch this evening.'

Carlyle bowed his head slightly. 'Thank you.'

'Do not thank me,' Chauzy said sharply. 'If it was my decision, you would not be walking away from these criminal acts so easily. But unfortunately, it is out of my hands. It would seem that your powerful friends in London have pulled some strings.'

Powerful friends? Carlyle wondered. *What powerful friends?*

'This has become a political issue,' Chauzy sighed. 'The Metropolitan Police made representations to the Department of Justice, and the British Consulate in Geneva also intervened.'

'You have to remember that I came here with a legitimate warrant,' Carlyle interjected.

Somehow, Chauzy managed to look even more unimpressed. 'That is a matter for some debate. However, we are prepared to accept that you personally did not shoot the Earl of Falkirk, and as you clearly know nothing about the person or persons who did . . .'

Sarcasm in Switzerland – who would have thought it?

'. . . we will not detain you any longer. There is a driver waiting for you outside. Just, please, do not return here. You will not be welcome in Switzerland again.' Pushing open the door, Chauzy stepped out into the corridor and was gone.

That sounds like a fair deal to me, thought Carlyle, as he savoured his rediscovered freedom. *Very fair indeed.*

Chapter Thirty-five

STANDING AT THE bar of the Royal China Club, a seafood restaurant on Baker Street, Carlyle scanned the front page of that morning's *Daily Mirror*. ROYAL EXECUTION screamed the 72-point headline, above a photograph of Falkirk partying somewhere with a girl on each arm. Inside, the story was spread across pages 4, 5, 6 and 7. Happily, it was all filler, speculation and reaction – with no mention of the inspector himself. Content that there was nothing in the reporting that could add to his problems, he quickly turned to the sports pages.

Having been summoned to the club by Commander Carole Simpson, he was anticipating a major bollocking. After almost half an hour, he had read the *Mirror* from front to back, and was feeling weak with hunger. Finally, he saw Simpson's dining companion rise from their table, give the commander a quick peck on the cheek, then take his leave. A few minutes later, the inspector was ushered over to the same table and invited to take the empty seat.

The dining room was full of diners and the noise-level was high. Carlyle sat with his hands on his lap, avoiding eye-contact. Blowing gently on her tea, Simpson adopted an air of serenity.

A drink would be nice, Carlyle thought. He looked around hopefully but the waiters knew better than to offer him anything and steadfastly refused to catch his eye. Deciding that his boss's inscrutable act had gone on for long enough, he leaned forward and rested his forearms on the table. 'Thanks for getting me out of jail.'

Simpson replaced her cup carefully on its saucer and signalled for the bill. 'What exactly happened over there?'

'Well . . .' Carlyle proceeded to give her the same story he had told to the Swiss police – throwing in a few extra irrelevant details to give some colour and the suggestion of candour.

Simpson listened impassively. When Carlyle had finished his little story, she said nothing for a few moments. He could sense the debate going on inside her about whether to call him on his dishonesty or whether just to let it slide. The bill arrived, and Carlyle eyed her corporate credit card enviously as it was slipped into the machine. After typing in her PIN and taking the receipt, Simpson looked him directly in the eye. 'It was a bloody nightmare,' she said, almost keeping a smile from creeping across her lips. 'In the end, I had to get the ambassador himself involved.'

'I thought it was the consul,' Carlyle grinned.

'You think it's funny, John,' she admonished, 'don't you?'

'What?'

'Going over to Switzerland – how can anyone cause trouble in Switzerland, for God's sake? It's the place where you go to die! – and creating just about the biggest international incident since World War Two.' She ran a hand through her hair. 'For goodness' sake, how do you manage it?'

'I was simply executing a warrant,' Carlyle said humbly.

Sticking her credit card and the receipt safely in her bag, she leaned over the table and lowered her voice. 'Just as long as you didn't execute a member of the ruddy royal family.'

'No, no.' Carlyle stiffened. 'As I said, I had nothing to do with that.'

'Nothing? Are you sure?'

'Completely,' he nodded solemnly. 'As you know, I was assaulted myself.'

'Don't try and play the victim with me, Inspector,' Simpson said tartly, 'it simply doesn't suit you. Those two goons you put in hospital have hired some ambulance-chaser over here in London. This isn't going to go away quietly – the Met is facing an embarrassing civil suit.'

'It won't be the first time,' Carlyle replied sullenly. He'd had enough of acting the penitent soldier, and wondered if there was going to be a point to this meeting.

'I have had to tell the authorities, both here and in Berne, that you will be disciplined very harshly.'

Here we go, Carlyle thought. 'Which means what?'

'Which means,' she said slowly, 'that you had better keep a very, very low profile for a very, very long time.'

Carlyle stared at her.

'Amazingly,' said Simpson, 'despite causing chaos abroad and a tabloid media frenzy here at home, there are still some people who think you have done a good job.'

Carlyle felt his stomach rumble. There were two small chocolates that the waiter had brought with the bill. He grabbed one. 'Some people as in you?' he asked, stuffing it in his mouth.

'No.' Simpson shook her head. 'I think that you have been very unprofessional.' She handed him the final chocolate. 'Not to mention economical with the truth.'

Caryle bit into the other one. It was easier to lie with something in your mouth. 'I have told you what I know,' he said, with a small shrug.

'Anyway,' said Simpson, obviously knowing when she was flogging a dead horse, 'Sir Ewen Mayflower seems to have taken quite a shine to you.'

'He didn't mention the vase, then?'

Simpson gave him a funny look. 'What?'

Carlyle coughed. 'Nothing.'

'He says that there are people in Buckingham Palace – "very high-up people", were his precise words – who are very pleased with your efforts.'

'What?' Carlyle laughed. 'You think the Queen herself wanted Falkirk offed?'

'I don't know,' Simpson grinned, getting to her feet, signalling that their little chat was at an end. 'Maybe the Duke of Edinburgh?'

'Yeah,' Carlyle laughed, finally catching the eye of a waiter and gesturing to him for a menu. 'I could understand that. You wouldn't want to mess with that old bugger.'

Chapter Thirty-six

SITTING AT HIS desk in Charing Cross, the inspector aimlessly surfed the internet while studiously avoiding doing any work. If Simpson wanted him to keep a low profile that was fine by him. Picking up his mobile, he rang Helen. It was a while since he had taken his wife to lunch, and he fancied a burrito from the Mexican place near her office. But the call went straight to voicemail, and he hung up without leaving a message. If she didn't call him back in time, he would grab a sandwich. Yawning, he returned his attention to the story of an Oscar-winning actress whose husband was being 'linked' with a tattoo model. 'Tattoo model,' Carlyle mused, marvelling at the girl's picture. 'Now that's what I call a proper job.'

Joe Szyszkowski appeared at his shoulder, holding an over-sized doughnut, covered in white icing, in front of his mouth. In his other hand he carried a page ripped from a magazine. 'Take a look at this,' he said, waving the story at Carlyle, 'from the *Sunday Times* Rich List. It says: "*like us, the Queen has suffered from the effects of falling share prices and property values . . .*" yada, yada,

yada . . . "*excluding the vast Crown Estate and royal art collection, worth more than £16 billion – but her wealth in jewellery, horses, stamps and paintings takes her to £270 million . . .*'"

Carlyle was still captivated by the tattoo model. 'My heart bleeds.'

'I thought it might.'

'Only in England could you try and claim someone worth more than sixteen billion quid was only worth two hundred and seventy million.'

Joe shook his head. 'Imagine being down to your last two hundred odd mill.'

'But she isn't,' Carlyle snapped. 'That's the point.'

'I suppose.' Taking a large, almost ceremonial bite of his doughnut, Joe sent pieces of icing flying all over Carlyle's desk.

'Hey!' Carlyle squawked in protest.

'Sorry,' said Joe, in a manner suggesting that he was not sorry in the slightest.

'Messy pig,' Carlyle fussed, sweeping the crumbs on to the floor.

Dropping the magazine story on Carlyle's desk, Joe pointed the remainder of his doughnut at the image on his boss's computer screen of a blonde bimbo in a tiny powder-blue bikini pouting for the camera. The tattoos covered so much of her body that it was impossible to work out exactly what they were supposed to represent. 'I see that you're broadening your taste in pornography then,' he joked.

'I'm not sure if I go for the excessively inky look,' Carlyle pondered.

'No need to be coy, Inspector.' Sticking the remainder of the doughnut in his mouth, Joe flopped into a nearby chair.

'Really?' huffed Carlyle. 'Would you go for something like that?'

'Who is she, anyway?'

'Don't you keep up with current affairs?' Carlyle laughed. He then explained the situation with the tattoo model, happy to be talking about something other than his Swiss adventure.

Joe chewed thoughtfully. 'There's no accounting for taste.'

'I guess not.'

'Speaking of which, did you hear that they've closed down Dolan's investment company?'

'United 14?'

'Yeah. Apparently it had assets of more than twenty million quid.'

Carlyle let out a low whistle. 'Not bad. Not exactly in Her Majesty's league, but not to be sniffed at.'

'And they think there might be more of it, stashed away in various companies in the Caymans and the British Virgin Islands. There were loads of documents in Dolan's garage – the finance guys are still going through them.'

'Mm.'

'He had a Porsche and a Range Rover there, too – almost a hundred grand's worth of motors. Plus, he had almost twenty grand in cash under his bed.'

'A real business big-shot,' Carlyle snorted.

'United 14 had almost thirty SO14 or former SO14 guys as its investors,' Joe continued. 'Of those still working, six have already resigned . . .'

'Including that little shit Charlie Adam?'

'Yeah,' Joe nodded, 'he was one of them.'

Carlyle thought about that for a second. 'So maybe he did rather more than just look the other way?'

'Another two have been suspended,' Joe carried on, 'pending a formal investigation. The ones that had already retired have had their police pensions frozen.'

'What about the connection to Falkirk?' Carlyle asked.

'Falkirk's company, Black Prince Elite, was also an investor in United 14.'

'What will happen to the cash?'

'It will either be confiscated or squandered on legal fees if they try and fight it in the courts.'

'Result!' Carlyle punched the air in triumph. 'With a bit of luck, those bent bastards will lose all their cash and run up big legal fees as well.'

'Yeah,' Joe laughed.

'And end up living in cardboard boxes under Charing Cross arches. Sleeping in their own piss and getting arse-raped for their last can of Special Brew.'

'You are a right vindictive bastard,' Joe said admiringly, 'aren't you?'

'Someone's got to be,' said Carlyle humbly.

'There's more,' said Joe, grinning. 'The chief financial officer at Black Prince was identified as the guy who was in that pod at the London Eye with the underage girl. He was picked up a couple of hours ago. CEOP are questioning him right now.'

'Fuck me sideways,' said Carlyle, grinning himself now. 'I didn't realise that it was bloody Christmas!' He grabbed the mobile from his desk. 'I'd better give Rose a call.'

JOE HAD SLOPED off again, presumably in search of another doughnut. He's putting on too much timber, Carlyle thought. The fitness levels required of policemen these days was abysmal but, even so, there were limits. Joe didn't look like he could run ten yards without suffering a coronary.

His mobile started vibrating on the desk. Helen? Or Rose? He answered it cautiously. 'Hello?'

'Hello, Inspector . . .'

The accent was familiar, but for a second he was thrown. 'This is Carlyle,' he said, sticking to what he knew.

'And this is Olga!'

Olga? Olga! Carlyle struggled to remember her real name. Alexandra . . . Alexandra something. This was not a call that he had ever expected to receive. Sifting one-handed through a pile of papers on his desk, he tried to concentrate. 'What can I do for you?'

'Nice to speak to you too,' Alex Gazizulin replied tartly.

'Where are you?'

'I'm here in London,' she said, her tone bright. 'Why else would I call you?'

Carlyle had long since given up trying to work out what was going on in this woman's head. Deciding to go with the flow, he tried relaxing into the conversation. 'I don't know why you would bother calling me,' he laughed, 'other than to show off, since you are always one step ahead.'

'Very true, Inspector,' she teased, 'but at least you are smart enough to understand that. That makes you much smarter than most men.'

It was a compliment of sorts. 'So? What can I do for you?'

'I have brought you a present.'

'Yes?'

'I have found the girl's mother,' Alex said, sounding highly pleased with herself. 'Alzbetha Tishtenko's mother. And I have brought her from the Ukraine to London.'

'Mm.' Carlyle thought of the small urn still sitting on top of the microwave in his kitchen at home.

'What's the matter?' Alex asked. 'Has the cat got your tongue? I thought you wanted to find her.'

'Yes, yes,' said Carlyle hastily. 'You have done a good thing. Thank you.'

'You are very welcome,' said Alex, sounding somewhat mollified.

'What about the father?'

'The father?' Alex laughed. 'Who knows? The mother certainly doesn't. Anyway, who cares?'

Carlyle grunted something that could have been considered assent. Getting to the bottom of his pile of papers, he still couldn't find what he was looking for. Cursing under his breath, he started again from the top, going through each sheet more carefully this time.

'Men,' Alex mused, 'are basically useless.'

'Yes.' Carlyle was familiar with this line of argument, from Helen's frequent lectures on the subject.

'This one,' Alex continued, warming to her theme, 'is a typical example. He abandoned his child and the mother of his child. Not an uncommon scenario where I come from.'

'Not an uncommon scenario anywhere,' Carlyle interjected.

'He probably drank himself to death years ago. At least, I hope so.'

'We need to meet up,' Carlyle said, thinking it through. 'I've had an idea for Alzbetha's ashes.' He explained his plan.

'Inspector Carlyle,' she purred, 'you are a very thoughtful man. Maybe a bit sentimental also, but that is good. Make the arrangements. I will call you back later.'

'What about you?' Carlyle asked swiftly. He had finally found the piece of paper he was looking for. Tossing everything else on to the floor, he placed the arrest warrant for Alexandra Gazizulin right in front of him.

'This will be my last trip to London for a while,' Alex said. 'We are pulling out of the UK. I have decided it's not worth trying to rebuild our operations here.'

'Now that Falkirk is dead?'

'That wasn't really the major consideration,' she said carefully, 'but it was a factor.'

'Thank you for saving my life, by the way,' Carlyle told her. 'Ihor turned up at just the right moment.'

'My pleasure, Inspector.' He could hear genuine warmth in her voice. 'I am glad that Ihor actually managed to do what he was told, for once.'

'What will happen to him?'

'That is not something you need to worry about,' she snapped, the warmth gone as quickly as it had appeared. 'He compromised our business here, and it will take him a long time to repair his reputation. He will, as the saying goes, be living in the dog's house for some time.'

Better than being dead, Carlyle thought. 'So where will you go next?'

'I don't know,' Alex sighed. 'There are plenty of opportunities. Choosing one is difficult.'

'I can imagine,' he said, though not having a clue.

'One thing I will promise you, however, is that there will be no more trafficking of children. I have put a stop to that. No one under sixteen will be sent away. That is my new rule.'

A misery merchant with a heart of gold! Carlyle didn't know whether to laugh or cry. 'Why not make the minimum age eighteen?' he replied finally.

'Half of our girls are under eighteen, Inspector,' she said calmly – like the CEO of a car-maker explaining the sales breakdown of his different models. 'You have to be realistic. Less than seven per cent of them are under sixteen. *We* have to be realistic. I had to argue for a long time even to get agreement on that. There are many people who do not have the same concerns about such things.'

This conversation was starting to drive Carlyle insane. 'Call me tomorrow,' he said, ending the call before his brain melted.

'DO YOU WANT me to reheat your coffee, or maybe make you a new one?'

In response, Carlyle handed over the untouched latte that had been sitting in front of him for the last twenty minutes. 'Thanks, Marcello.' Seated in the back booth of Il Buffone, with the *Closed* sign on the door, he wished he had the energy to do more than brood over his recent conversation with 'Olga'.

In many ways, the case had been successfully concluded. And now, as an unexpected bonus, it looked like he would get the chance to arrest Alex Gazizulin on suspicion of being an accessory to murder, attempted murder and child-trafficking. He knew that he should focus on the positives of his investigation, even as he continued to focus on the negatives. As the ancient Gaggia machine wheezed into action, he let out a heavy sigh. As far as he could see, the glass would always be half-empty.

Marcello placed the reheated coffee back on the table just as Joe Szyszkowski pushed his way through the door and slumped into the booth opposite Carlyle.

'We're closed,' said Marcello. 'Can't you read the sign on the bloody door?' But his smile gave him away. 'What you havin'?' he asked, as he retreated behind the counter.

Joe held up a hand. 'I'm good, Marcello, thanks. I just need a word with the inspector.'

Marcello grunted and disappeared into his storeroom at the back.

Carlyle took a sip of his coffee and waited for his sergeant to elucidate.

Out of his pocket, Joe pulled a small box, about half the size of a paperback book and a couple of inches thick. He placed it on the table next to Carlyle's mug. 'This arrived for you by courier this afternoon.'

Carlyle could see that the box, wrapped in brown paper, was addressed to him at the station. He looked up at Joe. 'Has it been X-rayed?'

'Yeah,' Joe nodded. 'The scan was a bit inconclusive, but I read the note and assumed it would be okay.' He handed over a crumpled envelope that had already been slit open along the top.

Carlyle unfolded a small sheet of paper and scanned the handwritten note:

Inspector Carlyle,

I wanted to thank you for completing the investigation into the background to Joe Dalton's suicide. From what I gather, my Joe was caught up in some very horrible things, but it is always better to know the truth.

Enclosed is a little memento from my studio, I hope you like it.

Kind regards, Fiona Allcock

ALWAYS BETTER TO know the truth? I'm not sure about that, Carlyle thought morosely, not much cheered by the fact that the taxidermist had sent him a present. He eyed the box suspiciously. 'Open it,' he said to *his* Joe.

Sensing his boss's uncertainty, the sergeant sat back in his seat and shook his head. 'It's addressed to you.'

'Oh, for fuck's sake!' Carlyle stood up and grabbed a knife from behind the counter. Returning to his seat, he carefully removed the wrapping paper. Inside was something resembling an over-sized matchbox. Pushing out the inner tray, he peered inside. Two little black eyes stared back up at him.

'Fuck!' With a shudder, he dropped the box back on to the table.

Laughing, Joe yelled out, 'Marcello, come and see this!'

Wiping his hands on a tea towel, the café proprietor moved round the end of the counter to stand by their table. 'What have you got?'

Carlyle gingerly tilted the box so that he could see inside.

Marcello's eyes grew wide. *'Madre di Dio!* Get that thing out of here! I can't have a dead mouse in my café!'

'But, Marcello,' said Joe, laughing even harder now, 'it's not a rodent – it's a work of art.'

Chapter Thirty-seven

'GET RID OF that bloody thing! I don't want it in the house!'

'But it's a piece of art,' Carlyle protested feebly. 'It's probably worth a few quid.'

'I don't care,' Helen hissed venomously. 'Get it out of here!'

'Okay,' Carlyle shrugged. Closing the box, he dropped the stiffed mouse into the Tesco plastic bag containing the rest of their non-recyclable rubbish. Tying the bag by the handles, he walked out of the kitchen and down the hall. Opening the front door, he placed it carefully beside their welcome mat on the landing. He would take it down to the street on his way to work next morning for the bin men to collect on their 7 a.m. round.

Returning to the kitchen, he boiled the kettle to make a cup of chamomile tea for his wife. In the living room, he found her sitting on the sofa, watching a cooking programme on the television.

'Sorry about the mouse,' he said, carefully handing over the steaming mug.

'Sometimes, John, really!' Helen said. Blowing on her tea, she took a tiny sip and signalled for him to sit beside her. On the screen, a fat bloke was shovelling forkfuls of food into his mouth while making vaguely orgasmic noises.

'We have a problem with Alice,' Helen said, staring at the screen.

'Great. Where is she, by the way?'

'She's having tea at a friend's house. She should be home by eight.'

'Okay, so what's the problem?'

Helen took another sip of her tea. 'She wants to give up karate.'

Carlyle sighed. This was an ongoing battle that he knew he would lose sooner or later. Getting Alice to go to her weekly karate lesson had become a war of attrition. The Wednesday-night class at Jubilee Hall, on the south side of the Covent Garden Piazza, was made up of a friendly group of kids ranging from six to sixteen. The teacher was an urban saint – not only a former World Champion, but also fantastic with the children. Alice had struggled towards her blue belt, but now was demanding that she be allowed to quit. The more her parents tried to persuade her to stick with it, the more insistent she got.

'She seems very determined,' Helen continued. 'She's even called a family meeting.'

The inspector made a face. Everyone in the Carlyle household had the right to call a formal 'family meeting' in order to try and resolve certain issues. It was part of the domestic democracy to which both he and Helen strongly subscribed. Meetings were invariably called by Alice, however, and they normally only had one or two a year. Sometimes they worked, sometimes they didn't. The point was that Alice felt she was being taken seriously.

'I said we'd take her out for her tea next week, to discuss it,' Helen told him.

'Sure,' said Carlyle, wondering if he could afford it.

'My treat,' said Helen, reading his mind.

'Fine,' he said, with no great enthusiasm.

Conversation over, Helen returned her attention to the cooking programme. Bored, Carlyle went back to the kitchen to make himself a cup of green tea. As he was dunking the bag in boiling water, his mobile started buzzing on the worktop next to the sink.

He picked it up. 'Hello?'

'John? It's Carole Simpson.'

'Commander . . .'

'Sorry to call you so late.'

Leaning against the sink, Carlyle took a sip of his tea. 'It's not a problem.'

'Good. Well, I just wanted to let you know of a few developments.'

She sounds distant, Carlyle thought, distracted. He wondered if that meant more problems with her husband. 'Joe already told me about United 14,' he ventured.

'Yes? Okay. I think that we'll get quite a lot out of that – thanks to Mr Dolan's record-keeping.'

'Good.'

'There are a couple of other things though. The first is that there is going to be a review into the workings of SO14. It will be announced next week. The commissioner will try to slip something out under the radar, but the media will probably get hold of it all the same.'

'Don't worry,' Carlyle told her. 'I will keep my mouth shut.'

'I wasn't suggesting—'

'I know, I know. But just for the avoidance of doubt, you don't have to worry about me blabbing to any journos.'

'Good. Thank you.'

'The whole thing will be a load of bollocks anyway,' Carlyle said sourly. 'There will be an investigation that takes months, if not years, then there will be a few cosmetic changes and everyone will go on wasting taxpayers' money with gay abandon.'

Simpson sighed. 'Doesn't being so cynical all the time tire you out?'

'It's not cynicism,' Carlyle harrumphed, 'it's realism.'

'The other thing,' said Simpson, clearly keen to move the conversation along, 'is Alexa Matthews and Heather Ramsden. The case is now being closed. Their deaths will be attributed to Dolan.'

'I think that he probably *was* responsible,' Carlyle mused. 'Anyway, thanks for letting me know.' He ended the call and looked out of the kitchen window, across the London gloom towards the Thames, and the lights of the London Eye, thinking of nothing.

THE NEXT DAY, wrapped up in an overcoat and scarf, Carlyle sat under one of the large paraffin heaters outside Bar Italia on Frith Street, cradling a demitasse containing the last drops of his double macchiato, in order to stop the over-zealous waitress snatching it away too soon. It was a beautiful morning, clear blue skies, with an invigorating nip in the air, and the good citizens of Soho were going about their business in their usual desultory fashion. Having nothing to say, Carlyle idly watched a young woman walking a trio of small dogs towards Soho Square. As she stopped to let one of her dogs take a piss on a bag of rubbish, a police car pulled up. A young officer got out of the passenger seat and crossed the road, heading towards the café. Seeing Carlyle, he nodded. Carlyle responded in kind and watched him disappear inside.

'Who was that?' Rose Scripps asked, popping the last bite of a ham and cheese panini into her mouth.

'No idea.' Carlyle shrugged. 'Maybe he works out of Charing Cross.'

'You're not very curious, are you?' she teased. 'For a policeman, I mean.'

'No,' Carlyle said, amused, 'I suppose not. You can't be interested in everything though, can you?' The waitress, a hard-looking Polish girl, appeared beside their table and made another grab for his cup. This time he gave it up. 'I'll have another one, please,' he said to her, then looked towards Rose.

'No, I'm fine, thanks,' she said.

'And I'll have the bill as well.'

The young woman nodded and headed back inside.

Carlyle stared into the middle distance. It was barely a week since they had come back from Switzerland, but things had moved on quickly. Their little adventure had already been consigned to the distant past, and that was the way Carlyle liked it.

The waitress reappeared with the bill, but not the coffee. Carlyle dropped a ten-pound note on the tray, digging some change out of his pocket to make up a half-decent tip.

'Thanks for breakfast,' said Rose.

'My pleasure,' said Carlyle. 'How are things at CEOP?'

'Fine,' she said brightly. 'Closing down Falkirk's enterprise is a big win for us. That will keep everyone happy for a while.'

'Yeah,' said Carlyle. 'But it never stops, does it?'

'No,' she sighed. 'I get my new partner next week. A woman this time, which is good. Maybe you know her?' She mentioned a name.

'Nope,' Carlyle said. The waitress brought the fresh coffee and took away his cash.

Rose watched her go. 'The *really* good news,' she said, 'is that Yulia Boyko has got a place in a British Council programme.'

'Well done.' Carlyle meant it, but he could hear the uncertainty in his own voice. Not wanting Rose to think that he was being insincere, he ploughed on, 'Really, I think that is great news.'

'It's early days,' Rose replied chirpily, 'but they say she's settling in well.'

'Let's hope she learns enough not to try and come back here.' He meant it as a joke, but the look on Rose's face told him that his remark had fallen very flat.

'We are going to keep in touch by email,' Rose said stiffly. 'I want to try and help her, if I can.'

'Let me know if I can do anything, too.'

'I will.' Her face softened and she leaned across the table to pat his hand. 'You can be sure of that.'

Not for the first time, Carlyle felt himself blush in her presence. After a moment, he removed his hand and placed it on his lap.

'I have to get going,' said Rose, pushing back her chair and getting to her feet. 'Did you hear about Shen?'

'No.' Looking up at her, Carlyle had to shield his eyes from the sun. 'What's happened?'

'He's quit the Force.'

'Interesting.'

'I reckon that his wife made him do it.'

I can believe that, Carlyle thought. 'Do you think he was bent?'

Rose frowned. 'I really don't know. Not worth worrying about now, I suppose.'

'Probably not.'

Rose hoisted her bag on to her shoulder. Hesitating, she offered Carlyle a hand in farewell. Without getting up, he shook it. 'Thanks for all your help,' he said awkwardly. 'It was good working together.'

'Yes,' she smiled, eyes lowered.

'I'll see you around.'

'Yes.'

She turned and crossed the road. Sipping his coffee, Carlyle watched her head into Old Compton Street and disappear.

FINISHING HIS SECOND macchiato, he became conscious of someone standing in front of him.

'Inspector Carlyle?'

'Yes?' Again he had to squint into the sun to look up at the tall man, easily six foot plus, with silver hair shaved close to the scalp. Dark rings under his watery blue eyes suggested someone who had enjoyed very little sleep in recent weeks.

'I am Kelvin Matthews, Alexa's father.' He gestured back across the road to a large woman standing just outside Ronnie Scott's Jazz Club; she was eyeing them both with a tortured expression on her face. 'And that's her mum, Sandra.'

Oh, Christ, thought Carlyle, his heart sinking. 'Nice to meet you, sir,' he said, trying not to let his expression collapse into a grimace. Getting quickly to his feet, he shook the man's hand. Across the road, the wife seemed to remain in some kind of trance, rooted to the spot.

'Alexa was our only child,' Kelvin said wistfully, delivering this line like it had been rehearsed many times at home, in front of a mirror.

Resisting the urge to turn and flee, Carlyle tried to think of something to say.

But Kelvin Matthews didn't seem to be looking for a dialogue. 'For that to happen to her . . . well, it's knocked the stuffing out of us.' He looked over his shoulder towards Ronnie Scott's and added, 'especially her mother.'

Carlyle placed a gentle hand on the man's shoulders. 'Is there anything I can do to help, sir?' he asked kindly.

'Alexa told us that you were assisting her with her transfer,' said Kelvin Matthews, staring at a space somewhere to Carlyle's left.

'Her move out of SO14?'

'Yes,' Matthews nodded. 'Her mother and I always thought that working for the royal family must be the best job going.' He finally managed to make eye-contact. 'So why would she want to pack it in?'

'I worked at the Palace myself for a while,' said Carlyle, relieved at the modesty of the man's demands, and even more relieved at how easy it was for him to invent a credible response on the spot. 'It was certainly a very . . . interesting place to work. The great thing about the Met though, is the variety of things you can do. In the end, I just wanted to try something different. I suspect that it was the same for Alexa.'

Matthews thought about it for a moment, as if not quite prepared to accept that this was the only answer he was going to get.

Carlyle glanced to check whether Mrs Matthews had moved yet. She hadn't.

'I see,' Matthews said finally. 'And did that have anything to do with her being burned alive?'

'Not as far as I am aware, sir,' the inspector said slowly, carefully making sure that the right words came out in the right order. 'I am not technically part of the investigation into your daughter's death, but I am, of course, taking a keen interest in how it is progressing. Can I ask one of the officers in charge to speak to you?'

'That's all right,' said Matthews, 'we are already in contact with an Inspector Petherick.'

The name didn't ring any bells. 'He's a good man,' said Carlyle.

'A woman,' replied Matthews.

Carlyle felt his buttocks clench in embarrassment. 'Ah, yes, of course.' He tapped his head lightly. 'My mistake.' How could he retrieve this situation? He glanced again at the woman across the road, who was radiating confusion and despair. 'Would you like me to talk to your wife, sir?'

'It's fine, thank you,' said Matthews stiffly. 'We just wanted to ask you the question.'

Carlyle dug a card out of his pocket and handed it to him. 'If I can be of any further assistance, sir, please let me know.'

Matthews put the card in his coat pocket without looking at it. 'I will, Inspector, thank you. And thank you for trying to help Alexa.'

Feeling like a total shit, Carlyle forced himself to look Kelvin Matthews directly in the eye. 'I'm sorry I couldn't do more,' he said gently. 'We had known each other for a long time.'

The man merely nodded, and they shook hands for a second time. Then, stepping off the pavement, he waited for a van to pass before crossing the road, back to his wife. Without apparently saying anything, he gave her a tender kiss on the forehead and took her hand, before they began walking slowly away, down the street.

Chapter Thirty-eight

THE RAIN CAME down like a blessing, little more than a fine mist offering the eternal promise of renewal. Pressing one toe of his Oliver Sweeney shoes into the damp lawn, Carlyle listened to the relentless background hum of traffic on Grosvenor Place, on the other side of the wall. Buttoning up his raincoat to protect his beloved, second-hand Paul Smith suit from the elements, he made sure his tie was properly done up. The inspector was wearing what his father would have called his Sunday best. Suited and booted for the first time in months, he had made an effort, just as Helen had done. They were both showing some respect as they gathered to scatter Alzbetha Tishtenko's ashes.

Sir Ewen Mayflower appeared at his shoulder. 'Are we ready?'

Carlyle looked around for Helen. She was standing fifty yards away, examining some plants that he didn't recognise. In one hand she clutched her bag, in the other the urn itself. There was not another soul around. The three of them had the whole of the Palace garden to themselves. He looked at his watch: Alexandra Gazizulin and the girl's mother were almost thirty minutes late.

That could just be a problem with traffic, but the inspector doubted it. Anyway, he couldn't keep the Head of the Royal Household waiting any longer.

'Yes,' he said, turning back to Mayflower. 'I think that we should get started.'

'Good.'

'Thank you again for making this happen.'

'Don't thank me,' said Mayflower benignly. He gestured back towards the Palace. 'You should thank the owners.'

Looking up, Carlyle thought he saw a small, grey figure at a ground-floor window, looking out across the lawn at this melancholy scene. He did a double-take and the figure was gone. Maybe he was imagining things. 'The owners of this place . . . do they know about Falkirk?'

Mayflower let out a sly smile. 'Yes and no.'

'What does that mean?'

'I would have thought that was fairly obvious. They know enough to know that they don't want to know.'

'Of course,' Carlyle replied. 'That's a key establishment skill – dodging the shit.'

'An interesting way of putting it, Inspector, but basically correct.'

'Whatever,' Carlyle said quietly, 'we are very grateful. I am sure that you will convey our sincere thanks to the relevant parties.'

'Of course,' Mayflower nodded. 'Of course.' He hooked his arm under Carlyle's and started walking them both across the lawn towards Helen. 'There is also,' he said, after a few moments, 'something that you can do for me.'

'I will certainly try,' said Carlyle, wondering what favour he could possibly do for this distinguished old gent.

'I want you to keep an eye on Carole Simpson.'

'What do you mean?' Carlyle frowned. 'She's my boss.'

'Yes,' Mayflower grabbed his arm more tightly, 'but she respects you and you respect her.'

Well, kind of, Carlyle thought.

'And now is a time when the poor woman desperately needs the help and support of those close to her.'

And that means me? Carlyle wondered. Poor woman indeed.

Mayflower halted them about ten feet away from Helen. 'Her husband is still in hospital.'

'Still?'

'Yes, they've found something nasty. Cancer of the colon, I believe. It looks like Joshua will now be released from prison early on compassionate grounds. The expectation is that he has maybe six months.'

'Carole Simpson told you all this?'

Mayflower looked at him sadly. 'Not everyone is as buttoned up as you, Inspector.'

Buttoned up? Carlyle thought. We've met, what – three times – and you're dissecting my character already? However, realising that this was not about him, he quickly pulled himself together. 'How is she going to look after him?'

'I think that Joshua may be back home only a few weeks before entering a hospice.'

'Jesus!'

'So, you can see, Carole needs all the kindness and under-standing she can get at this time.'

'Yes, of course. I will do whatever I can.' Carlyle looked up to the grey heavens, wondering what exactly that might be.

Mayflower patted his arm. 'God bless you, Inspector.'

As they finally reached Helen, a mobile started ringing to the tune of 'Land of Hope and Glory'. Mayflower pulled a handset out of his jacket pocket. 'Yes, I see,' he said. He looked over at Carlyle. 'Your guests are here.'

'Excellent timing,' said Carlyle.

'Very well,' Mayflower spoke into the handset, 'I'll be right there.' Ending the call, he excused himself and headed back across the lawn towards the Palace.

Carlyle stepped up to Helen. Putting his arm around her, he gently kissed her forehead. 'Are you okay?'

'I'm fine,' Helen smiled. She gestured with the urn towards an empty flower bed. 'This is where Sir Ewen said we should put her ashes.'

'Not very glamorous,' Carlyle commented.

'They will plant some summer damasks next year,' Helen said. 'Then it will be nice.'

Carlyle, who wouldn't have known a summer damask from a hole in the ground, grunted his assent. Over Helen's shoulder he watched Mayflower reappear with two women in tow. One he didn't recognise – short and stumpy, she was looking around like she had just arrived on Mars. If her jaw dropped any further, it would soon hit the turf. The other woman he did know: she was tall, elegant and, even at this distance, obviously beautiful. Dressed in a dark business suit under a Burberry raincoat, she could have been simply passing through on her way to a much more classy engagement.

As Alexandra Gazizulin came closer, the inspector stiffened slightly, recognising the amused twinkle in her eye, and belatedly wondered whether having Helen in tow was such a good idea. It was too late to do anything about it now. Giving his wife another kiss, he whispered, 'Thank you for coming.'

Taking his arm, Helen pulled him closer. 'How else would I ever get the run of the gardens at Buckingham Palace?'

'You know what I mean.'

She watched the trio approach. 'You are a good man, John. Doing this for the poor girl and her mother.'

'It's not much.'

'But it's above and beyond the call of duty. And you also had to think of the idea in the first place.'

'Maybe,' Carlyle sighed. 'I suppose so.'

'I'm only sorry that there wasn't a happy ending here.'

He breathed his wife's perfume and gave silent thanks for all that she was; all that he had; his immense good fortune. Reflecting on all that Alzbetha Tishtenko, and Yulia Boyko, and God knows how many others didn't have. 'There are no happy endings,' he declared morosely.

She grabbed his arm tighter. 'Don't be so gloomy,' she chided softly. 'Remember that old Carlyle saying: it'll be all right in the end . . .'

'Yes,' Carlyle laughed. 'And if it's not all right, that just means that it's not yet the end!'

'Exactly.' Stepping away from him, Helen moved forward to greet the others.

ALEXANDRA GAZIZULIN MADE the introductions, translating for the benefit of Alzbetha's mother, who nodded once or twice but said nothing. Carlyle watched the woman sway slightly, her eyes glassy and unfocused. He wondered if she was on medication. Helen carefully handed her the urn and they retreated to a respectful distance, while she spread the ashes in the designated spot.

Helen then took Sir Ewen by the arm and whisked him off to a nearby bench in order to buttonhole him about Avalon, the international medical charity where she worked. Carlyle had been aghast at her plan to try and use the day for a bit of networking, but she had primly informed him that this was a unique opportunity that could not be passed up. For his part, the old man was clearly delighted to be cornered by this handsome younger woman. Sitting down together, they were quickly engaged in an animated conversation.

Alex followed his gaze. 'You have a lovely wife,' she remarked, with only the slightest edge in her voice.

'I do,' he replied. 'I am very lucky.' He watched Alzbetha's mother empty the last of the urn, replace the lid and mumble something to herself. 'What will she do now?' he asked.

'She wants to go shopping.' Alex looked at the expression on Carlyle's face and laughed. 'Why not?'

'It's not exactly what you would expect after you've lost a child,' Carlyle huffed.

'She had six kids,' Alex shrugged. 'She looked after three of them; gave the other three away. That's not bad by Ukrainian standards. She did her best. You can't afford to be too sentimental.'

'Fair enough.' It was Carlyle's turn to shrug. Who was he to judge?

'I've given her £200 to go and spend in Harrods on her way back to the airport. Harrods, imagine! She is very excited by it all.'

'Thank you for bringing her over.'

'It was my responsibility.' Alex stared into the middle distance. 'We made a bad mistake. The best I can do is to make sure that we don't do it again. There are limits.'

'Yes,' Carlyle agreed, 'there are.'

Just then, Alzbetha's mother appeared in front of them. Eyes lowered, she murmured something to Alex and handed her the urn. Without acknowledging Carlyle in any way, she turned and stomped away across the lawn.

'Harrods time,' Carlyle said to no one in particular. He turned to Alex. 'You know, I've lived my whole life in London and I don't think I've ever gone there.'

She arched an eyebrow. 'I'm not surprised. It's only for classy people.'

'Thanks a lot!' he gasped, in mock indignation.

'I'm more of a Harvey Nichols girl myself,' Alex told him.

'I can imagine,' Carlyle replied. And he could. It was clear that the term 'high maintenance' did not even begin to cover Alexandra Gazizulin.

'Hopefully they will open a franchise in Kiev one day. Here.' Alex handed the urn to Carlyle. 'She wants you to keep it.'

Carlyle turned it over in his hands. A squat brown box, it looked like a tea caddy. 'Thanks.'

Alex sighed. 'It is time for me to go.'

'Shall I get Sir Ewen to show you out?'

'No. It looks like he is getting on well with your wife,' she murmured. 'I would not wish to interrupt. We can see ourselves out.'

'Okay.'

'Don't worry,' Alex teased, 'we will not steal anything on the way to the gate.'

Carlyle laughed, but said nothing.

'We might visit the gift shop though.'

'It's expensive.'

'I guess they need the money.' She gestured towards the Palace. 'It's a bit run-down, no? It could do with a makeover.'

He shrugged. 'These type of places always need a lot of upkeep, I suppose.'

Bored with the conversation, she held out a hand. 'Good to know you, John Carlyle.'

Carlyle hesitated. Then he took her hand, holding it for the shortest moment. 'Good to know you . . . "Olga".'

She leaned over and kissed him lightly on the cheek. 'In your dreams, policeman,' she whispered. '"Olga" would have eaten you alive, many times over.'

Feeling himself blush violently, Carlyle looked over towards his wife. Mercifully, Helen was still deep in conversation with Mayflower, so didn't pay him any attention.

By the time he had composed himself, Alex was almost half-way across the lawn. A firm breeze caught him in the face, and he realised that it had stopped raining. A tiny patch of blue had appeared in the sky, displaying token resistance against the inexorable advance of winter. Sticking his hands deep into the pockets of his raincoat, Carlyle watched Alexandra Gazizulin catch up with Alzbetha's mother and lead her towards an attendant who was waiting by a doorway, ready to show them off the premises.

As they disappeared from view, the inspector pulled an envelope from one of his pockets. Inside it was the warrant for Alexandra Gazizulin's arrest. Tearing the document up, he tossed the pieces into the air, watching as they were carried off on the breeze. When the last shred of paper had vanished, he walked over to join his wife and her new friend.

Chapter Thirty-nine

CARNIVAL, FOOTBALL, SAMBA!

Bollocks.

It was a cold, dark, wet evening and the wind whipping spitefully off the Thames made it harder to imagine any place on God's earth less like Brazil. Checking the time on his mobile phone, Carlyle hurried across Charing Cross footbridge, cursing under his breath. He was supposed to be at a performance by the South American Circus at the Royal Festival Hall, but that had started ten minutes ago.

Damn, damn, damn.

Helen had spent a fortune on tickets for the show. Afterwards they were going for a pizza at one of the restaurants on the South Bank – a relaxed setting for their family meeting. That, at least, had been the idea. A train rumbled noisily past on the railway bridge nearby as he felt his phone buzzing angrily in his pocket. Another text from Helen, no doubt, wondering where the hell he was. He only hoped that she and Alice had taken their seats and left his ticket at the desk in the foyer. If not, he could meet them in the interval, assuming that there even was one. At the very least, he could pay for their dinner as a gesture of goodwill.

He struggled forward. The footbridge was barely eight feet wide. There was just enough space for four people, two moving in each direction, less if people stopped to take photographs or just admire the view. 'Excuse me!' Slaloming round an elderly woman, Carlyle barged past a man standing by the railings, looking west, towards the Houses of Parliament. Ignoring the man's complaint, he tried to increase his pace.

His phone started vibrating again and he glanced at the screen. It was Joe Szyszkowski. The inspector knew what it would be about, so he let it go to voicemail. They had both been delayed by the latest mini-drama at the Charing Cross station where a WPC had launched a sexual harassment claim against the Met and various officers at Charing Cross. It was a nasty little dispute – involving too much alcohol and too many sex toys – that was rapidly heading towards a tribunal and the pages of the tabloid newspapers. Carlyle didn't want to have anything to do with the whole sorry mess. He only knew the principals in the vaguest terms and had been less than pleased to find himself pulled into an interview room earlier in the afternoon and required to give a formal statement on the matter. He was even less pleased when the Met's lawyer then proceeded to spend almost an hour going through a list of seemingly random questions to which the inspector had no answers.

None of that would cut any ice with Helen, however. His wife assumed that work only got in the way if you let it. At the very least, she would consider Carlyle's tardiness symptomatic of a subconscious desire to avoid dealing with Alice's karate issue. Trying to press on, he found his way blocked by a young woman deep in earnest conversation with a homeless guy selling the *Big*

Issue. Carlyle tried to swerve round her, but his path was blocked by a group of schoolkids coming the other way, led by a teacher. Carlyle glared at the magazine seller who, sensing his frustration, smiled mockingly.

As the schoolkids snaked past, the inspector felt someone push up behind him. That wasn't a surprise, given the bottleneck, but then he felt something hard being rammed into the base of his spine.

Carlyle half-turned.

'Eyes front,' a voice hissed. 'This Walther P99 goes off, and the best scenario is that you will be spending the rest of your life in a wheelchair. And that's absolutely the best-case scenario.'

Carlyle recognised the voice but said nothing.

A hand between his shoulderblades pushed him forwards.

'Step over there . . . to the side. Put your hands on the rail, where I can see them.'

Carlyle did as he was told. He stared down at the grey-brown soup that was the River Thames, and shivered.

The man with the gun stepped close up behind him, almost like they were spooning, giving Carlyle no room for manoeuvre while keeping the semi-automatic out of sight of other people crossing the bridge.

Carlyle turned his head slightly, so that his words wouldn't get lost on the wind. 'So what are you going to do now, Charlie?' he asked. 'Shoot me or fuck me?'

Charlie Adam dug the gun deeper into the small of Carlyle's back. 'You always were a complete arse,' he said with contempt. 'I'm just going to finish a job that should have been done years ago. Undesirables like you should never be allowed in the Force. You should have left SO14 in a box.'

'Like Tommy Dolan?'

'Dolan was a far better copper that you could ever hope to be.'

'Yeah . . . right.' Carlyle watched the schoolkids disappear towards the train station. He could feel his pulse racing and his heart was threatening to jump out of his chest. Breathing in deeply, he wondered quite how he was going to resolve this situation. Nothing immediately sprang to mind. 'I got Dolan, so what?' he said calmly. 'What do you care?'

'I don't give a damn about Tommy Dolan,' Adam whined, the adrenaline and stress sounding clear in his voice, which was now at least an octave higher than usual, 'He's the only one anyone ever talks about. I had more than a million in that bloody firm. What about me?'

'United 14?'

'God, Carlyle, you can be really slow sometimes. Yes, United bloody 14. A million bloody quid! That was a lifetime's work . . .'

A lifetime's graft more like, Carlyle thought. Serves you right for being a bent bastard. 'Well,' he said, 'that's gone. I can't get it back for you.'

Tears welled up in Adam's eyes. Maybe it was due to the wind. Maybe it was the frustration. Maybe it was the thought of a poverty-stricken old age. 'I know you can't,' he snarled. 'My retirement is gone – up the fucking Swanee.'

'So what do you want from me?' Carlyle snarled back. He was getting bored with this. In the absence of a better plan, he decided that he would just have to smack the little twat in the face and take his chances.

Adam waited as another train went by. 'I want to see you jump.'

'What?' Carlyle snorted. 'You've got to be fucking kidding.'

'Jump, or I shoot you and push you in.'

Would the little shit have the bottle to kill him? The inspector seriously doubted it. On the other hand, he didn't really want to put it to the test. 'Fuck off!'

Adam moved the gun a fraction of an inch away from Carlyle's spine. 'Jump and you might survive.'

Like fuck I might. If I don't drown, all the poison in there will kill me. Carlyle imagined Adam's index finger tightening on the trigger. Had he taken the safety-catch off? Above all, he wondered how he might dodge the bullet.

'I beg your pardon?'

Adam took half a step back and Carlyle turned to see a tall man with white hair and a white beard standing in front of them. In his hand was a German-language *City Guide to London*. Behind the man stood a middle-aged woman and two teenage girls, presumably the pair's daughters.

'We are looking for the London Eye,' announced the man, speaking in the kind of precise, clear English that only the Germans used. 'We have a booking for a flight in thirty minutes.'

Adam and Carlyle both turned to look at the 400-foot wheel, lighting up the night sky as it revolved serenely, barely 100 yards from where they were standing.

Charlie Adam turned back to the clueless tourist. 'What the bloody hell do you think that is?' he growled.

The man glanced at the Eye and then, realising his mistake, smiled apologetically. As he did so, Carlyle took a small step towards Adam. Moving up on to his toes, the inspector smashed his right elbow into the chief superintendent's face. Adam's legs sagged and Carlyle gave him the elbow a second time. As Adam's hands went to his face, he dropped the Walther. The German family looked on disbelievingly as they watched the pistol bounce once, twice on the bridge before disappearing through the railings and into the river.

Everything was happening in slow motion. Carlyle's blood was up now. Grabbing Adam by the collar of his coat, he threw him against the railings and launched a drop kick between his legs.

'Ooof!' As he struggled for breath, Adam tried to spit blood from his mouth. Carlyle could see that the fire had gone out of his eyes. It was time to end it. Stepping forward, he wound up a right hook to the man's chin, which connected perfectly. Adam's head snapped back. He tried to hold on to the rail, but stumbled sideways and slumped to the ground.

Seeing that Adam was done, Carlyle turned to the small crowd that had gathered to watch. He fumbled in the pocket of his trousers and pulled out his warrant card. Waving it above his head, he made eye-contact with as many of the onlookers as possible. 'Has anyone called the police?' he shouted.

The sirens approaching on the Embankment below gave their own answer.

'Oh, my God!' A woman started screaming.

Carlyle turned round to find that Charlie Adam had disappeared. By the time he stepped to the rail and gazed down into the floodlit murk, there was no sign of the man at all.

Chapter Forty

IN A RESTAURANT just to the north of the piazza in Covent Garden, Carlyle looked at the Rajasthani puppets hanging from the ceiling. The scene depicted a royal wedding: bridegroom seated on a traditional white horse, surrounded by an array of priests, acrobats, musicians and dancers. In one corner, he spied a group of snake charmers and smiled. Across the table from him were Helen and Alice. It was time for their belated 'family meeting'.

Charlie Adam's body had been washed up on the south bank of the Thames near Tower Bridge two days earlier. The four German tourists had corroborated Carlyle's version of events, missing their flight on the London Eye in the process. Now, finally, the case was closed.

Returning home in the early hours of the following morning, Carlyle had given Helen an only slightly sanitised version of what had happened. After some deliberation, he was excused, if not forgiven, for having missed the circus. He still had to take them to dinner.

Taking a gulp of his Cobra beer, the inspector sat back in his chair. He already knew what he wanted to eat but waited patiently while Helen played with her tap water and carefully scanned a menu that she had seen many times before. Alice, her head deep in a vampire story called *Never Bite a Boy on the First Date*, ignored them both.

'I think I'll have the dhaba rogan josh.' Helen placed the menu on the table and turned to Alice. 'What about you?'

'Not hungry,' said the voice behind the book.

'You've got to have something,' her father snapped.

'No, I don't!' Alice protested, briefly looking up from her book. 'Just because you managed to turn up this time, you think you can tell me exactly what to do. Well, you can't.'

Out of his depth, Carlyle felt a wave of consternation wash over him. What was all that about?

Helen gave him an amused look that said, *Welcome to my world, Mister Policeman.*

The brewing argument was interrupted by the cheery hum of a mobile phone. Carlyle and Helen both checked their phones, but neither had received a call.

'It's for me,' Alice said, her petulance immediately giving way to a genuine cheeriness, as she pulled a mobile out of the back pocket of her jeans.

Finishing his beer, Carlyle gave his wife a hard stare, which she ignored.

'Hello? Stuart . . . hi!' Jumping to her feet, Alice jogged towards the door, nearly sending a waiter and his tray of thalis flying.

Carlyle felt a migraine building at the base of his skull. He watched Alice standing on the street, talking away animatedly. His Alice? Still? Not yet a young woman, but not his little girl any more.

He gestured to the waiter for another beer.

'When did she get that phone?' he asked his wife.

'She bought it with money my mother sent her.'

'Great,' Carlyle sighed.

'Come on,' Helen shrugged, 'you've got to "get real", as Alice would say. All the girls in her class at school have got one. Anyway, she needs it to be able to call us when she's out and about . . .'

She's never called me. Carlyle looked helplessly at his wife. 'And who the bloody hell is Stuart, anyway?'

Acknowledgements

This is the third John Carlyle novel and, quite rightly, the list of people I need to thank continues to grow. Among others, I am very pleased to acknowledge the help and support of: Polly James, Paul Ridley, Michael Doggart, Luke Speed, Andrea von Schilling, Celso F. Lopez and Peter Lavery, as well as Mary Dubberly and all the staff at Waterstone's in Covent Garden.

Particular mention has to go to Chris McVeigh and Beth McFarland at 451 for all their help in promoting John Carlyle online. Of course, nothing would have come of any of this without the efforts of Krystyna Green, Rob Nichols, Martin Palmer, Emily Burns, Jamie-Lee Nardone, Jo Stansall, Clive Hebard and all of the team at Constable. Thanks too to copy editor Joan Deitch and the eagle-eyed Richard Lewis.

Above all, however, I have to thank Catherine and Cate who have put up with all of this when I should have been doing other things. This book, and all the others, is for them.

About the Author

JAMES CRAIG has worked in London as a journalist and consultant for almost thirty years. He lives in Covent Garden with his family.

www.james-craig.co.uk

Discover great authors, exclusive offers, and more at hc.com.